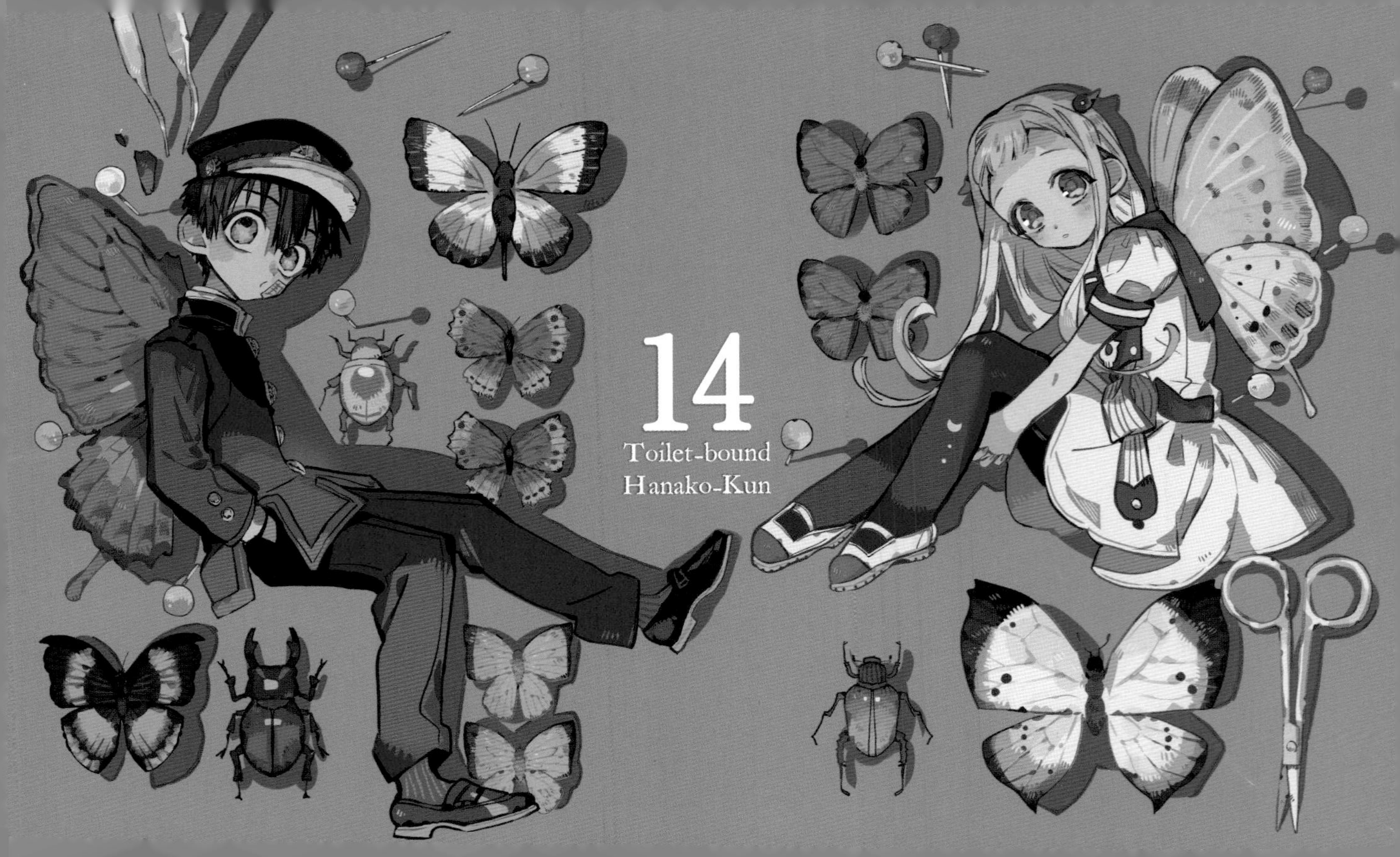
14
Toilet-bound
Hanako-Kun

Contents

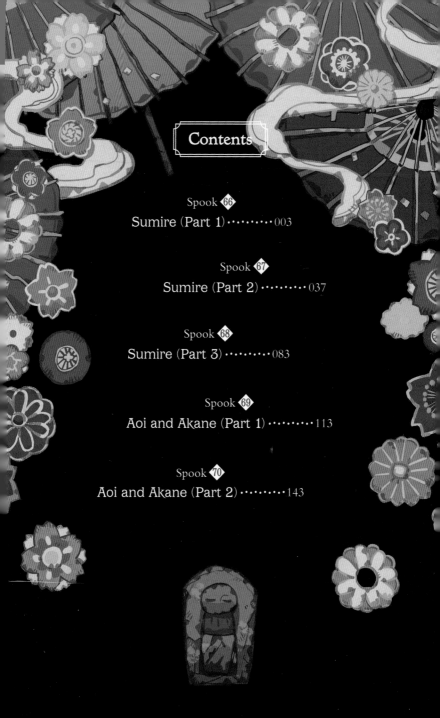

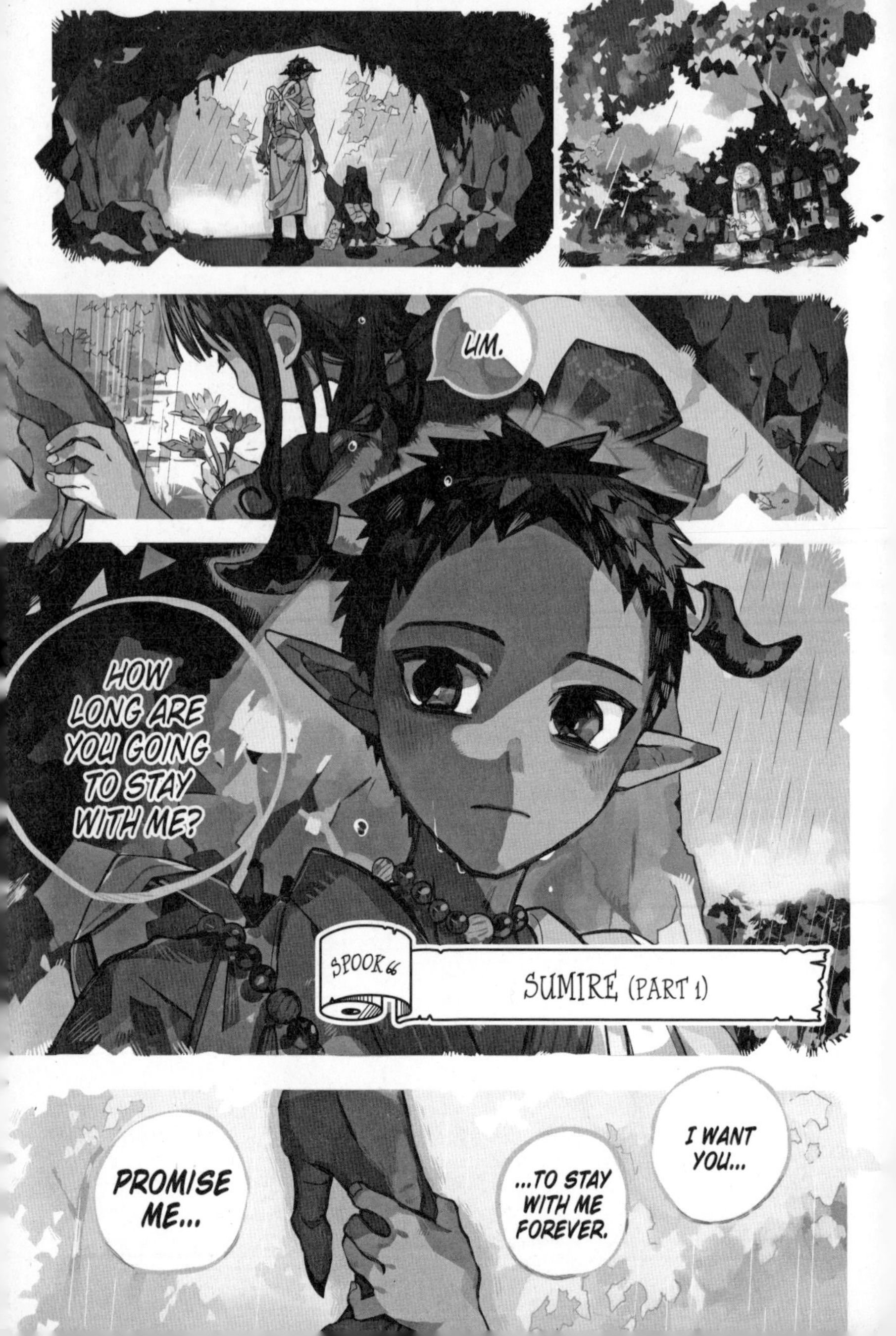
UM.
HOW LONG ARE YOU GOING TO STAY WITH ME?
SPOOK 66
SUMIRE (PART 1)
I WANT YOU...
...TO STAY WITH ME FOREVER.
PROMISE ME...

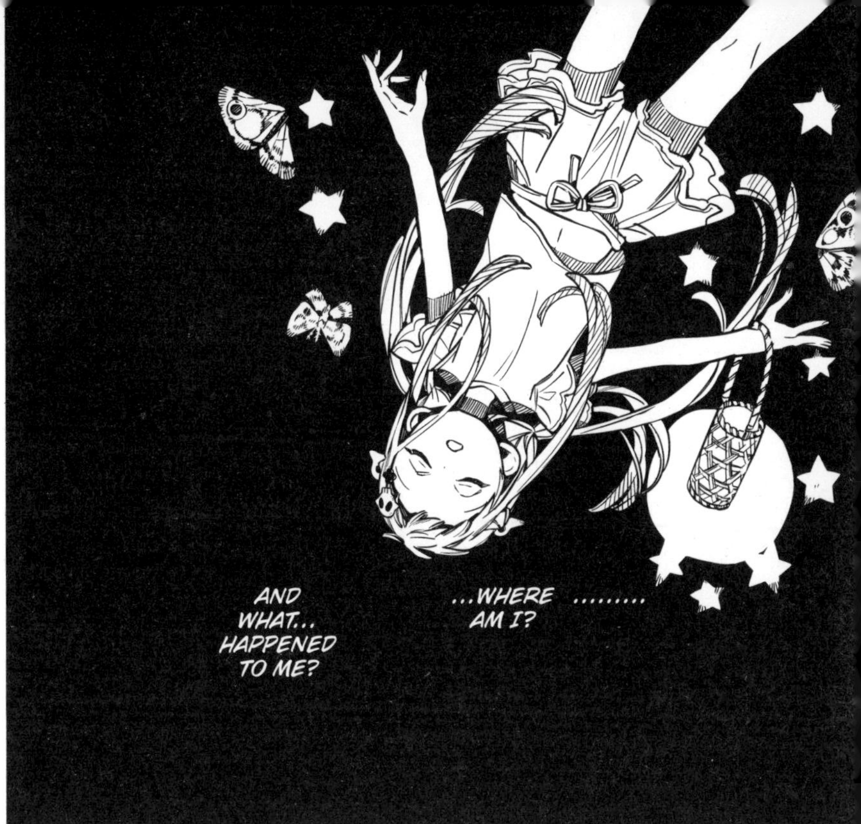
....
...WHERE AM I?
AND WHAT... HAPPENED TO ME?

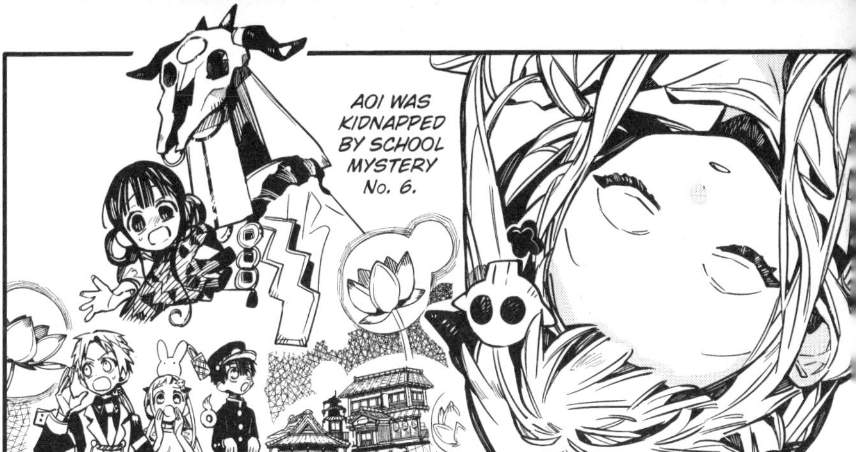
AOI WAS KIDNAPPED BY SCHOOL MYSTERY No. 6.

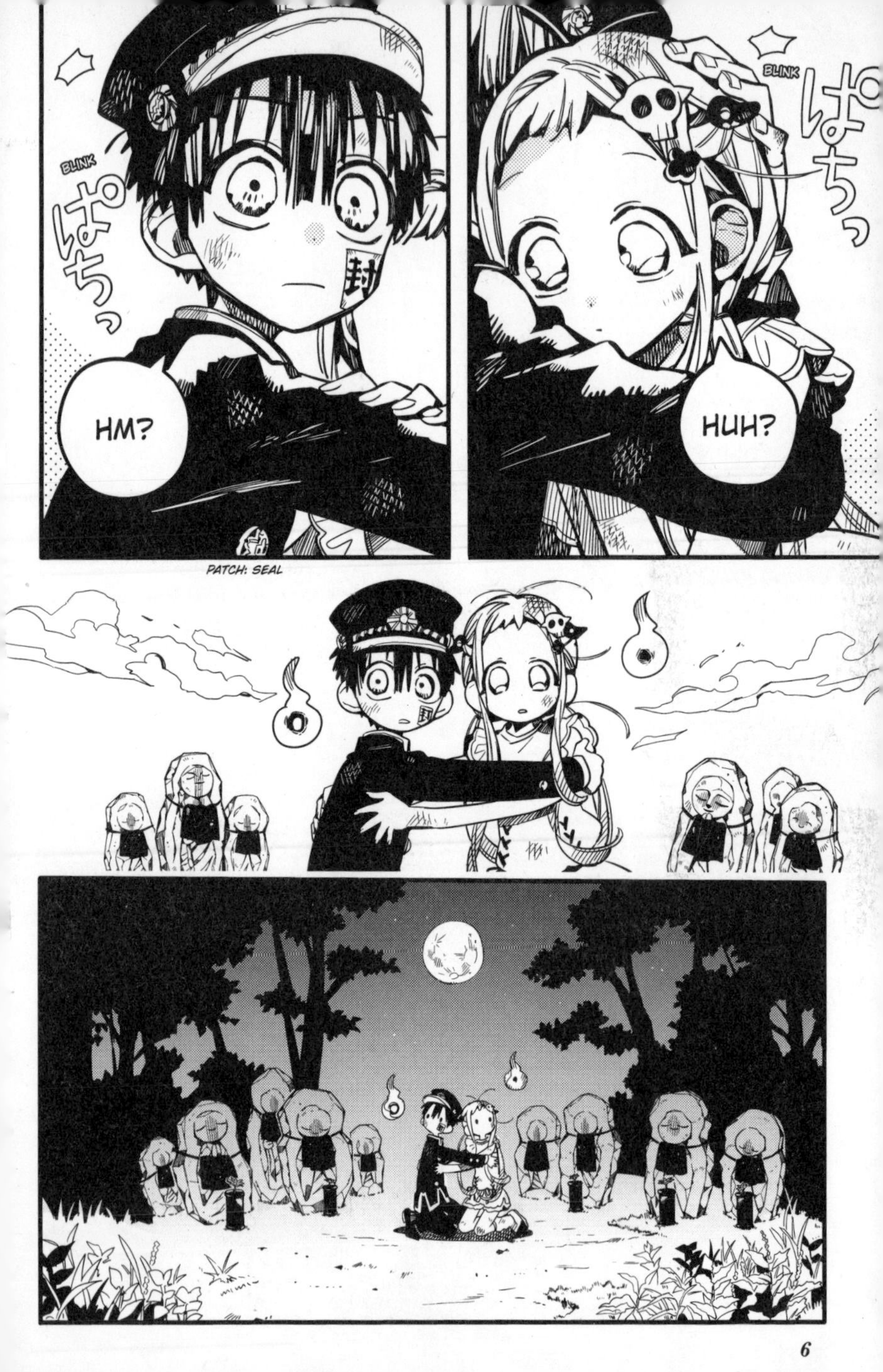
BLINK
ぱちっ
HUH?
BLINK
ぱちっ
HM?
PATCH: SEAL

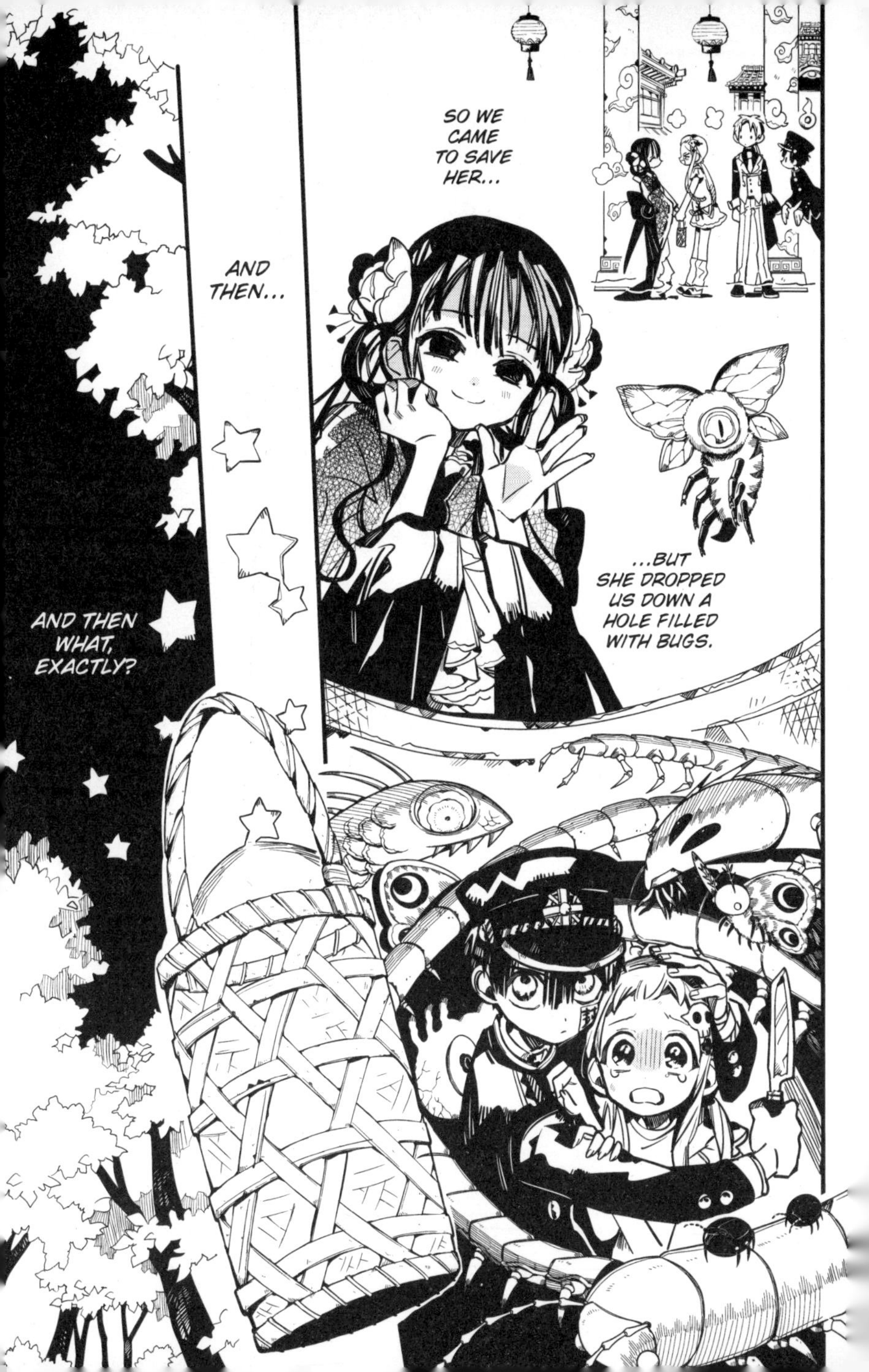
SO WE CAME TO SAVE HER...
AND THEN...
...BUT SHE DROPPED US DOWN A HOLE FILLED WITH BUGS.
AND THEN WHAT, EXACTLY?

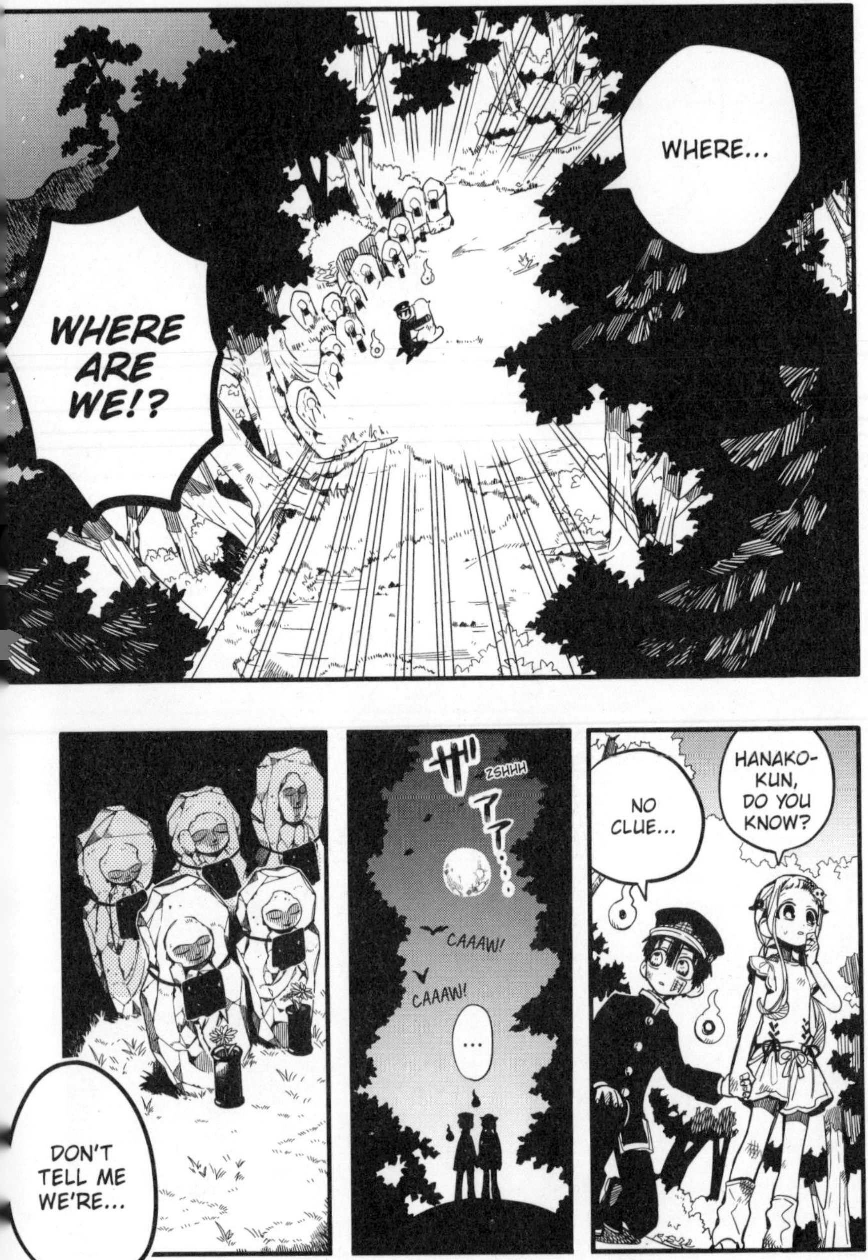
WHERE...
WHERE ARE WE!?
HANAKO-KUN, DO YOU KNOW?
NO CLUE...
ZSHHH
CAAAW!
CAAAW!
...
DON'T TELL ME WE'RE...

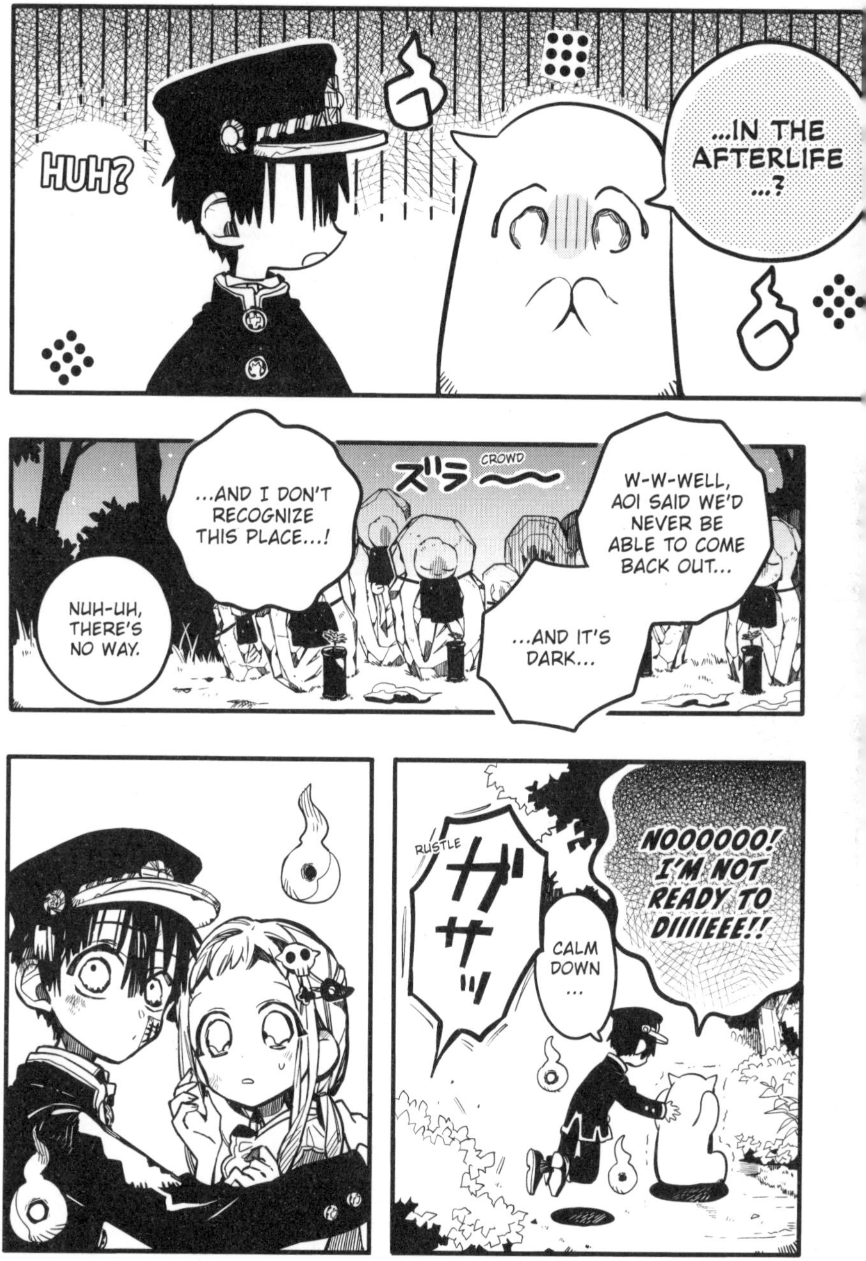
...IN THE AFTERLIFE ...?
HUH?
W-W-WELL, AOI SAID WE'D NEVER BE ABLE TO COME BACK OUT...
CROWD
ズラ〜〜
...AND I DON'T RECOGNIZE THIS PLACE...!
...AND IT'S DARK...
NUH-UH, THERE'S NO WAY.
NOOOOOO! I'M NOT READY TO DIIIIEEE!!
CALM DOWN ...
RUSTLE
ガサッ

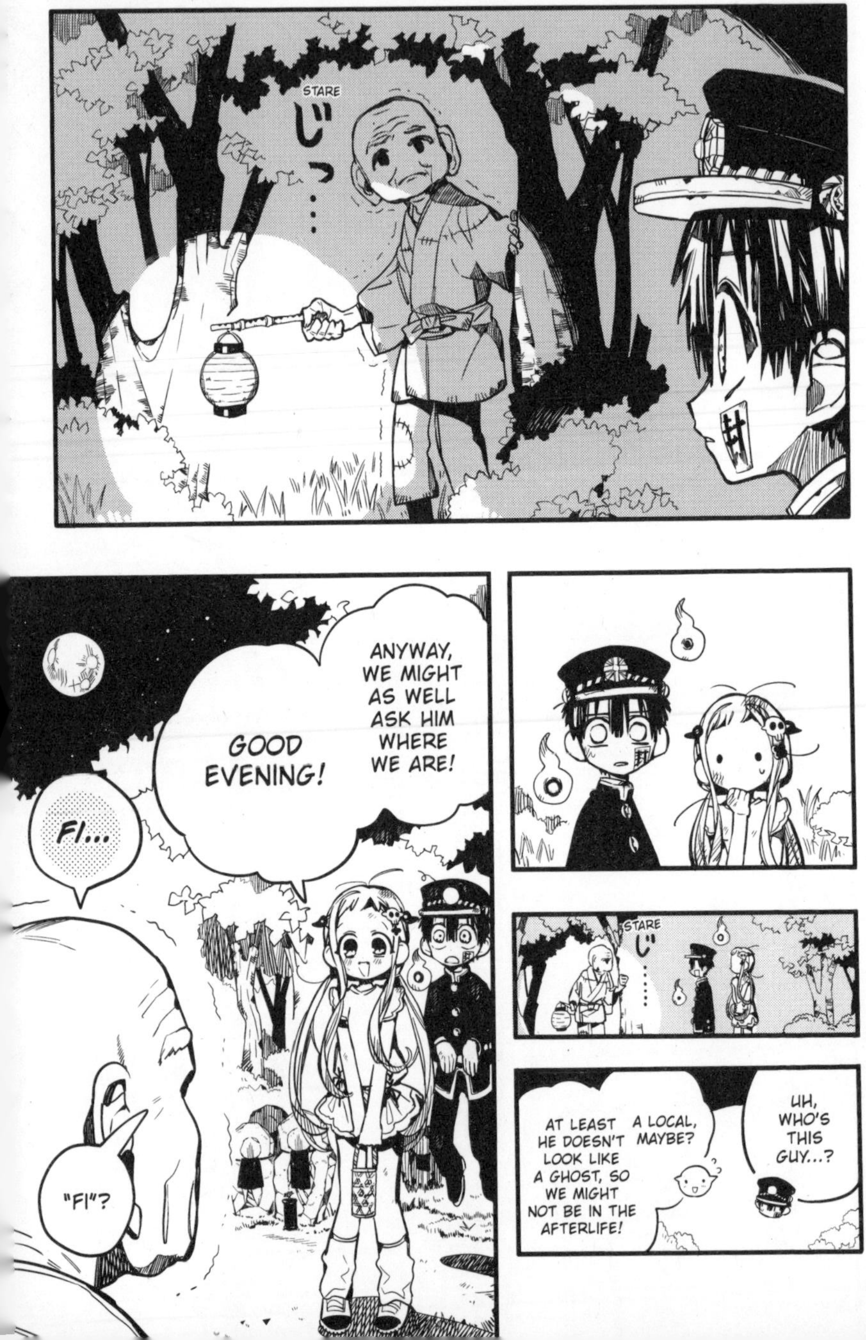
STARE
じっ…
STARE
じ……
UH, WHO'S THIS GUY...?
A LOCAL, MAYBE?
AT LEAST HE DOESN'T LOOK LIKE A GHOST, SO WE MIGHT NOT BE IN THE AFTERLIFE!
ANYWAY, WE MIGHT AS WELL ASK HIM WHERE WE ARE!
GOOD EVENING!
FI...
"FI"?

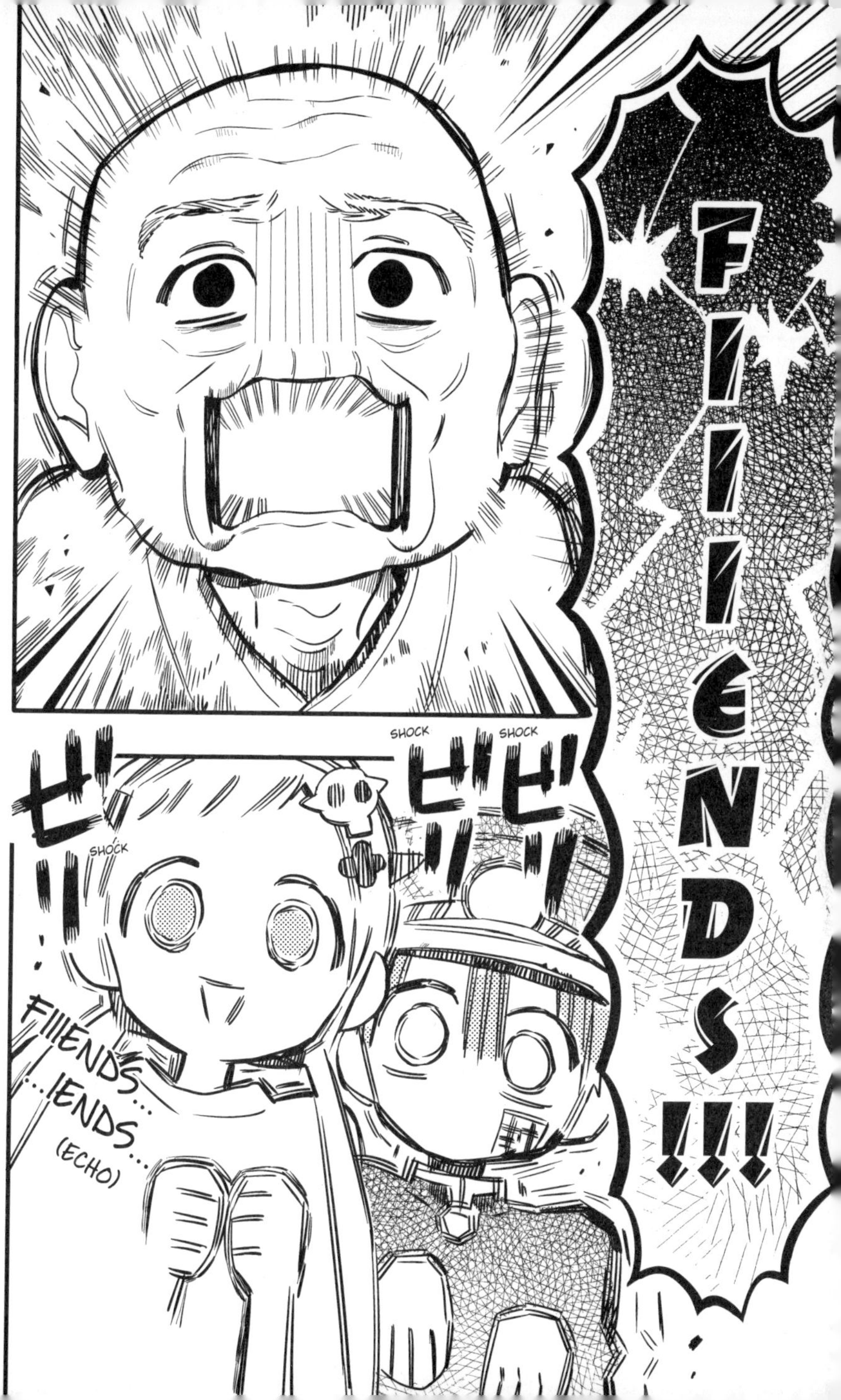
FIIIENDS!!!
SHOCK
SHOCK
ビ!! ビ!!
ゼ!!
SHOCK
FIIIENDS...
...IENDS...
(ECHO)

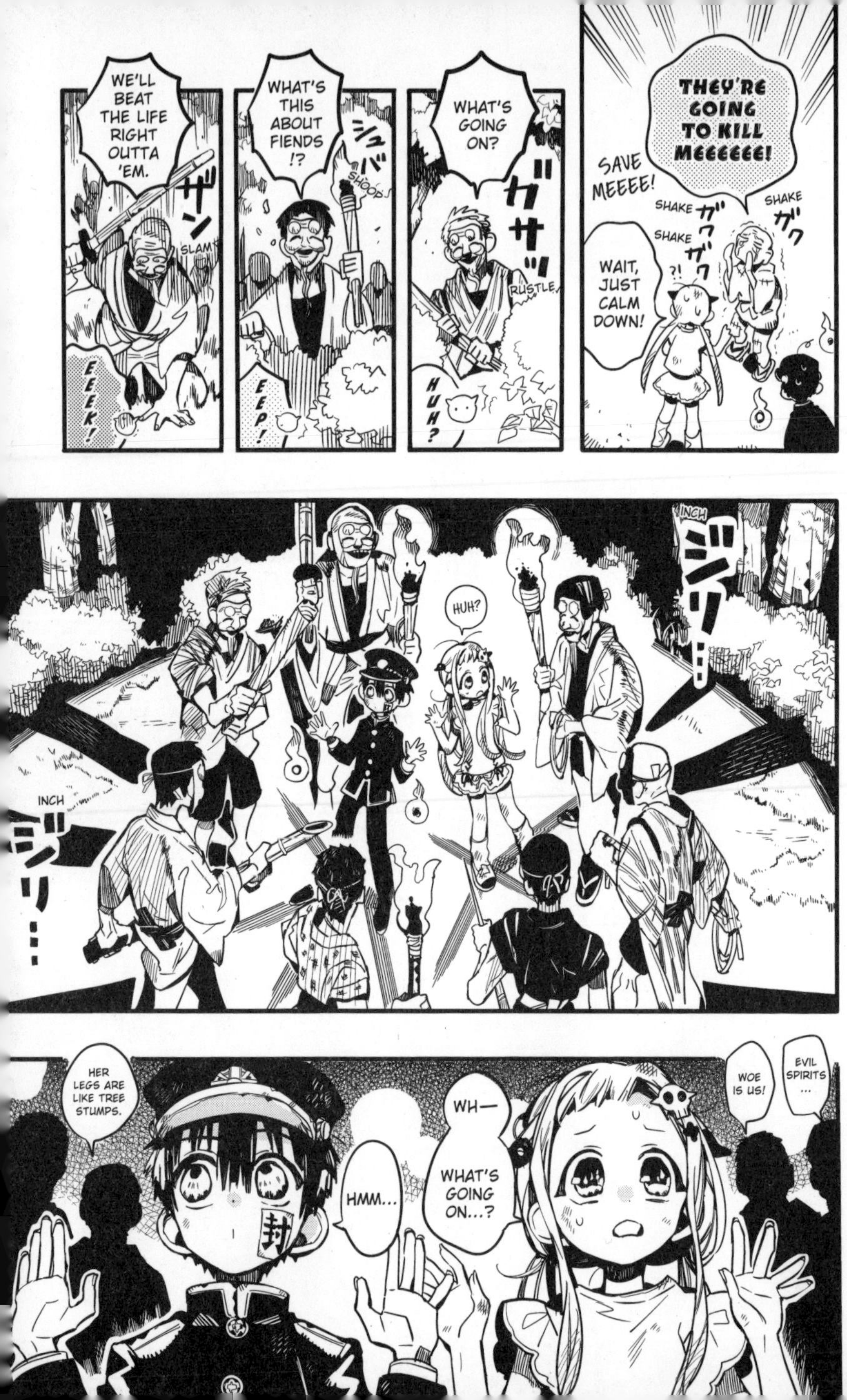
THEY'RE GOING TO KILL MEEEEEEE!
SAVE MEEEE!
SHAKE
ガク
SHAKE
ガクガク
SHAKE
?!
WAIT, JUST CALM DOWN!
WHAT'S GOING ON?
ガサッ
RUSTLE
HUH?
WHAT'S THIS ABOUT FIENDS!?
シュバ
SHOOP
EEP!
WE'LL BEAT THE LIFE RIGHT OUTTA 'EM.
ザン
SLAM
EEEEK!
INCH
ジリ…
HUH?
INCH
ジリ…
EVIL SPIRITS...
WOE IS US!
WH—
WHAT'S GOING ON...?
HMM...
HER LEGS ARE LIKE TREE STUMPS.

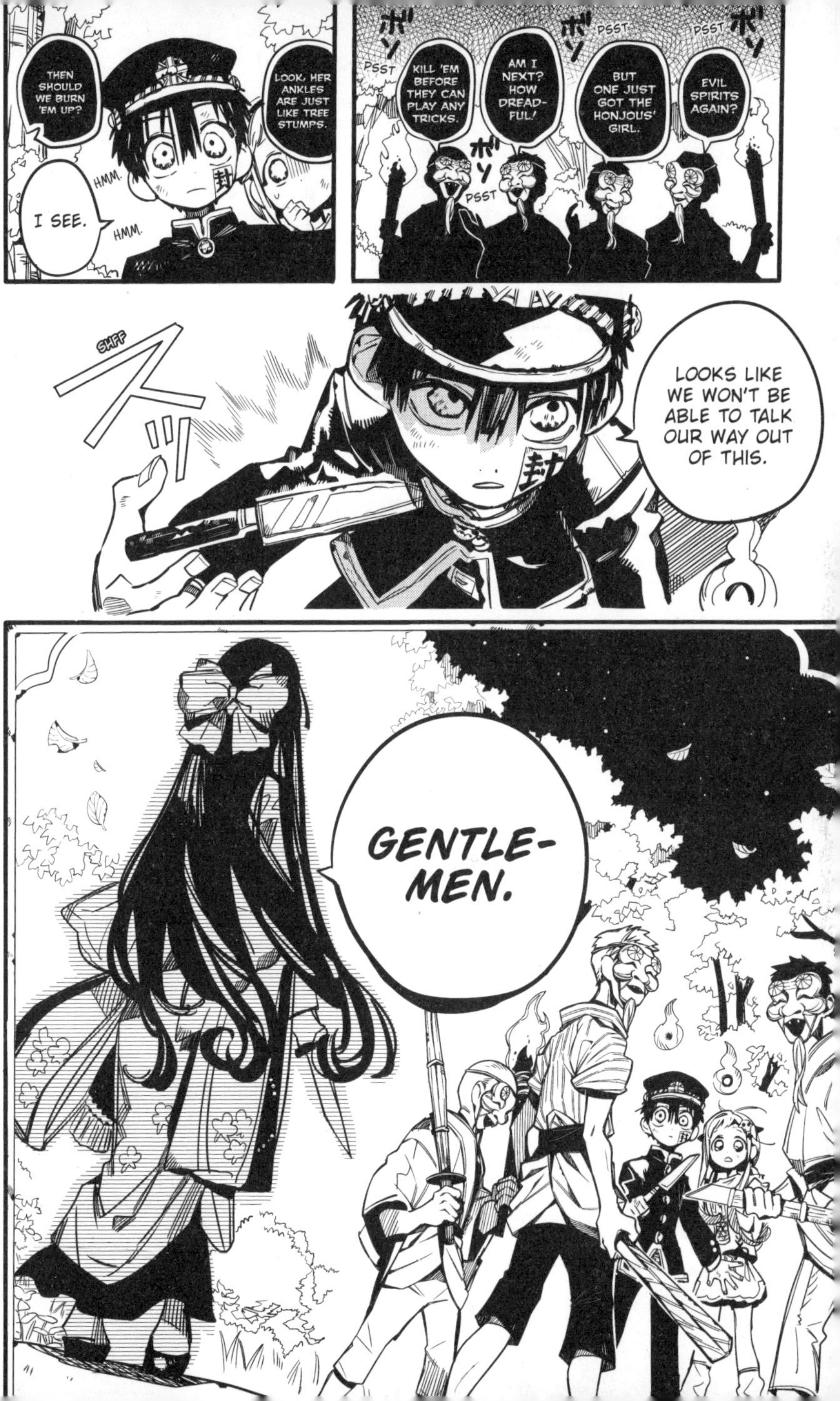
PSST
ボソ
EVIL SPIRITS AGAIN?
PSST
ボソ
BUT ONE JUST GOT THE HONJOUS' GIRL.
ボソ
AM I NEXT? HOW DREAD-FUL!
ボソ
PSST
ボソ
PSST
KILL 'EM BEFORE THEY CAN PLAY ANY TRICKS.
LOOK, HER ANKLES ARE JUST LIKE TREE STUMPS.
THEN SHOULD WE BURN 'EM UP?
HMM.
I SEE.
HMM.
LOOKS LIKE WE WON'T BE ABLE TO TALK OUR WAY OUT OF THIS.
SHFF
スッ
GENTLE-MEN.

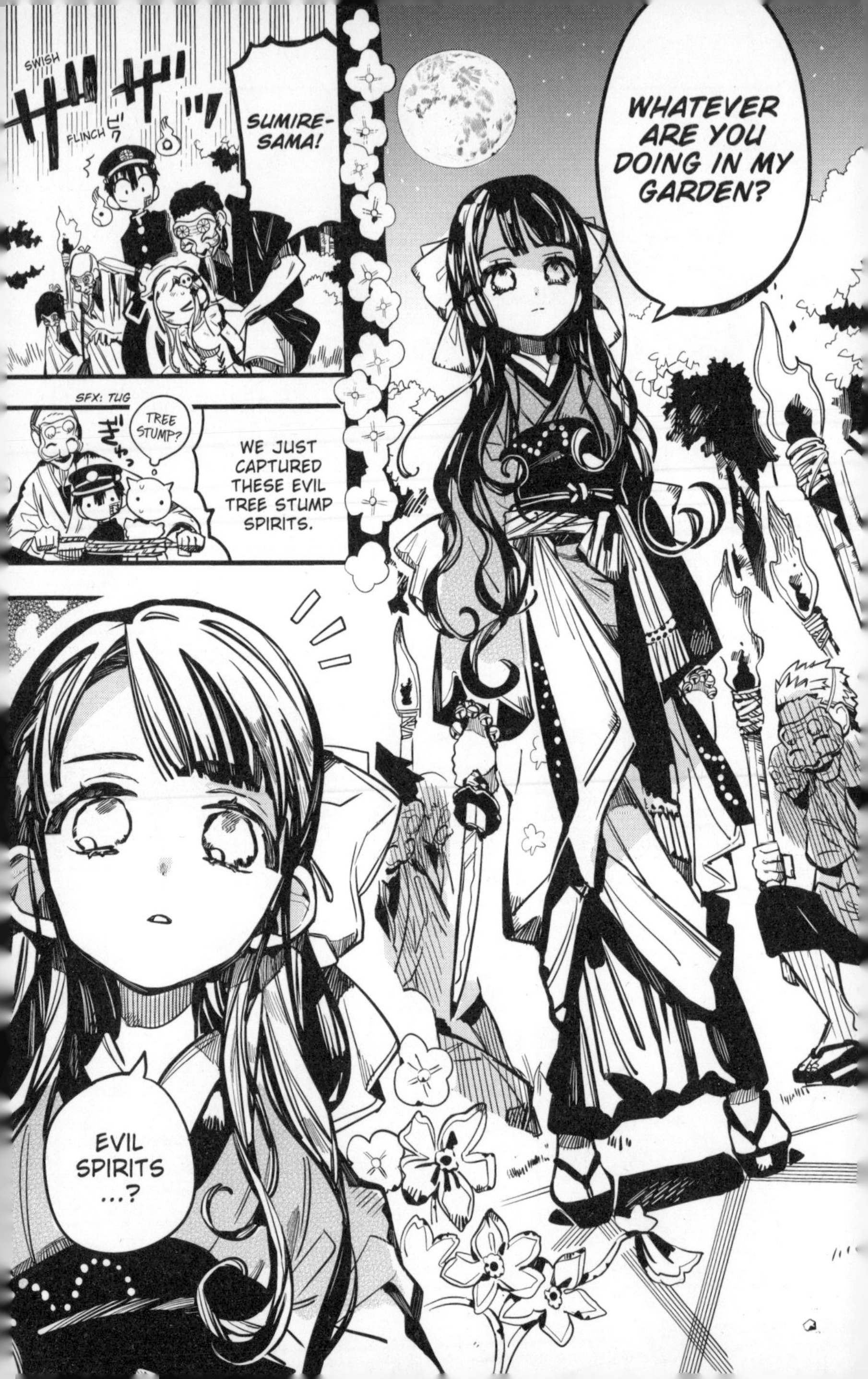
WHATEVER ARE YOU DOING IN MY GARDEN?
SWISH
FLINCH
SUMIRE-SAMA!
SFX: TUG
WE JUST CAPTURED THESE EVIL TREE STUMP SPIRITS.
TREE STUMP?
EVIL SPIRITS ...?

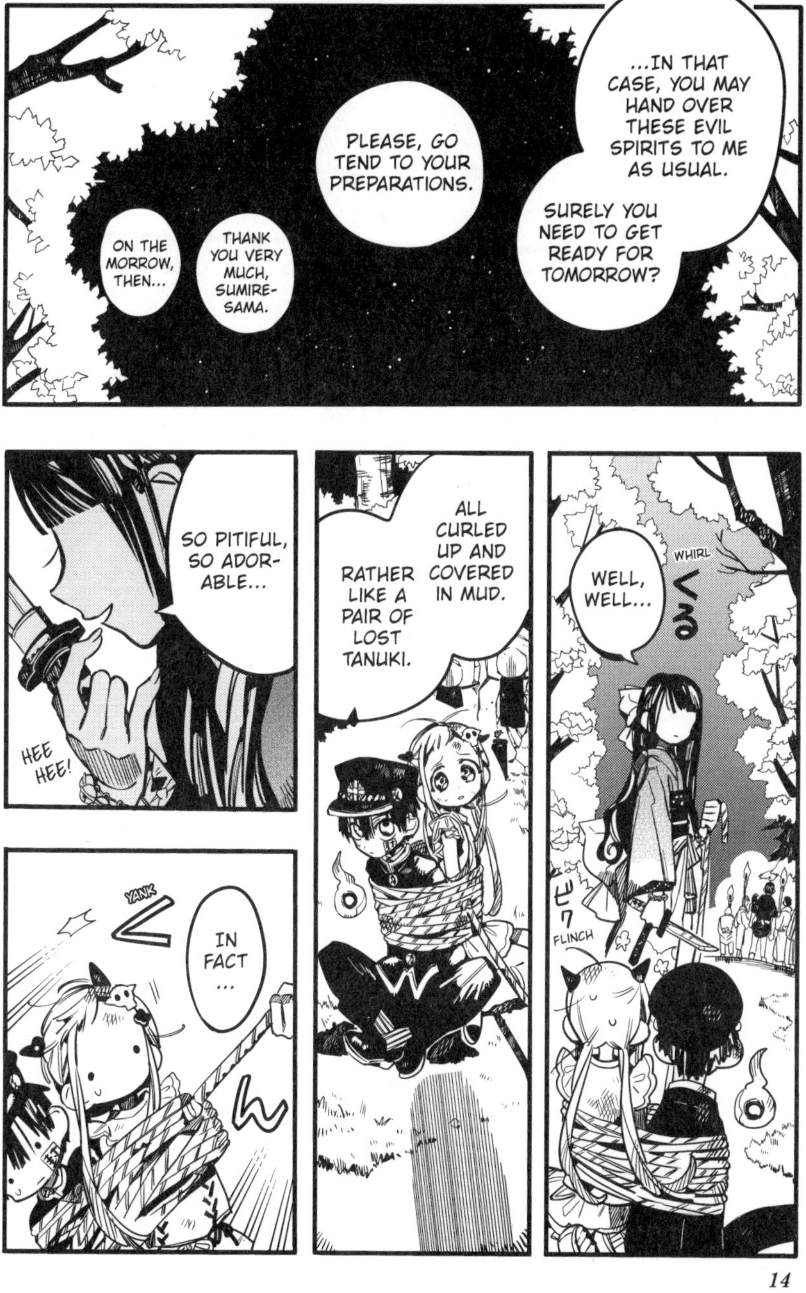
...IN THAT CASE, YOU MAY HAND OVER THESE EVIL SPIRITS TO ME AS USUAL.
SURELY YOU NEED TO GET READY FOR TOMORROW?
PLEASE, GO TEND TO YOUR PREPARATIONS.
THANK YOU VERY MUCH, SUMIRE-SAMA.
ON THE MORROW, THEN...
WHIRL
くる
WELL, WELL...
ビク
FLINCH
ALL CURLED UP AND COVERED IN MUD.
RATHER LIKE A PAIR OF LOST TANUKI.
SO PITIFUL, SO ADORABLE...
HEE HEE!
YANK
IN FACT ...

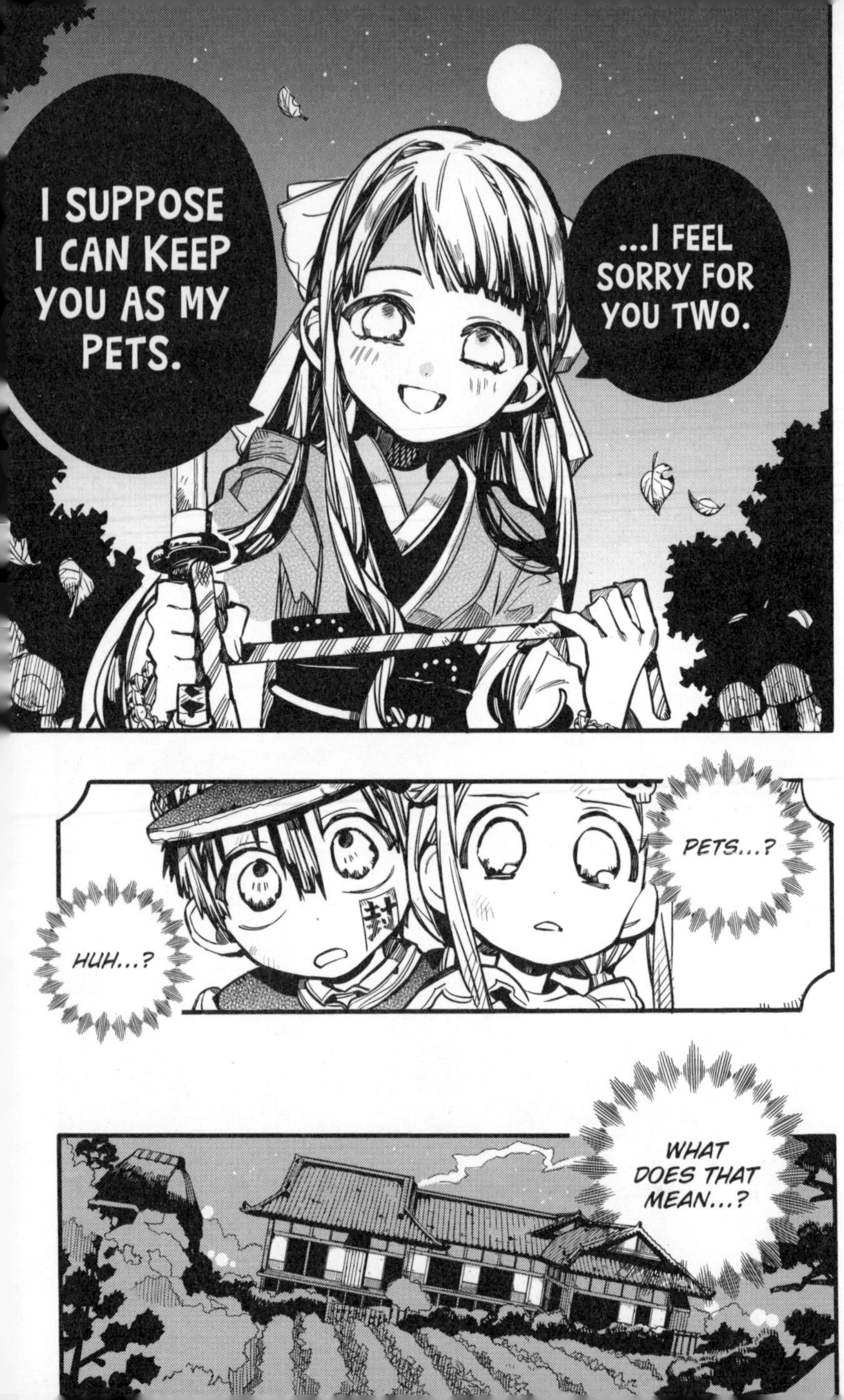
...I FEEL SORRY FOR YOU TWO.
I SUPPOSE I CAN KEEP YOU AS MY PETS.
PETS...?
HUH...?
WHAT DOES THAT MEAN...?

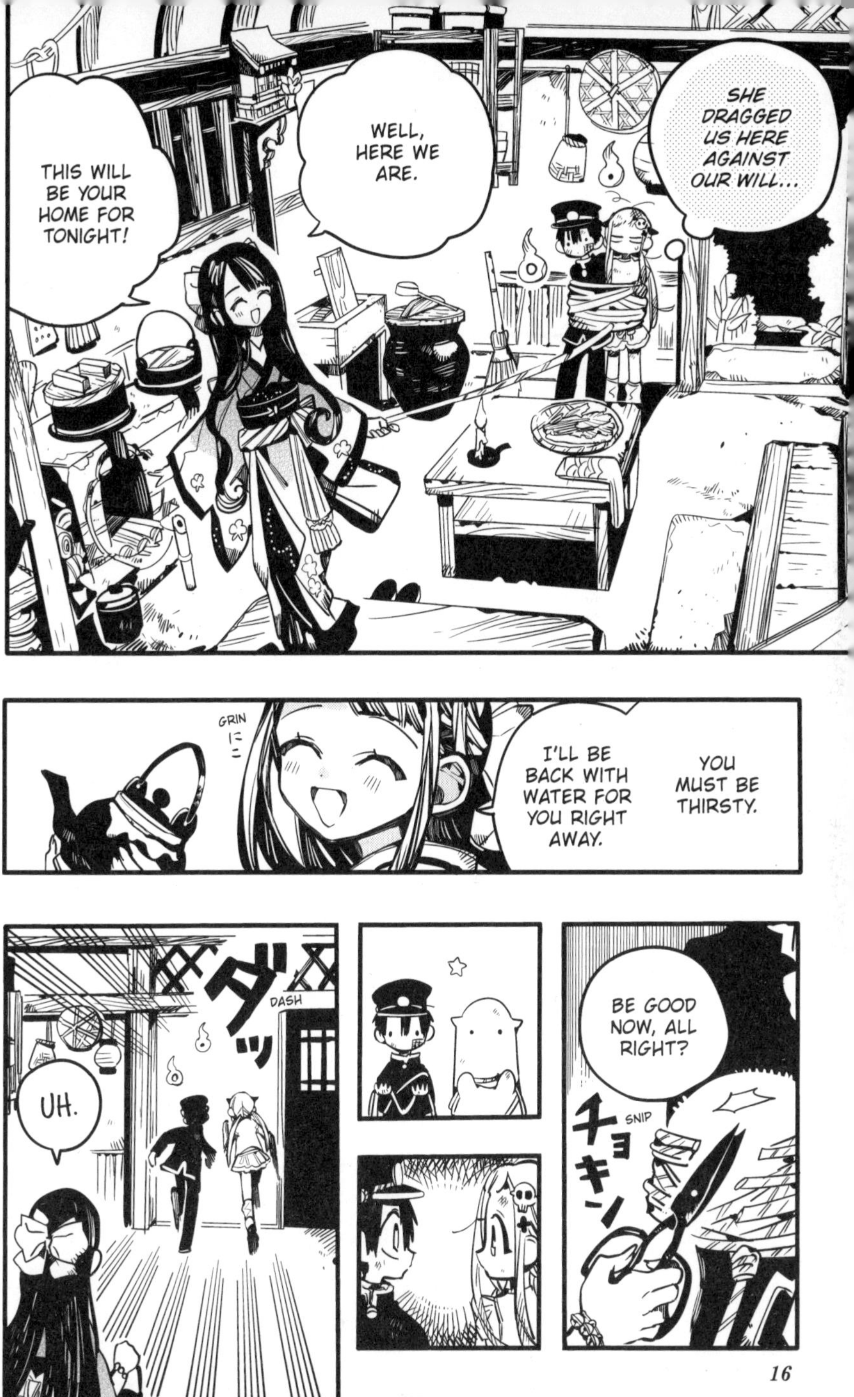
SHE DRAGGED US HERE AGAINST OUR WILL...
WELL, HERE WE ARE.
THIS WILL BE YOUR HOME FOR TONIGHT!
YOU MUST BE THIRSTY.
I'LL BE BACK WITH WATER FOR YOU RIGHT AWAY.
GRIN
にこ
BE GOOD NOW, ALL RIGHT?
チョキン
SNIP
ダッ
DASH
UH.

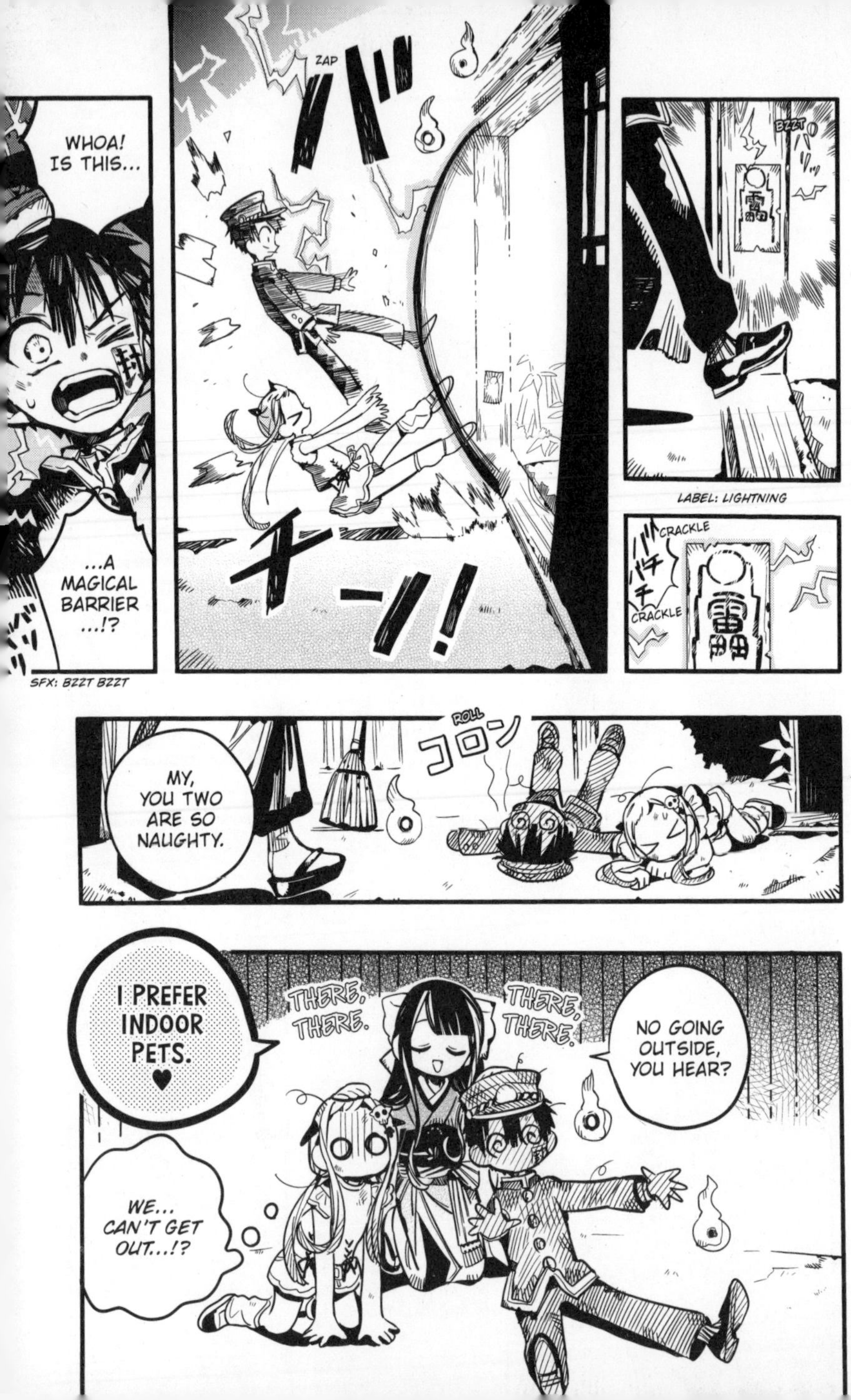
BZZT
LABEL: LIGHTNING
CRACKLE
CRACKLE
ZAP
WHOA! IS THIS...
...A MAGICAL BARRIER ...!?
SFX: BZZT BZZT
ROLL
MY, YOU TWO ARE SO NAUGHTY.
NO GOING OUTSIDE, YOU HEAR?
THERE, THERE.
THERE, THERE.
I PREFER INDOOR PETS. ♥
WE... CAN'T GET OUT...!?

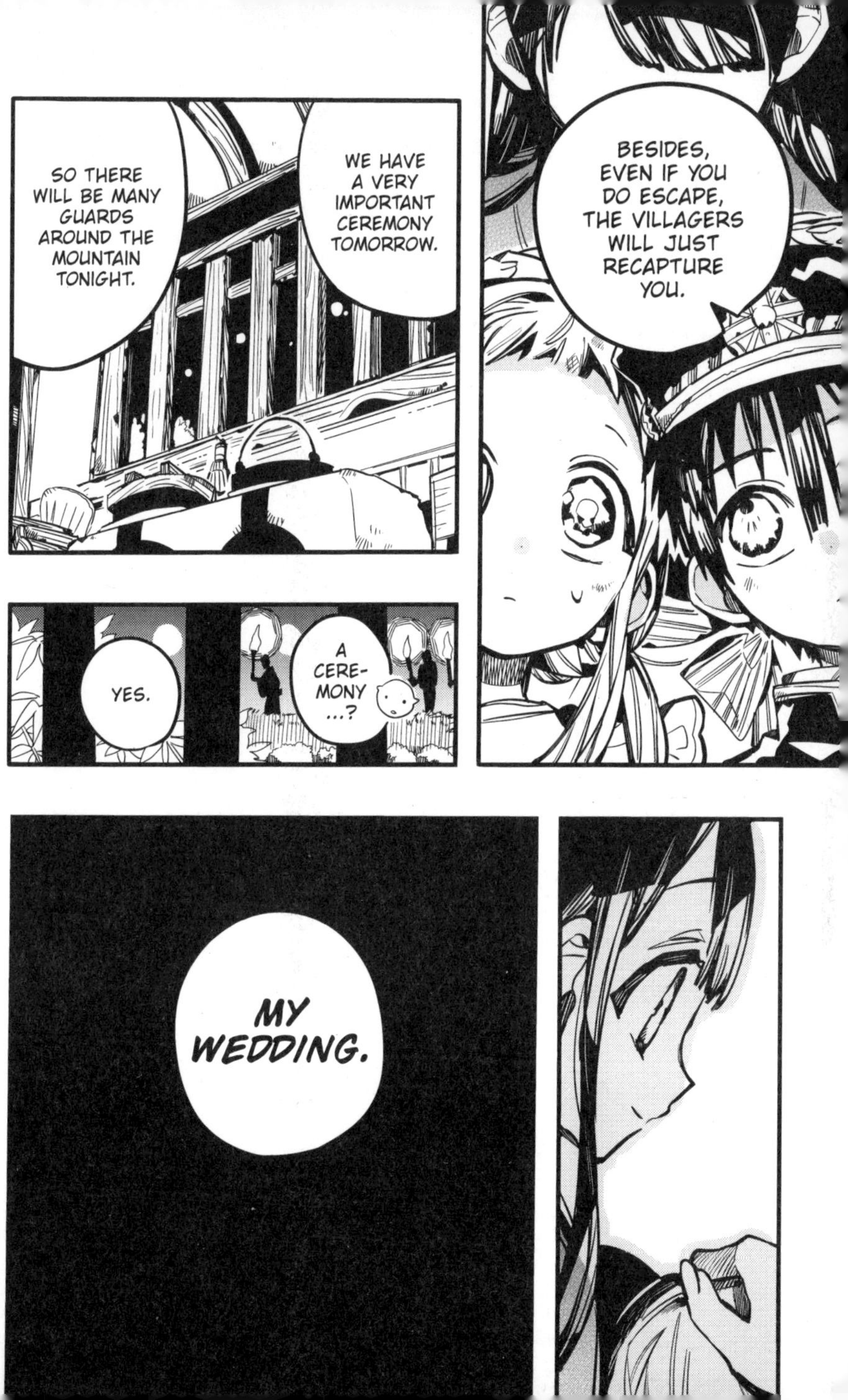
BESIDES, EVEN IF YOU DO ESCAPE, THE VILLAGERS WILL JUST RECAPTURE YOU.
WE HAVE A VERY IMPORTANT CEREMONY TOMORROW.
SO THERE WILL BE MANY GUARDS AROUND THE MOUNTAIN TONIGHT.
A CERE-MONY ...?
YES.
MY WEDDING.

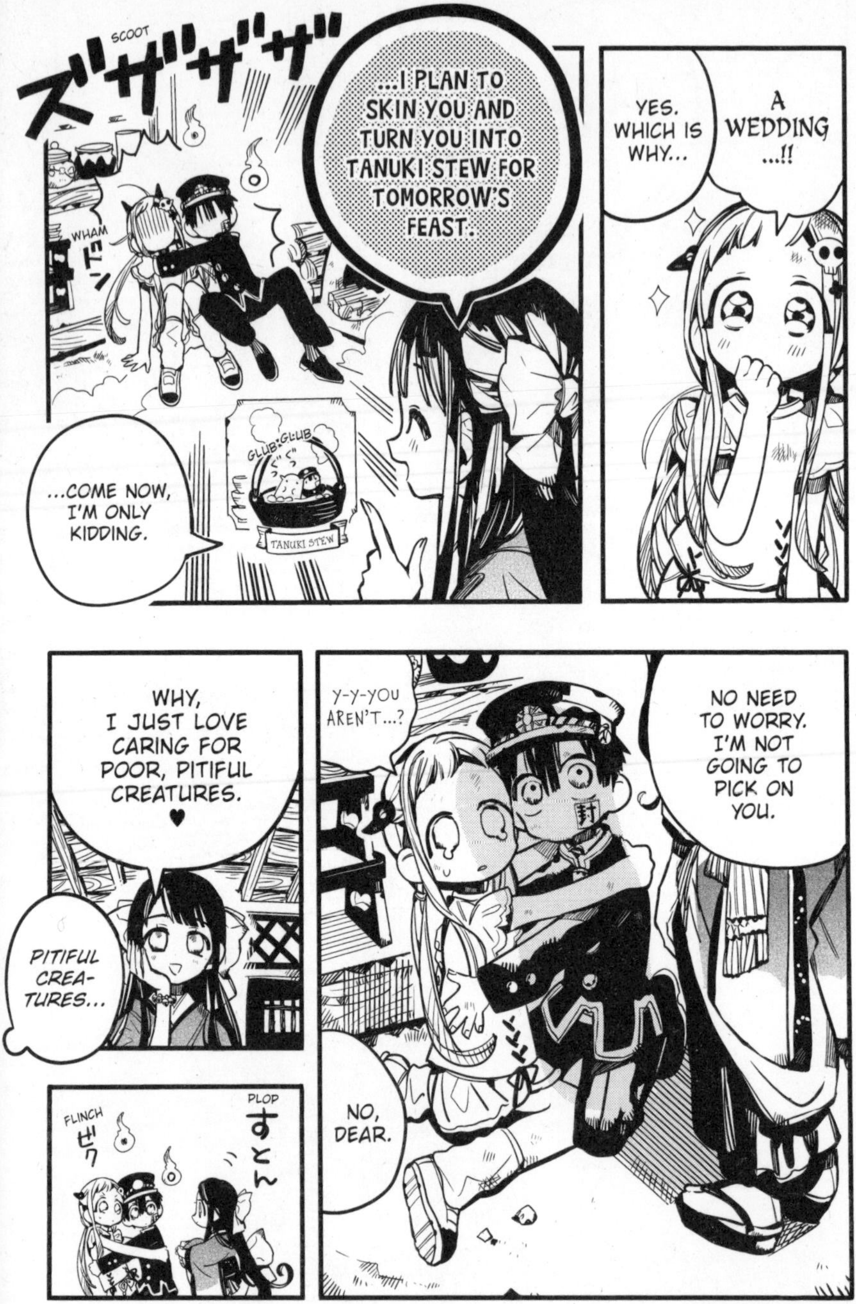
A WEDDING ...!!
YES. WHICH IS WHY...
...I PLAN TO SKIN YOU AND TURN YOU INTO TANUKI STEW FOR TOMORROW'S FEAST.
SCOOT
ズザザザ
WHAM
ドン
GLUB GLUB
TANUKI STEW
...COME NOW, I'M ONLY KIDDING.
NO NEED TO WORRY. I'M NOT GOING TO PICK ON YOU.
Y-Y-YOU AREN'T...?
NO, DEAR.
WHY, I JUST LOVE CARING FOR POOR, PITIFUL CREATURES. ♥
PITIFUL CREA-TURES...
PLOP
すとん
FLINCH
ビク

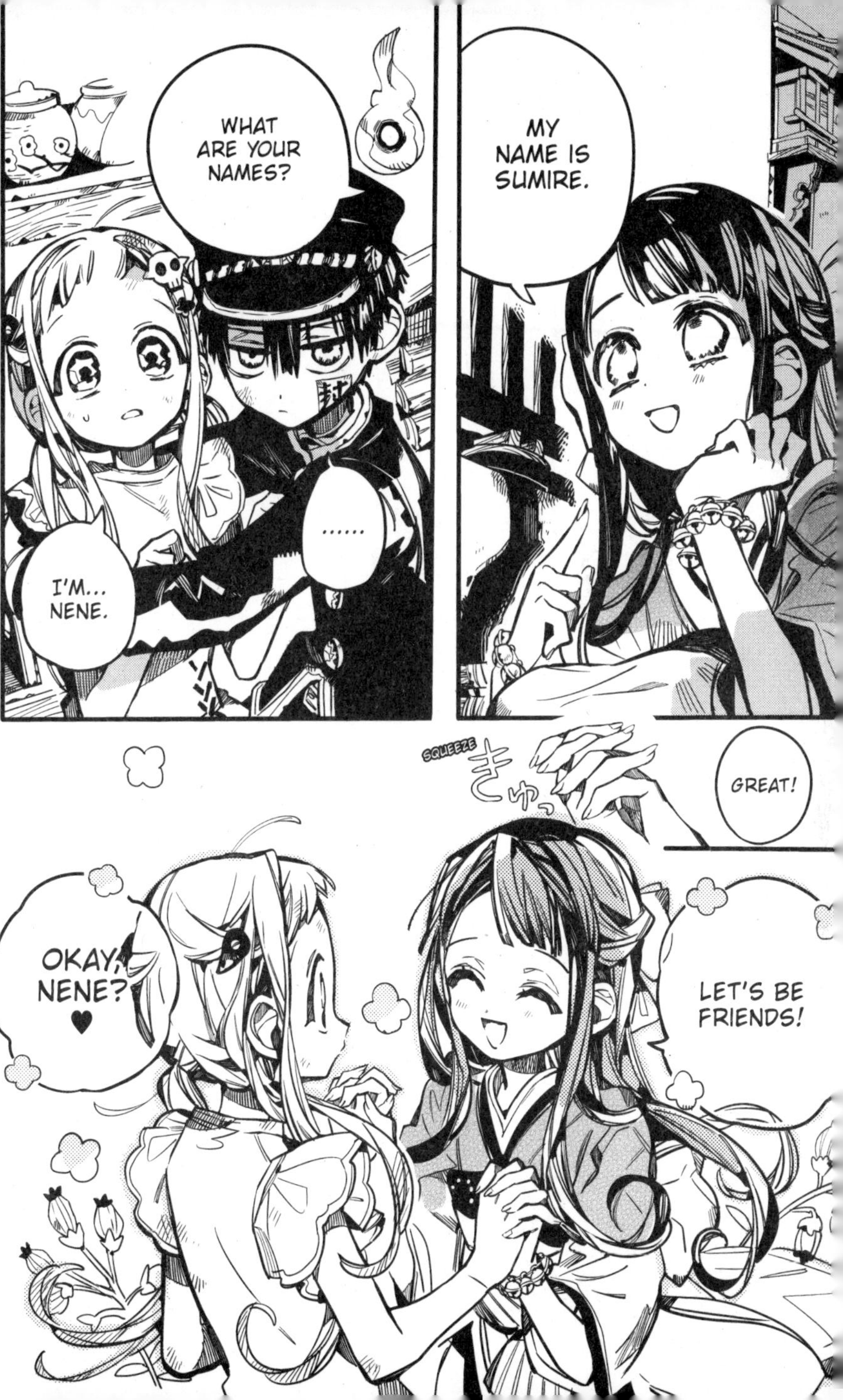
MY NAME IS SUMIRE.
WHAT ARE YOUR NAMES?
......
I'M... NENE.
GREAT!
SQUEEZE
きゅっ
LET'S BE FRIENDS!
OKAY, NENE? ♥

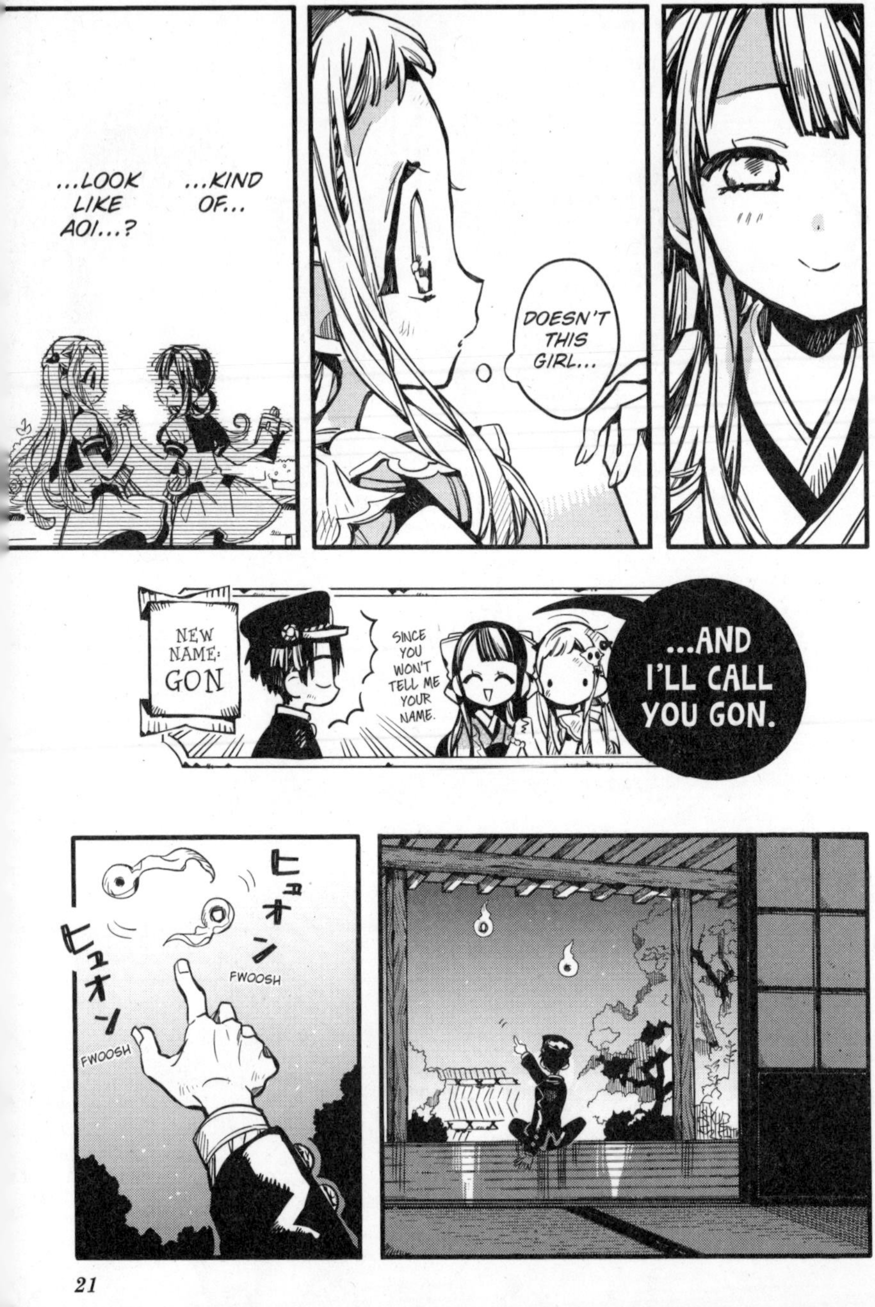
DOESN'T THIS GIRL...
...KIND OF...
...LOOK LIKE AOI...?
...AND I'LL CALL YOU GON.
SINCE YOU WON'T TELL ME YOUR NAME.
NEW NAME: GON
ヒュオン
FWOOSH
ヒュオン
FWOOSH

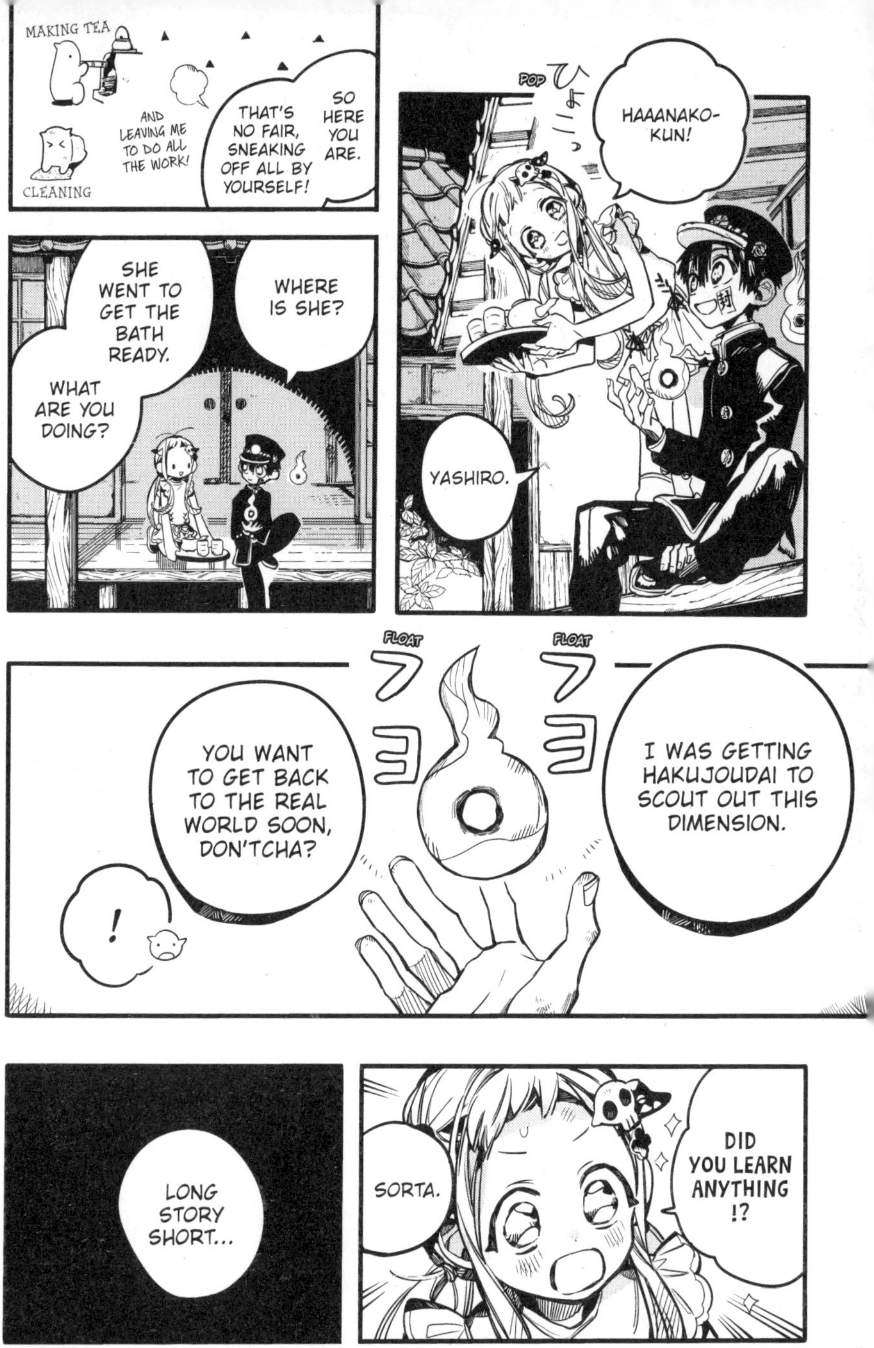
POP
HAAANAKO-KUN!
YASHIRO.
SO HERE YOU ARE.
THAT'S NO FAIR, SNEAKING OFF ALL BY YOURSELF!
AND LEAVING ME TO DO ALL THE WORK!
MAKING TEA
CLEANING
WHERE IS SHE?
SHE WENT TO GET THE BATH READY.
WHAT ARE YOU DOING?
FLOAT
FLOAT
I WAS GETTING HAKUJOUDAI TO SCOUT OUT THIS DIMENSION.
YOU WANT TO GET BACK TO THE REAL WORLD SOON, DON'TCHA?
!
DID YOU LEARN ANYTHING !?
SORTA.
LONG STORY SHORT...

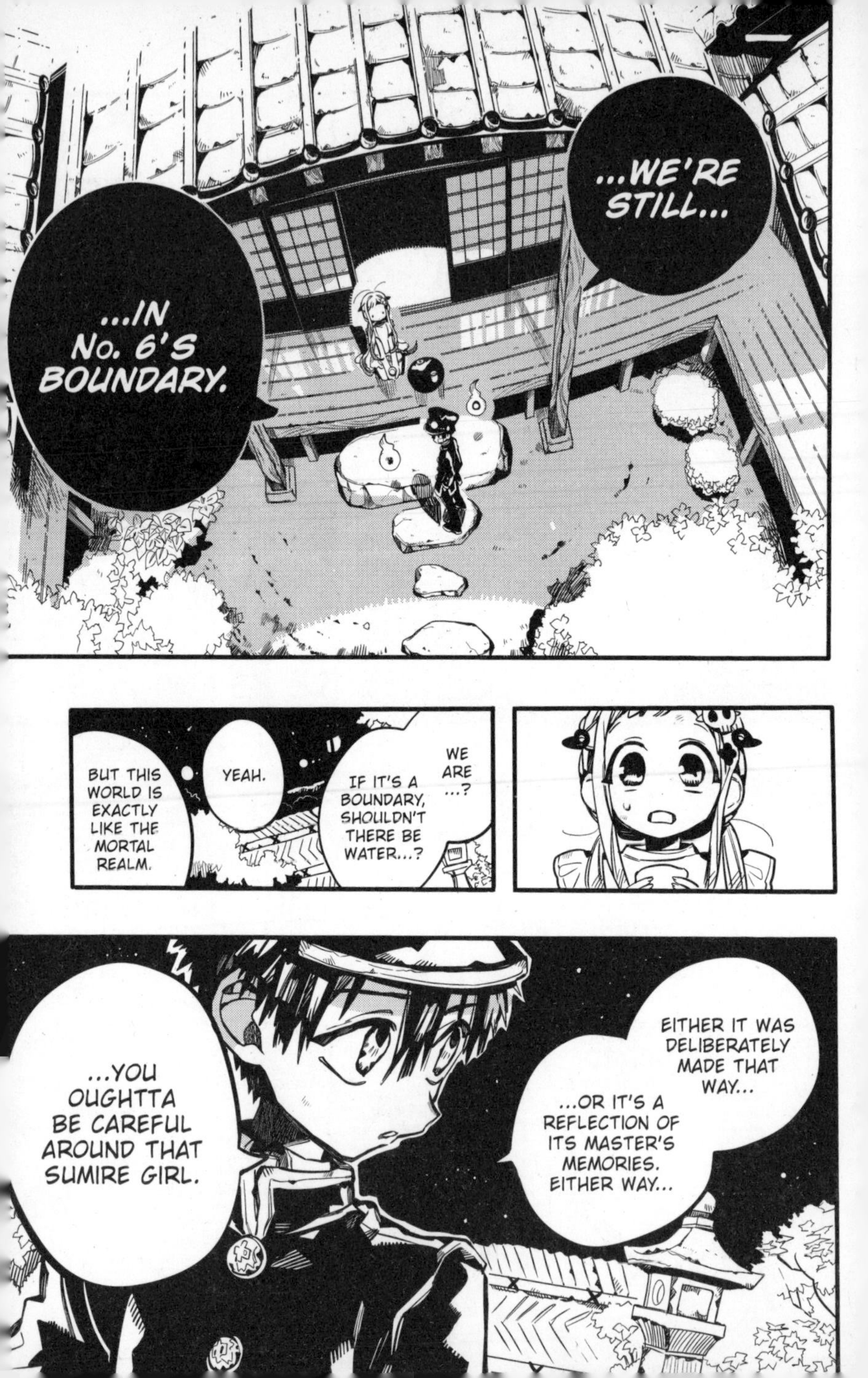
...WE'RE STILL...
...IN No. 6'S BOUNDARY.
WE ARE ...?
IF IT'S A BOUNDARY, SHOULDN'T THERE BE WATER...?
YEAH.
BUT THIS WORLD IS EXACTLY LIKE THE MORTAL REALM.
EITHER IT WAS DELIBERATELY MADE THAT WAY...
...OR IT'S A REFLECTION OF ITS MASTER'S MEMORIES. EITHER WAY...
...YOU OUGHTTA BE CAREFUL AROUND THAT SUMIRE GIRL.

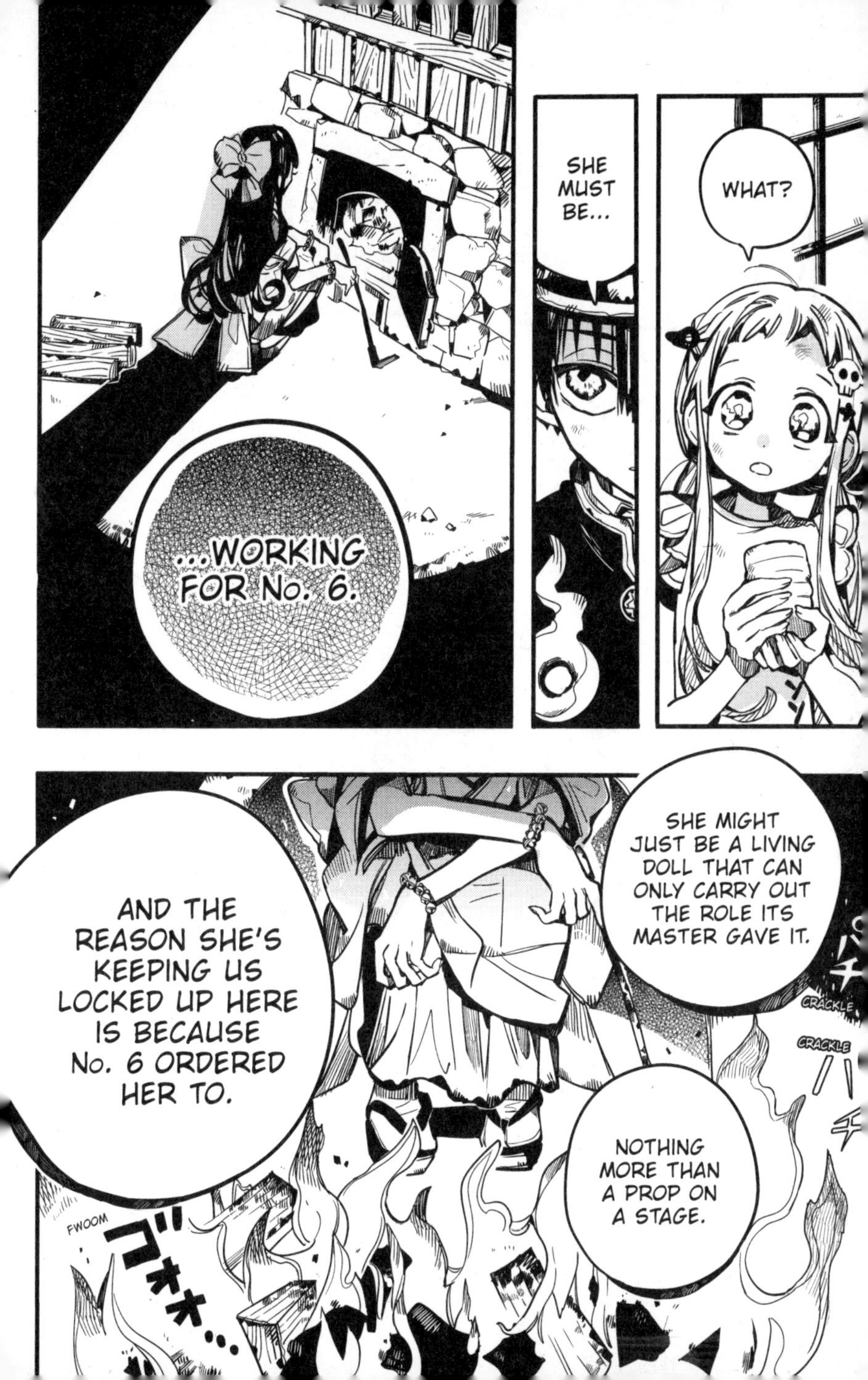
WHAT?
SHE MUST BE...
...WORKING FOR No. 6.
SHE MIGHT JUST BE A LIVING DOLL THAT CAN ONLY CARRY OUT THE ROLE ITS MASTER GAVE IT.
CRACKLE
CRACKLE
NOTHING MORE THAN A PROP ON A STAGE.
AND THE REASON SHE'S KEEPING US LOCKED UP HERE IS BECAUSE No. 6 ORDERED HER TO.
FWOOM

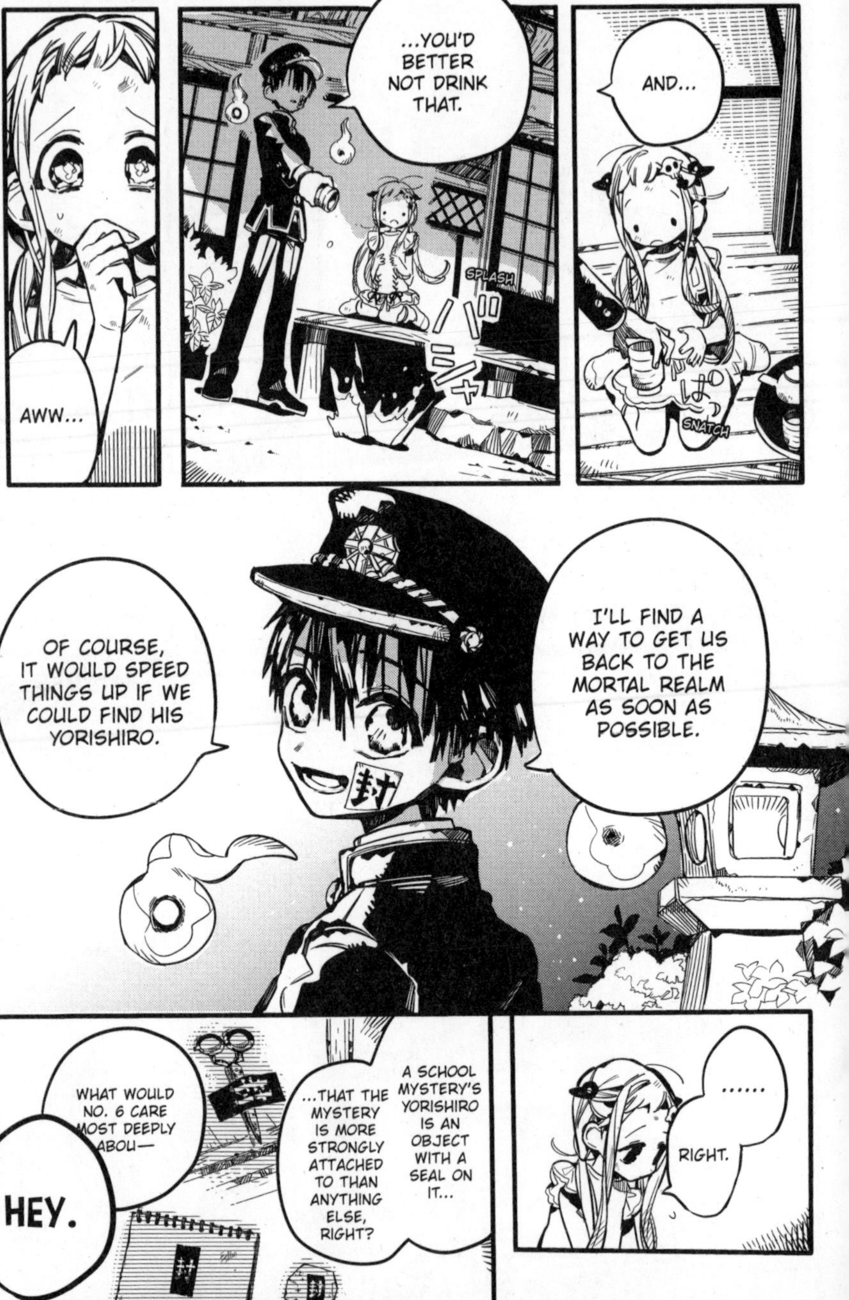
AND...
SNATCH
...YOU'D BETTER NOT DRINK THAT.
SPLASH
AWW...
I'LL FIND A WAY TO GET US BACK TO THE MORTAL REALM AS SOON AS POSSIBLE.
OF COURSE, IT WOULD SPEED THINGS UP IF WE COULD FIND HIS YORISHIRO.
......
RIGHT.
A SCHOOL MYSTERY'S YORISHIRO IS AN OBJECT WITH A SEAL ON IT...
...THAT THE MYSTERY IS MORE STRONGLY ATTACHED TO THAN ANYTHING ELSE, RIGHT?
WHAT WOULD NO. 6 CARE MOST DEEPLY ABOU—
HEY.

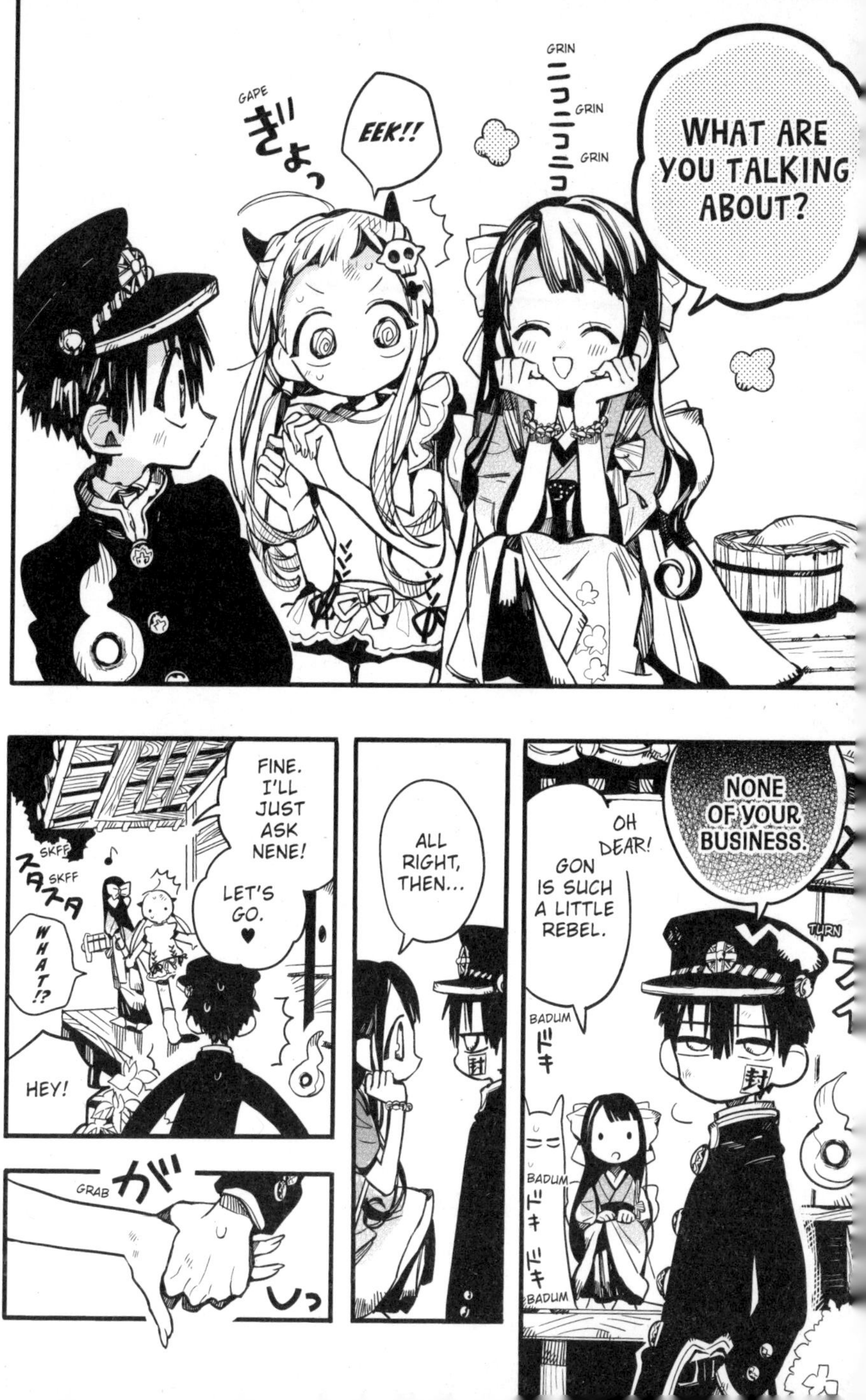
WHAT ARE YOU TALKING ABOUT?
GRIN
GRIN
GRIN
EEK!!
GAPE
ぎょっ
NONE OF YOUR BUSINESS.
TURN
OH DEAR!
GON IS SUCH A LITTLE REBEL.
BADUM
ドキ
BADUM
ドキ
ドキ
BADUM
ALL RIGHT, THEN...
FINE. I'LL JUST ASK NENE!
LET'S GO. ♥
SKFF
SKFF
スタスタ
WHAT!?
HEY!
GRAB
がし
しっ

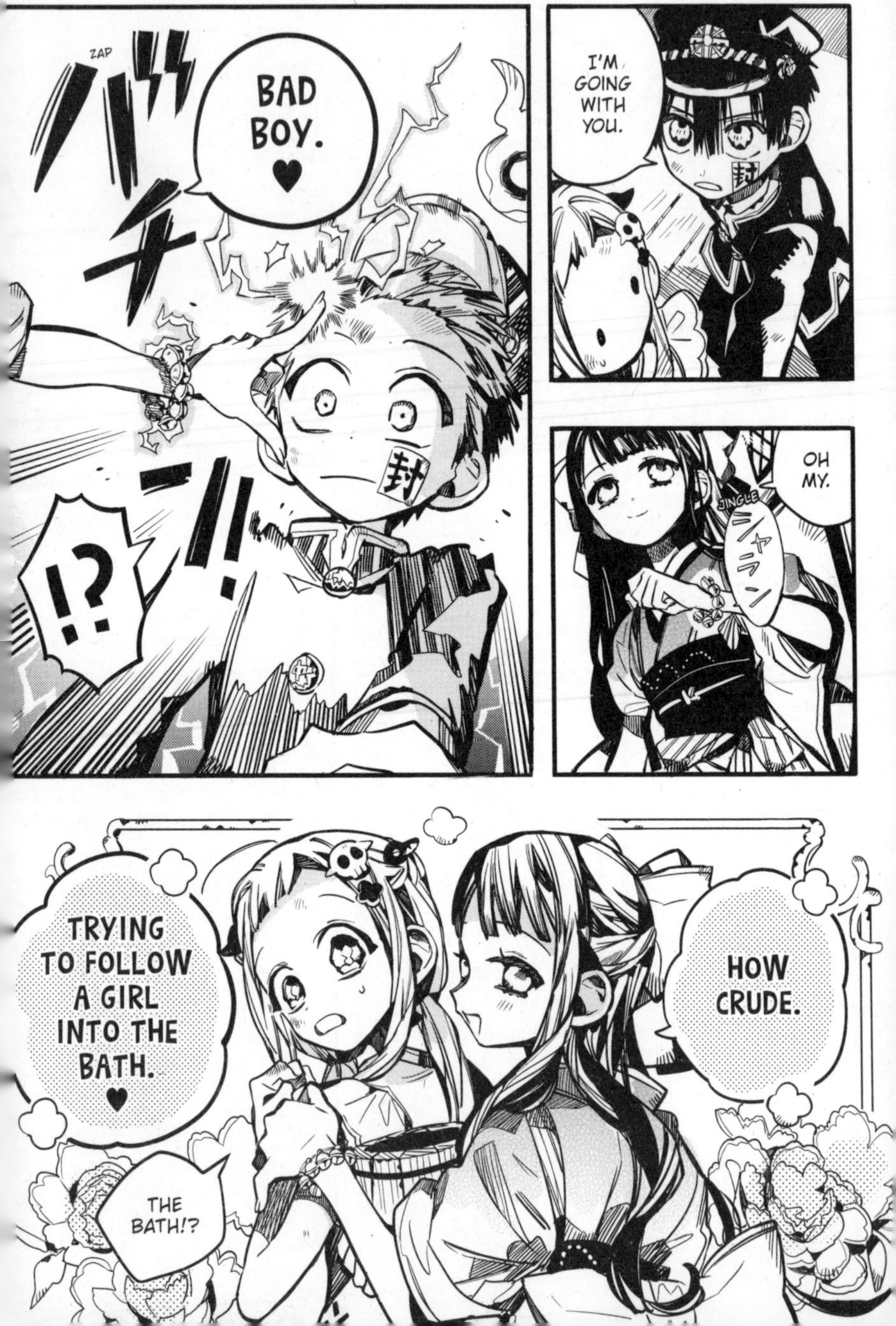
I'M GOING WITH YOU.
OH MY.
JINGLE
ZAP
BAD BOY. ♥
!?
HOW CRUDE.
TRYING TO FOLLOW A GIRL INTO THE BATH. ♥
THE BATH!?

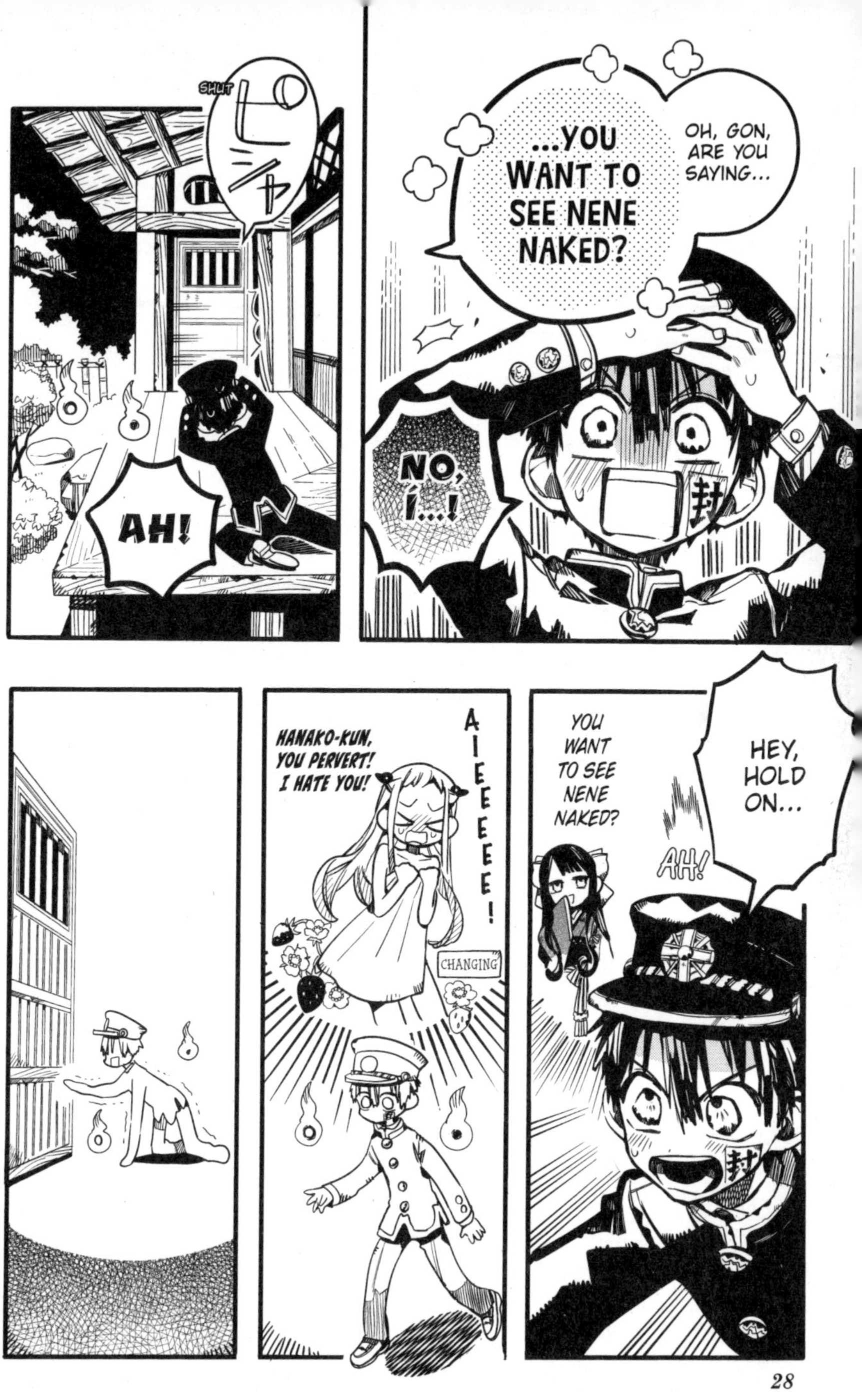
OH, GON, ARE YOU SAYING...
...YOU WANT TO SEE NENE NAKED?
NO, I...!
SHUT
AH!
HEY, HOLD ON...
AH!
YOU WANT TO SEE NENE NAKED?
HANAKO-KUN, YOU PERVERT! I HATE YOU!
AIEEEEEE!
CHANGING

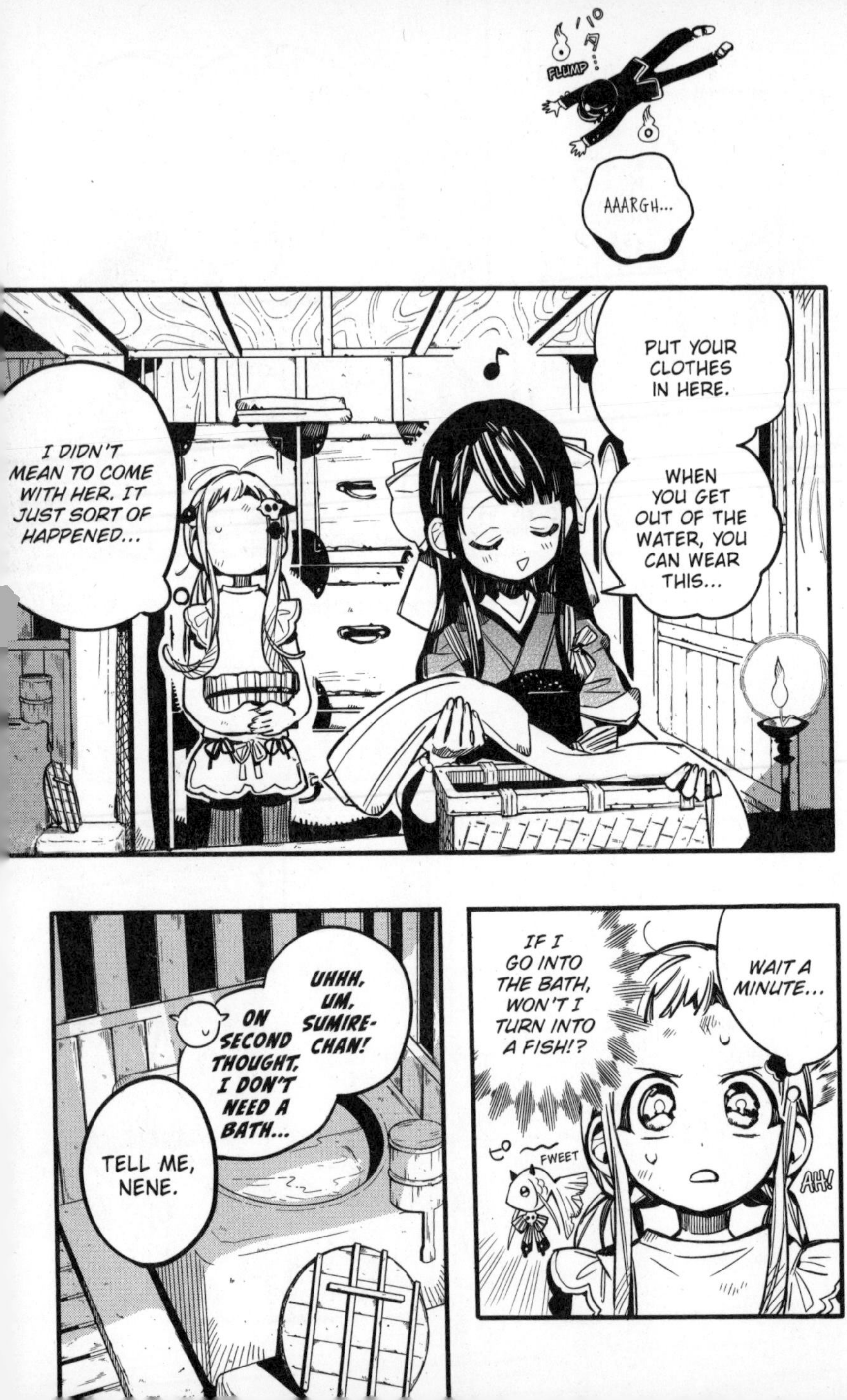
パタ…
FLUMP
AAARGH...
PUT YOUR CLOTHES IN HERE.
WHEN YOU GET OUT OF THE WATER, YOU CAN WEAR THIS...
I DIDN'T MEAN TO COME WITH HER. IT JUST SORT OF HAPPENED...
WAIT A MINUTE...
IF I GO INTO THE BATH, WON'T I TURN INTO A FISH!?
AH!
ピ〜
FWEET
UHHH, UM, SUMIRE-CHAN!
ON SECOND THOUGHT, I DON'T NEED A BATH...
TELL ME, NENE.

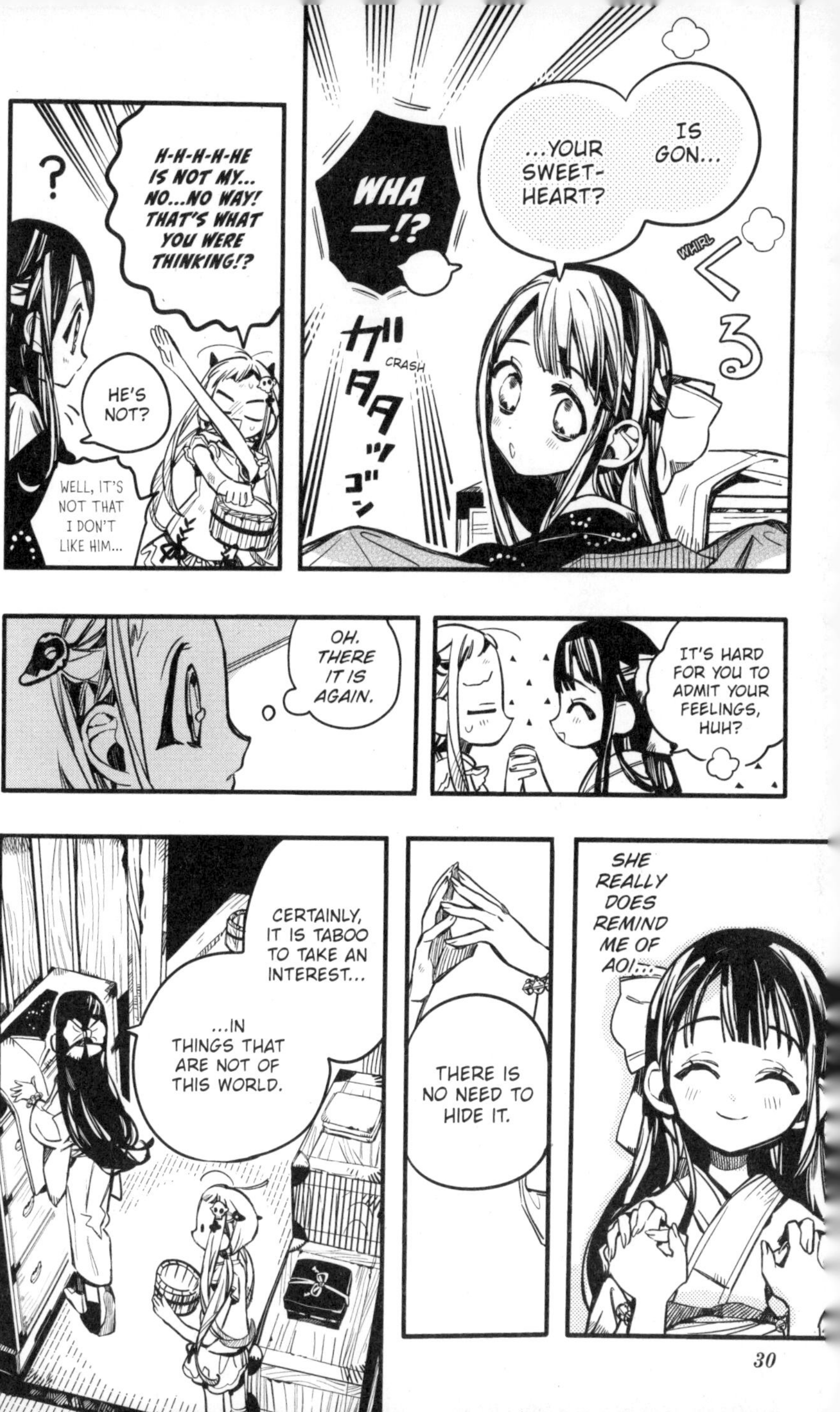
IS GON...
...YOUR SWEET-HEART?
WHIRL
WHA—!?
CRASH
H-H-H-H-HE IS NOT MY... NO...NO WAY! THAT'S WHAT YOU WERE THINKING!?
?
HE'S NOT?
WELL, IT'S NOT THAT I DON'T LIKE HIM...
IT'S HARD FOR YOU TO ADMIT YOUR FEELINGS, HUH?
OH. THERE IT IS AGAIN.
SHE REALLY DOES REMIND ME OF AOI...
THERE IS NO NEED TO HIDE IT.
CERTAINLY, IT IS TABOO TO TAKE AN INTEREST...
...IN THINGS THAT ARE NOT OF THIS WORLD.

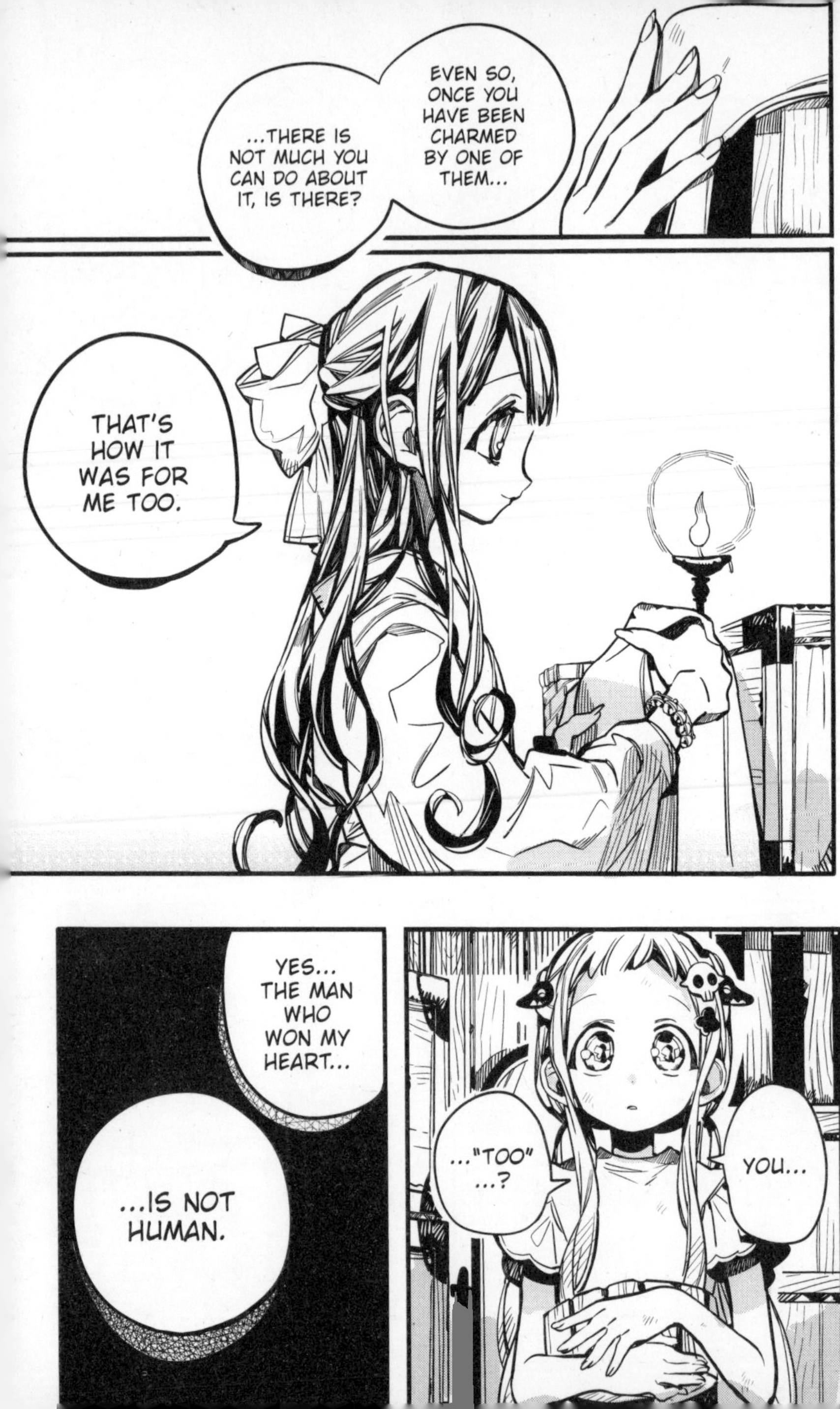
EVEN SO, ONCE YOU HAVE BEEN CHARMED BY ONE OF THEM...
...THERE IS NOT MUCH YOU CAN DO ABOUT IT, IS THERE?
THAT'S HOW IT WAS FOR ME TOO.
YOU...
..."TOO" ...?
YES... THE MAN WHO WON MY HEART...
...IS NOT HUMAN.

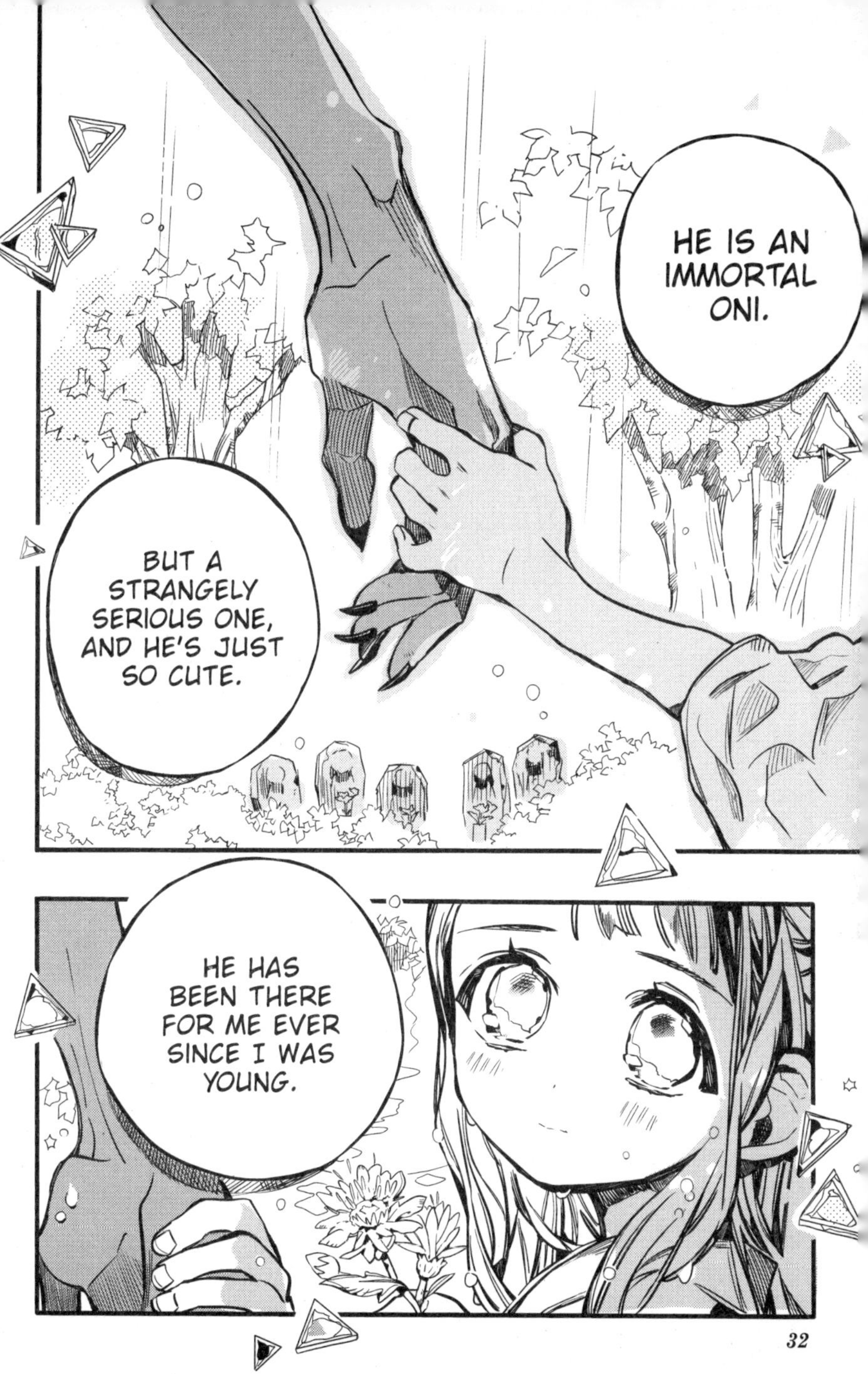
HE IS AN IMMORTAL ONI.
BUT A STRANGELY SERIOUS ONE, AND HE'S JUST SO CUTE.
HE HAS BEEN THERE FOR ME EVER SINCE I WAS YOUNG.

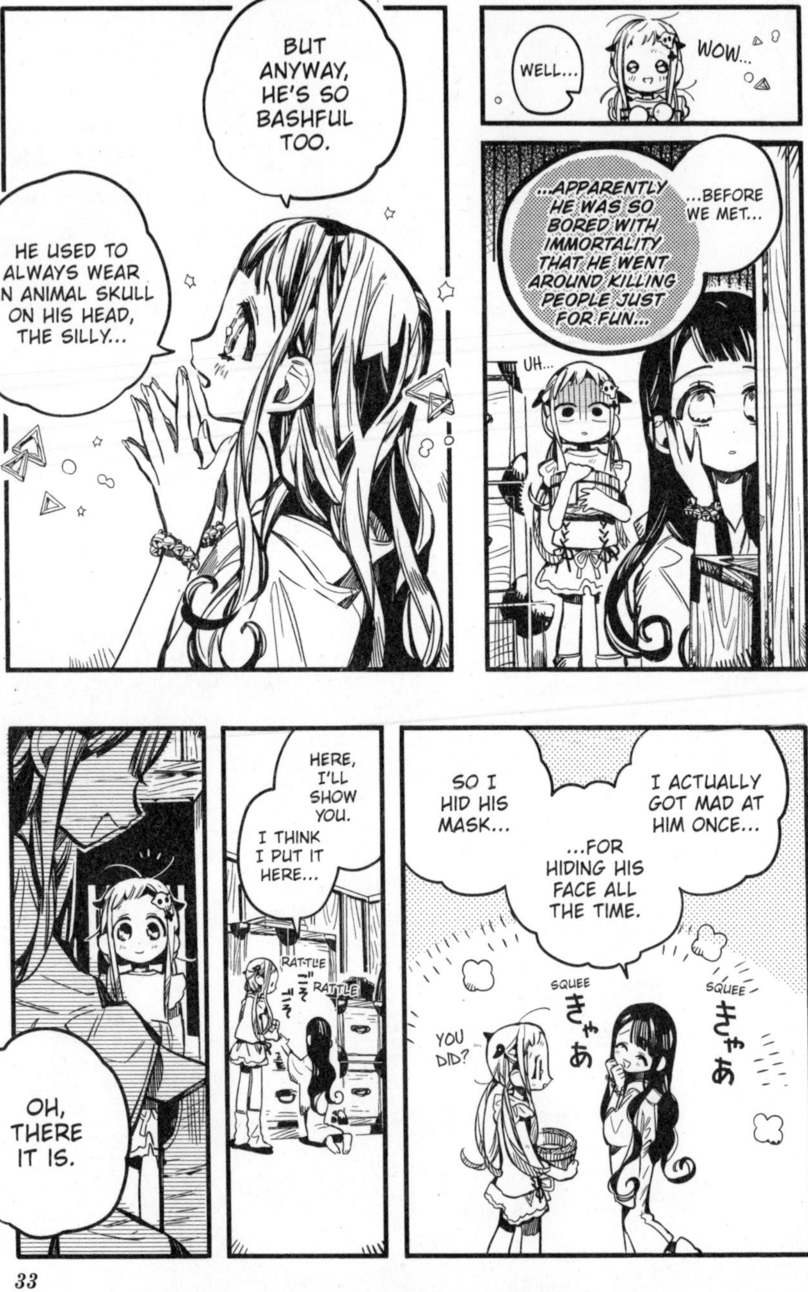
WOW...
WELL...
...BEFORE WE MET...
...APPARENTLY HE WAS SO BORED WITH IMMORTALITY THAT HE WENT AROUND KILLING PEOPLE JUST FOR FUN...
UH...
BUT ANYWAY, HE'S SO BASHFUL TOO.
HE USED TO ALWAYS WEAR AN ANIMAL SKULL ON HIS HEAD, THE SILLY...
I ACTUALLY GOT MAD AT HIM ONCE...
SO I HID HIS MASK...
...FOR HIDING HIS FACE ALL THE TIME.
SQUEE
きゃあ
SQUEE
きゃあ
YOU DID?
HERE, I'LL SHOW YOU.
I THINK I PUT IT HERE...
RATTLE
ごそ
ごそ
RATTLE
OH, THERE IT IS.

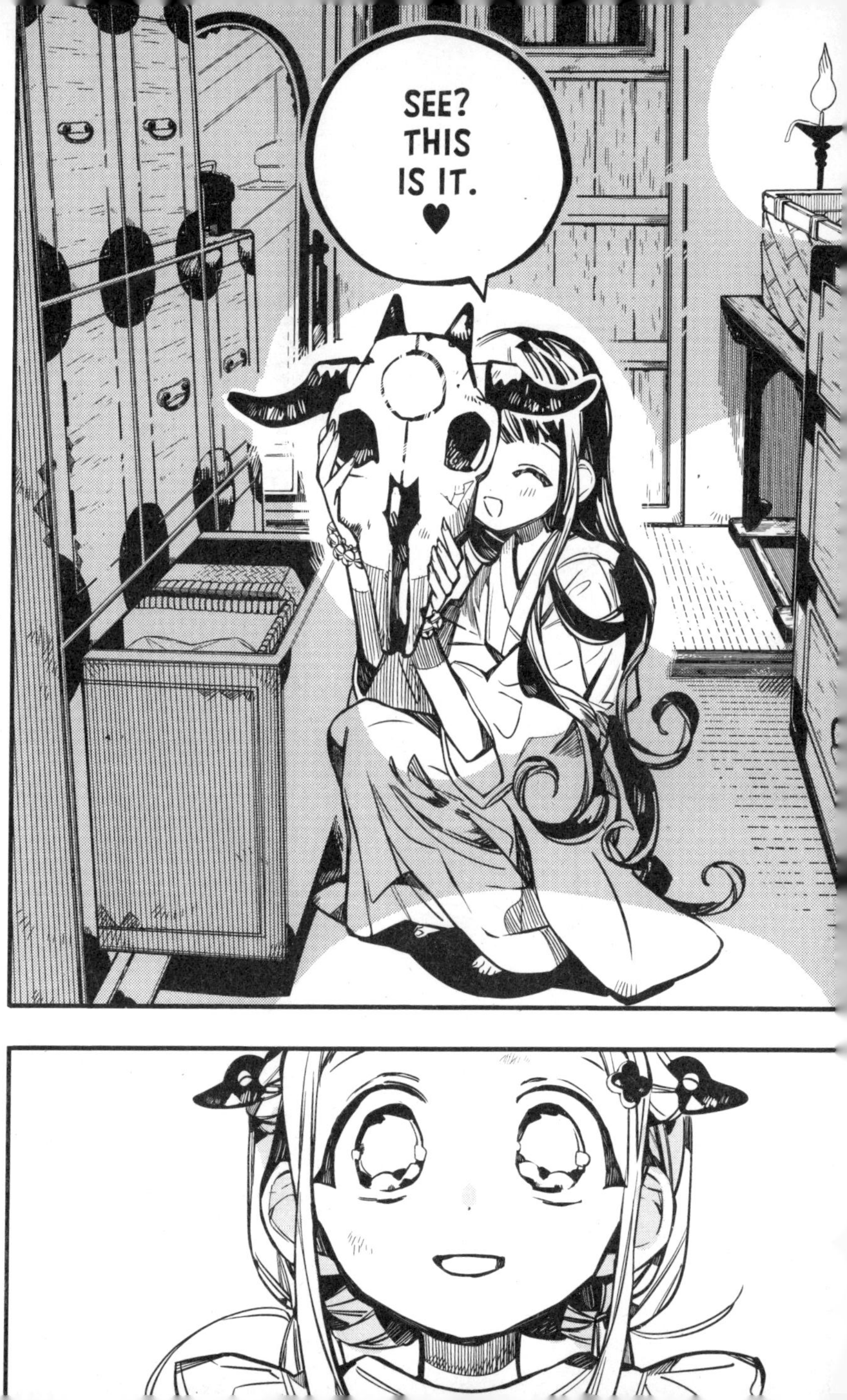
SEE? THIS IS IT. ♥

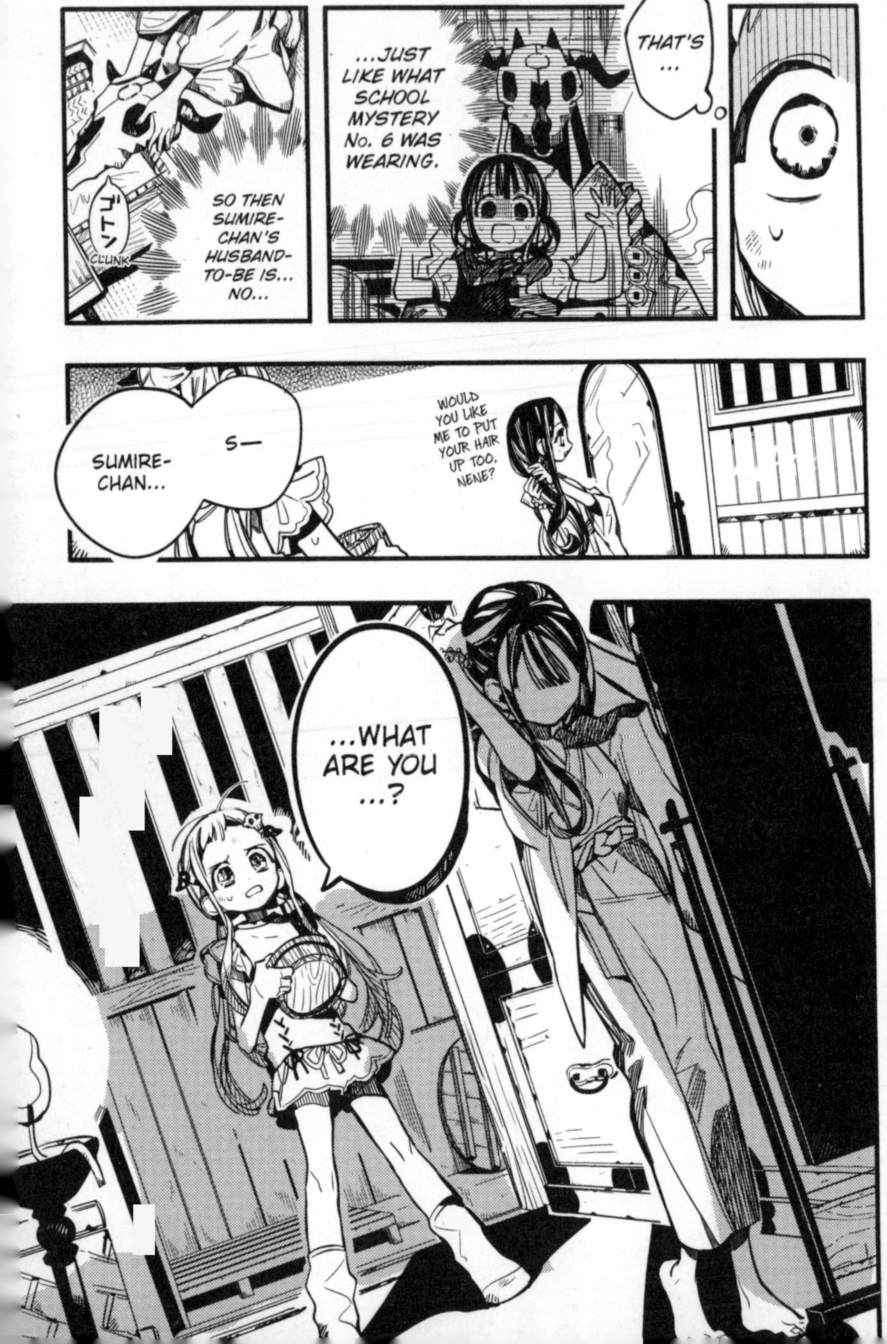
THAT'S ...
...JUST LIKE WHAT SCHOOL MYSTERY No. 6 WAS WEARING.
SO THEN SUMIRE-CHAN'S HUSBAND-TO-BE IS... NO...
ゴトン
CLUNK
WOULD YOU LIKE ME TO PUT YOUR HAIR UP TOO, NENE?
S— SUMIRE-CHAN...
...WHAT ARE YOU ...?

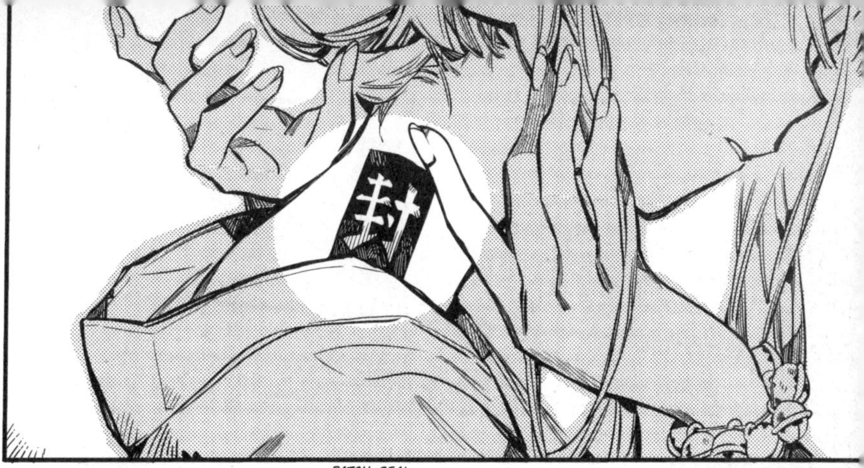

PATCH: SEAL

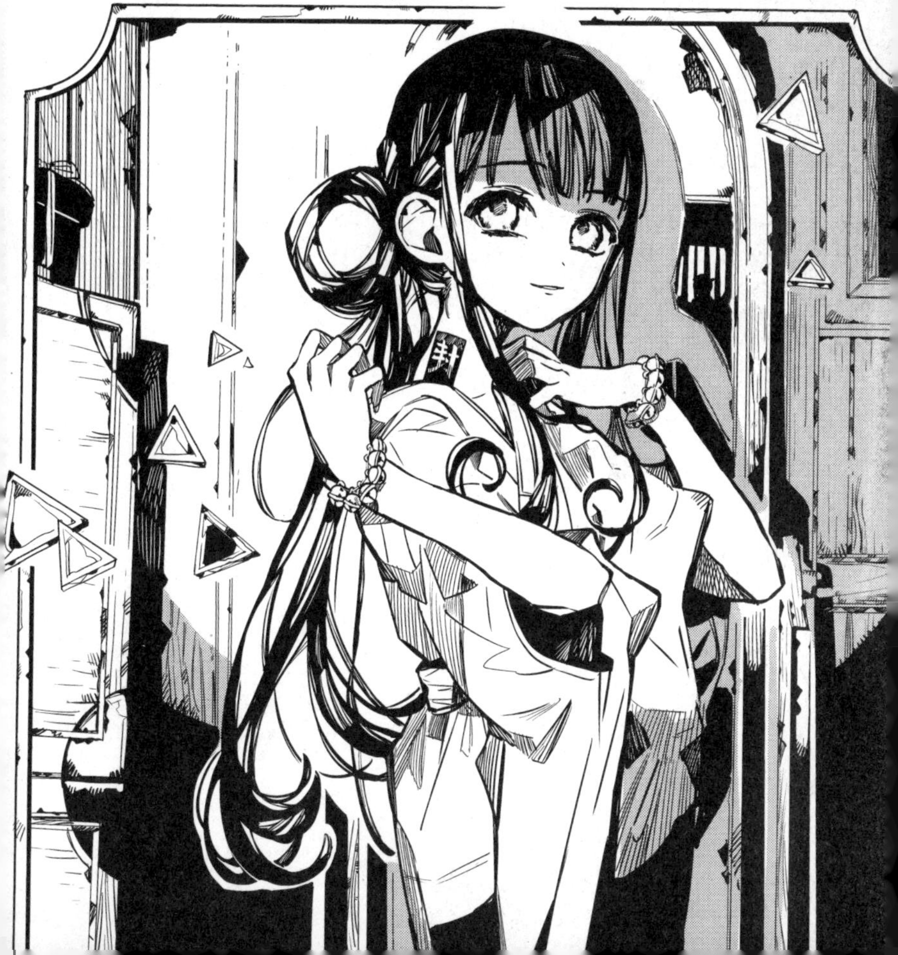

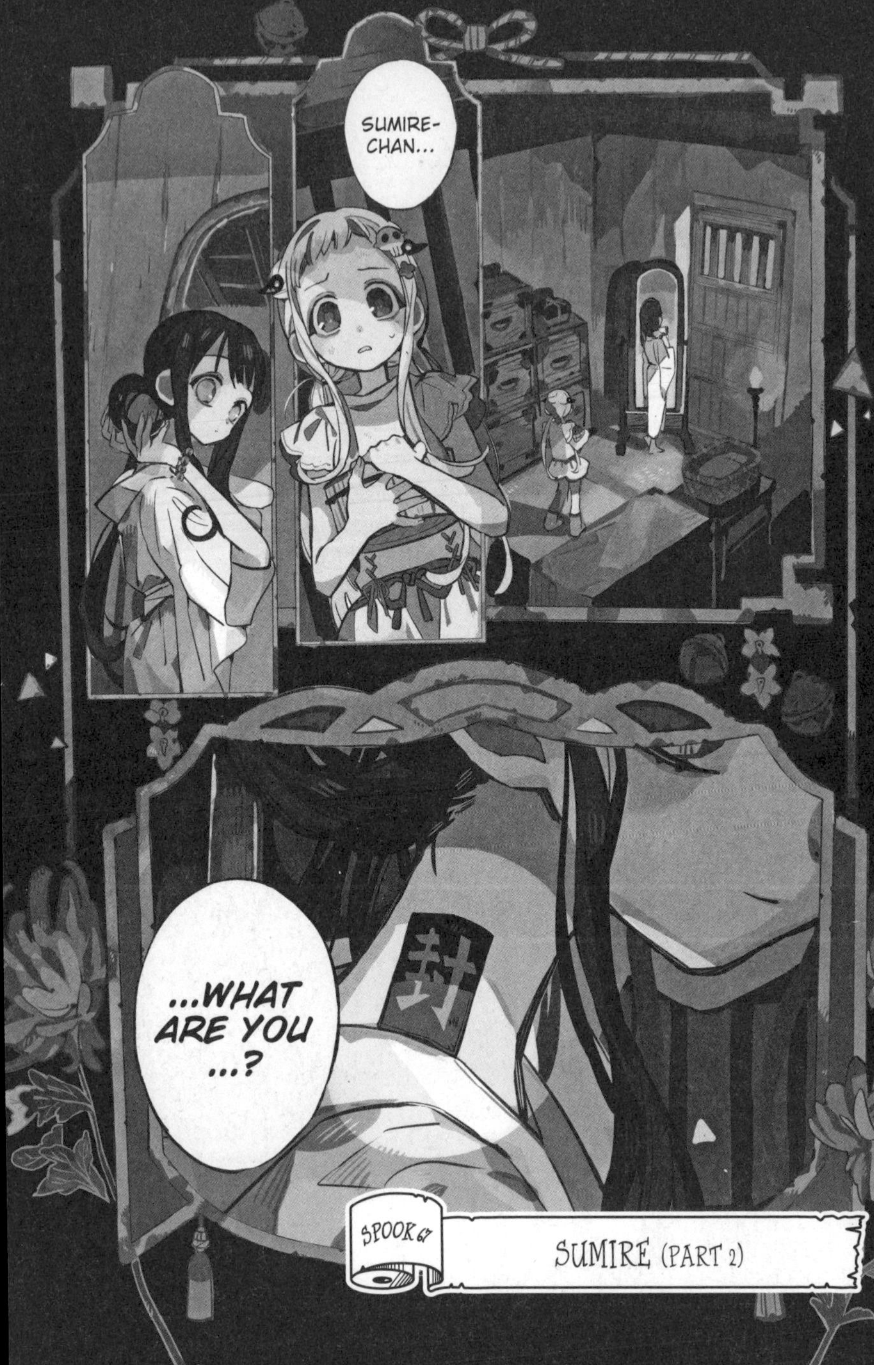
SUMIRE-CHAN...
...WHAT ARE YOU ...?
SPOOK 67
SUMIRE (PART 2)

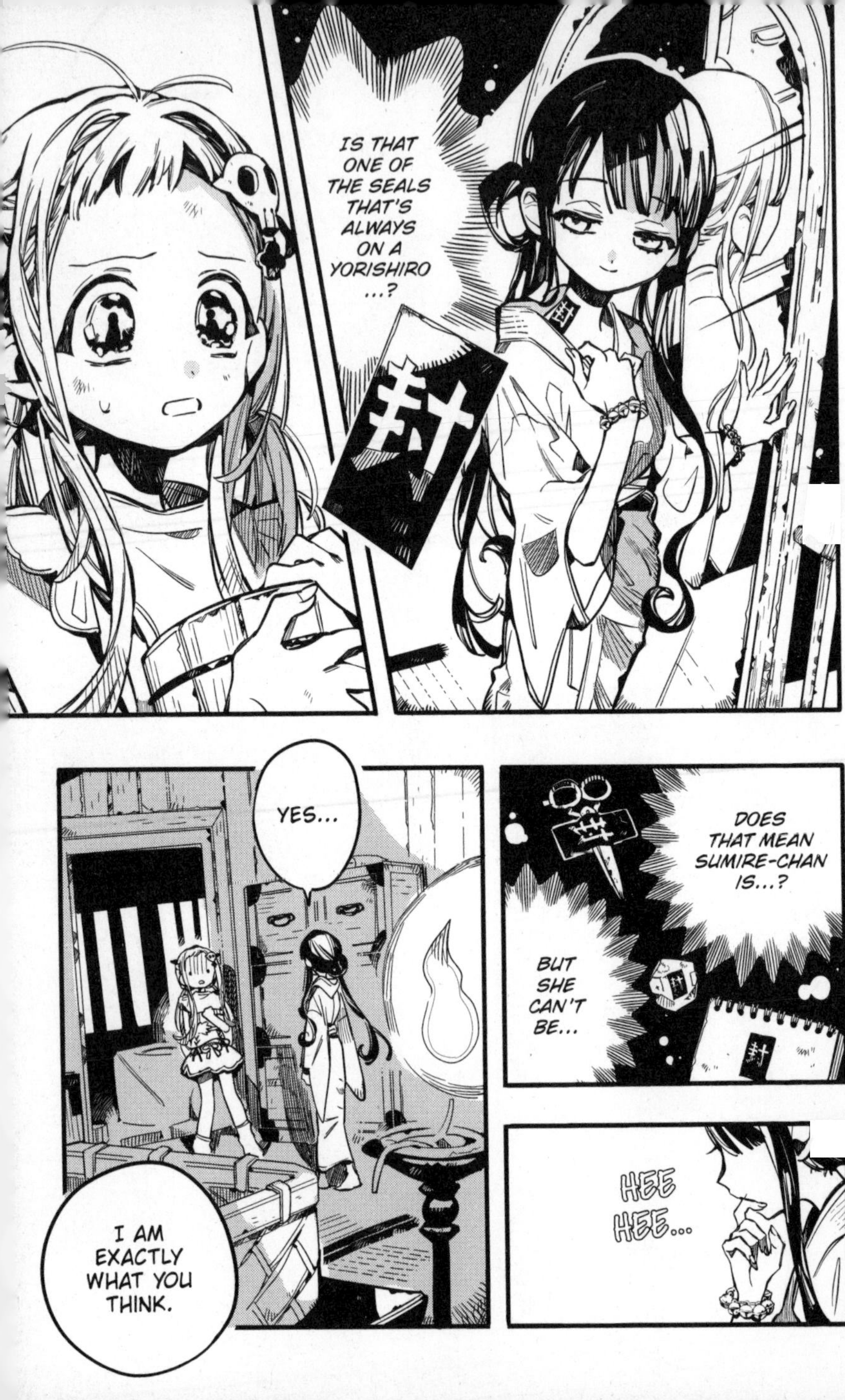
IS THAT ONE OF THE SEALS THAT'S ALWAYS ON A YORISHIRO ...?
DOES THAT MEAN SUMIRE-CHAN IS...?
BUT SHE CAN'T BE...
HEE HEE...
YES...
I AM EXACTLY WHAT YOU THINK.

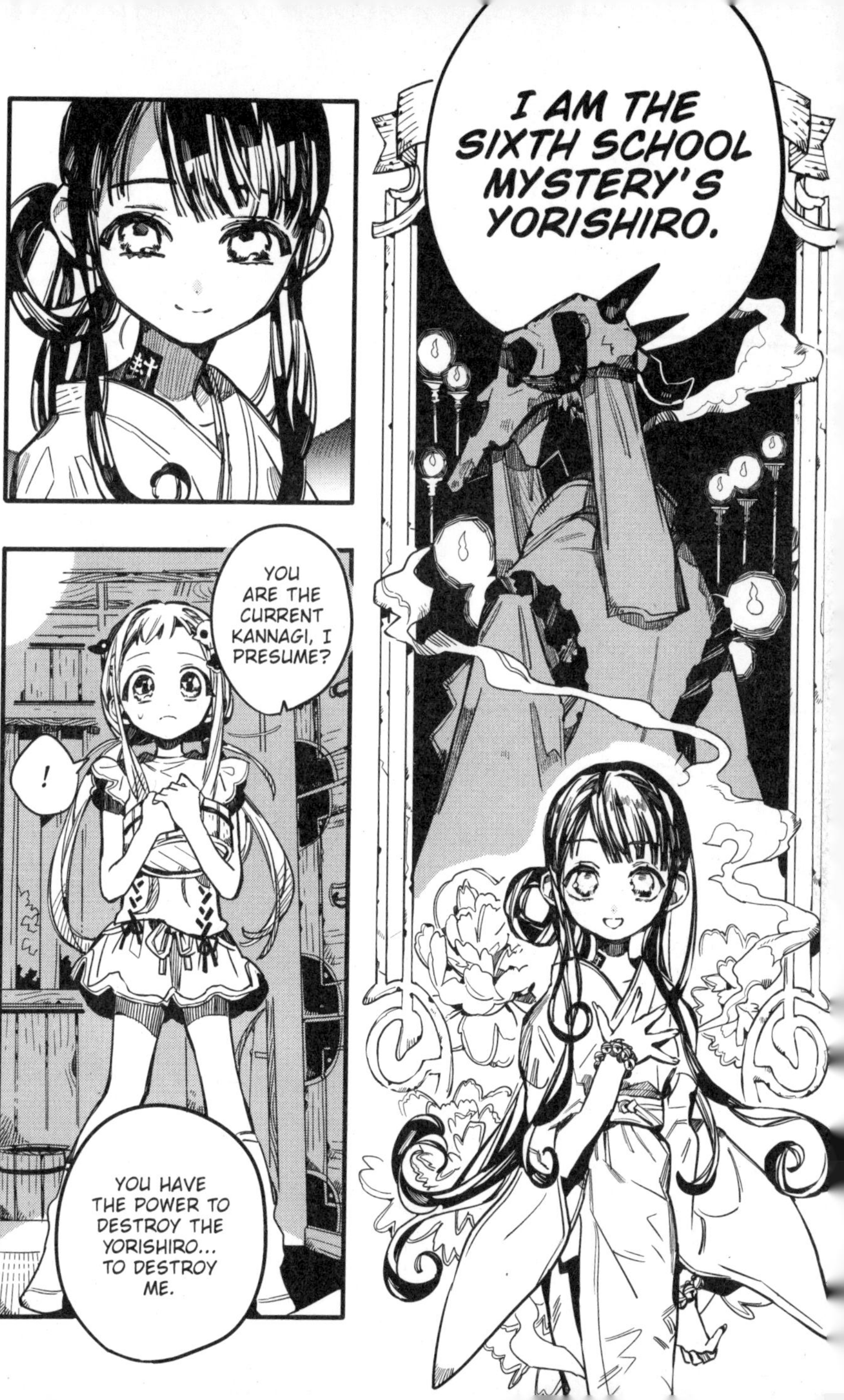
I AM THE SIXTH SCHOOL MYSTERY'S YORISHIRO.
YOU ARE THE CURRENT KANNAGI, I PRESUME?
!
YOU HAVE THE POWER TO DESTROY THE YORISHIRO... TO DESTROY ME.

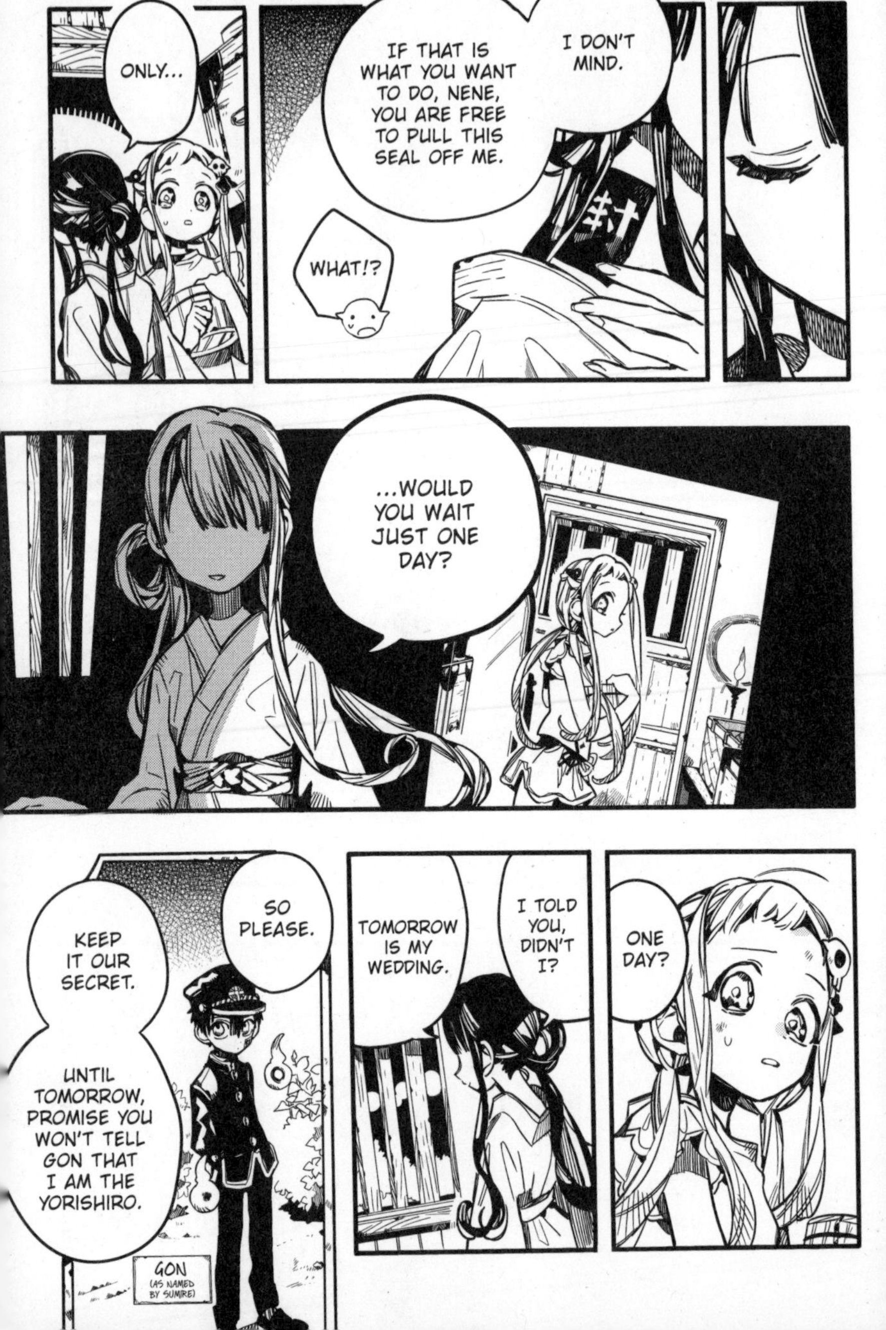
I DON'T MIND.
IF THAT IS WHAT YOU WANT TO DO, NENE, YOU ARE FREE TO PULL THIS SEAL OFF ME.
封
WHAT!?
ONLY...
...WOULD YOU WAIT JUST ONE DAY?
ONE DAY?
I TOLD YOU, DIDN'T I?
TOMORROW IS MY WEDDING.
SO PLEASE.
KEEP IT OUR SECRET.
UNTIL TOMORROW, PROMISE YOU WON'T TELL GON THAT I AM THE YORISHIRO.
GON (AS NAMED BY SUMIRE)

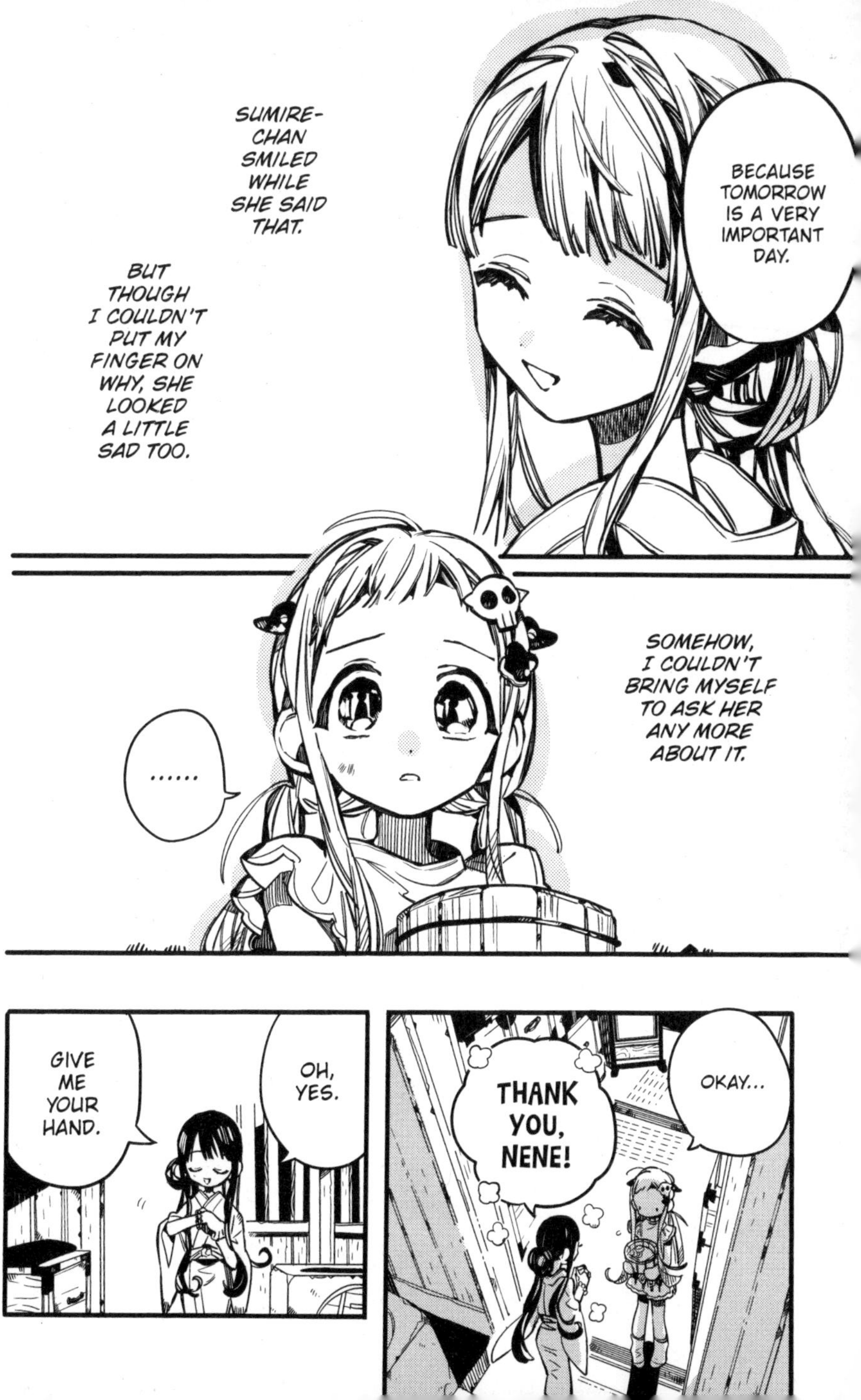
BECAUSE TOMORROW IS A VERY IMPORTANT DAY.
SUMIRE-CHAN SMILED WHILE SHE SAID THAT.
BUT THOUGH I COULDN'T PUT MY FINGER ON WHY, SHE LOOKED A LITTLE SAD TOO.
SOMEHOW, I COULDN'T BRING MYSELF TO ASK HER ANY MORE ABOUT IT.
......
OKAY...
THANK YOU, NENE!
OH, YES.
GIVE ME YOUR HAND.

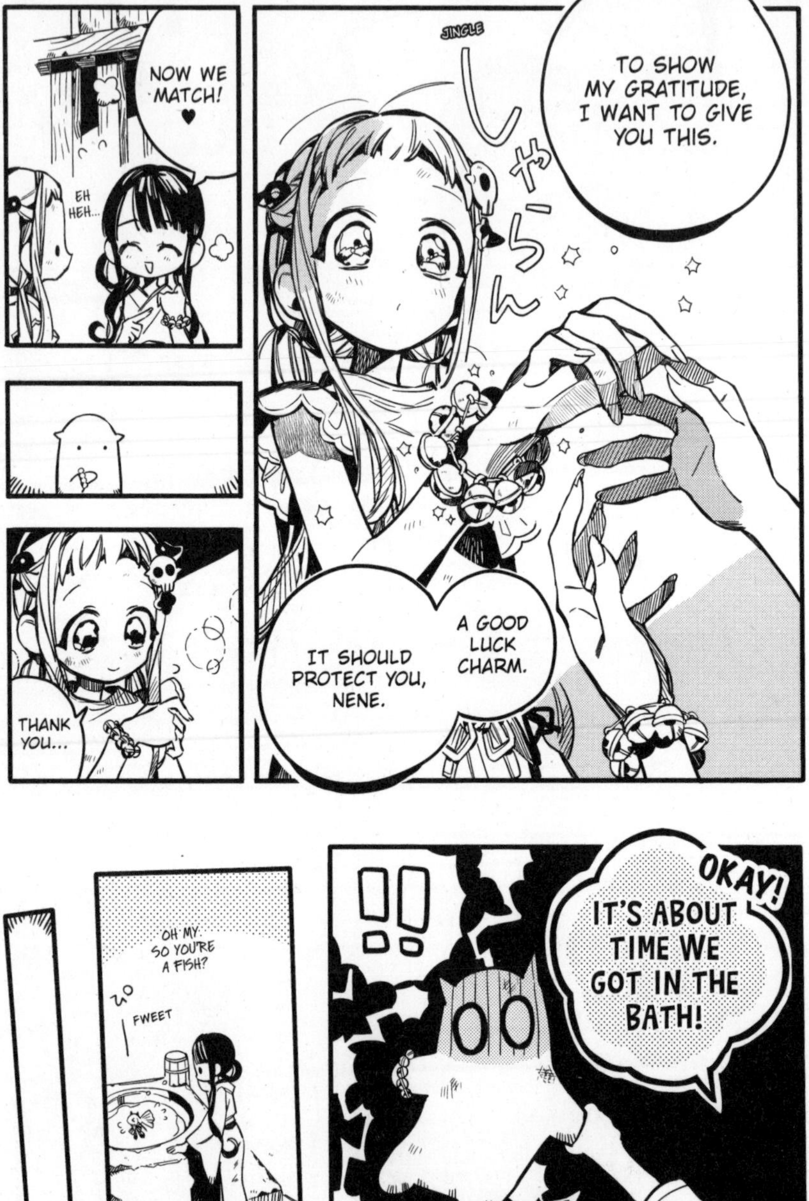
JINGLE
しゃらーん
TO SHOW MY GRATITUDE, I WANT TO GIVE YOU THIS.
A GOOD LUCK CHARM.
IT SHOULD PROTECT YOU, NENE.
NOW WE MATCH! ♥
EH HEH...
THANK YOU...
!!
OKAY!
IT'S ABOUT TIME WE GOT IN THE BATH!
OH MY. SO YOU'RE A FISH?
FWEET

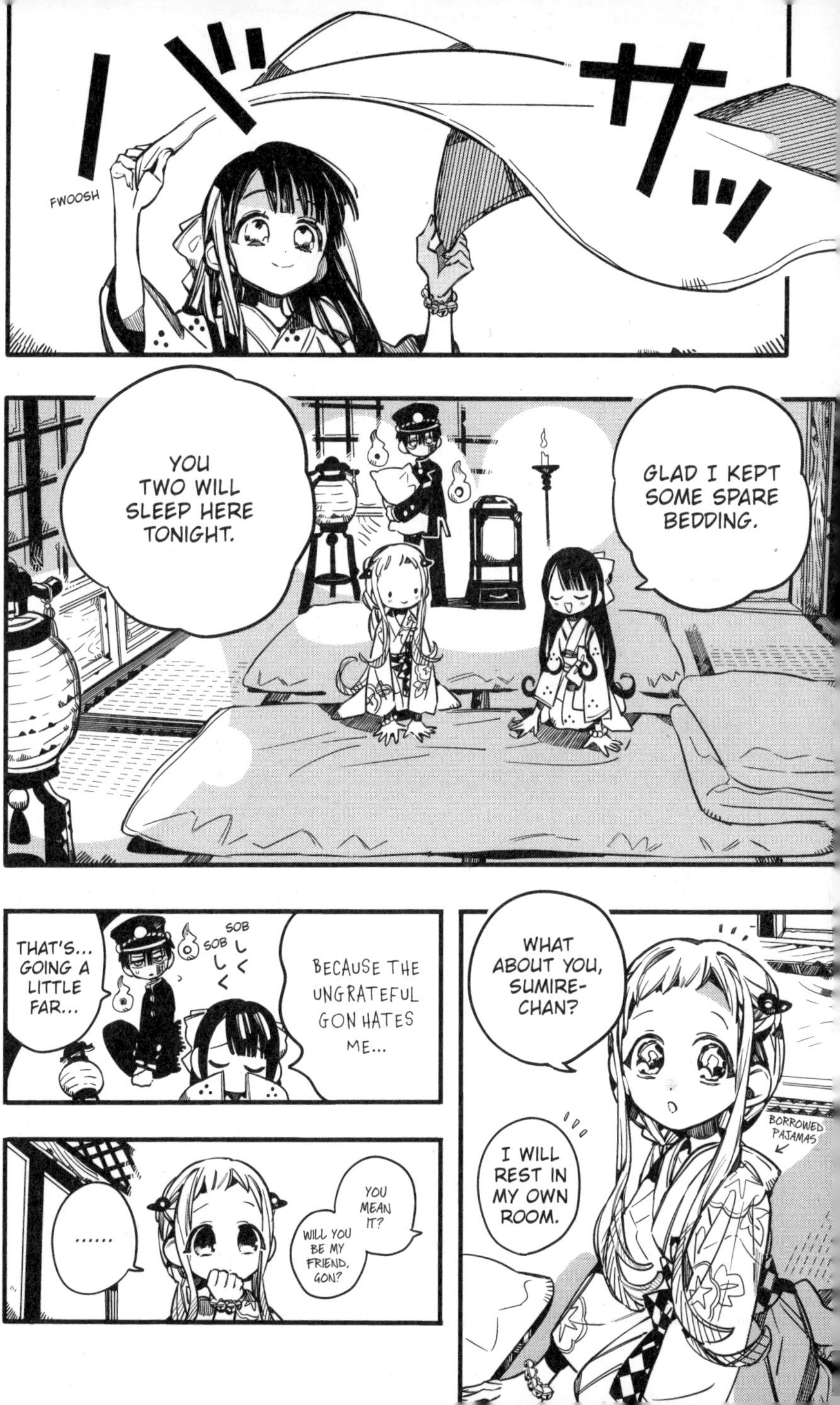
バサッ
FWOOSH
GLAD I KEPT SOME SPARE BEDDING.
YOU TWO WILL SLEEP HERE TONIGHT.
WHAT ABOUT YOU, SUMIRE-CHAN?
I WILL REST IN MY OWN ROOM.
BORROWED PAJAMAS
BECAUSE THE UNGRATEFUL GON HATES ME...
SOB しく
SOB しく
THAT'S... GOING A LITTLE FAR...
YOU MEAN IT?
WILL YOU BE MY FRIEND, GON?
......

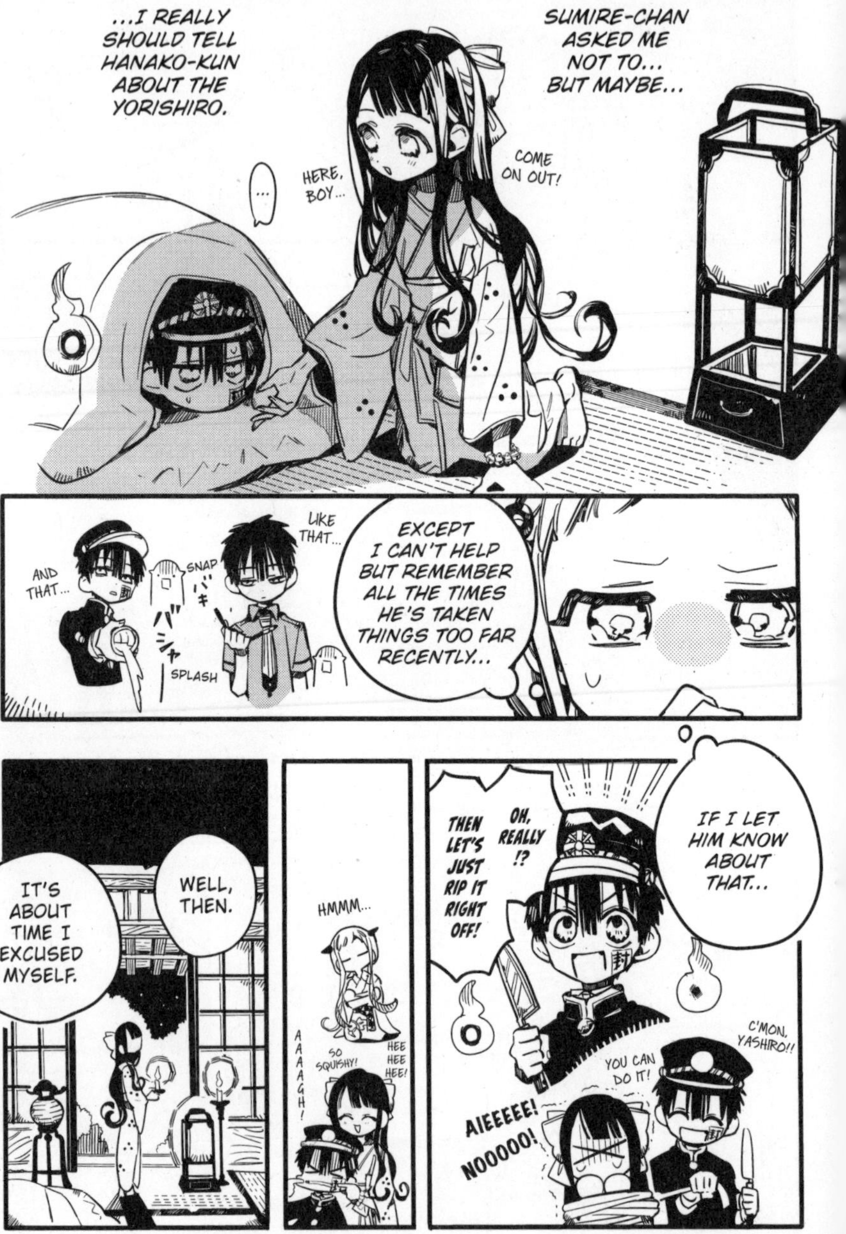
SUMIRE-CHAN ASKED ME NOT TO... BUT MAYBE...
...I REALLY SHOULD TELL HANAKO-KUN ABOUT THE YORISHIRO.
COME ON OUT!
HERE, BOY...
...
EXCEPT I CAN'T HELP BUT REMEMBER ALL THE TIMES HE'S TAKEN THINGS TOO FAR RECENTLY...
LIKE THAT...
バキ
SNAP
AND THAT...
バシャ
SPLASH
IF I LET HIM KNOW ABOUT THAT...
OH, REALLY!?
THEN LET'S JUST RIP IT RIGHT OFF!
C'MON, YASHIRO!!
YOU CAN DO IT!
AIEEEEE!
NOOOOO!
HMMM...
HEE HEE HEE!
SO SQUISHY!
AAAAGH!
WELL, THEN.
IT'S ABOUT TIME I EXCUSED MYSELF.

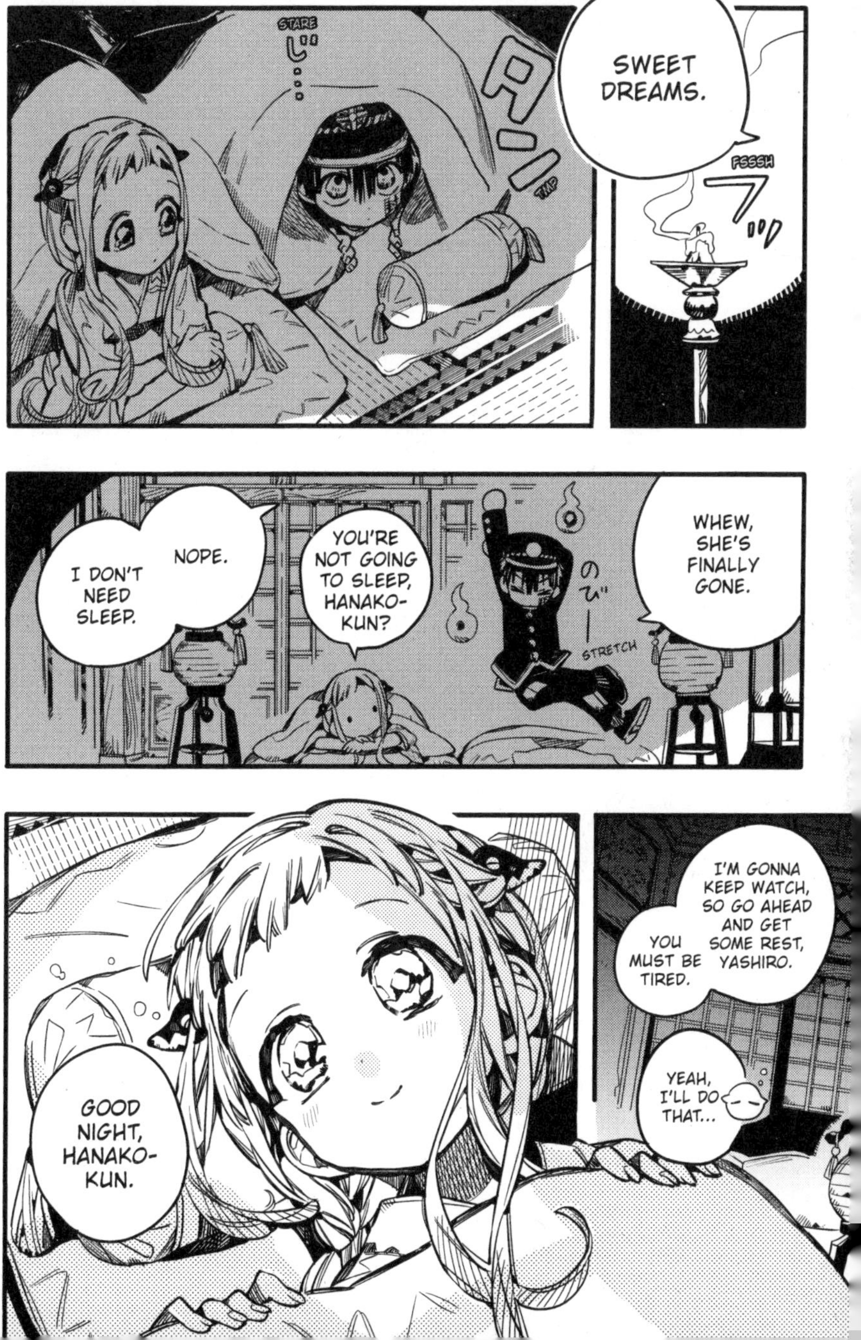
SWEET DREAMS.
FSSSH
STARE
TMP
WHEW, SHE'S FINALLY GONE.
STRETCH
YOU'RE NOT GOING TO SLEEP, HANAKO-KUN?
NOPE.
I DON'T NEED SLEEP.
I'M GONNA KEEP WATCH, SO GO AHEAD AND GET SOME REST, YASHIRO.
YOU MUST BE TIRED.
YEAH, I'LL DO THAT...
GOOD NIGHT, HANAKO-KUN.

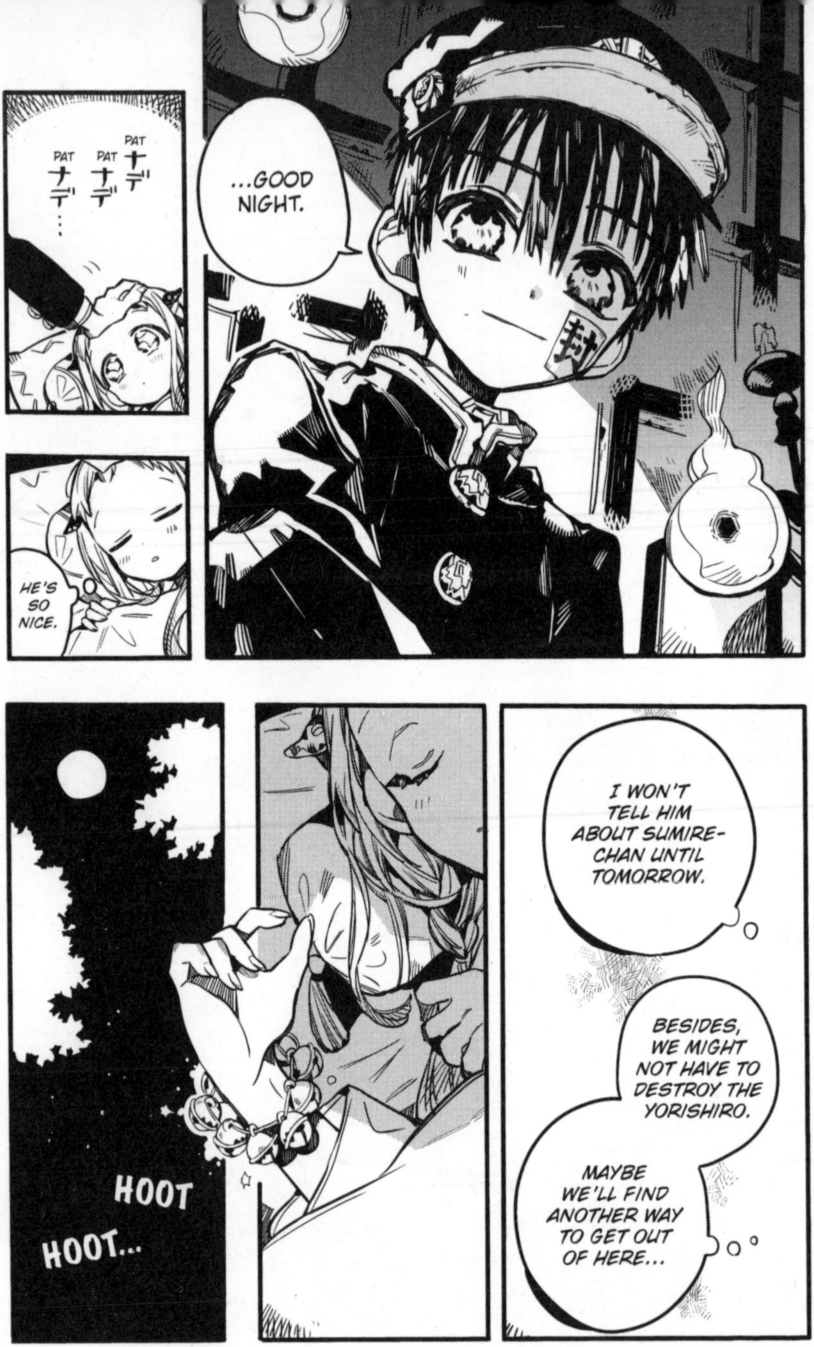
...GOOD NIGHT.
PAT PAT PAT
ナデナデナデ…
HE'S SO NICE.
I WON'T TELL HIM ABOUT SUMIRE-CHAN UNTIL TOMORROW.
BESIDES, WE MIGHT NOT HAVE TO DESTROY THE YORISHIRO.
MAYBE WE'LL FIND ANOTHER WAY TO GET OUT OF HERE...
HOOT
HOOT...

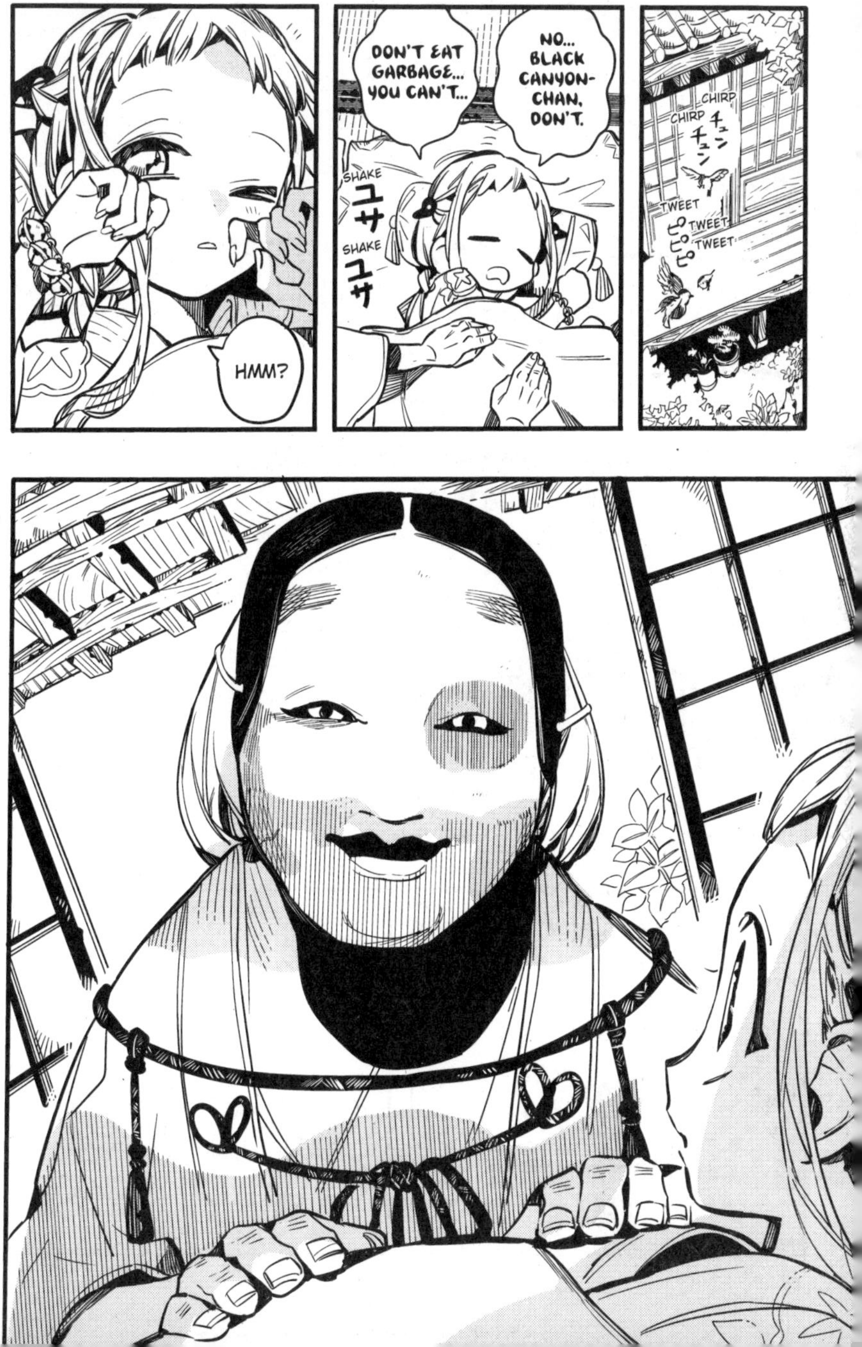
CHIRP
チュン
CHIRP
チュン
TWEET
ピ
TWEET
ピ
TWEET
ピ
NO... BLACK CANYON-CHAN, DON'T.
DON'T EAT GARBAGE... YOU CAN'T...
SHAKE
ユサ
SHAKE
ユサ
HMM?

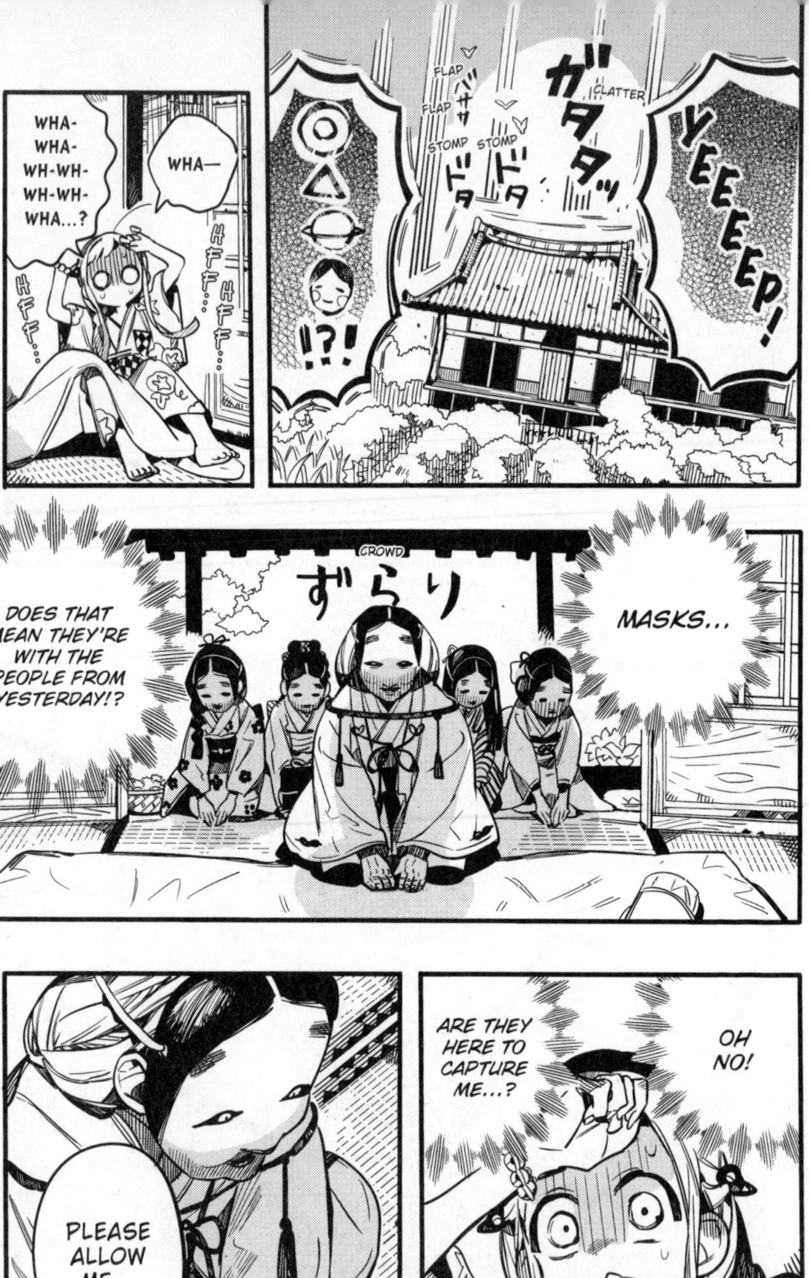
ガタタッ
CLATTER
FLAP
バサ
FLAP
ササ
STOMP
ドタ
STOMP
ドタ
YEEEEP!
!?!
WHA—
WHA-
WHA-
WH-WH-
WH-WH-
WHA...?
HFFF...
HFFF...
HFFF...
CROWD
ずらり
MASKS...
DOES THAT MEAN THEY'RE WITH THE PEOPLE FROM YESTERDAY!?
OH NO!
ARE THEY HERE TO CAPTURE ME...?
PLEASE ALLOW ME...

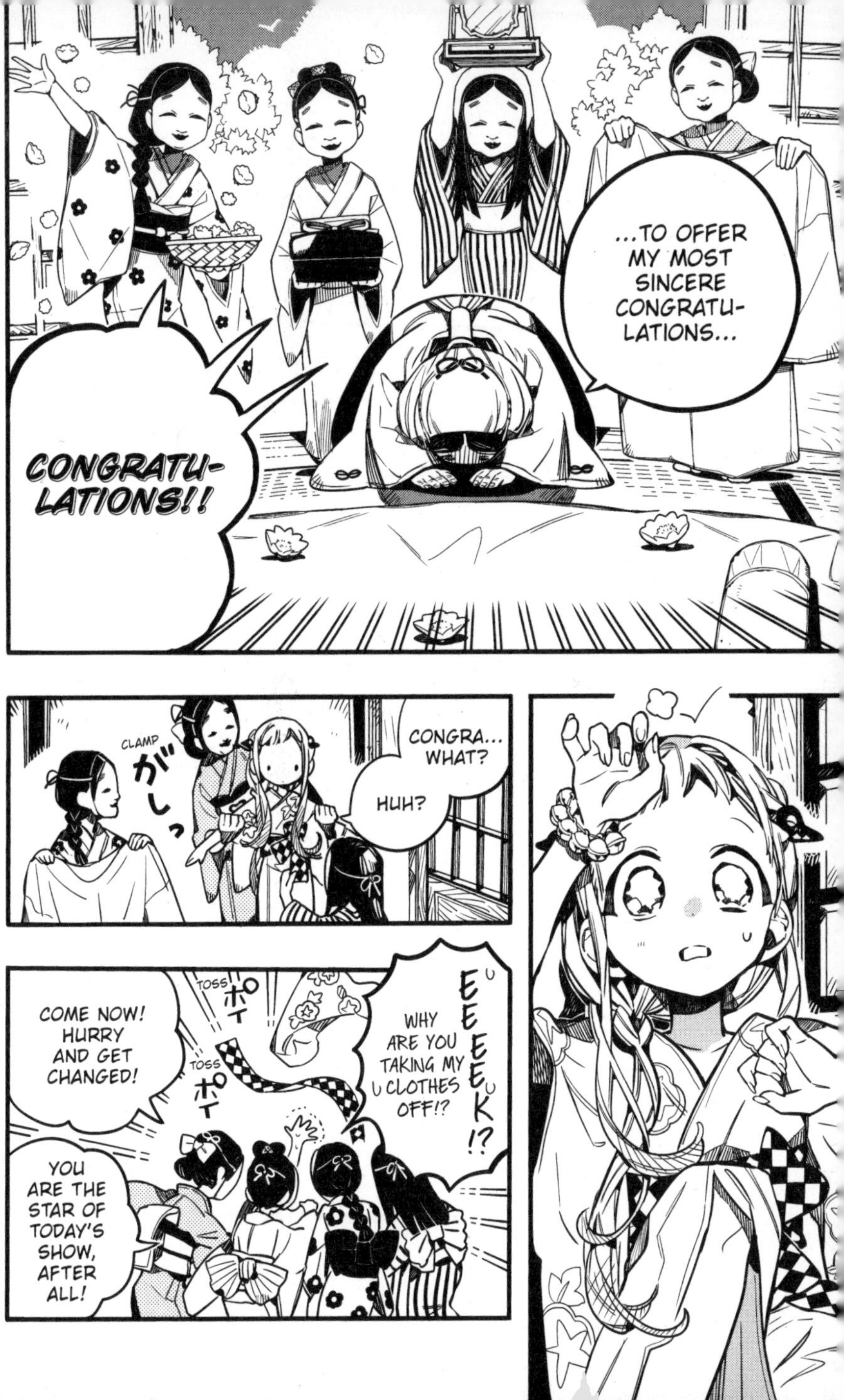
...TO OFFER MY MOST SINCERE CONGRATULATIONS...
CONGRATULATIONS!!
CONGRA... WHAT?
HUH?
がしっ
CLAMP
EEEEK!?
WHY ARE YOU TAKING MY CLOTHES OFF!?
ポイ
TOSS
ポイ
TOSS
COME NOW! HURRY AND GET CHANGED!
YOU ARE THE STAR OF TODAY'S SHOW, AFTER ALL!

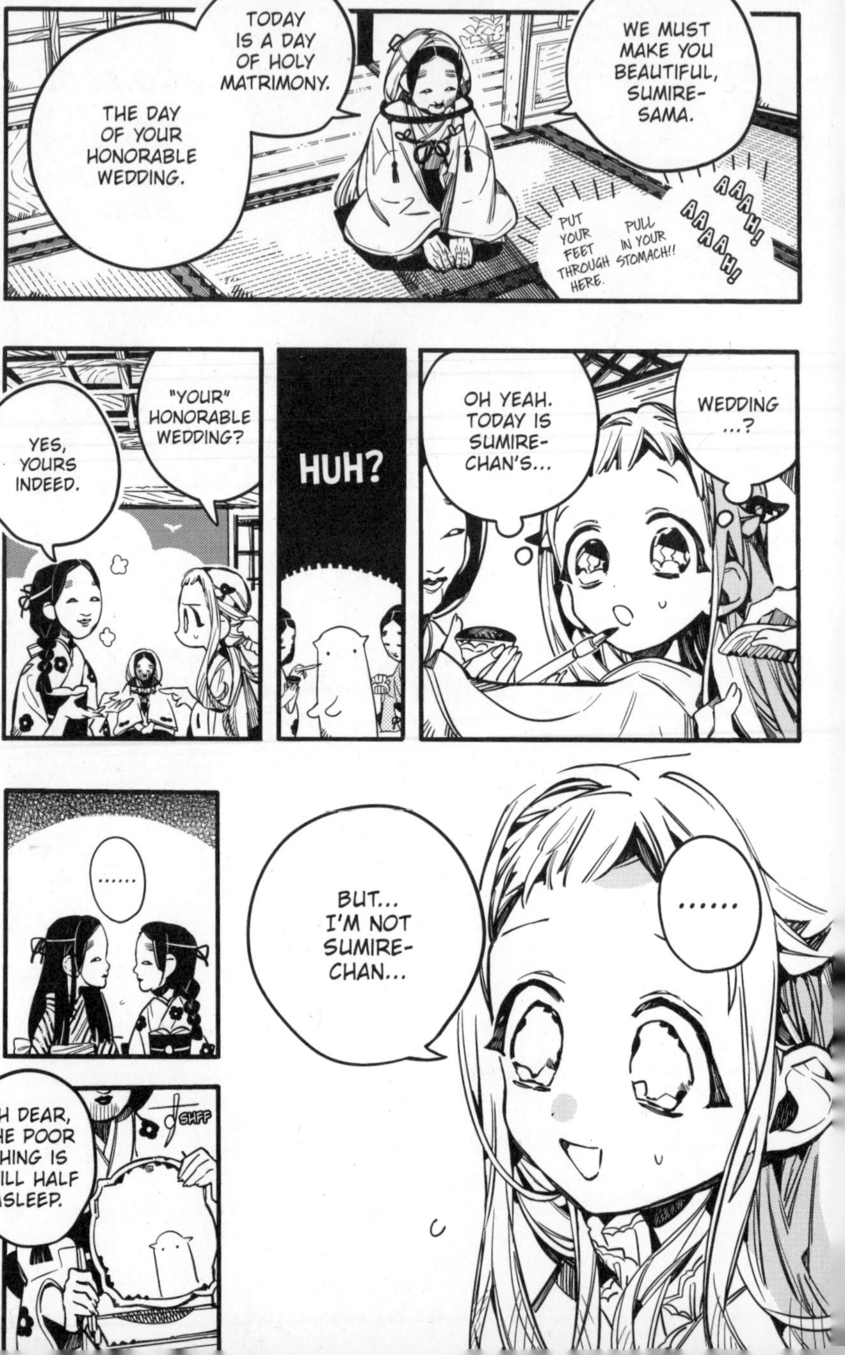
WE MUST MAKE YOU BEAUTIFUL, SUMIRE-SAMA.
TODAY IS A DAY OF HOLY MATRIMONY.
THE DAY OF YOUR HONORABLE WEDDING.
AAAAH! AAAAH!
PULL IN YOUR STOMACH!!
PUT YOUR FEET THROUGH HERE.
WEDDING ...?
OH YEAH. TODAY IS SUMIRE-CHAN'S...
HUH?
"YOUR" HONORABLE WEDDING?
YES, YOURS INDEED.
......
BUT... I'M NOT SUMIRE-CHAN...
......
SHFF
OH DEAR, THE POOR THING IS STILL HALF ASLEEP.

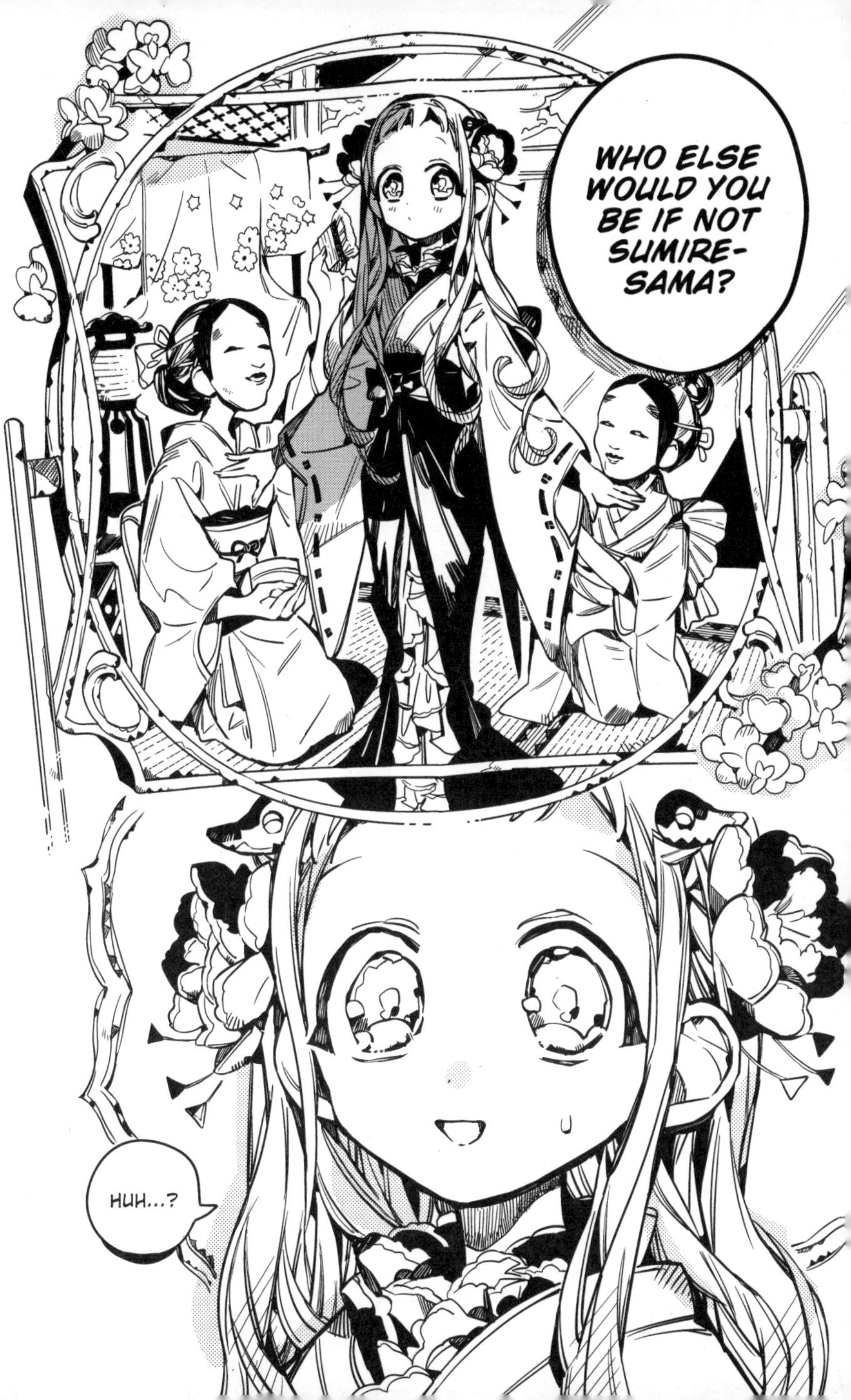
WHO ELSE WOULD YOU BE IF NOT SUMIRE-SAMA?
HUH...?

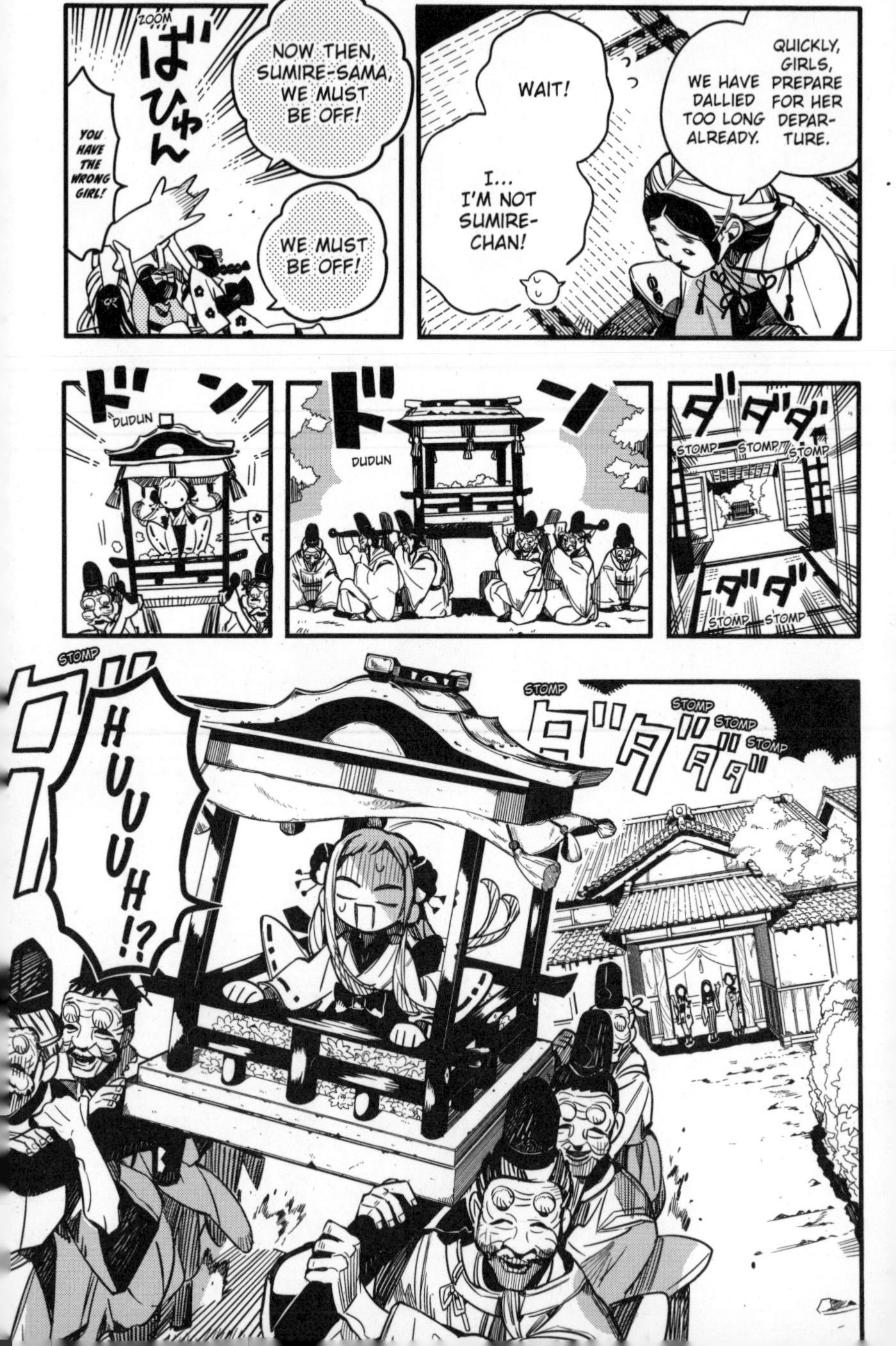
QUICKLY, GIRLS, PREPARE FOR HER DEPAR-TURE.
WE HAVE DALLIED TOO LONG ALREADY.
WAIT!
I... I'M NOT SUMIRE-CHAN!
NOW THEN, SUMIRE-SAMA, WE MUST BE OFF!
ZOOM
ばひゅん
YOU HAVE THE WRONG GIRL!
WE MUST BE OFF!
ダダダ
STOMP STOMP STOMP
ダダ
STOMP STOMP
ドン
DUDUN
ドン
DUDUN
ダダダダダ
STOMP STOMP STOMP STOMP
HUUUUH!?
STOMP

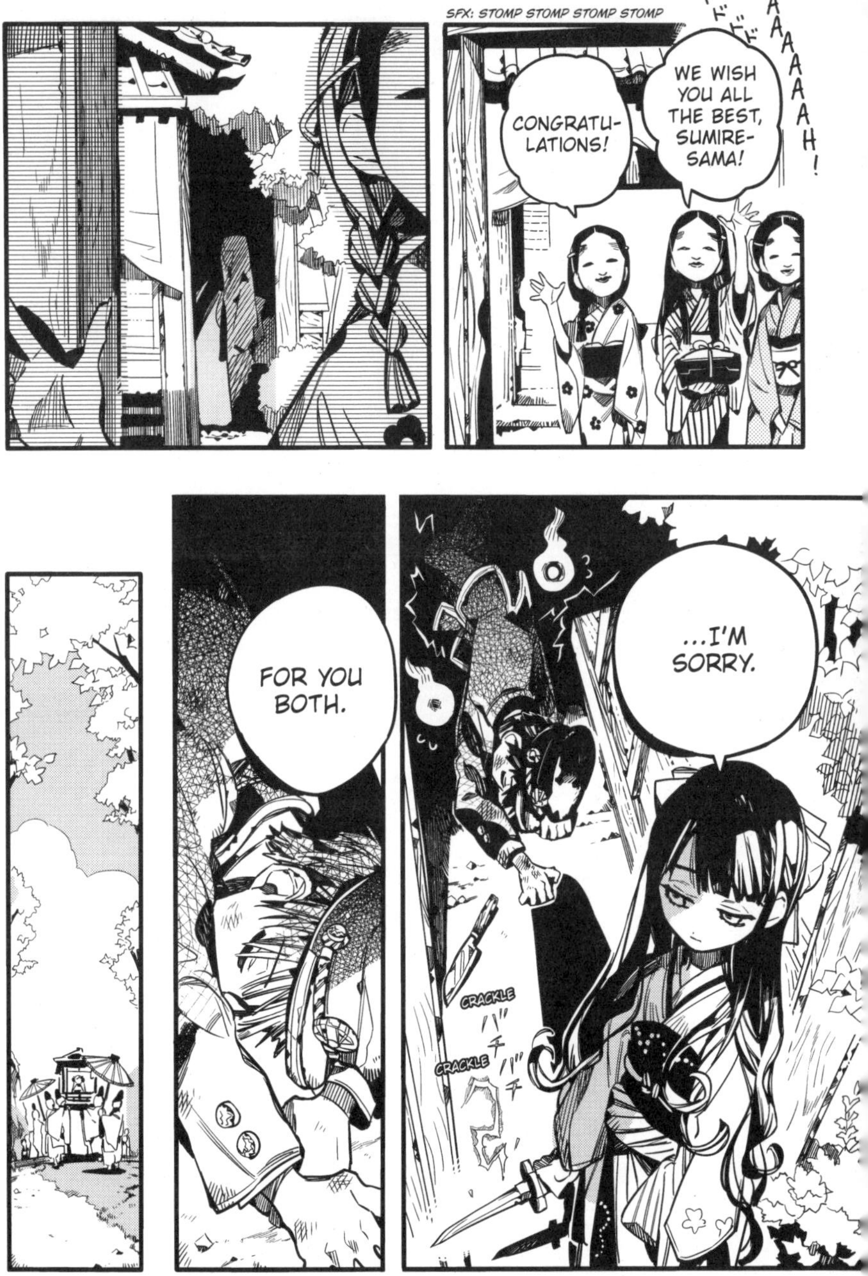
SFX: STOMP STOMP STOMP STOMP
AAAAAAAH!
WE WISH YOU ALL THE BEST, SUMIRE-SAMA!
CONGRATU-LATIONS!
...I'M SORRY.
CRACKLE
CRACKLE
FOR YOU BOTH.

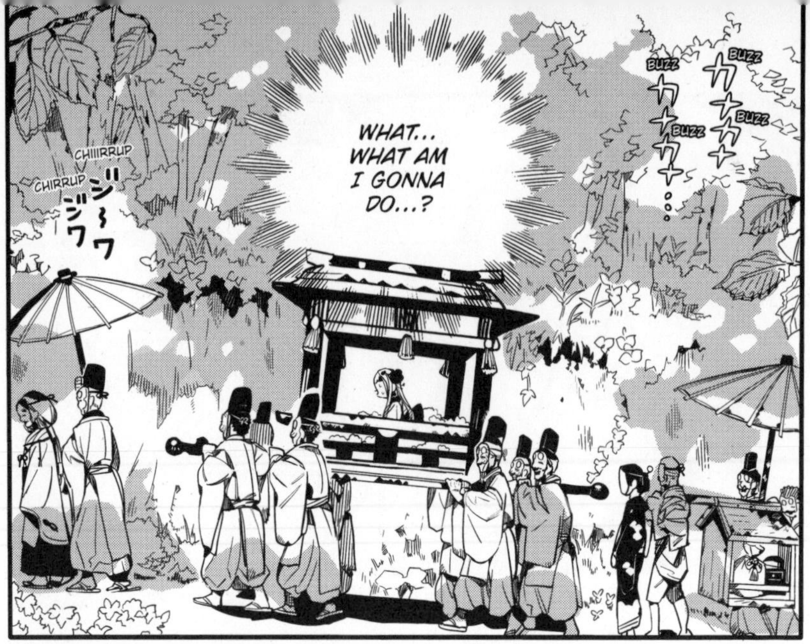
BUZZ
BUZZ
BUZZ
BUZZ
カナカナ…
WHAT... WHAT AM I GONNA DO...?
CHIIIRRUP
CHIRRUP
ジ~ワ ジワ

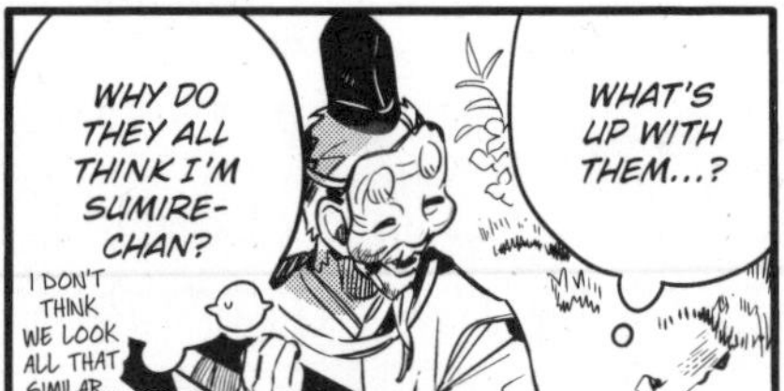
WHAT'S UP WITH THEM...?
WHY DO THEY ALL THINK I'M SUMIRE-CHAN?
I DON'T THINK WE LOOK ALL THAT SIMILAR...

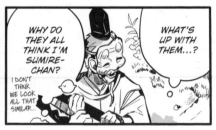

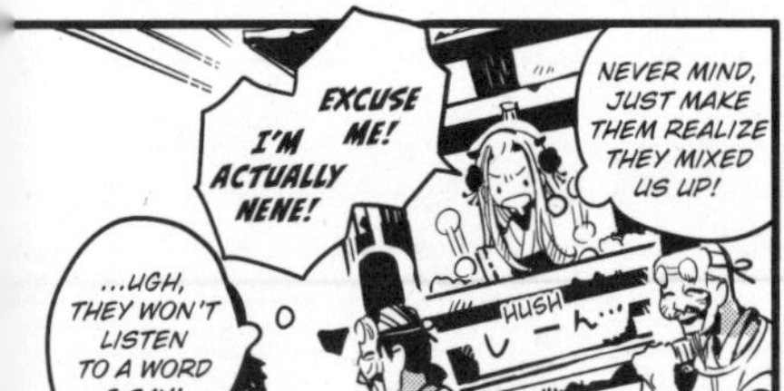
NEVER MIND, JUST MAKE THEM REALIZE THEY MIXED US UP!
EXCUSE ME! I'M ACTUALLY NENE!
HUSH
しーん…
...UGH, THEY WON'T LISTEN TO A WORD I SAY!

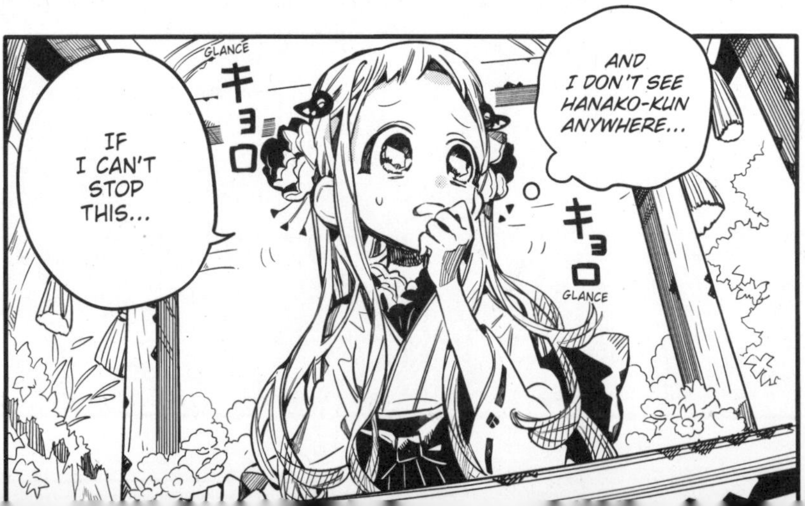
AND I DON'T SEE HANAKO-KUN ANYWHERE...
キョロ
GLANCE
GLANCE
キョロ
IF I CAN'T STOP THIS...

...AM I... GOING TO END UP MARRYING No. 6...!?
DO YOU PROMISE TO LOVE AND CHERISH HER?
LOVE NENE.
NOTE: BARELY REMEMBERS HIM
WILL MAKE HAPPY.
YOU MAY KISS THE BRIDE...
I CAN'T LET THAT HAPPEN!
WHOOSH
ばっ

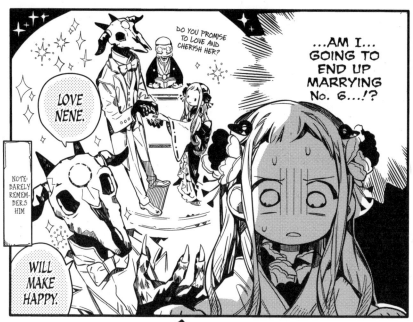

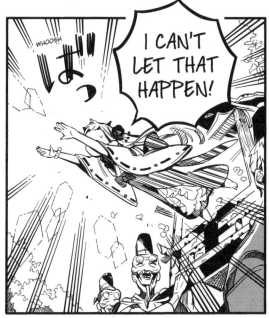

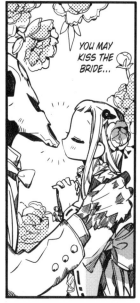

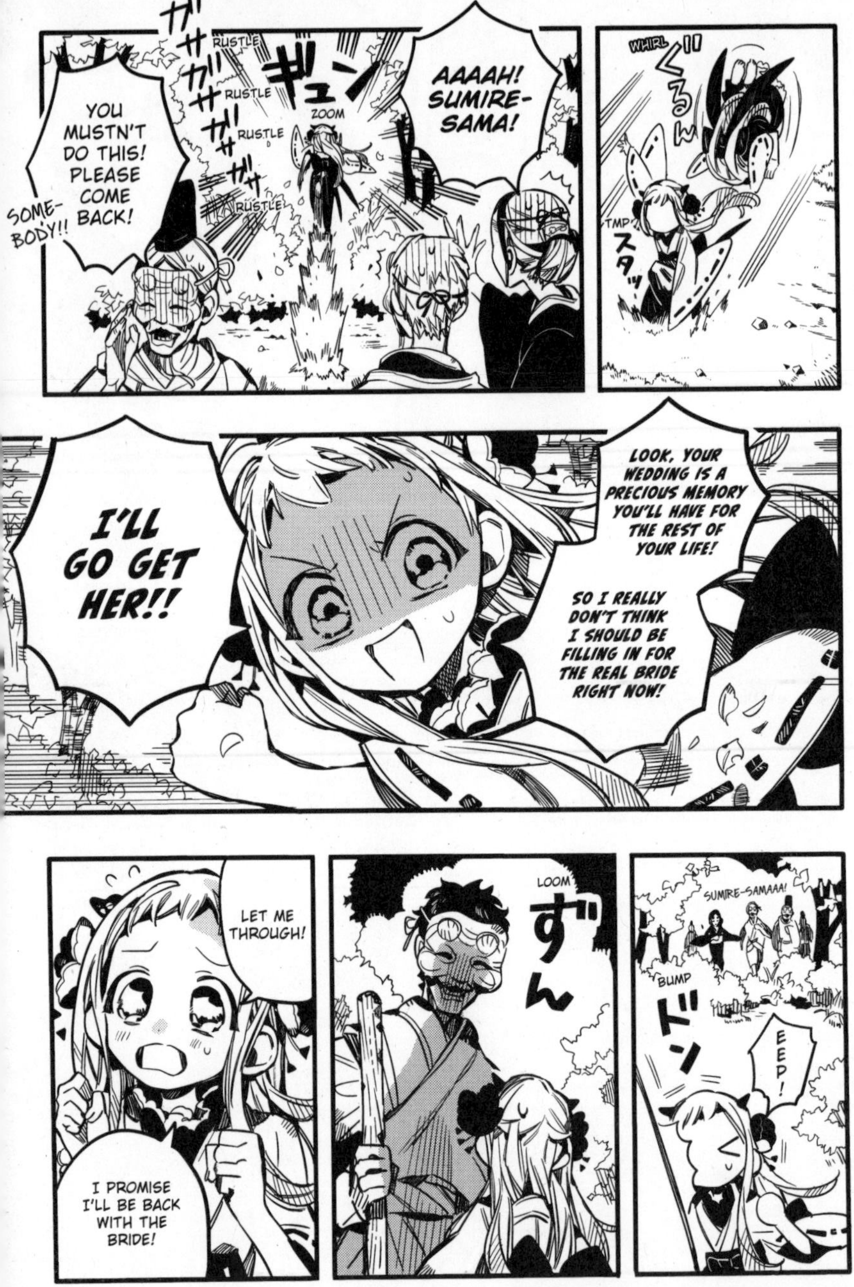
WHIRL
TMP
AAAAH! SUMIRE-SAMA!
ZOOM
RUSTLE
RUSTLE
RUSTLE
RUSTLE
YOU MUSTN'T DO THIS! PLEASE COME BACK!
SOME-BODY!!
LOOK, YOUR WEDDING IS A PRECIOUS MEMORY YOU'LL HAVE FOR THE REST OF YOUR LIFE!
SO I REALLY DON'T THINK I SHOULD BE FILLING IN FOR THE REAL BRIDE RIGHT NOW!
I'LL GO GET HER!!
SUMIRE-SAMAAA!
BUMP
EEP!
LOOM
LET ME THROUGH!
I PROMISE I'LL BE BACK WITH THE BRIDE!

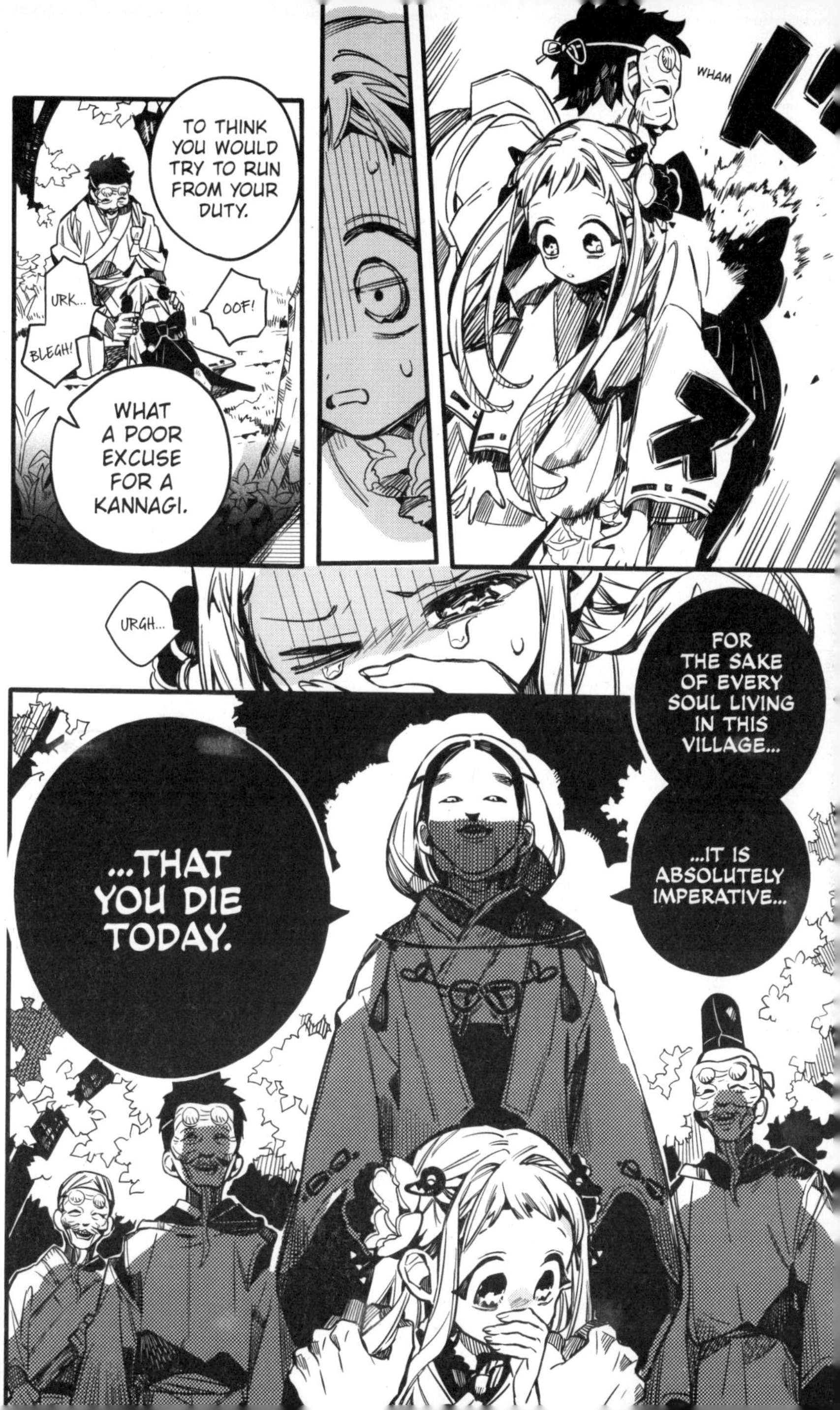
WHAM
TO THINK YOU WOULD TRY TO RUN FROM YOUR DUTY.
OOF!
URK...
BLEGH!
WHAT A POOR EXCUSE FOR A KANNAGI.
URGH...
FOR THE SAKE OF EVERY SOUL LIVING IN THIS VILLAGE...
...IT IS ABSOLUTELY IMPERATIVE...
...THAT YOU DIE TODAY.

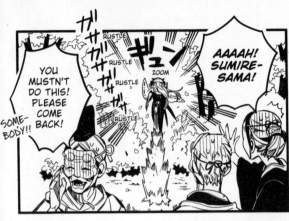
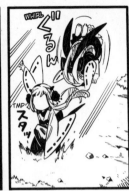
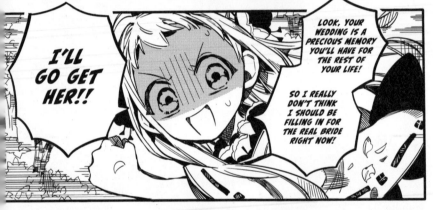
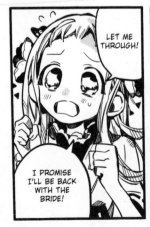
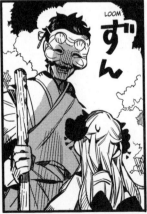
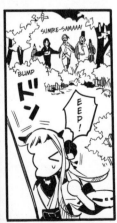

57

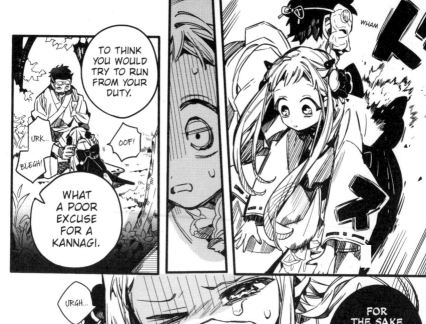

TO THINK YOU WOULD TRY TO RUN FROM YOUR DUTY.

URK...

OOF!

BLEGH!

WHAT A POOR EXCUSE FOR A KANNAGI.

WHAM

URGH...

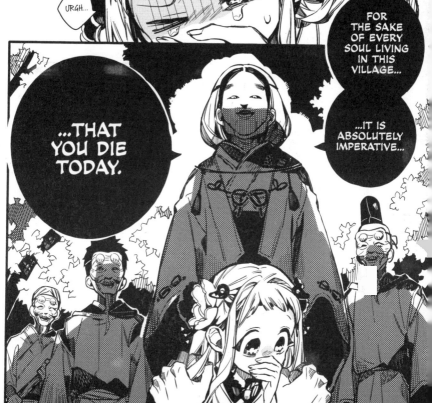

FOR THE SAKE OF EVERY SOUL LIVING IN THIS VILLAGE...

...THAT YOU DIE TODAY.

...IT IS ABSOLUTELY IMPERATIVE...

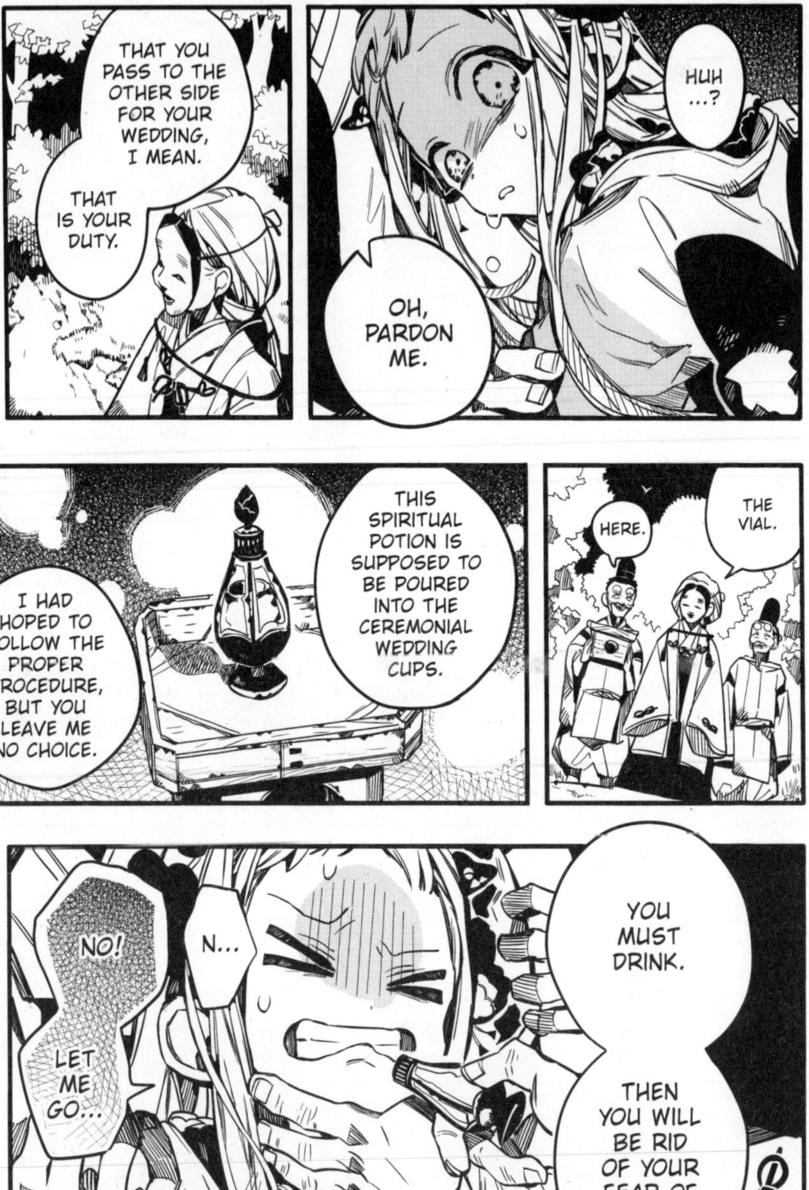
HUH ...?
OH, PARDON ME.
THAT YOU PASS TO THE OTHER SIDE FOR YOUR WEDDING, I MEAN.
THAT IS YOUR DUTY.
THE VIAL.
HERE.
THIS SPIRITUAL POTION IS SUPPOSED TO BE POURED INTO THE CEREMONIAL WEDDING CUPS.
I HAD HOPED TO FOLLOW THE PROPER PROCEDURE, BUT YOU LEAVE ME NO CHOICE.
YOU MUST DRINK.
THEN YOU WILL BE RID OF YOUR FEAR OF DEATH.
N...
NO!
LET ME GO...

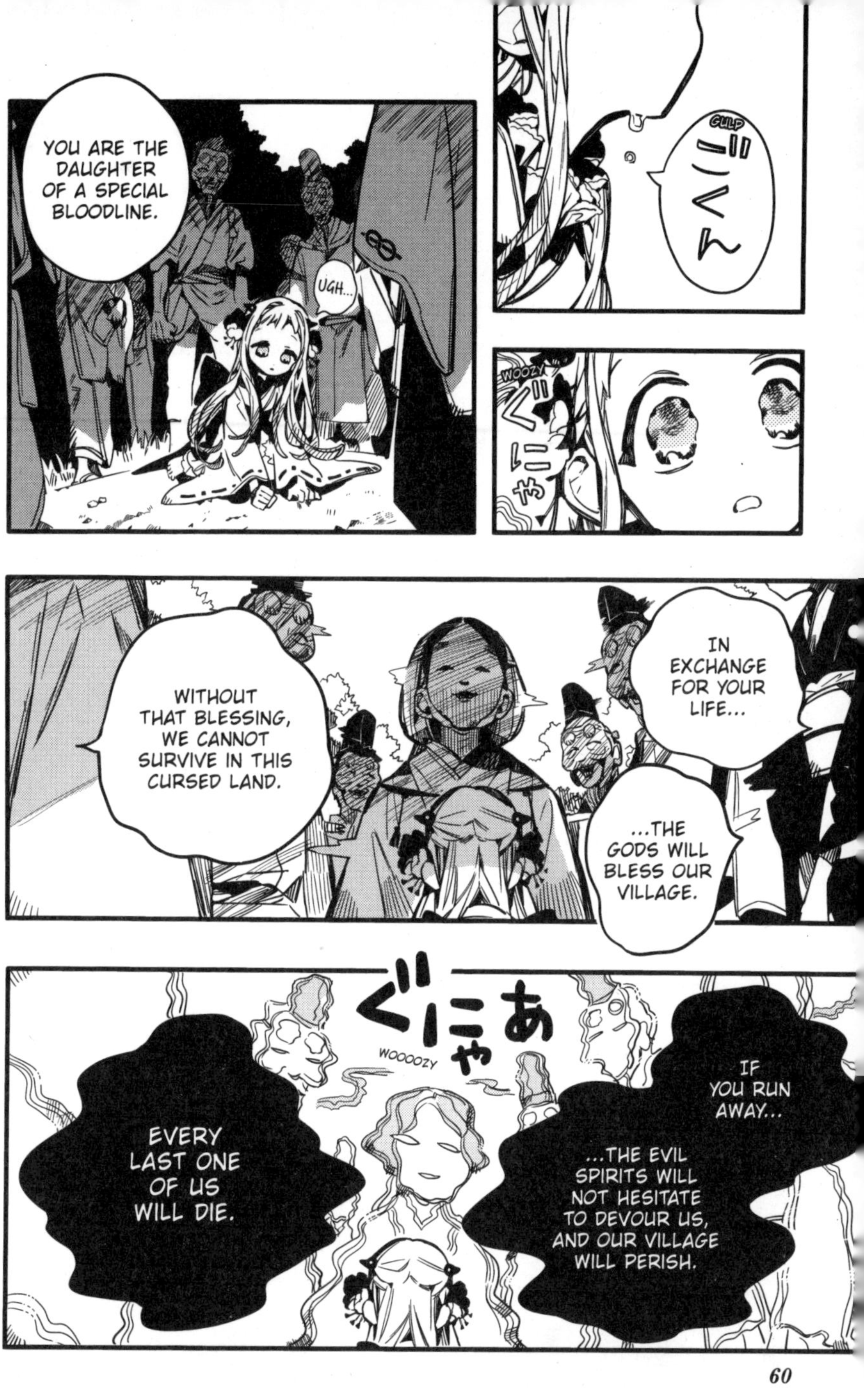
ごくん
GULP
ぐにゃ
WOOZY
YOU ARE THE DAUGHTER OF A SPECIAL BLOODLINE.
UGH...
IN EXCHANGE FOR YOUR LIFE...
...THE GODS WILL BLESS OUR VILLAGE.
WITHOUT THAT BLESSING, WE CANNOT SURVIVE IN THIS CURSED LAND.
ぐにゃあ
WOOOOZY
IF YOU RUN AWAY...
...THE EVIL SPIRITS WILL NOT HESITATE TO DEVOUR US, AND OUR VILLAGE WILL PERISH.
EVERY LAST ONE OF US WILL DIE.

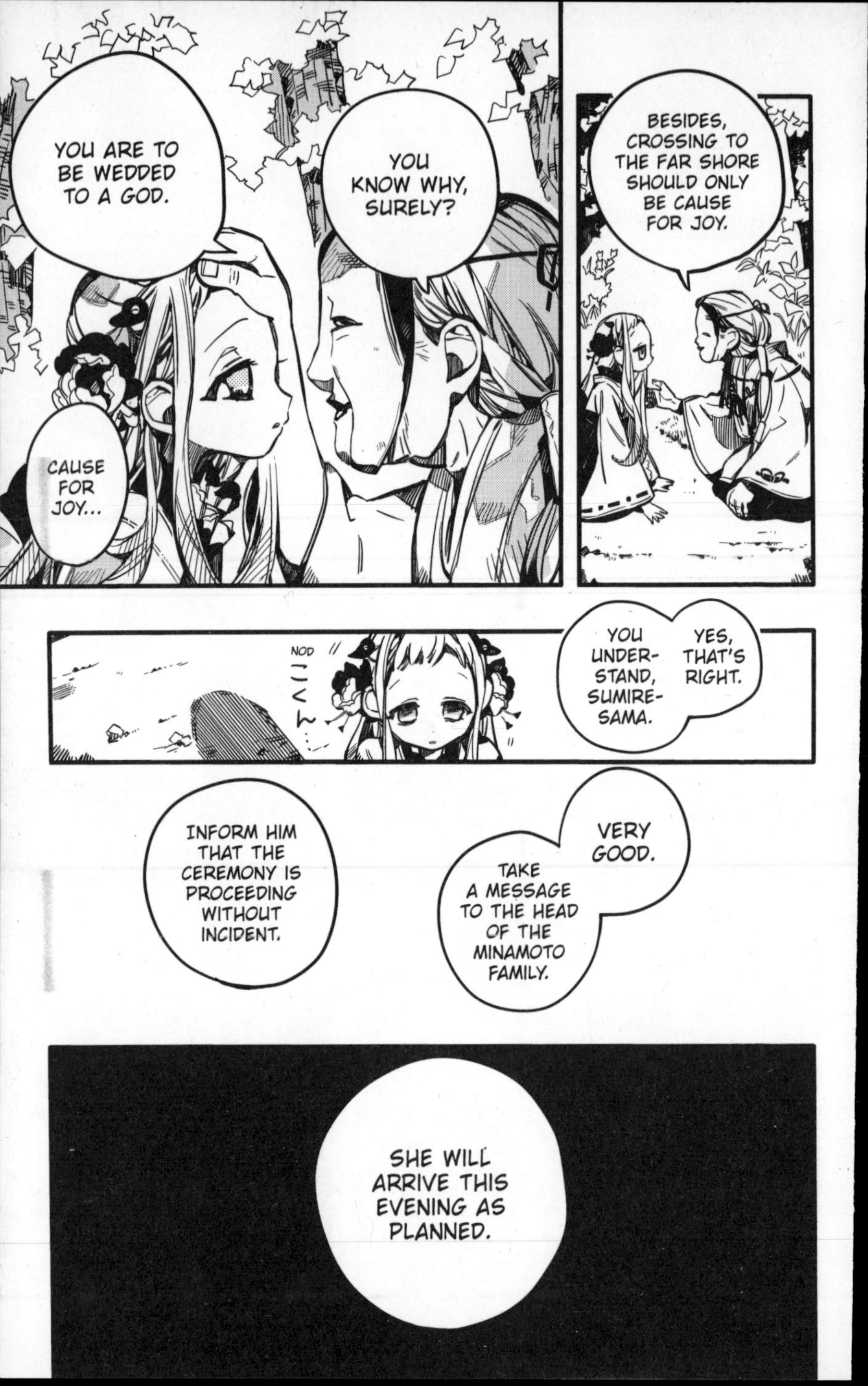
BESIDES, CROSSING TO THE FAR SHORE SHOULD ONLY BE CAUSE FOR JOY.
YOU KNOW WHY, SURELY?
YOU ARE TO BE WEDDED TO A GOD.
CAUSE FOR JOY...
YES, THAT'S RIGHT.
YOU UNDERSTAND, SUMIRE-SAMA.
NOD
VERY GOOD.
TAKE A MESSAGE TO THE HEAD OF THE MINAMOTO FAMILY.
INFORM HIM THAT THE CEREMONY IS PROCEEDING WITHOUT INCIDENT.
SHE WILL ARRIVE THIS EVENING AS PLANNED.

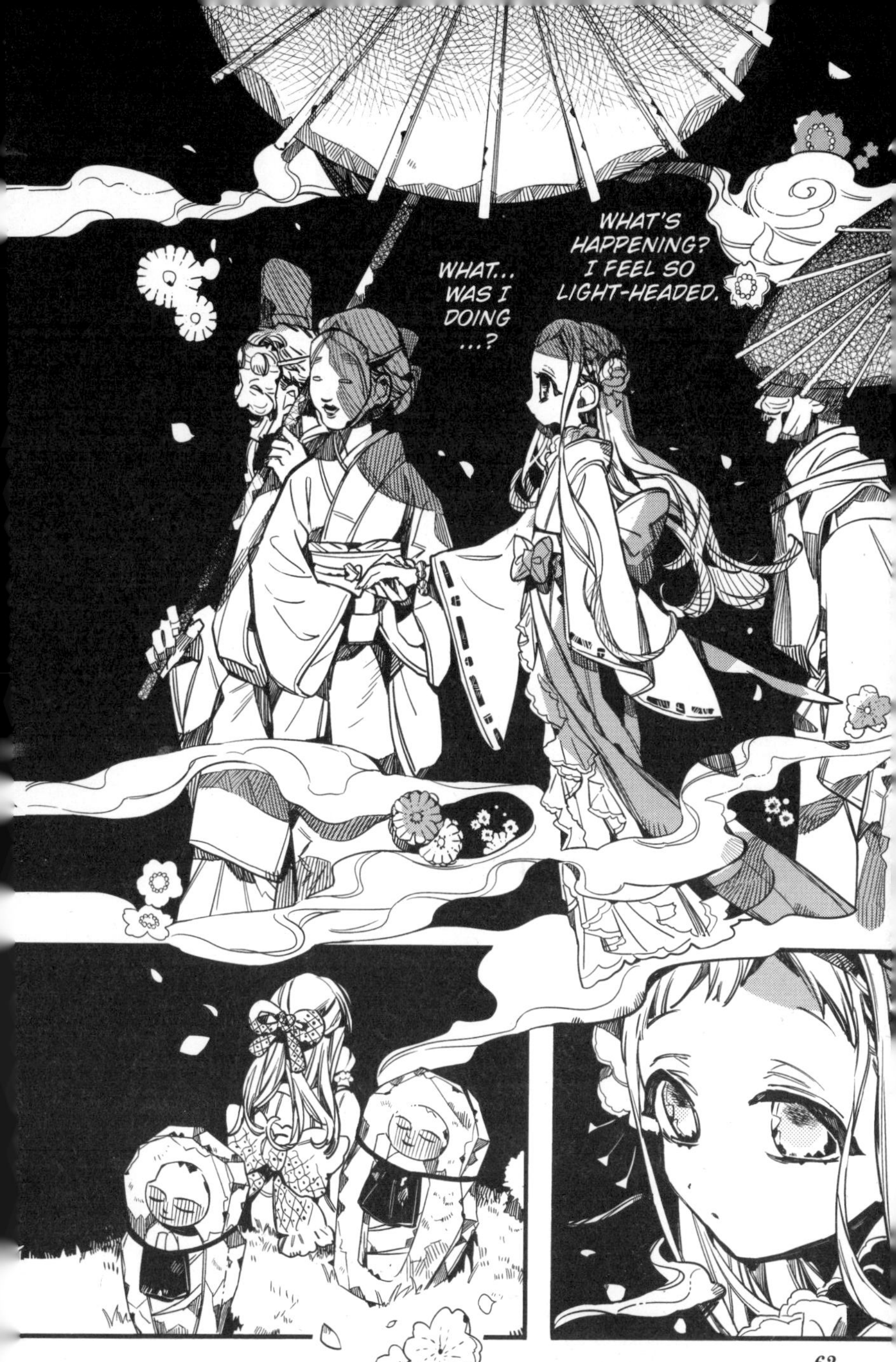
WHAT'S HAPPENING? I FEEL SO LIGHT-HEADED.
WHAT... WAS I DOING ...?

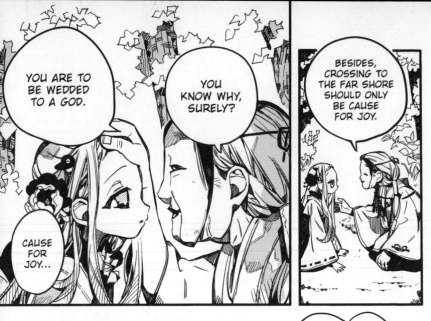

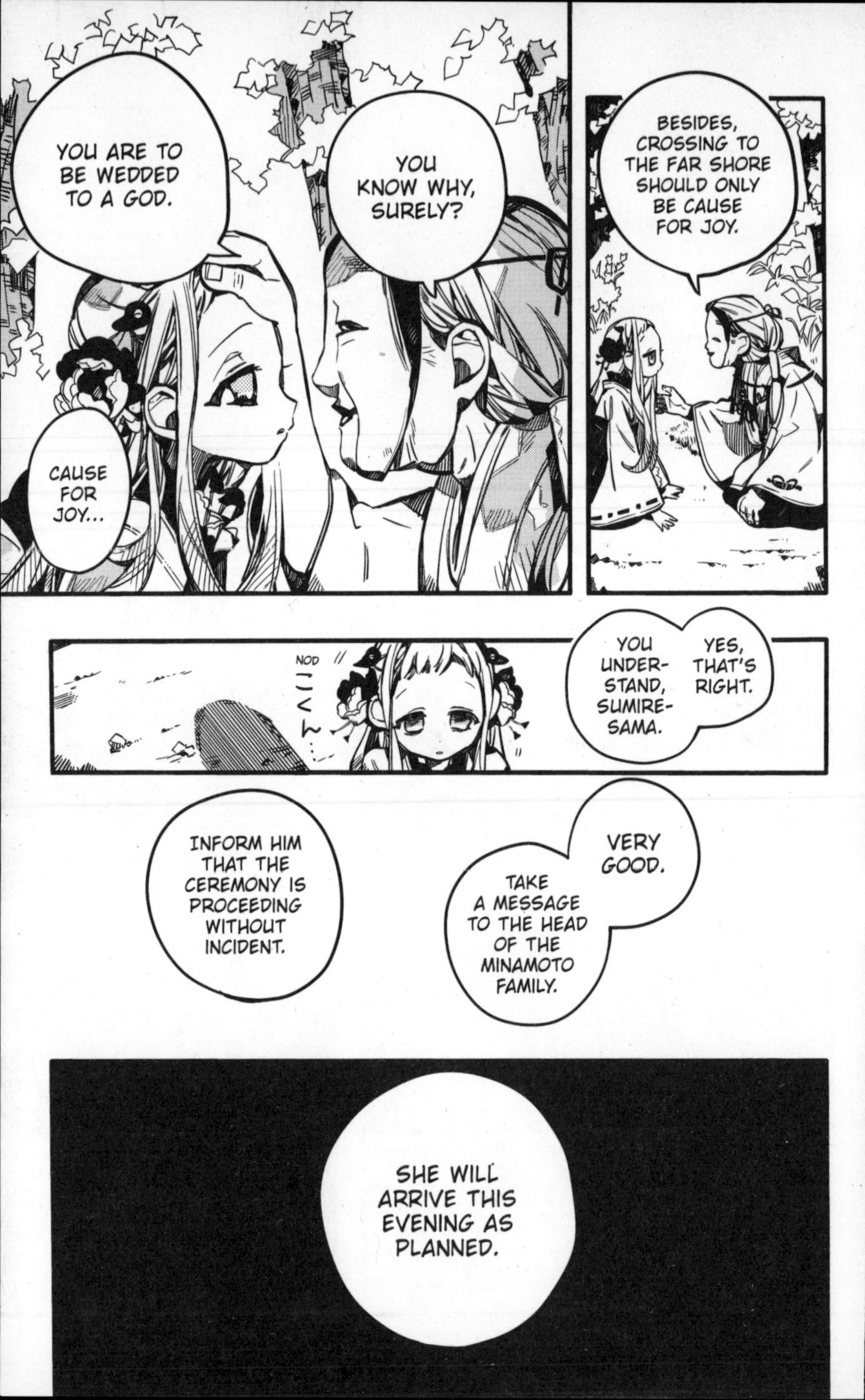

YOU ARE TO BE WEDDED TO A GOD.

YOU KNOW WHY, SURELY?

CAUSE FOR JOY...

BESIDES, CROSSING TO THE FAR SHORE SHOULD ONLY BE CAUSE FOR JOY.

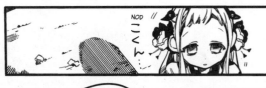

NOD

YOU UNDER-STAND, SUMIRE-SAMA.

YES, THAT'S RIGHT.

INFORM HIM THAT THE CEREMONY IS PROCEEDING WITHOUT INCIDENT.

TAKE A MESSAGE TO THE HEAD OF THE MINAMOTO FAMILY.

VERY GOOD.

SHE WILL ARRIVE THIS EVENING AS PLANNED.

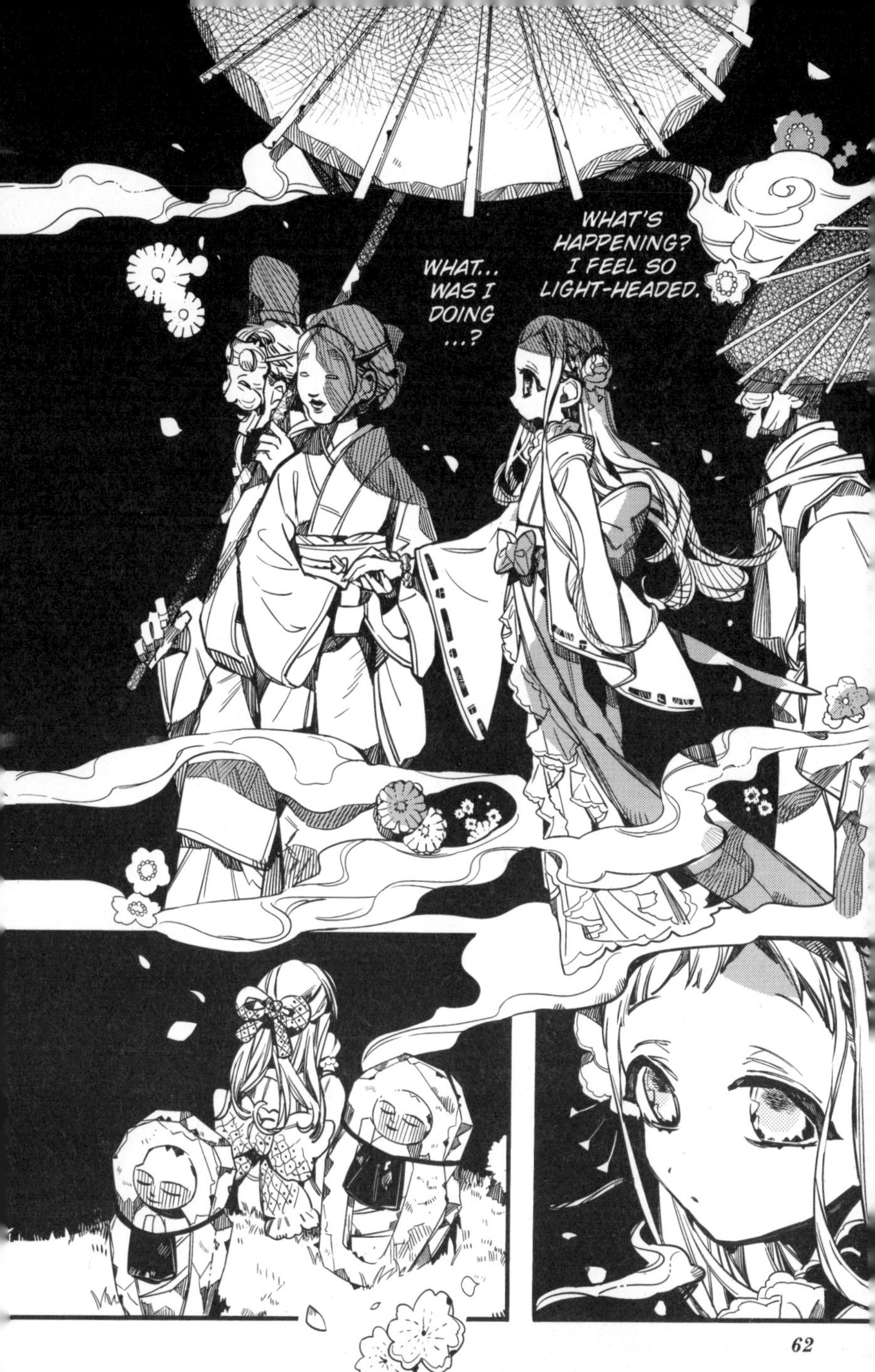
WHAT'S HAPPENING? I FEEL SO LIGHT-HEADED.
WHAT... WAS I DOING ...?

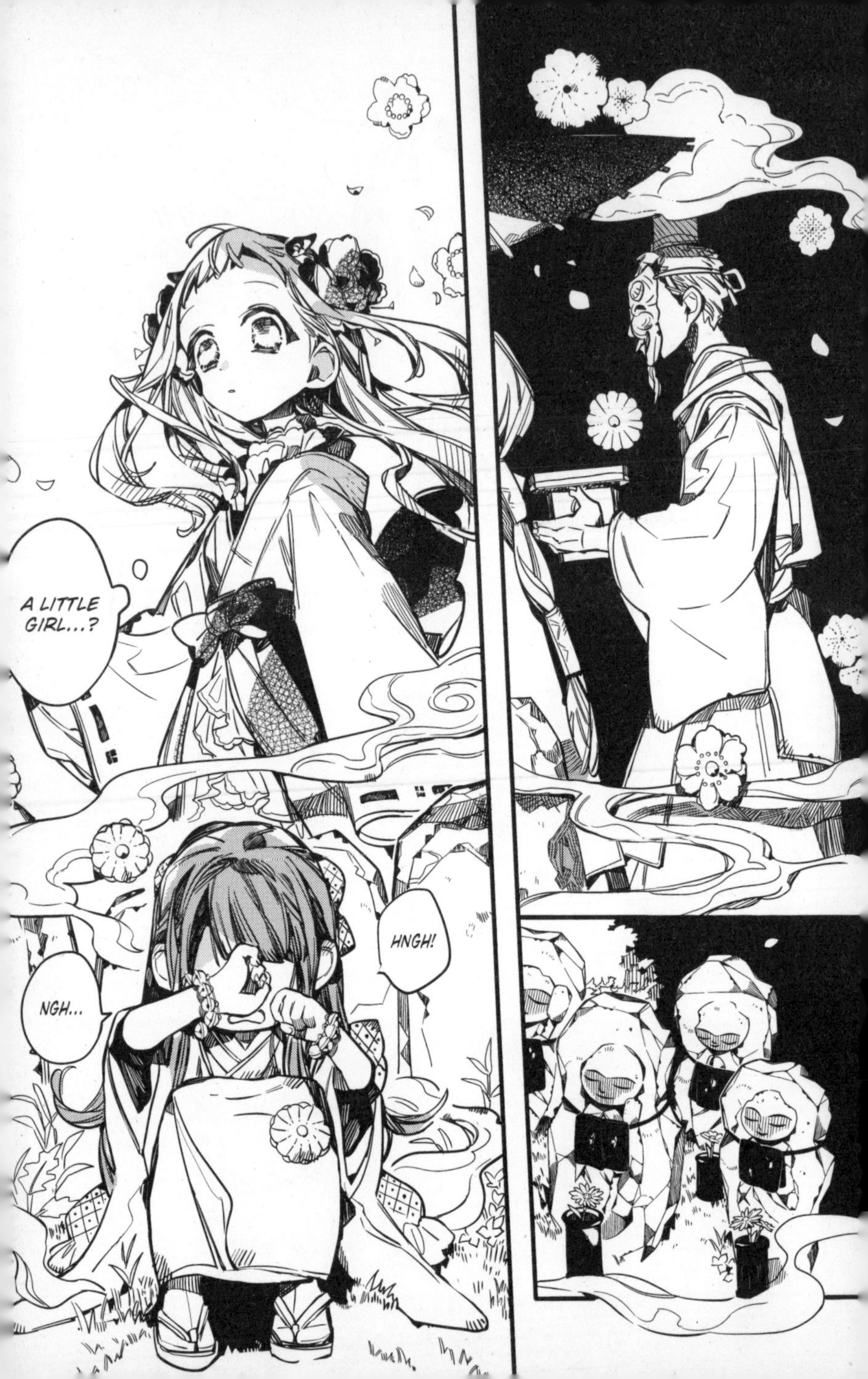
A LITTLE GIRL...?
HNGH!
NGH...

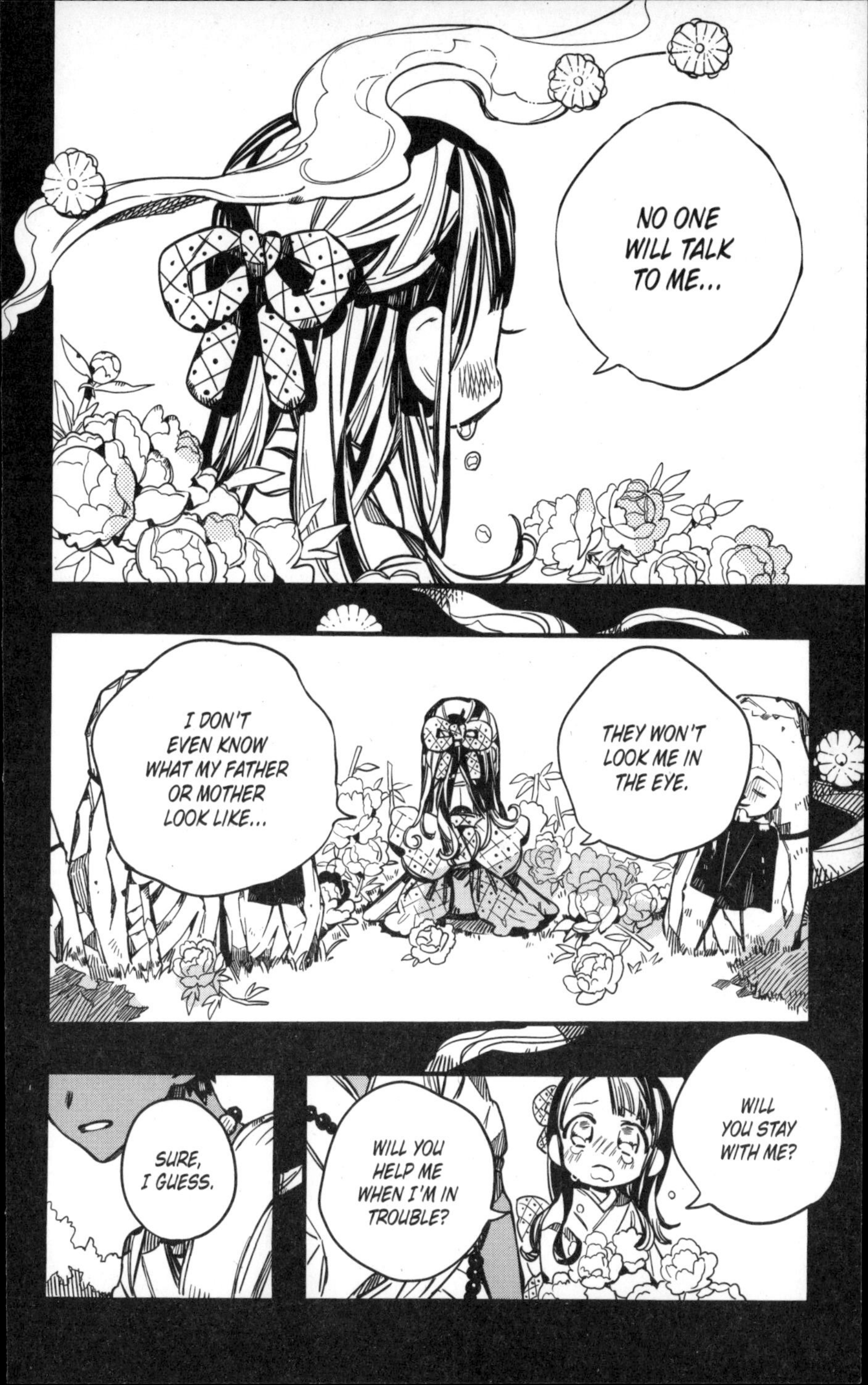
NO ONE WILL TALK TO ME...
THEY WON'T LOOK ME IN THE EYE.
I DON'T EVEN KNOW WHAT MY FATHER OR MOTHER LOOK LIKE...
WILL YOU STAY WITH ME?
WILL YOU HELP ME WHEN I'M IN TROUBLE?
SURE, I GUESS.

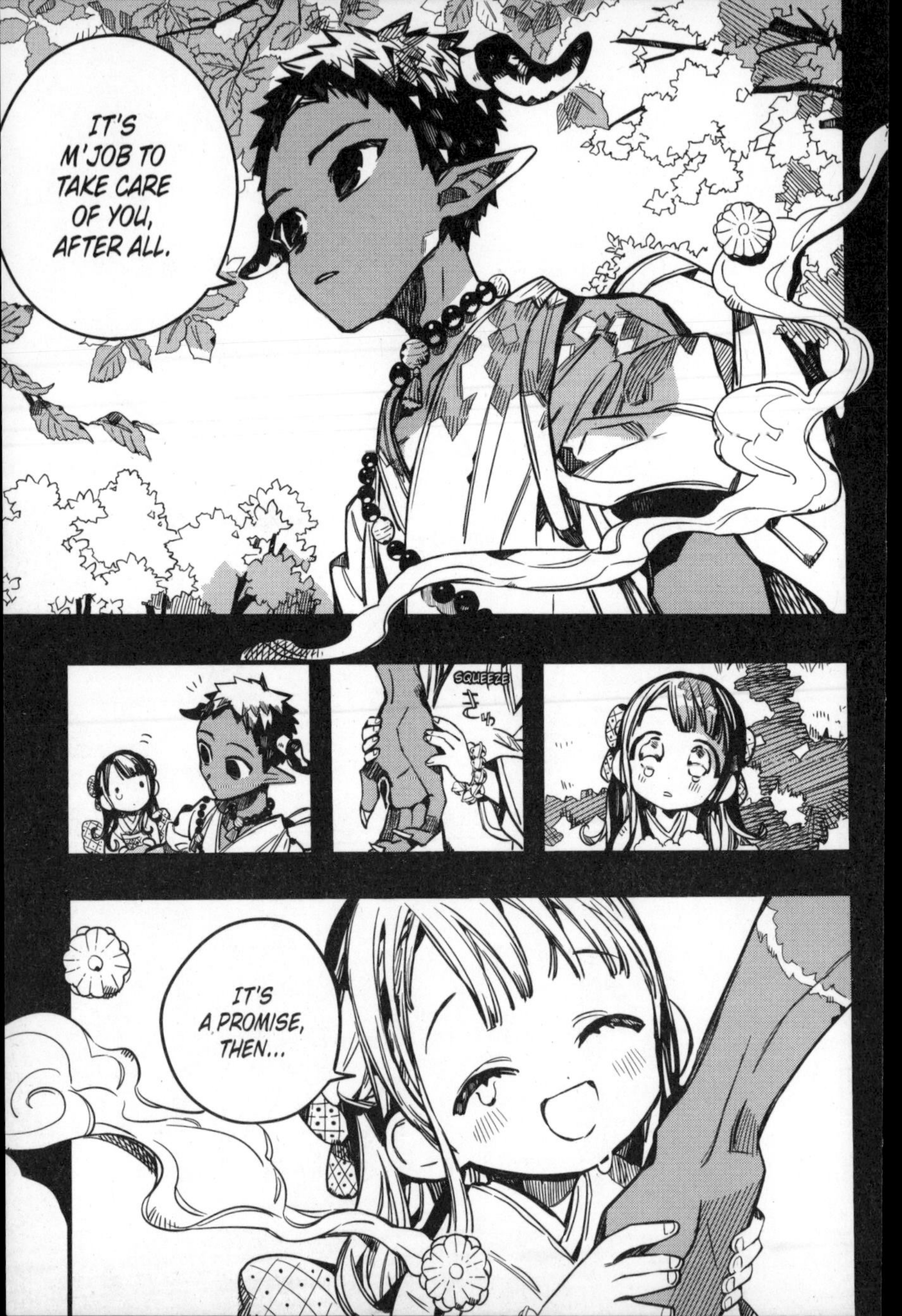
IT'S M'JOB TO TAKE CARE OF YOU, AFTER ALL.
SQUEEZE
きゅ
IT'S A PROMISE, THEN...

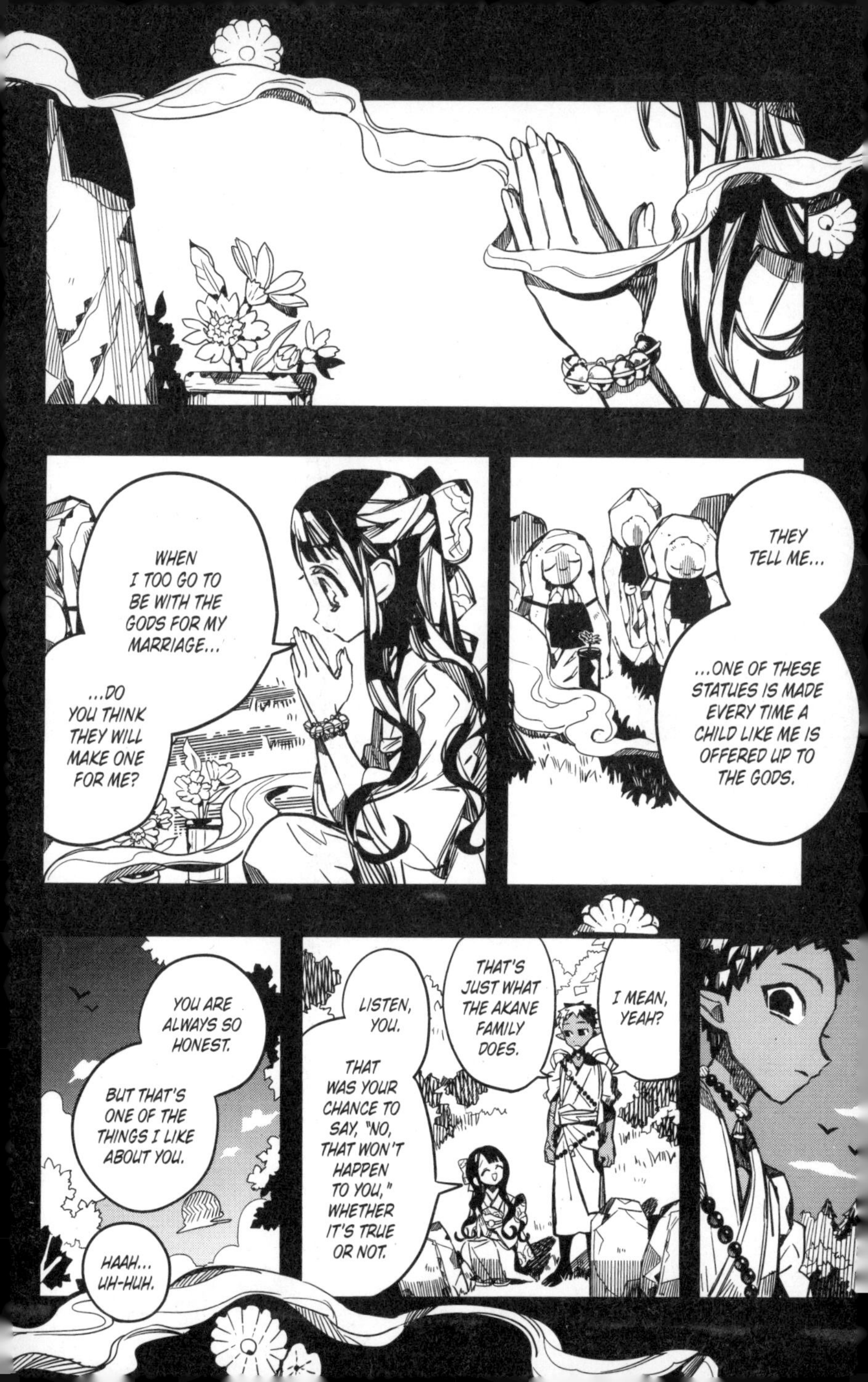
THEY TELL ME...
...ONE OF THESE STATUES IS MADE EVERY TIME A CHILD LIKE ME IS OFFERED UP TO THE GODS.
WHEN I TOO GO TO BE WITH THE GODS FOR MY MARRIAGE...
...DO YOU THINK THEY WILL MAKE ONE FOR ME?
I MEAN, YEAH?
THAT'S JUST WHAT THE AKANE FAMILY DOES.
LISTEN, YOU.
THAT WAS YOUR CHANCE TO SAY, "NO, THAT WON'T HAPPEN TO YOU," WHETHER IT'S TRUE OR NOT.
YOU ARE ALWAYS SO HONEST.
BUT THAT'S ONE OF THE THINGS I LIKE ABOUT YOU.
HAAH... UH-HUH.

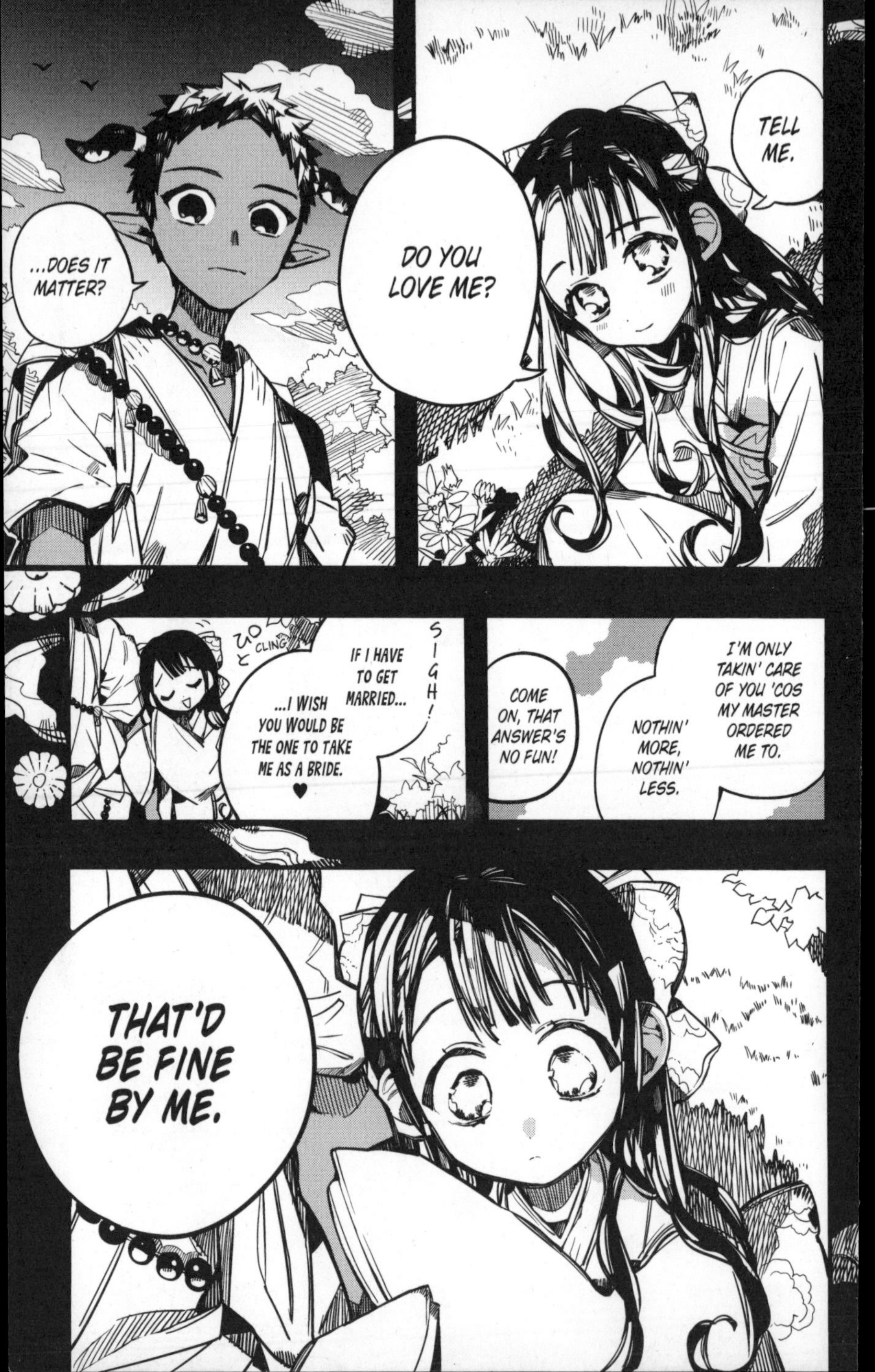
TELL ME.
DO YOU LOVE ME?
...DOES IT MATTER?
I'M ONLY TAKIN' CARE OF YOU 'COS MY MASTER ORDERED ME TO.
NOTHIN' MORE, NOTHIN' LESS.
COME ON, THAT ANSWER'S NO FUN!
SIGH!
IF I HAVE TO GET MARRIED...
...I WISH YOU WOULD BE THE ONE TO TAKE ME AS A BRIDE. ♥
CLING
THAT'D BE FINE BY ME.

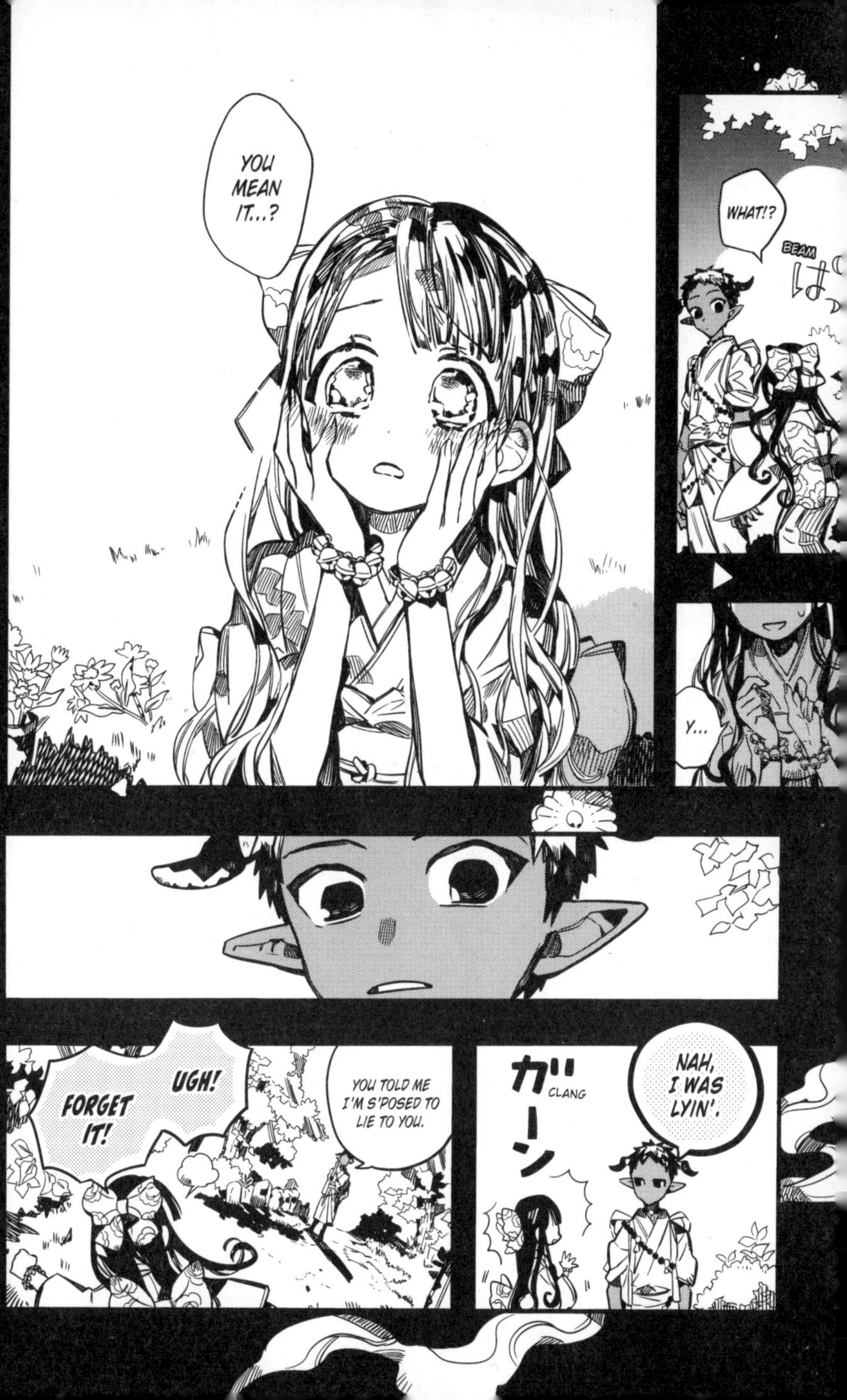
WHAT!?
BEAM
Y...
YOU MEAN IT...?
NAH, I WAS LYIN'.
ガーン
CLANG
YOU TOLD ME I'M S'POSED TO LIE TO YOU.
UGH!
FORGET IT!

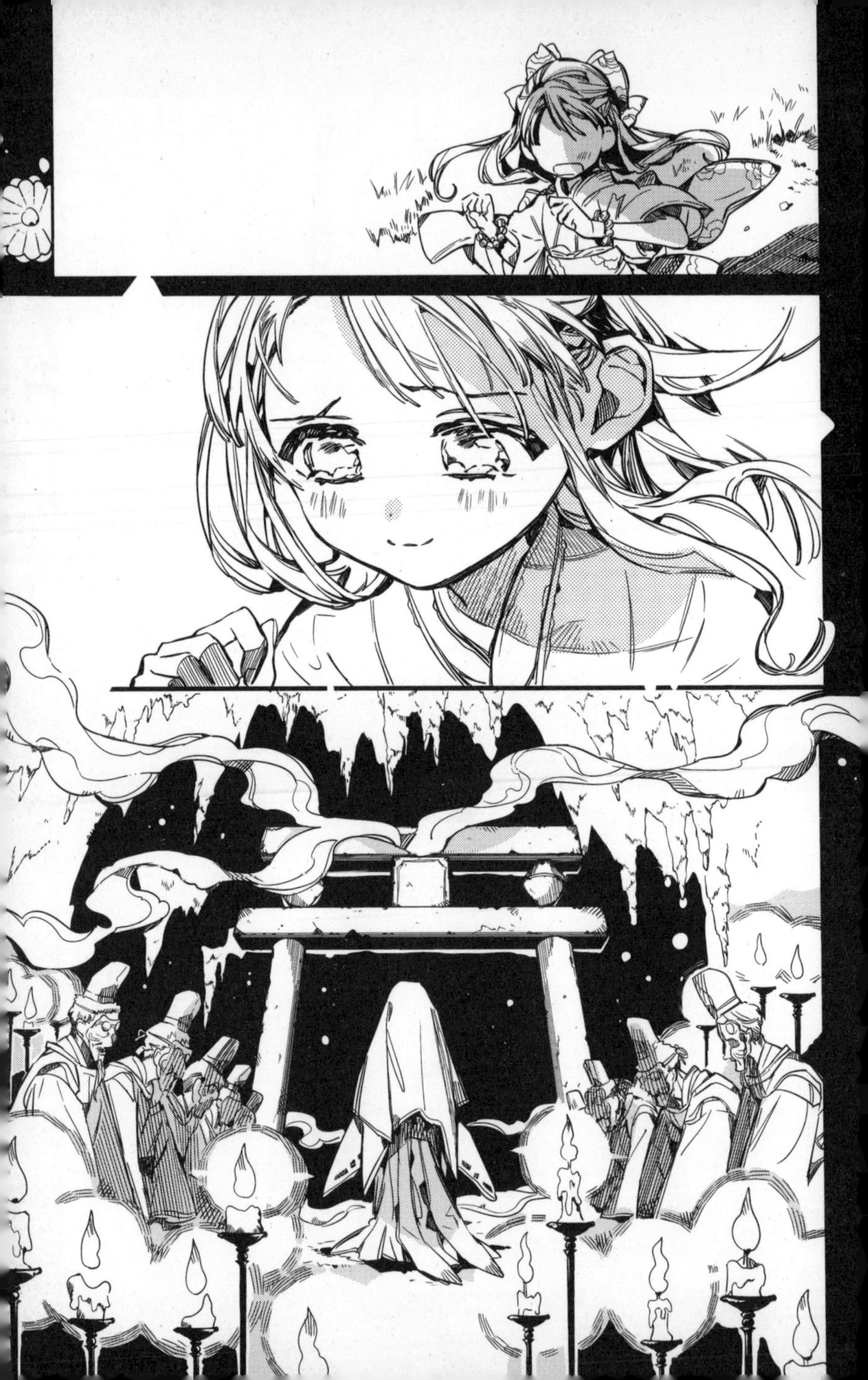

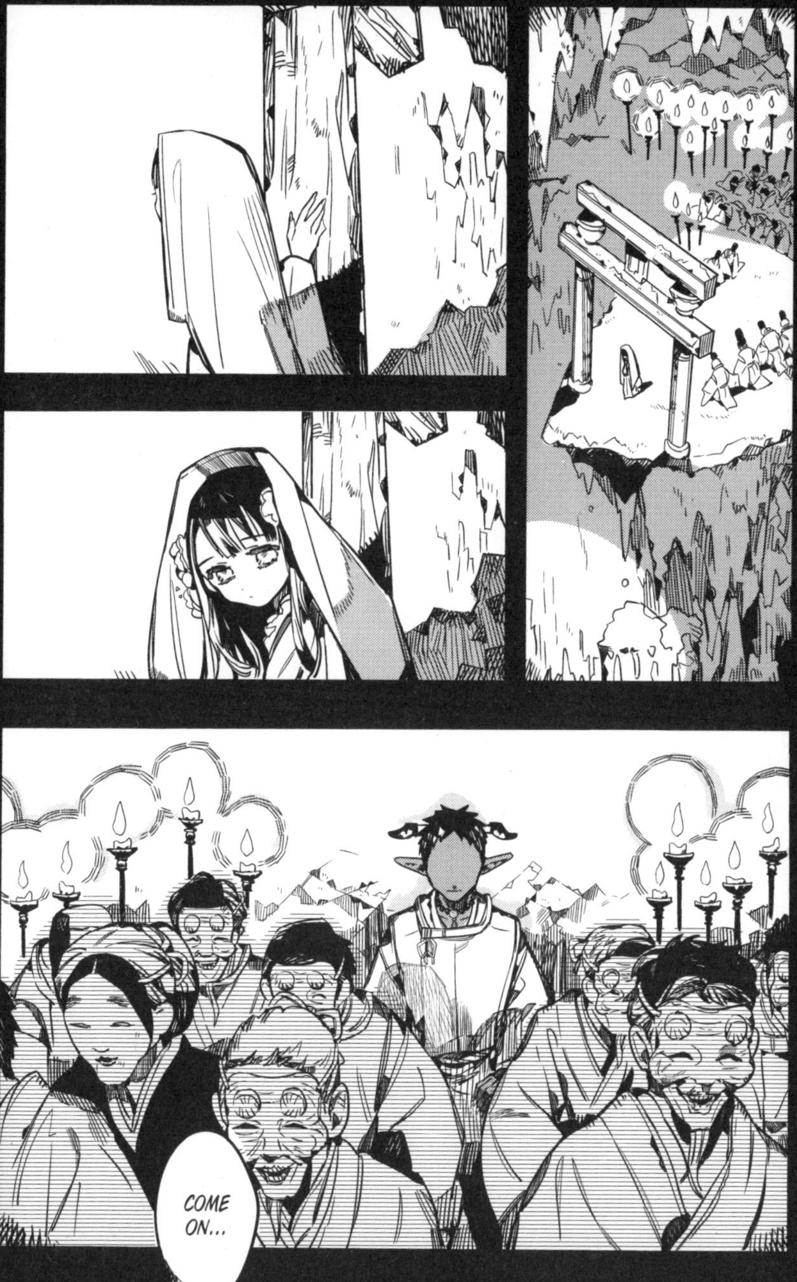COME ON...

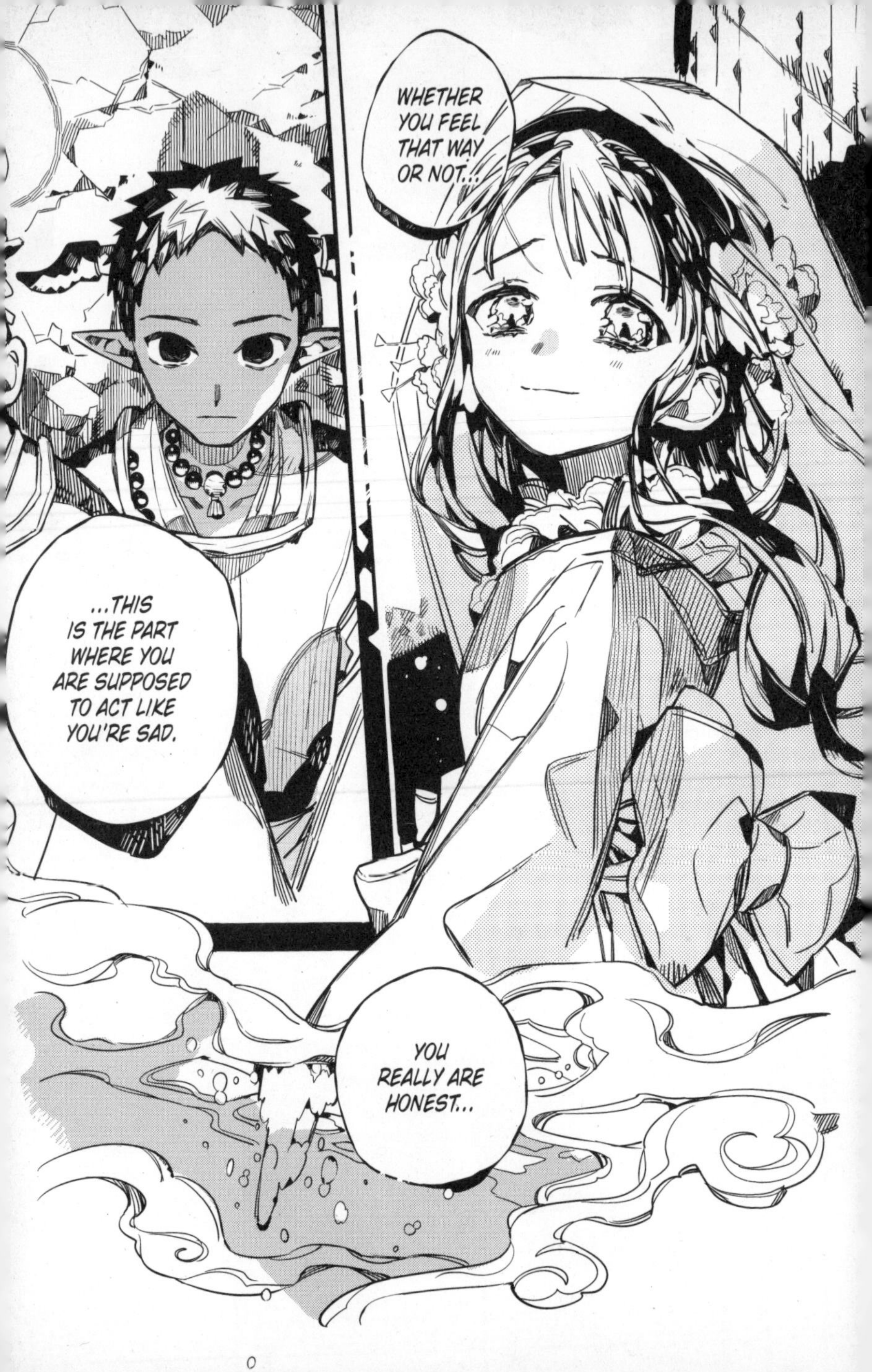
WHETHER YOU FEEL THAT WAY OR NOT...
...THIS IS THE PART WHERE YOU ARE SUPPOSED TO ACT LIKE YOU'RE SAD.
YOU REALLY ARE HONEST...

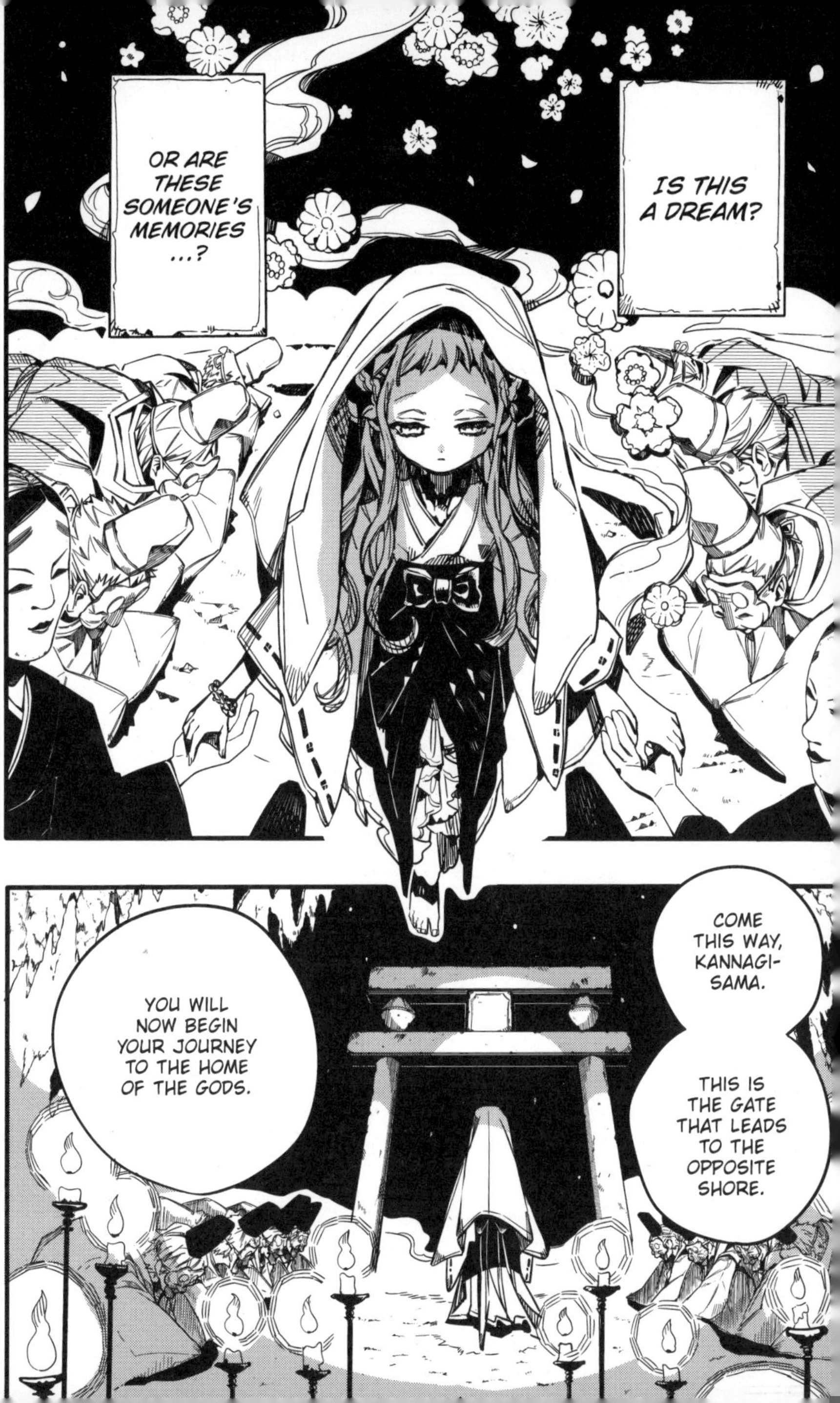
IS THIS A DREAM?
OR ARE THESE SOMEONE'S MEMORIES ...?
COME THIS WAY, KANNAGI-SAMA.
THIS IS THE GATE THAT LEADS TO THE OPPOSITE SHORE.
YOU WILL NOW BEGIN YOUR JOURNEY TO THE HOME OF THE GODS.

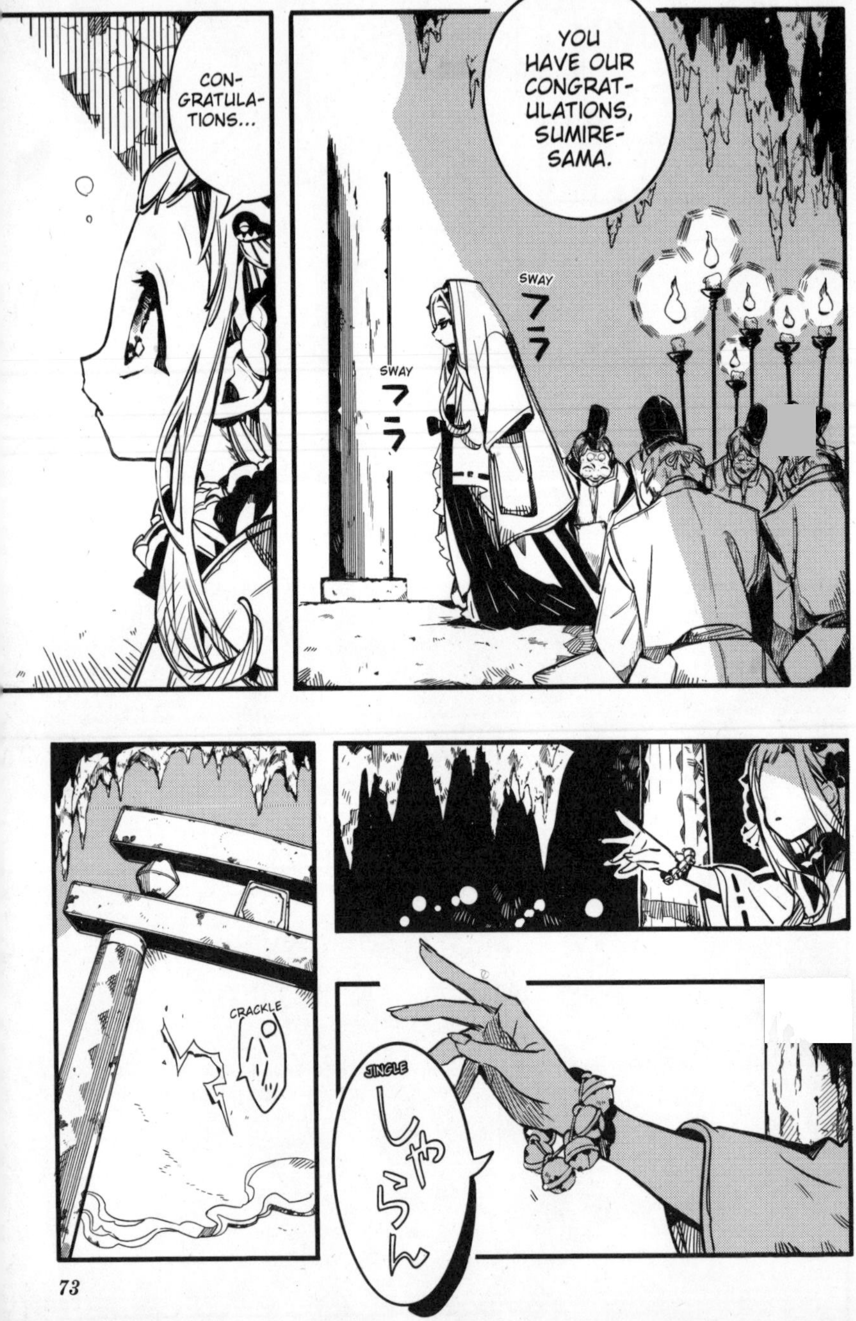
YOU HAVE OUR CONGRAT-ULATIONS, SUMIRE-SAMA.
SWAY
フラ
SWAY
フラ
CON-GRATULA-TIONS...
JINGLE
しゃらん
CRACKLE

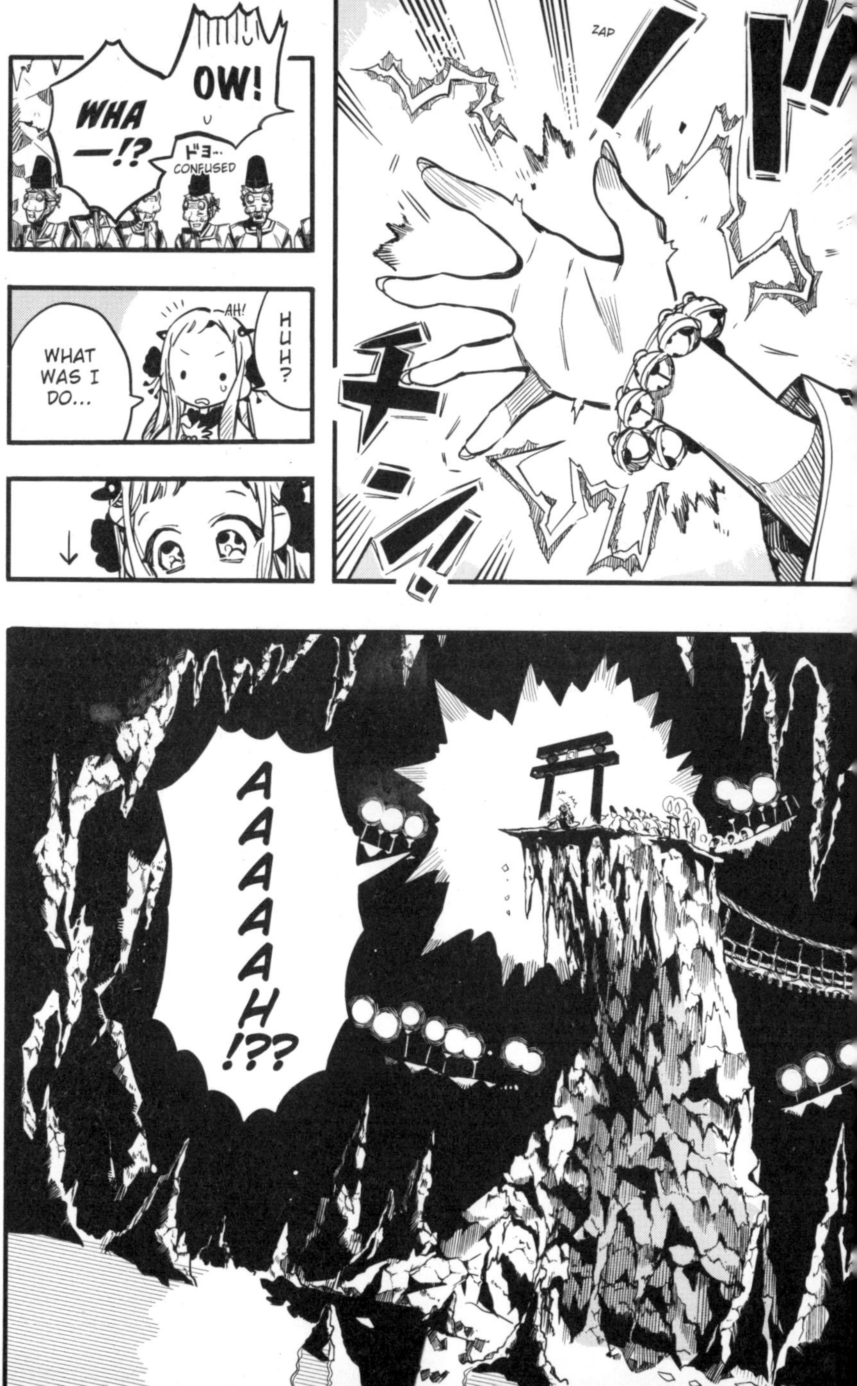
ZAP
OW!
WHA—!?
ドヨ… CONFUSED
HUH?
AH!
WHAT WAS I DO…
AAAAAAH!??

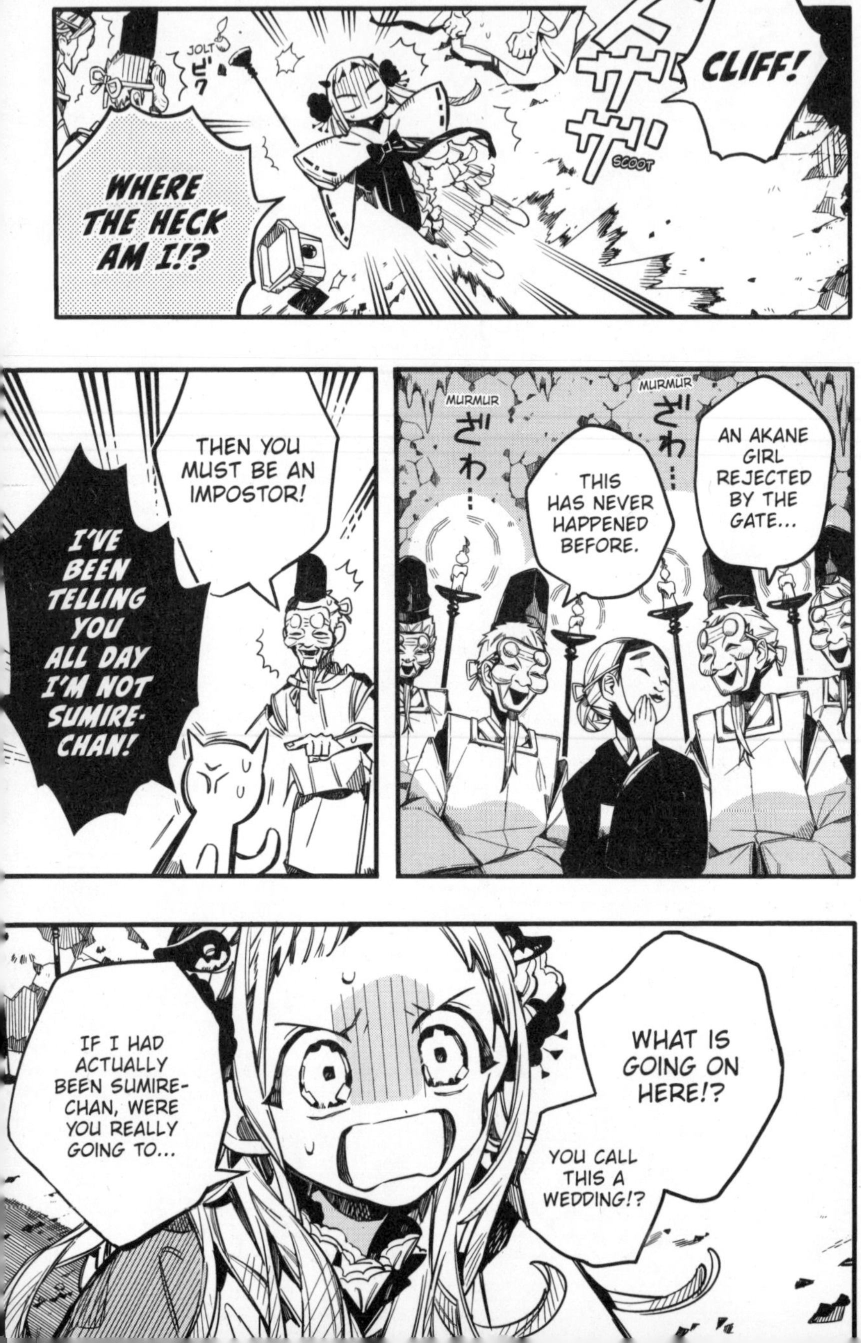
ズザザザ
SCOOT
CLIFF!
JOLT
ビク
WHERE THE HECK AM I!?
MURMUR
ざわ…
AN AKANE GIRL REJECTED BY THE GATE...
MURMUR
ざわ…
THIS HAS NEVER HAPPENED BEFORE.
THEN YOU MUST BE AN IMPOSTOR!
I'VE BEEN TELLING YOU ALL DAY I'M NOT SUMIRE-CHAN!
WHAT IS GOING ON HERE!?
YOU CALL THIS A WEDDING!?
IF I HAD ACTUALLY BEEN SUMIRE-CHAN, WERE YOU REALLY GOING TO...

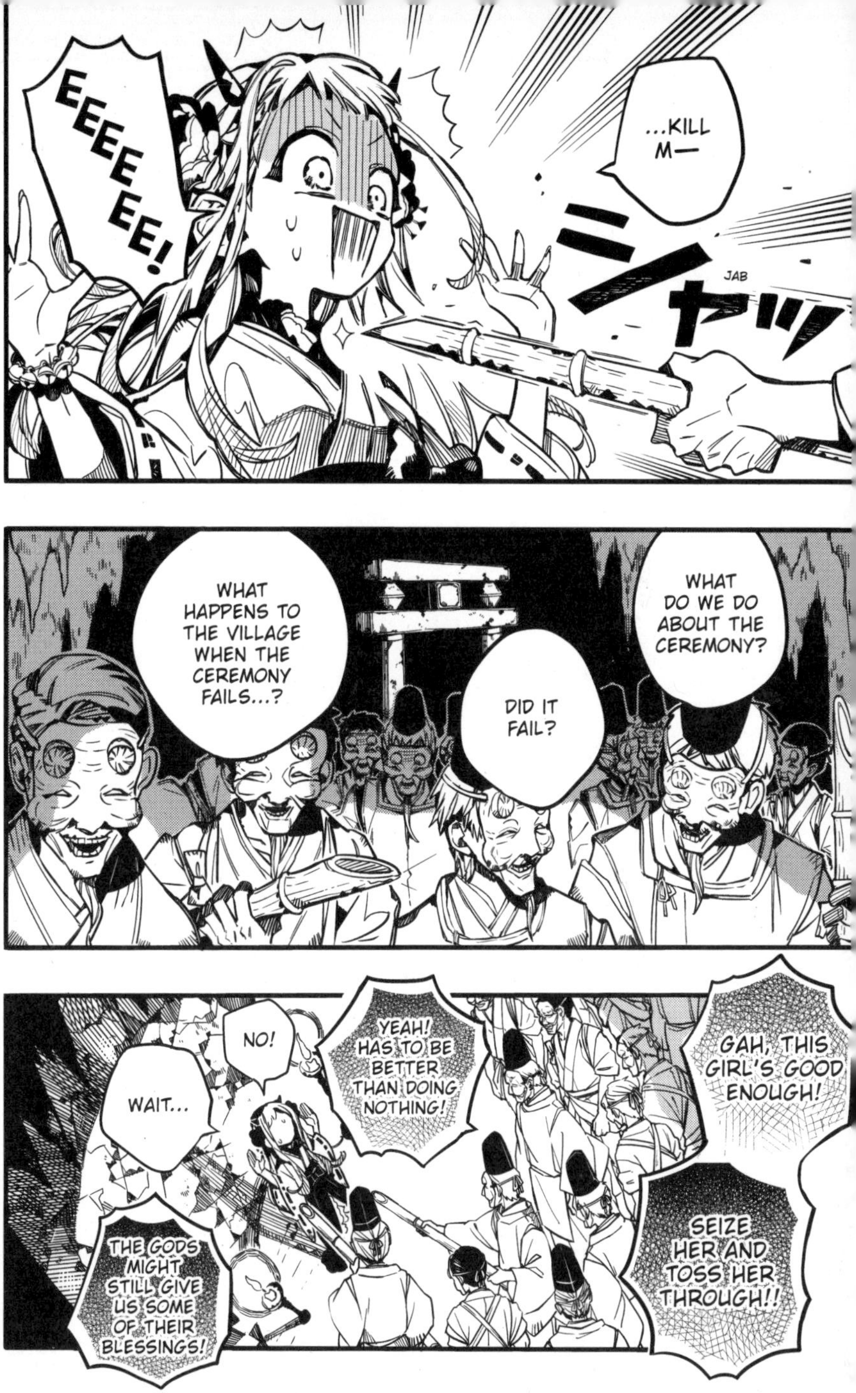
...KILL M—
JAB
EEEEEEEE!
WHAT DO WE DO ABOUT THE CEREMONY?
DID IT FAIL?
WHAT HAPPENS TO THE VILLAGE WHEN THE CEREMONY FAILS...?
GAH, THIS GIRL'S GOOD ENOUGH!
SEIZE HER AND TOSS HER THROUGH!!
YEAH! HAS TO BE BETTER THAN DOING NOTHING!
NO!
WAIT...
THE GODS MIGHT STILL GIVE US SOME OF THEIR BLESSINGS!

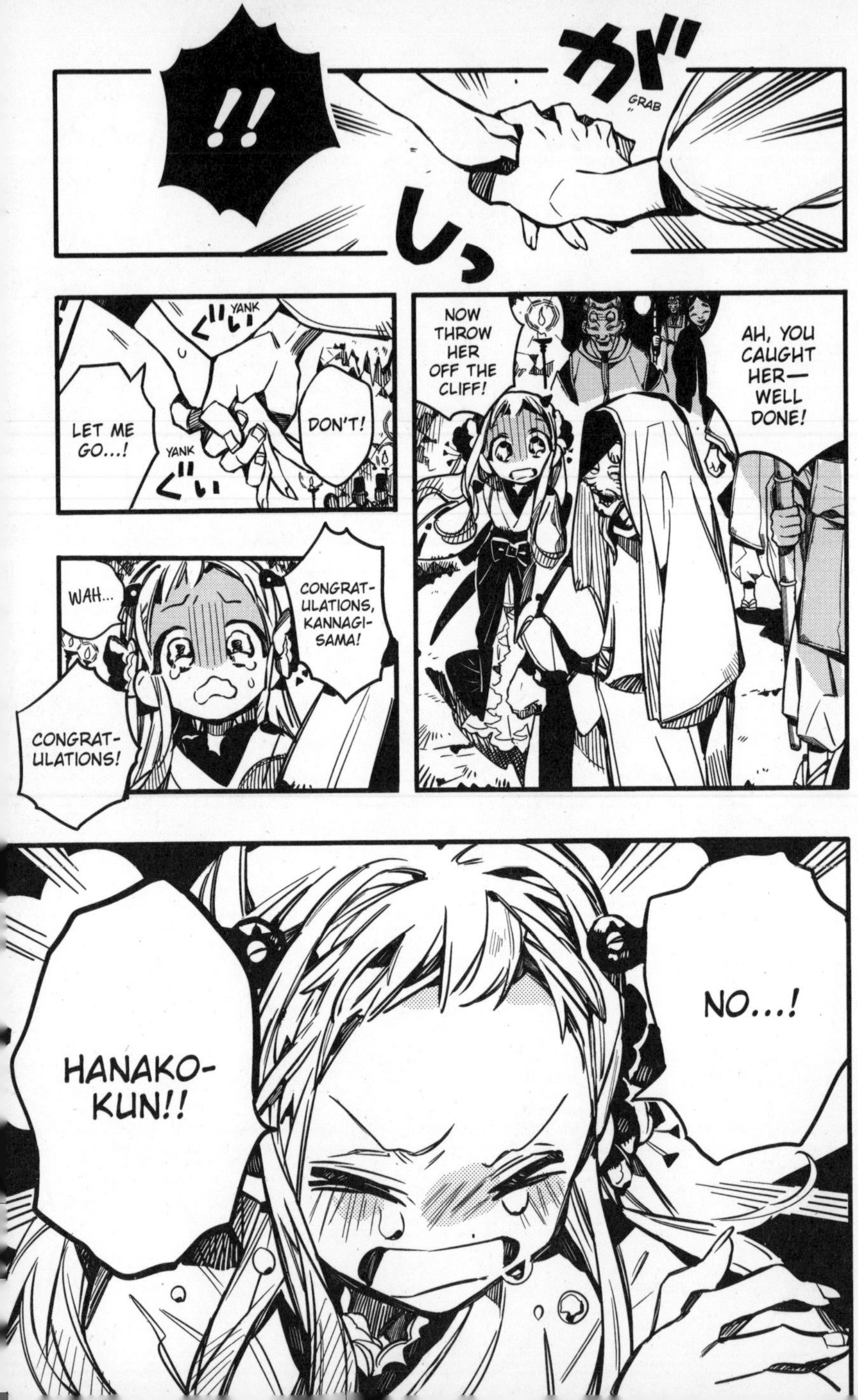

が
GRAB
!!
しっ
AH, YOU CAUGHT HER—WELL DONE!
NOW THROW HER OFF THE CLIFF!
ぐい YANK
DON'T!
LET ME GO...!
YANK ぐい
CONGRATULATIONS, KANNAGI-SAMA!
WAH...
CONGRATULATIONS!
NO...!
HANAKO-KUN!!

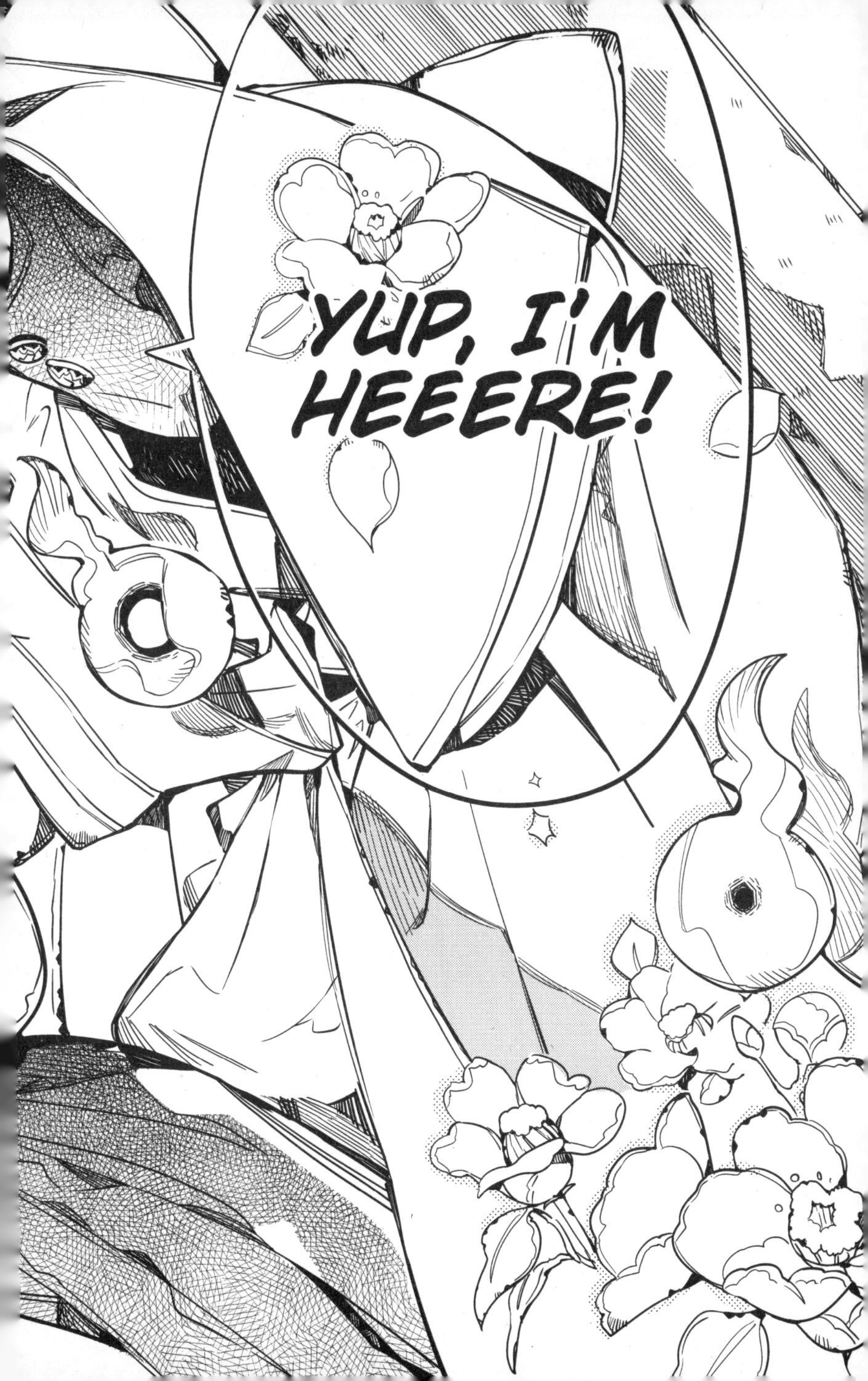
YUP, I'M HEEERE!

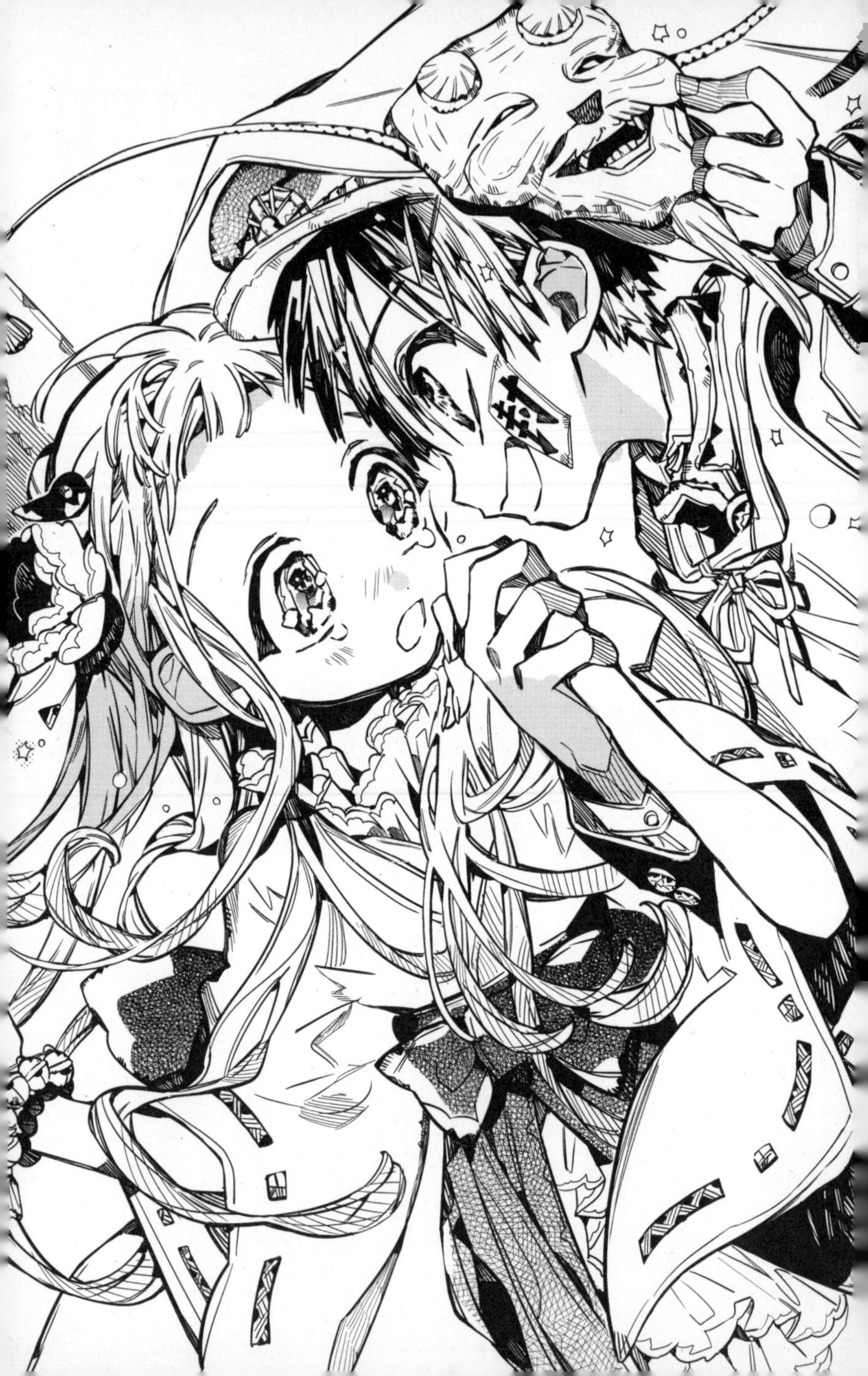

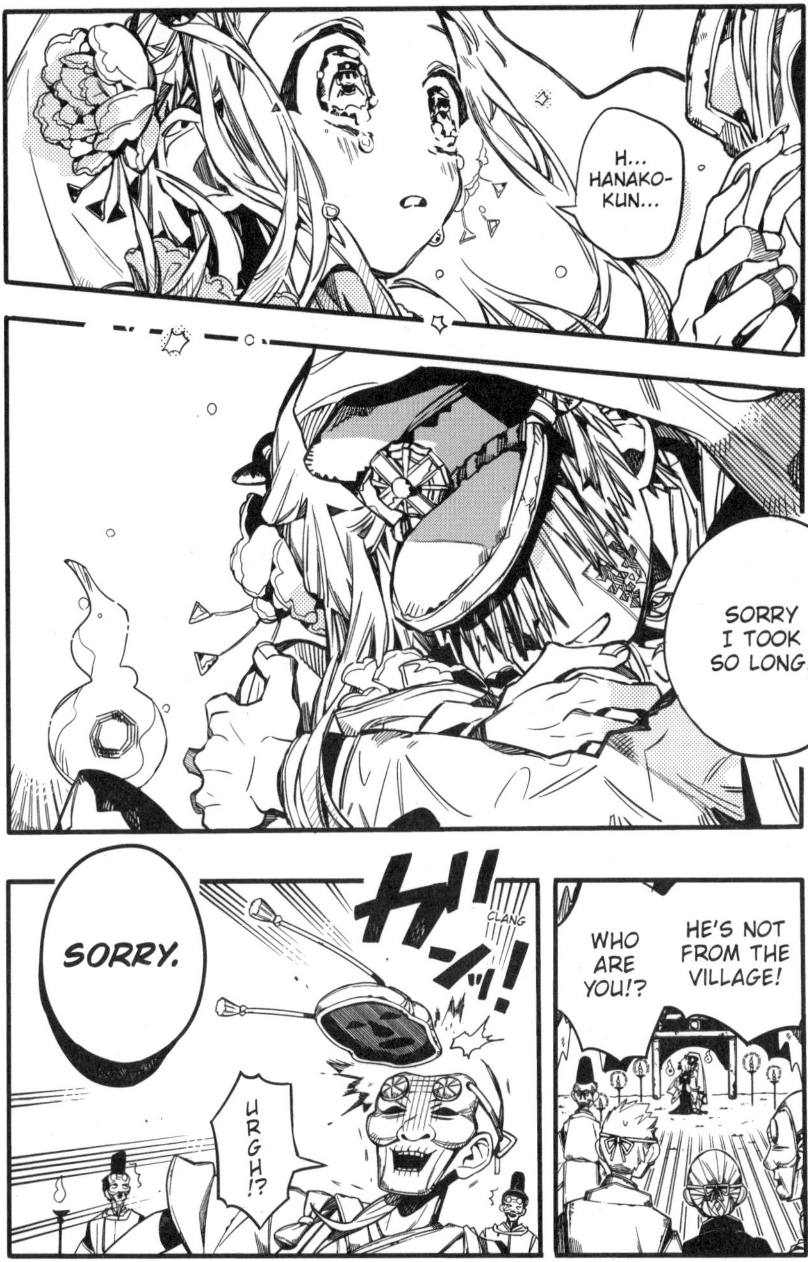
H... HANAKO-KUN...
SORRY I TOOK SO LONG.
HE'S NOT FROM THE VILLAGE!
WHO ARE YOU!?
CLANG
SORRY.
URGH!?

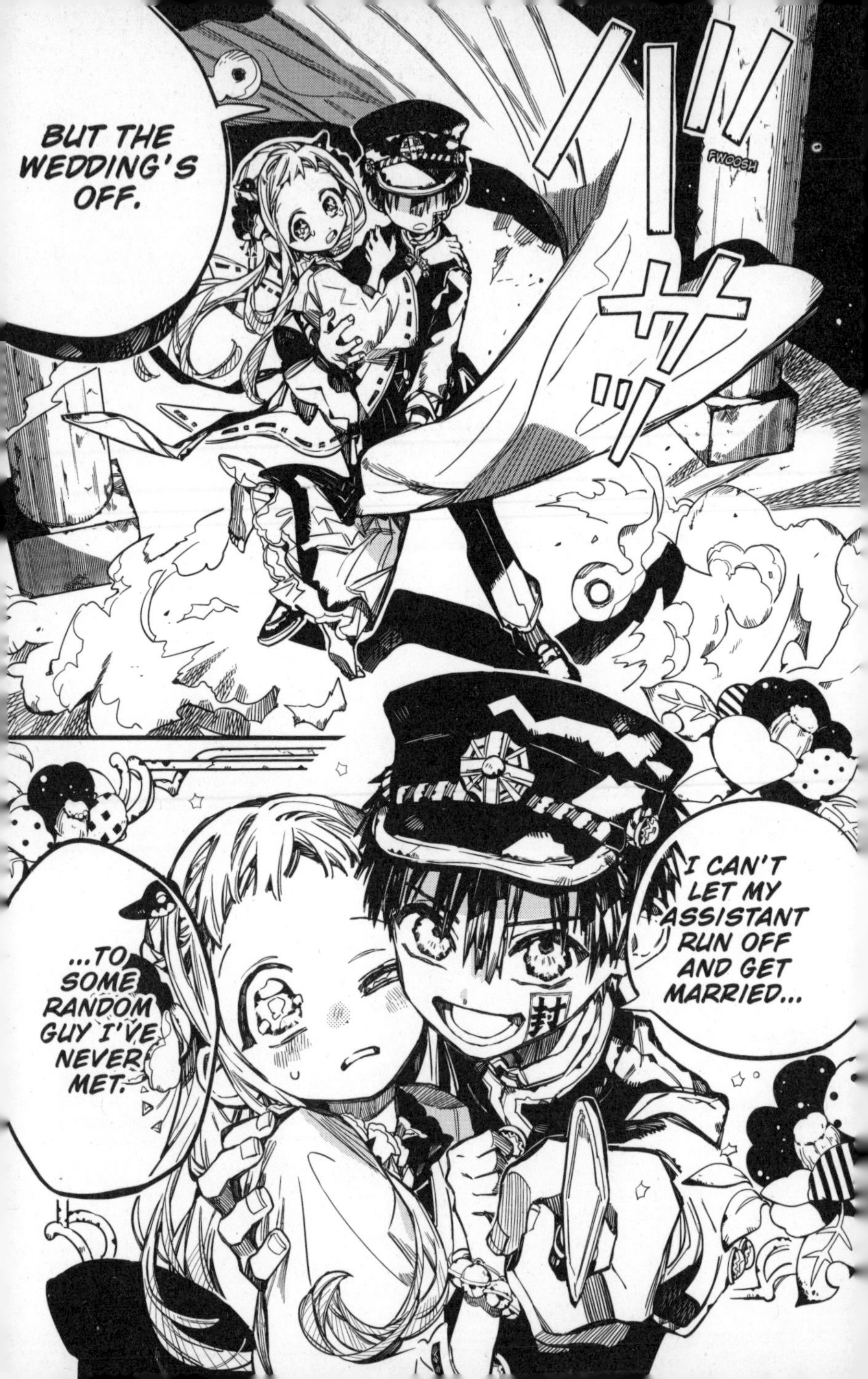
FWOOSH
BUT THE WEDDING'S OFF.
I CAN'T LET MY ASSISTANT RUN OFF AND GET MARRIED...
...TO SOME RANDOM GUY I'VE NEVER MET.

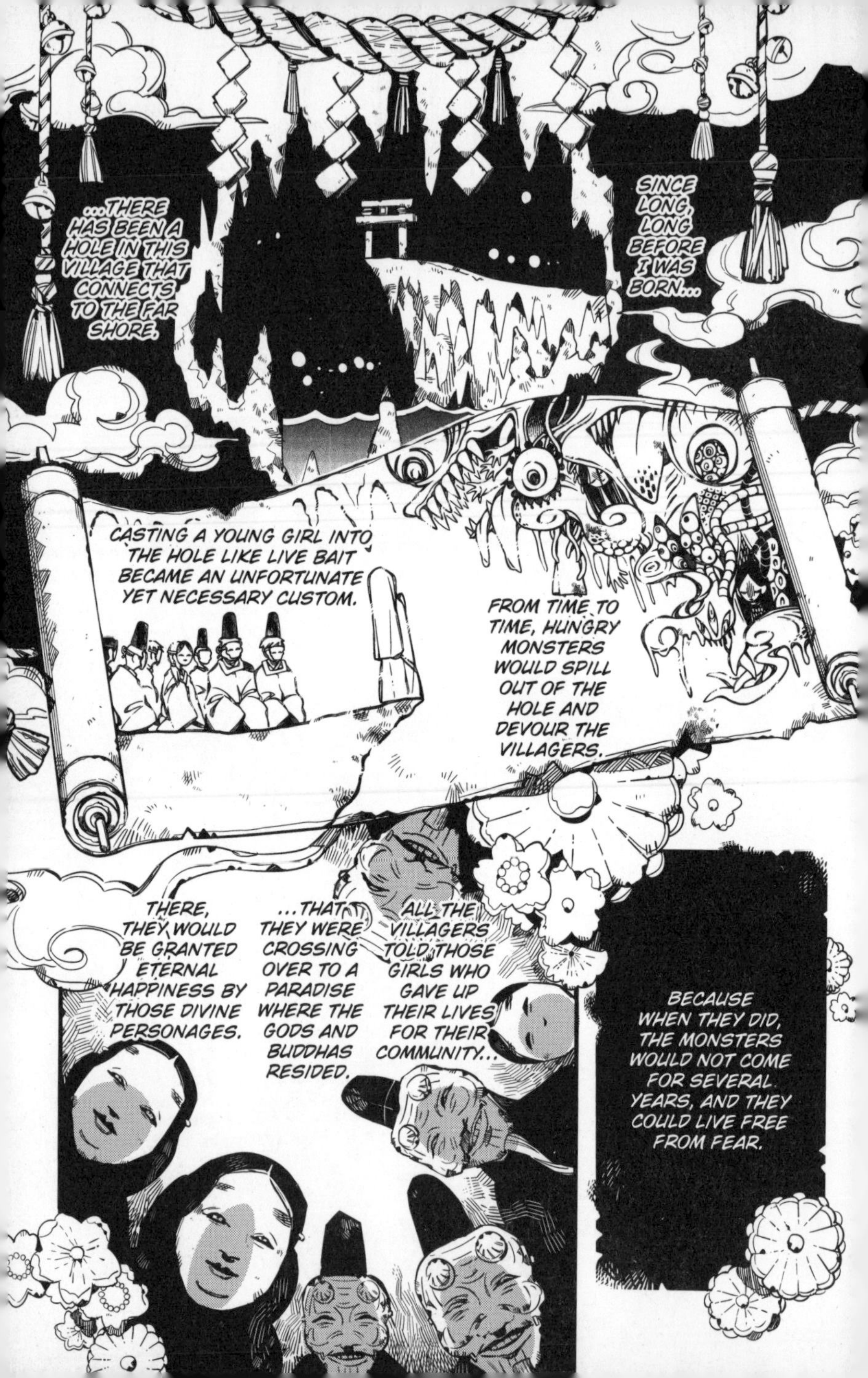
SINCE LONG, LONG BEFORE I WAS BORN...
...THERE HAS BEEN A HOLE IN THIS VILLAGE THAT CONNECTS TO THE FAR SHORE.
FROM TIME TO TIME, HUNGRY MONSTERS WOULD SPILL OUT OF THE HOLE AND DEVOUR THE VILLAGERS.
CASTING A YOUNG GIRL INTO THE HOLE LIKE LIVE BAIT BECAME AN UNFORTUNATE YET NECESSARY CUSTOM.
BECAUSE WHEN THEY DID, THE MONSTERS WOULD NOT COME FOR SEVERAL YEARS, AND THEY COULD LIVE FREE FROM FEAR.
ALL THE VILLAGERS TOLD THOSE GIRLS WHO GAVE UP THEIR LIVES FOR THEIR COMMUNITY...
...THAT THEY WERE CROSSING OVER TO A PARADISE WHERE THE GODS AND BUDDHAS RESIDED.
THERE, THEY WOULD BE GRANTED ETERNAL HAPPINESS BY THOSE DIVINE PERSONAGES.

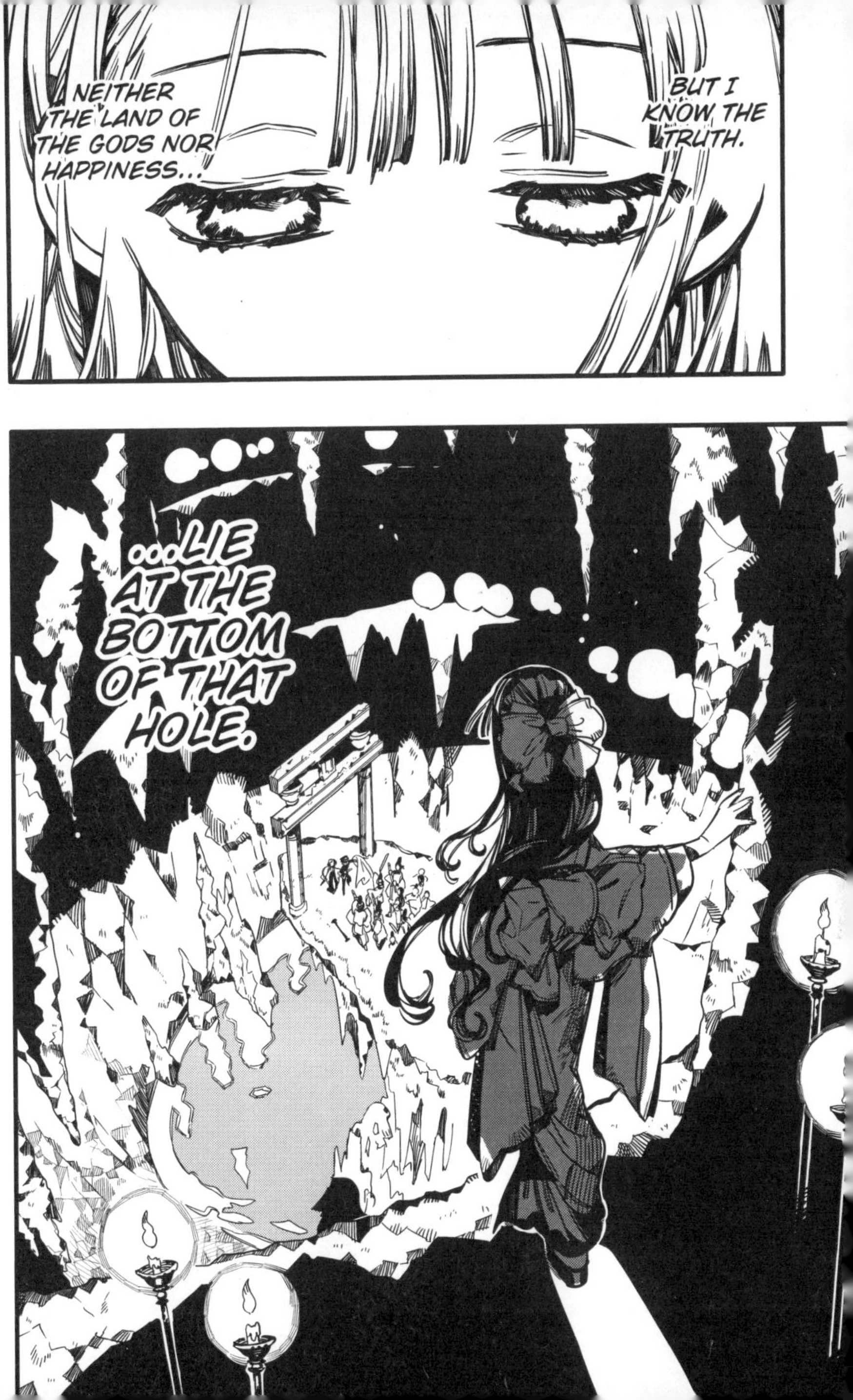
BUT I KNOW THE TRUTH.
NEITHER THE LAND OF THE GODS NOR HAPPINESS...
...LIE AT THE BOTTOM OF THAT HOLE.

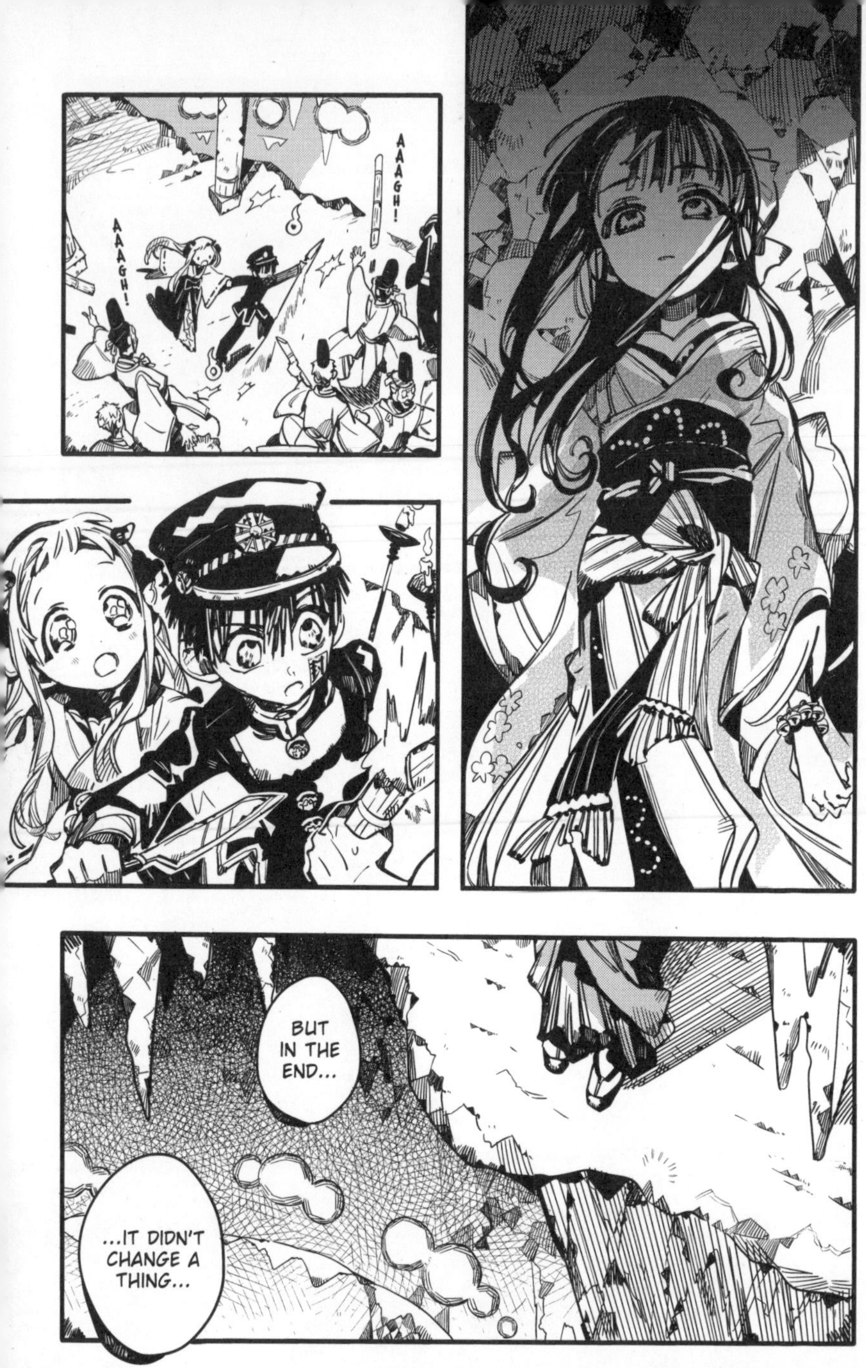
AAAGH!
AAAGH!
BUT IN THE END...
...IT DIDN'T CHANGE A THING...

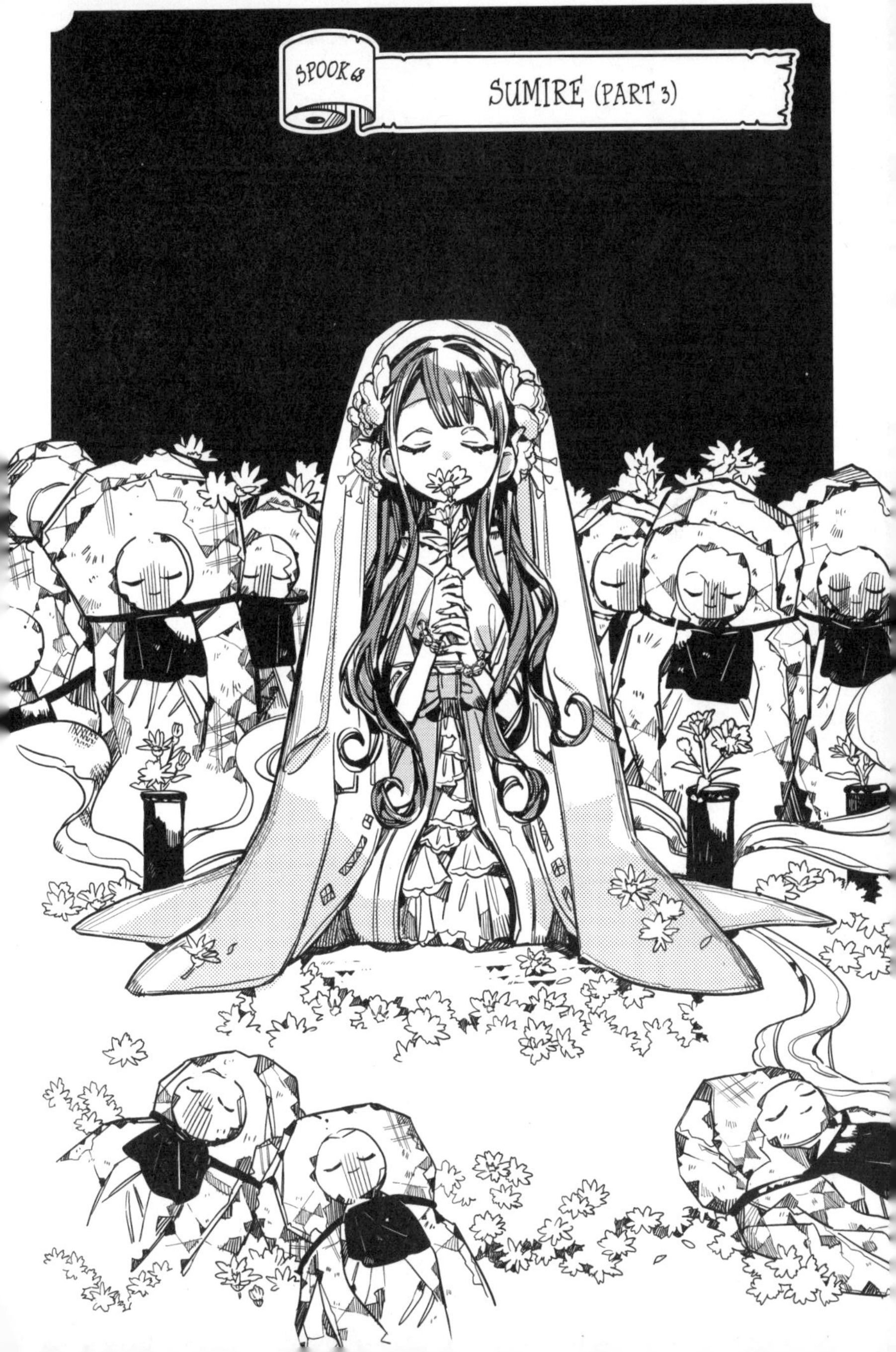
SPOOK 68
SUMIRE (PART 3)

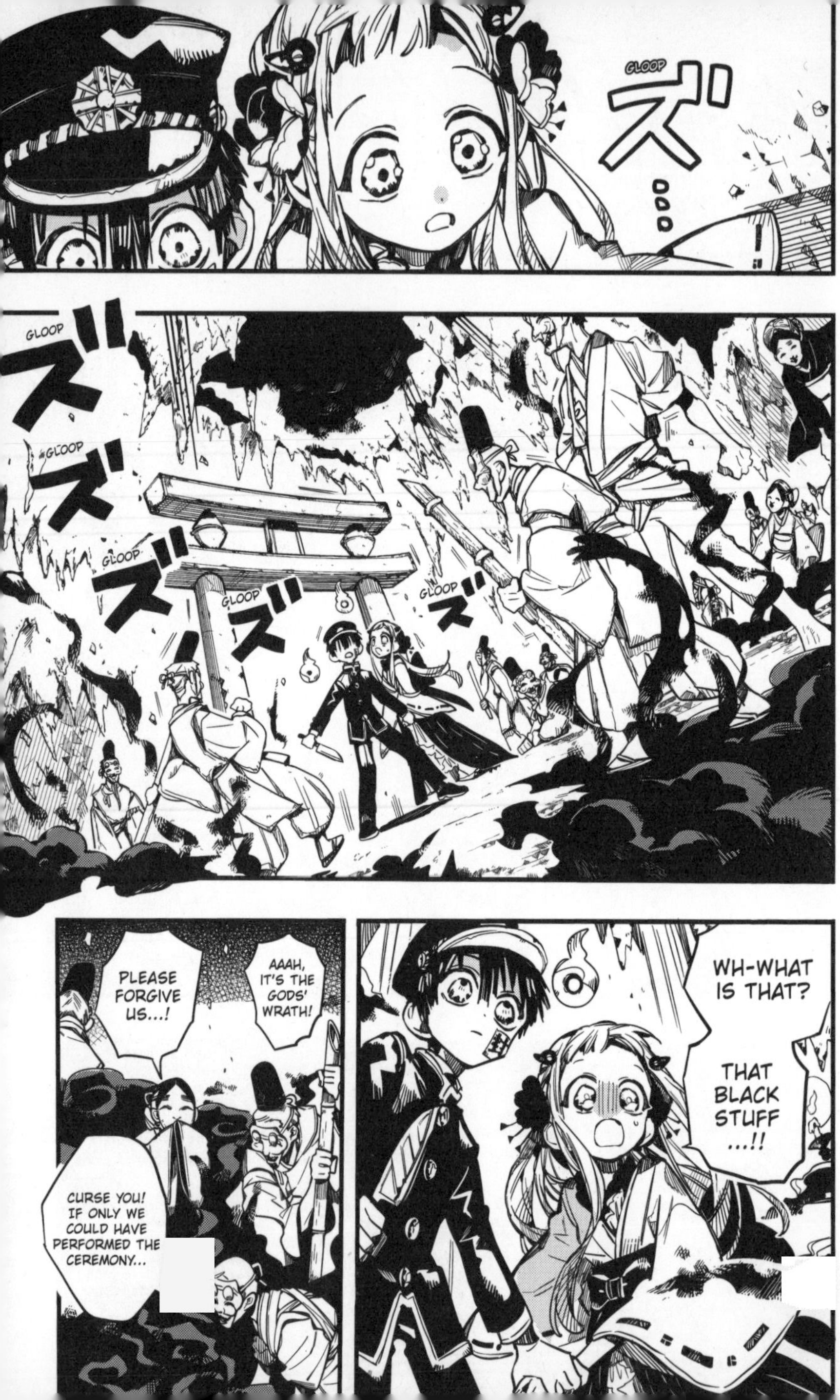

GLOOP
ズ...
GLOOP
ズ
GLOOP
ズ
GLOOP
ズ
GLOOP
ズ
GLOOP
ズ
WH-WHAT IS THAT?
THAT BLACK STUFF ...!!
AAAH, IT'S THE GODS' WRATH!
PLEASE FORGIVE US...!
CURSE YOU! IF ONLY WE COULD HAVE PERFORMED THE CEREMONY...

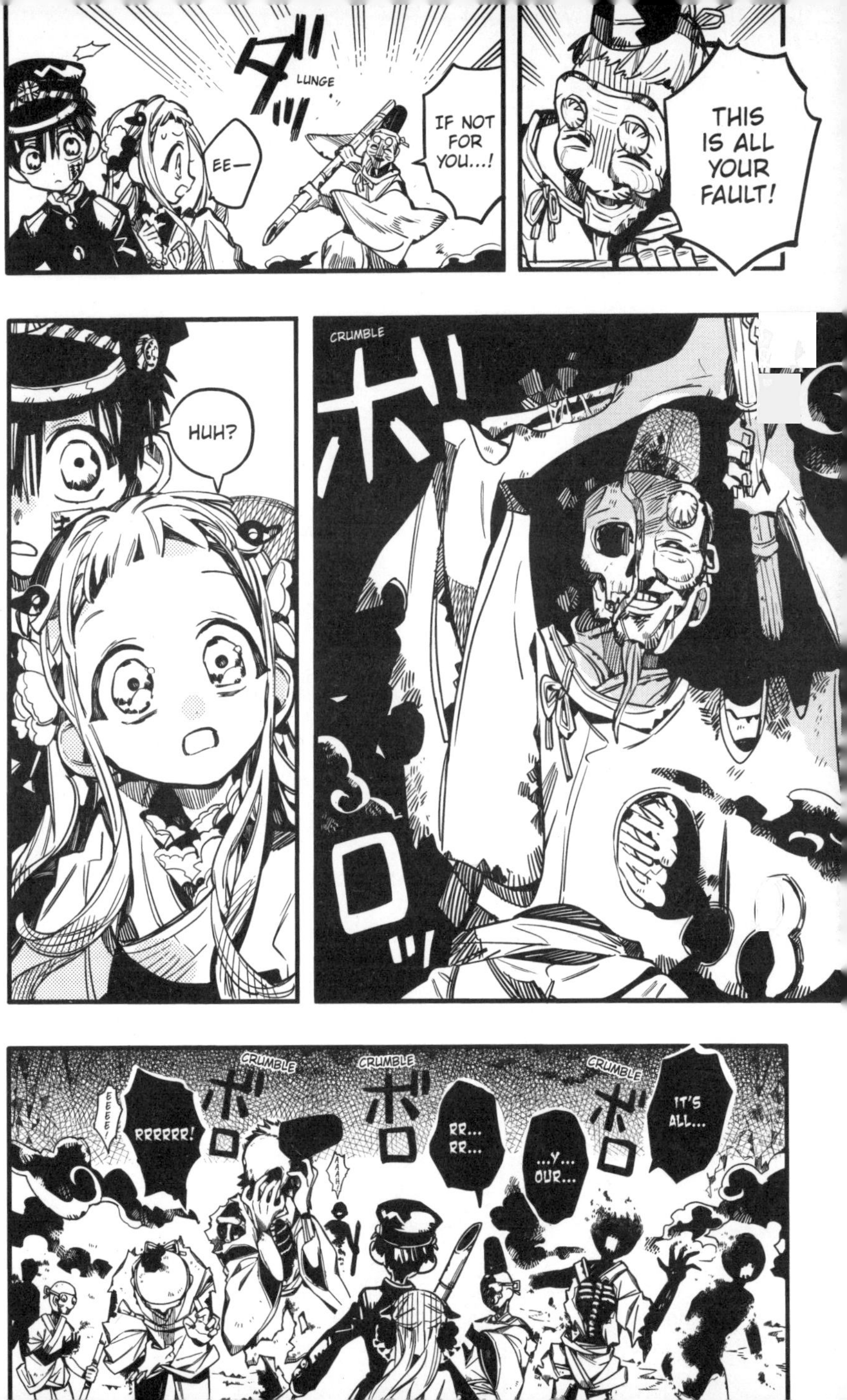
THIS IS ALL YOUR FAULT!
IF NOT FOR YOU...!
LUNGE
EE—
CRUMBLE
HUH?
IT'S ALL...
CRUMBLE
...Y... OUR...
RR... RR...
CRUMBLE
AAAH!
CRUMBLE
RRRRRR!
EEEE!

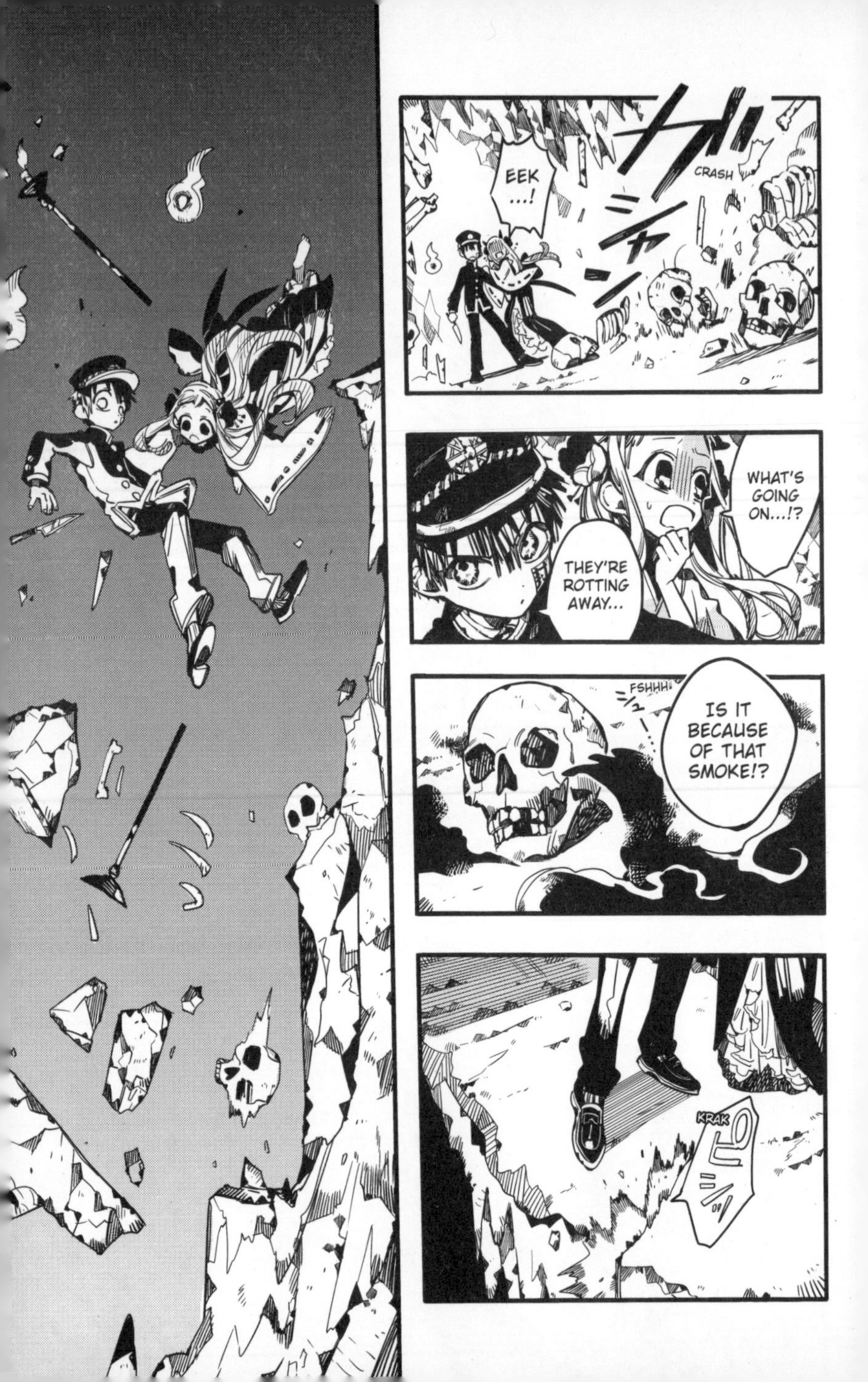
CRASH
EEK ...!
WHAT'S GOING ON...!?
THEY'RE ROTTING AWAY...
IS IT BECAUSE OF THAT SMOKE!?
FSHHH
KRAK

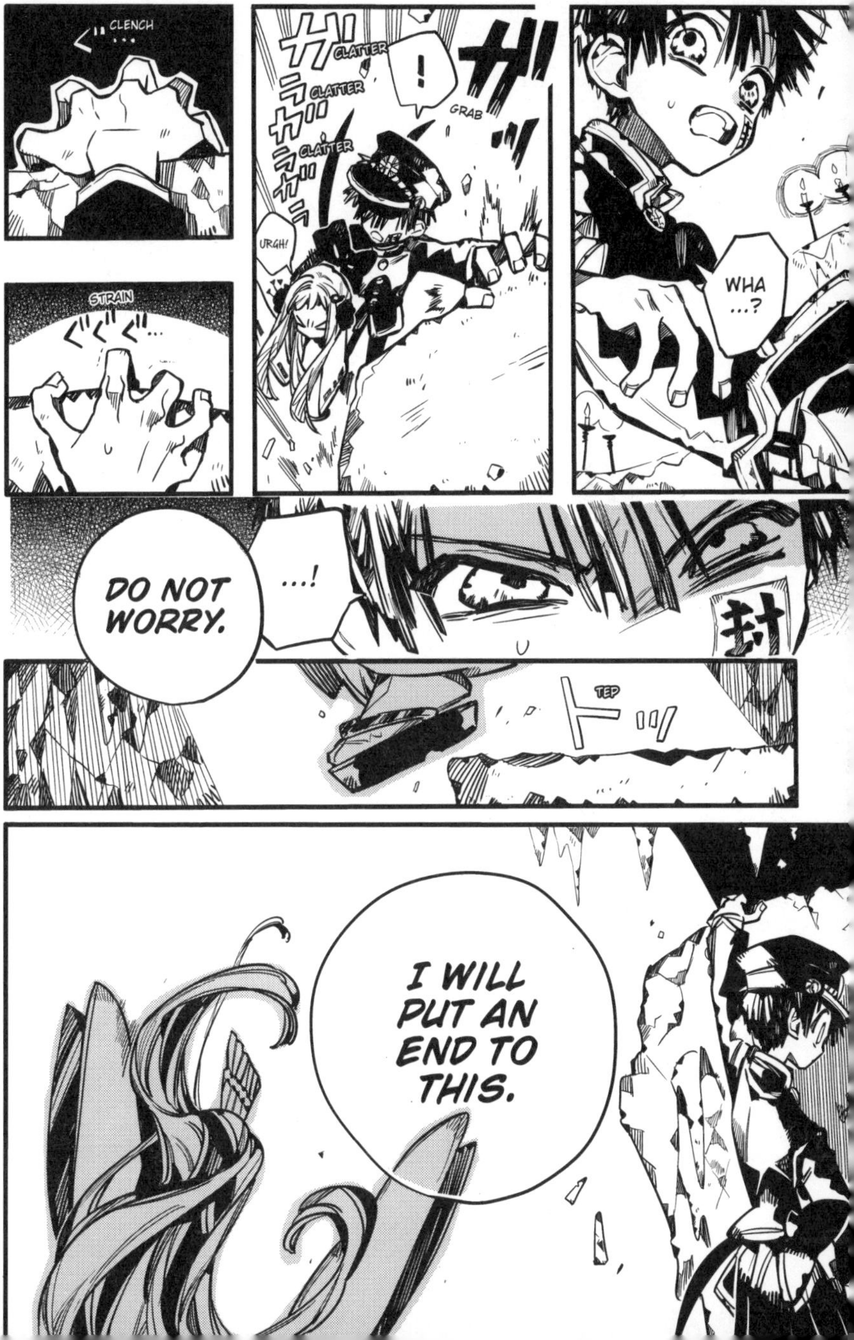
WHA ...?
GRAB
!
CLATTER
CLATTER
CLATTER
URGH!
CLENCH
STRAIN
...!
DO NOT WORRY.
TEP
I WILL PUT AN END TO THIS.

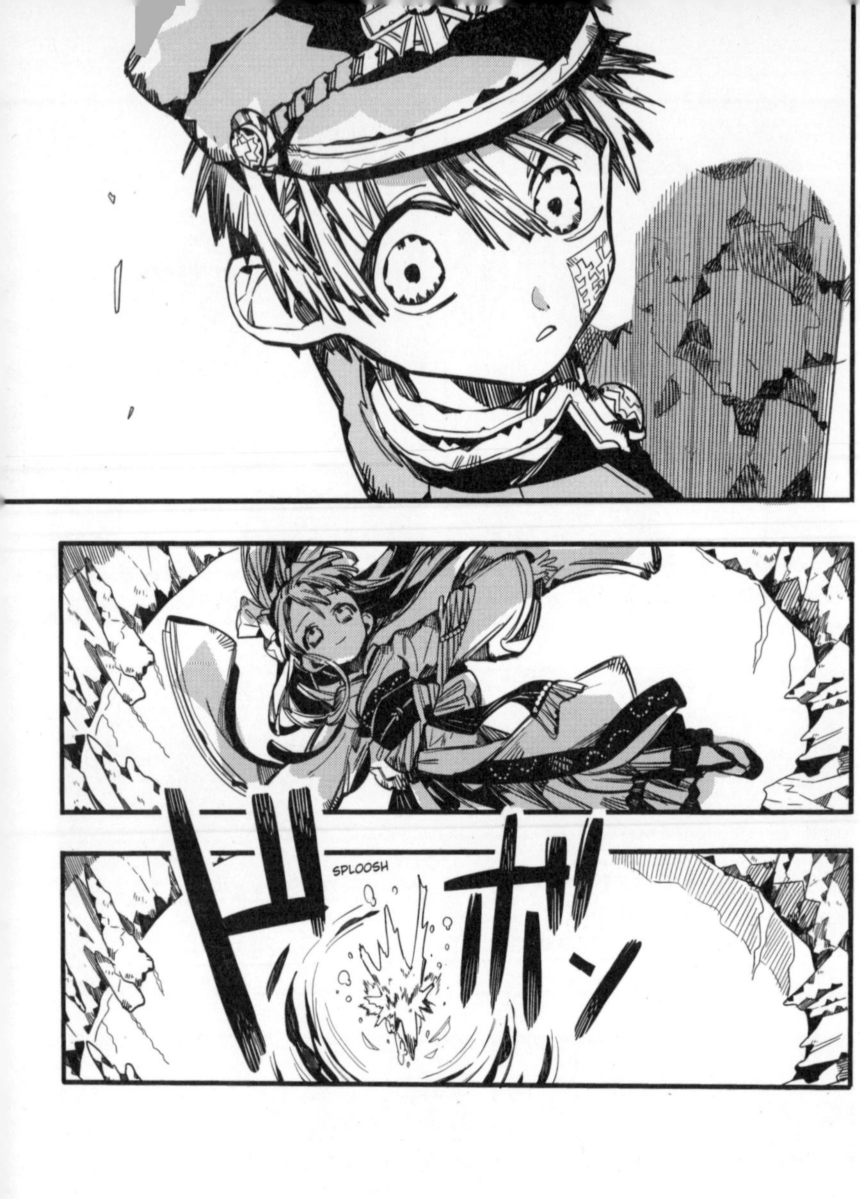
SPLOOSH

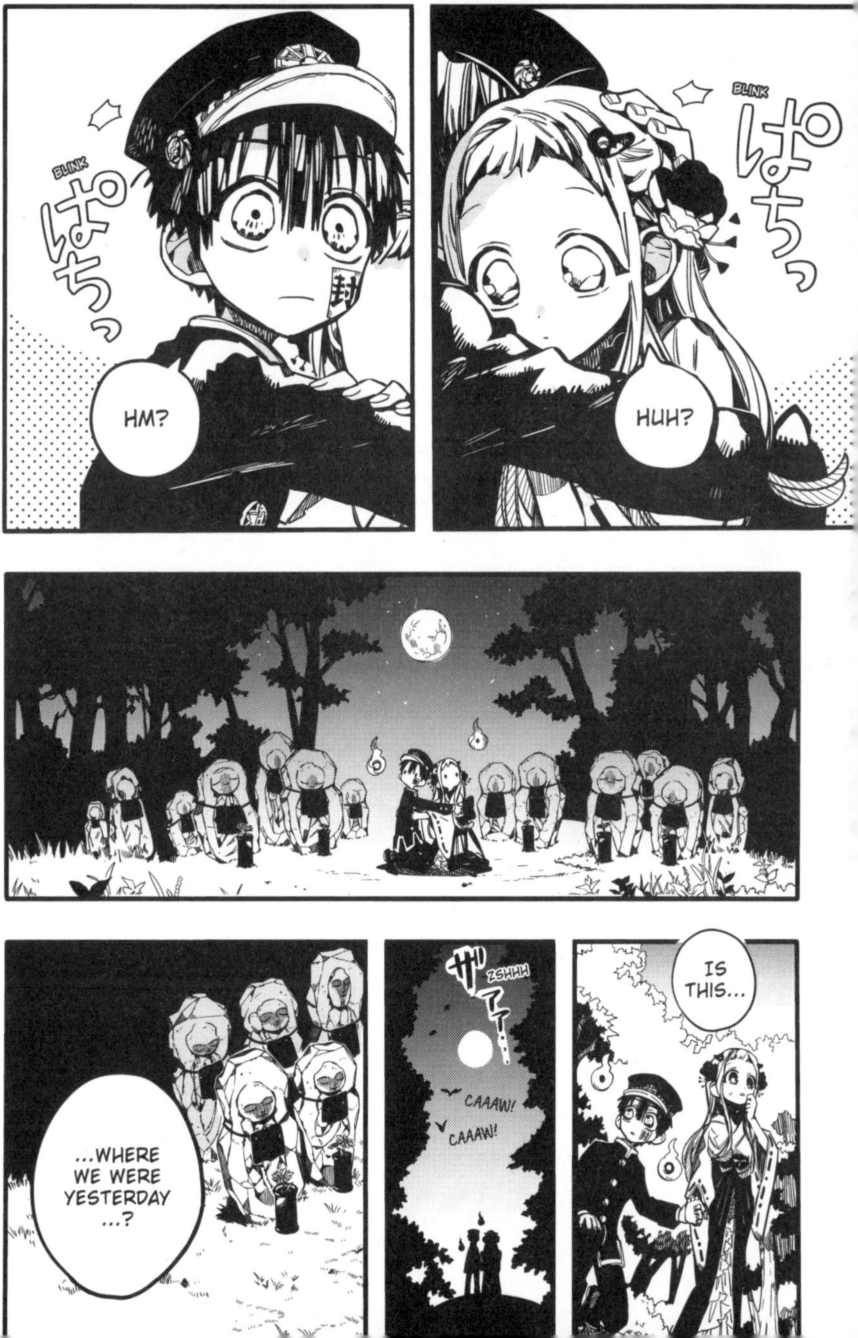
BLINK
ぱちっ
HUH?
BLINK
ぱちっ
HM?
IS THIS...
ザァァ...
ZSHHH
CAAAW!
CAAAW!
...WHERE WE WERE YESTERDAY ...?

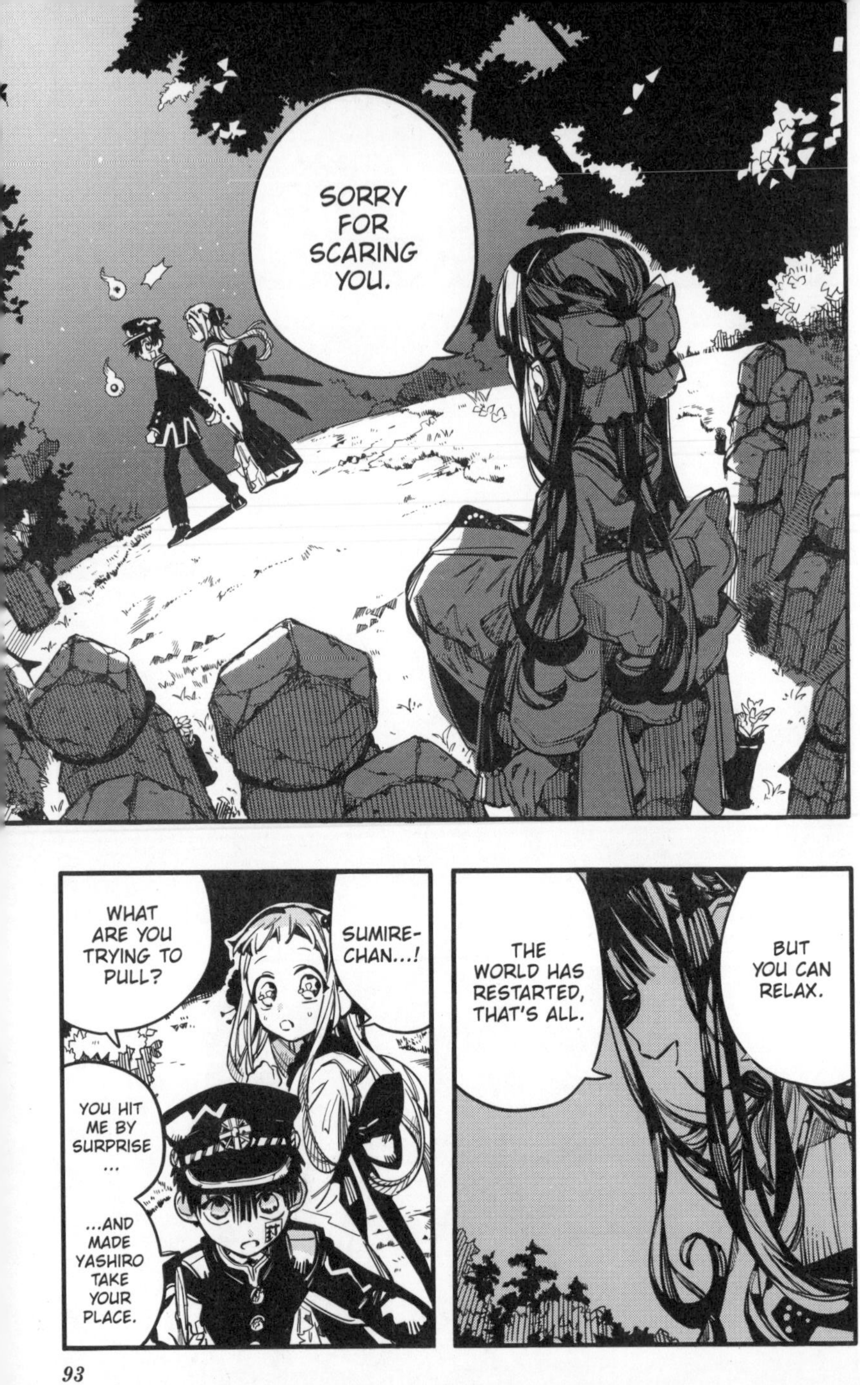
SORRY FOR SCARING YOU.
BUT YOU CAN RELAX.
THE WORLD HAS RESTARTED, THAT'S ALL.
SUMIRE-CHAN...!
WHAT ARE YOU TRYING TO PULL?
YOU HIT ME BY SURPRISE...
...AND MADE YASHIRO TAKE YOUR PLACE.

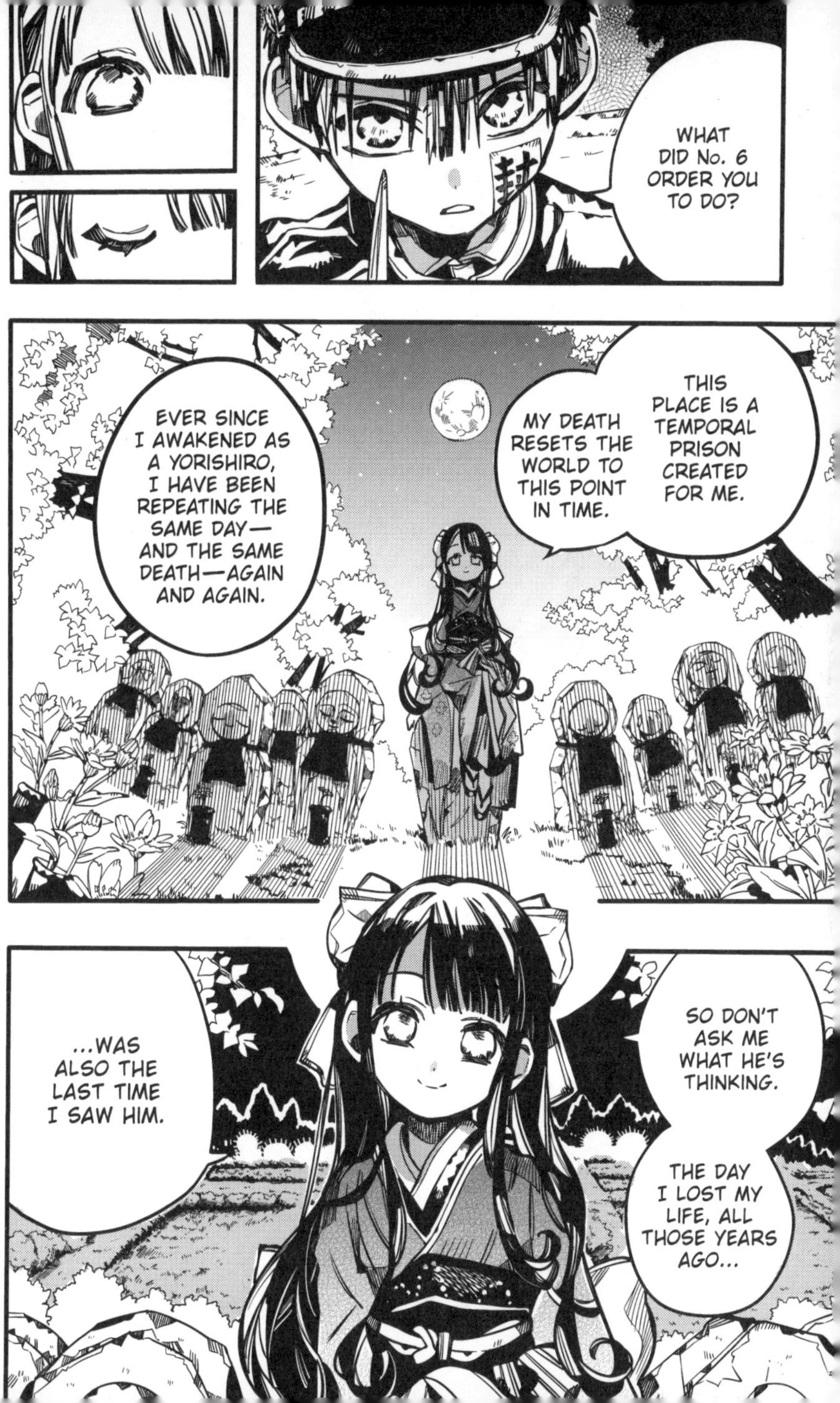
WHAT DID No. 6 ORDER YOU TO DO?
THIS PLACE IS A TEMPORAL PRISON CREATED FOR ME.
MY DEATH RESETS THE WORLD TO THIS POINT IN TIME.
EVER SINCE I AWAKENED AS A YORISHIRO, I HAVE BEEN REPEATING THE SAME DAY—AND THE SAME DEATH—AGAIN AND AGAIN.
SO DON'T ASK ME WHAT HE'S THINKING.
THE DAY I LOST MY LIFE, ALL THOSE YEARS AGO...
...WAS ALSO THE LAST TIME I SAW HIM.

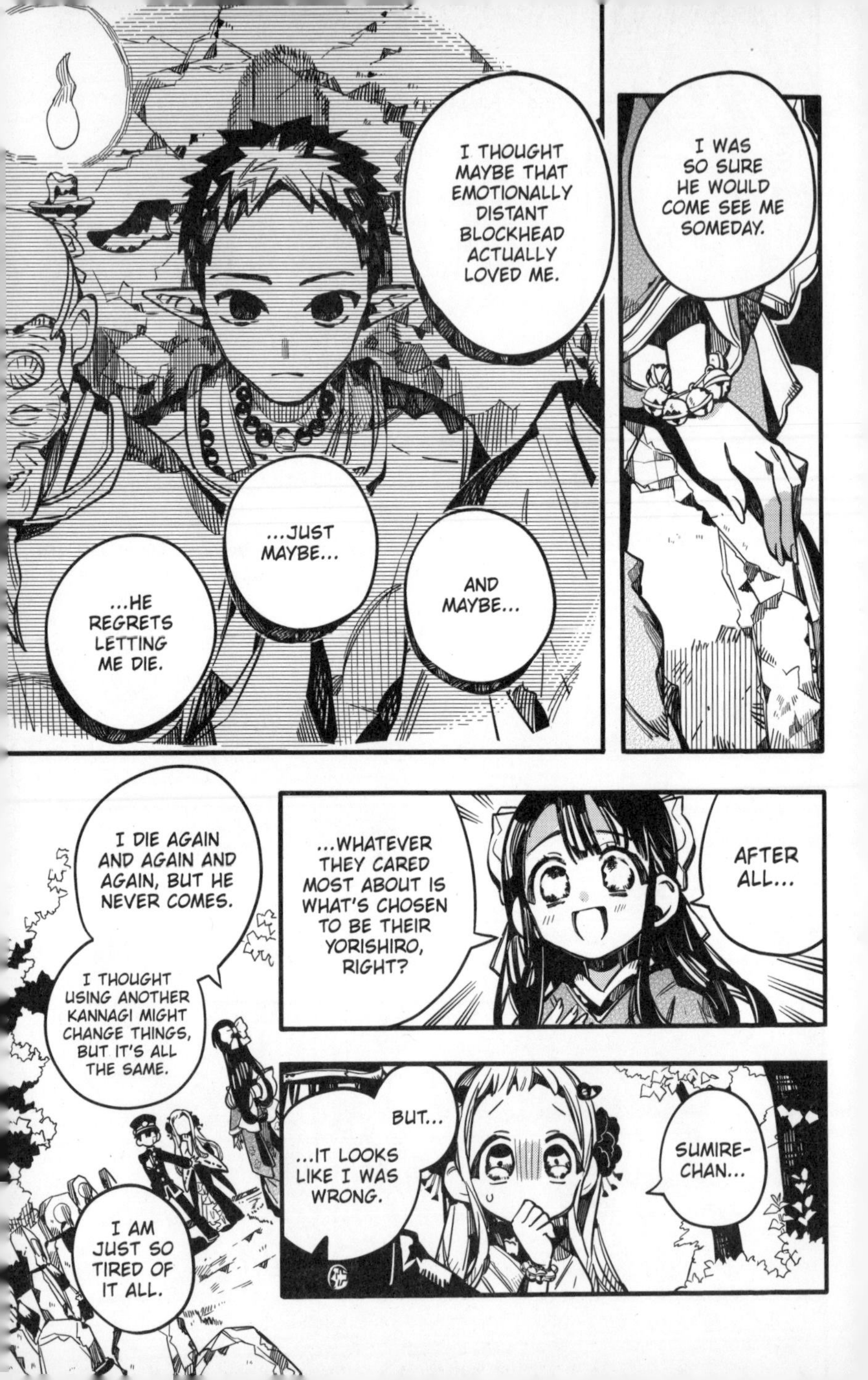
I WAS SO SURE HE WOULD COME SEE ME SOMEDAY.
I THOUGHT MAYBE THAT EMOTIONALLY DISTANT BLOCKHEAD ACTUALLY LOVED ME.
AND MAYBE...
...JUST MAYBE...
...HE REGRETS LETTING ME DIE.
AFTER ALL...
...WHATEVER THEY CARED MOST ABOUT IS WHAT'S CHOSEN TO BE THEIR YORISHIRO, RIGHT?
SUMIRE-CHAN...
BUT...
...IT LOOKS LIKE I WAS WRONG.
I DIE AGAIN AND AGAIN AND AGAIN, BUT HE NEVER COMES.
I THOUGHT USING ANOTHER KANNAGI MIGHT CHANGE THINGS, BUT IT'S ALL THE SAME.
I AM JUST SO TIRED OF IT ALL.

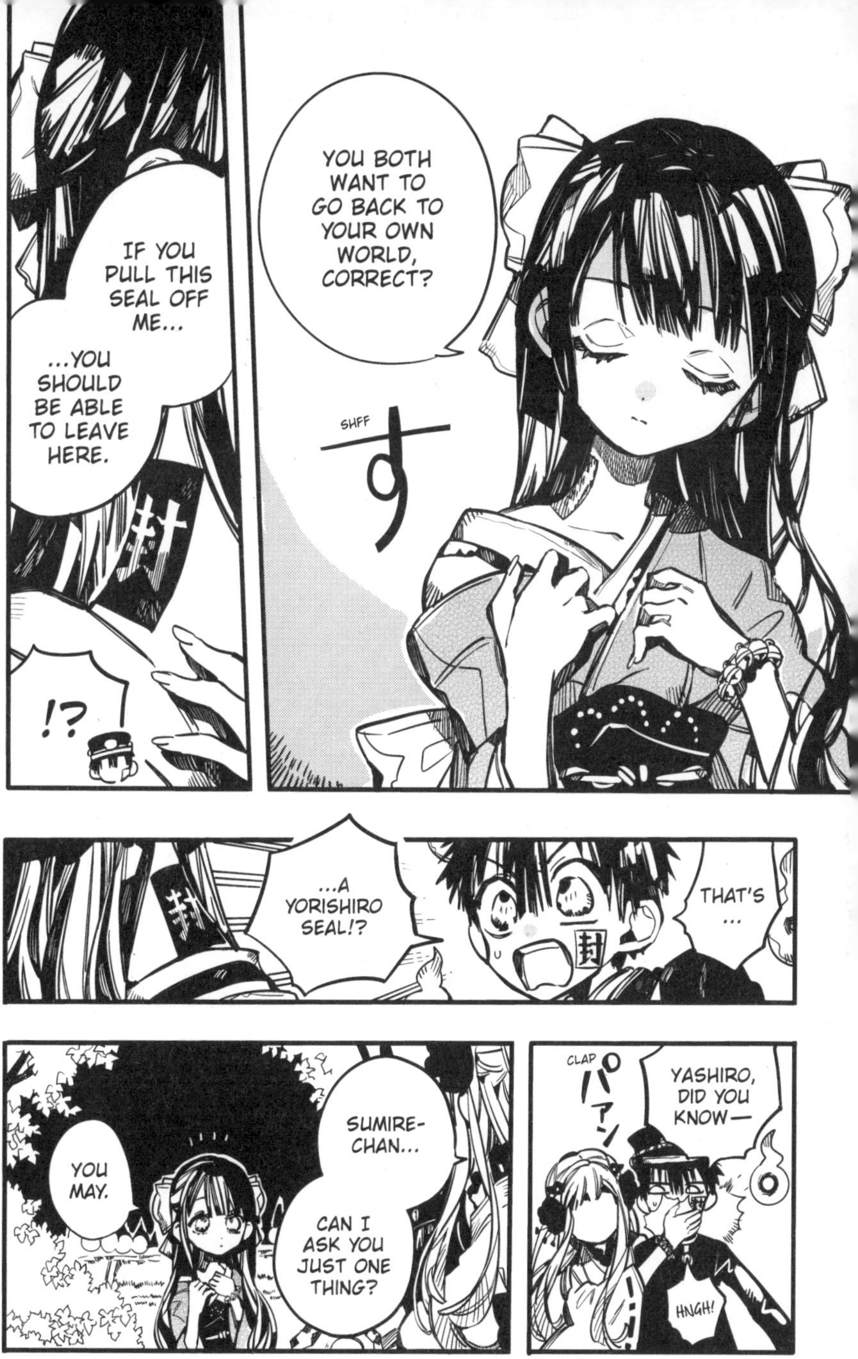
YOU BOTH WANT TO GO BACK TO YOUR OWN WORLD, CORRECT?
SHFF
す
IF YOU PULL THIS SEAL OFF ME...
...YOU SHOULD BE ABLE TO LEAVE HERE.
!?
THAT'S ...
...A YORISHIRO SEAL!?
YASHIRO, DID YOU KNOW—
CLAP
パァン
HNGH!
SUMIRE-CHAN...
CAN I ASK YOU JUST ONE THING?
YOU MAY.

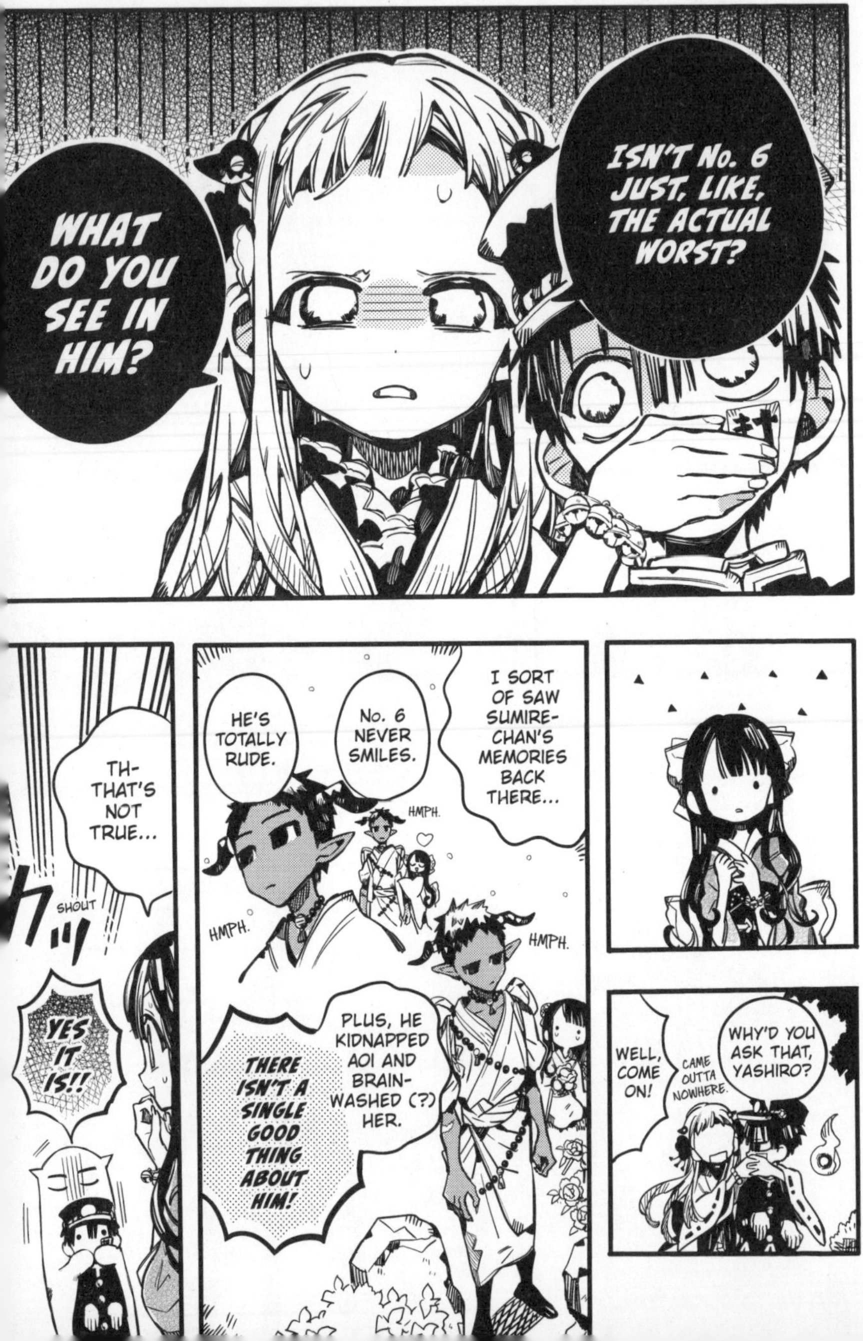
ISN'T No. 6 JUST, LIKE, THE ACTUAL WORST?
WHAT DO YOU SEE IN HIM?
WHY'D YOU ASK THAT, YASHIRO?
CAME OUTTA NOWHERE.
WELL, COME ON!
I SORT OF SAW SUMIRE-CHAN'S MEMORIES BACK THERE...
No. 6 NEVER SMILES.
HE'S TOTALLY RUDE.
HMPH.
HMPH.
HMPH.
PLUS, HE KIDNAPPED AOI AND BRAIN-WASHED (?) HER.
THERE ISN'T A SINGLE GOOD THING ABOUT HIM!
TH-THAT'S NOT TRUE...
SHOUT
YES IT IS!!

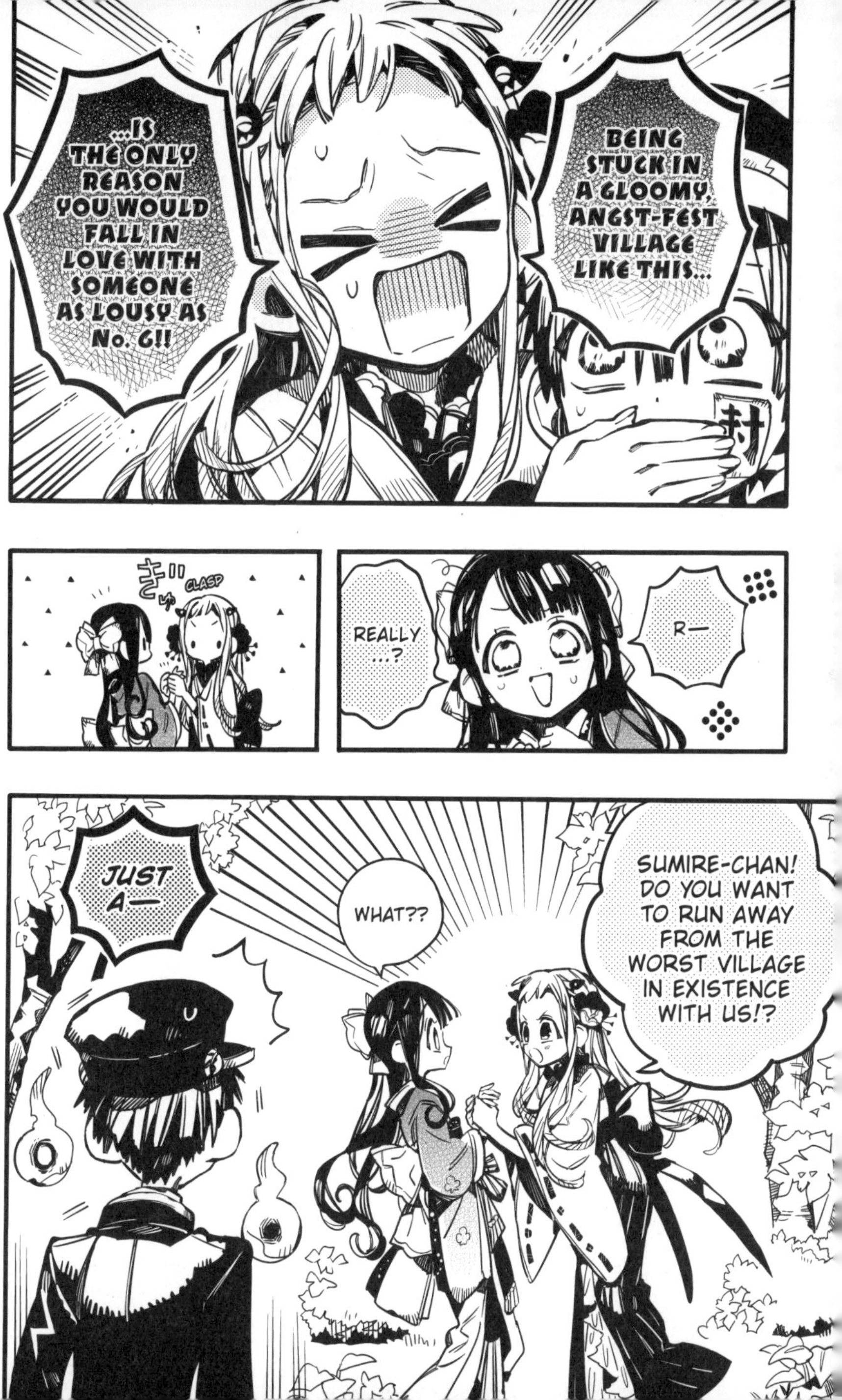
BEING STUCK IN A GLOOMY, ANGST-FEST VILLAGE LIKE THIS...
...IS THE ONLY REASON YOU WOULD FALL IN LOVE WITH SOMEONE AS LOUSY AS No. 6!!
R—
REALLY ...?
CLASP
SUMIRE-CHAN! DO YOU WANT TO RUN AWAY FROM THE WORST VILLAGE IN EXISTENCE WITH US!?
WHAT??
JUST A—

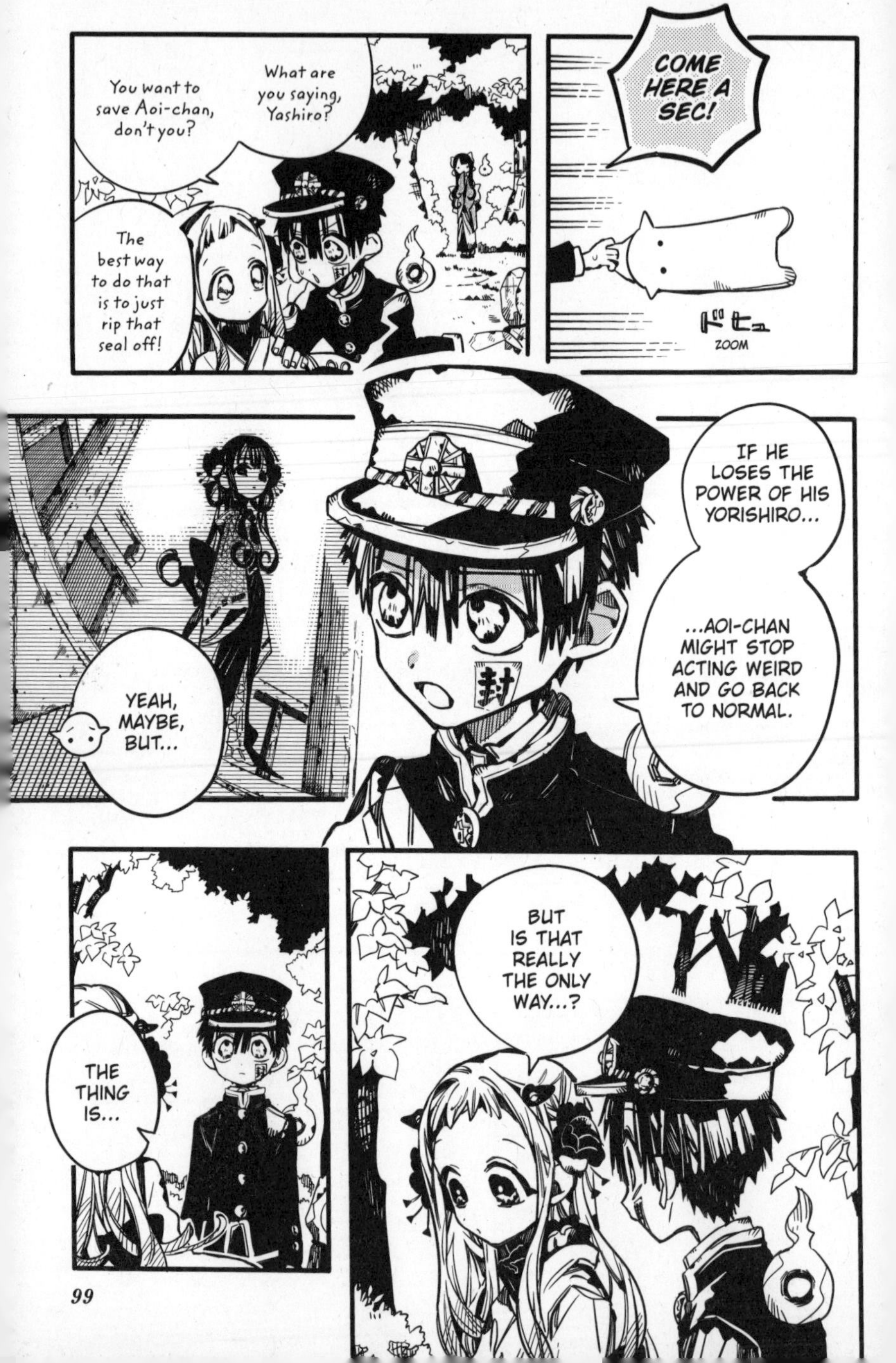
COME HERE A SEC!
ドヒュ
ZOOM
What are you saying, Yashiro?
You want to save Aoi-chan, don't you?
The best way to do that is to just rip that seal off!
IF HE LOSES THE POWER OF HIS YORISHIRO...
...AOI-CHAN MIGHT STOP ACTING WEIRD AND GO BACK TO NORMAL.
YEAH, MAYBE, BUT...
BUT IS THAT REALLY THE ONLY WAY...?
THE THING IS...

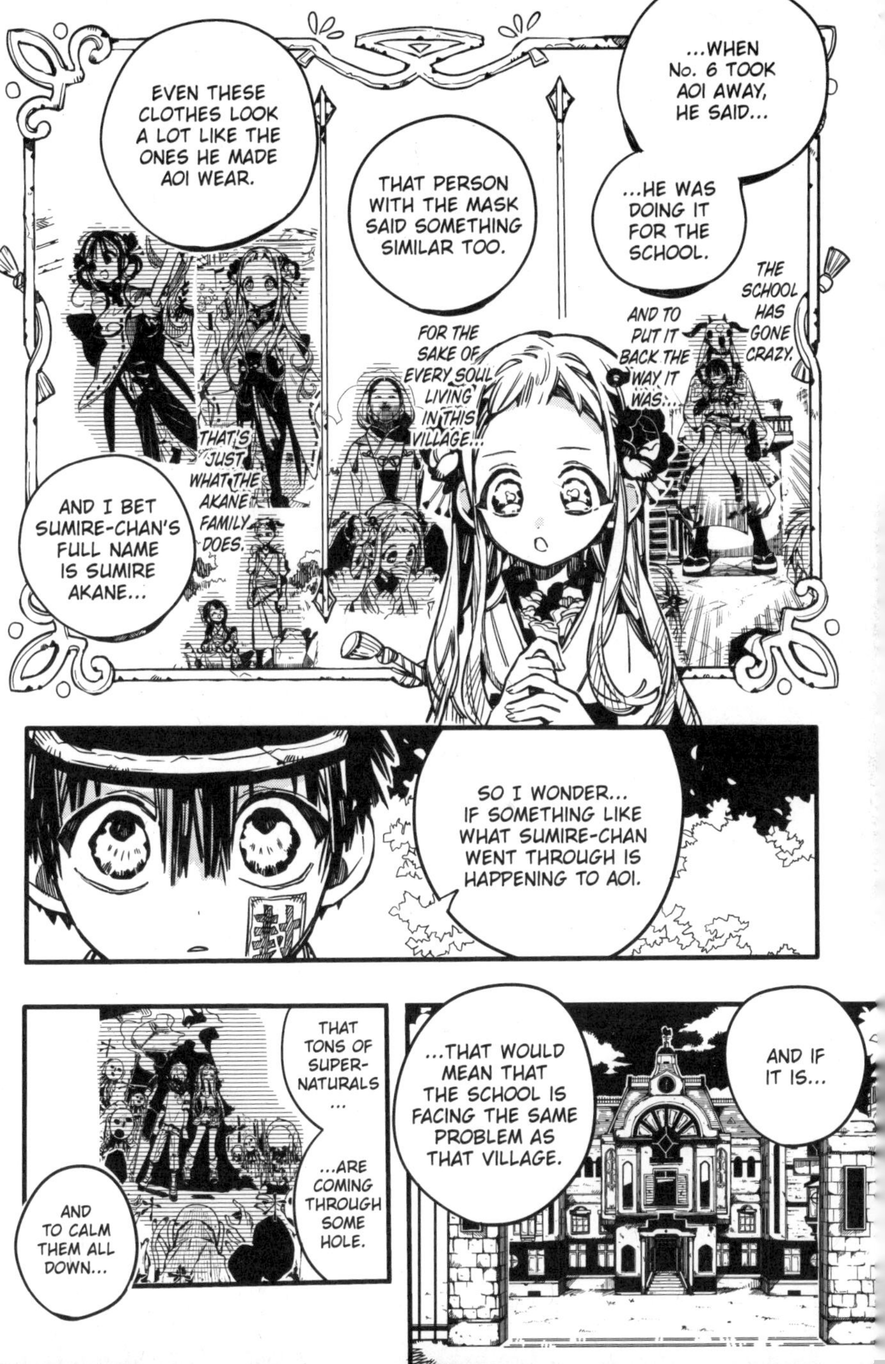
...WHEN No. 6 TOOK AOI AWAY, HE SAID...
...HE WAS DOING IT FOR THE SCHOOL.
THE SCHOOL HAS GONE CRAZY.
AND TO PUT IT BACK THE WAY IT WAS...
THAT PERSON WITH THE MASK SAID SOMETHING SIMILAR TOO.
FOR THE SAKE OF EVERY SOUL LIVING IN THIS VILLAGE...
EVEN THESE CLOTHES LOOK A LOT LIKE THE ONES HE MADE AOI WEAR.
THAT'S JUST WHAT THE AKANE FAMILY DOES.
AND I BET SUMIRE-CHAN'S FULL NAME IS SUMIRE AKANE...
SO I WONDER... IF SOMETHING LIKE WHAT SUMIRE-CHAN WENT THROUGH IS HAPPENING TO AOI.
AND IF IT IS...
...THAT WOULD MEAN THAT THE SCHOOL IS FACING THE SAME PROBLEM AS THAT VILLAGE.
THAT TONS OF SUPER-NATURALS...
...ARE COMING THROUGH SOME HOLE.
AND TO CALM THEM ALL DOWN...

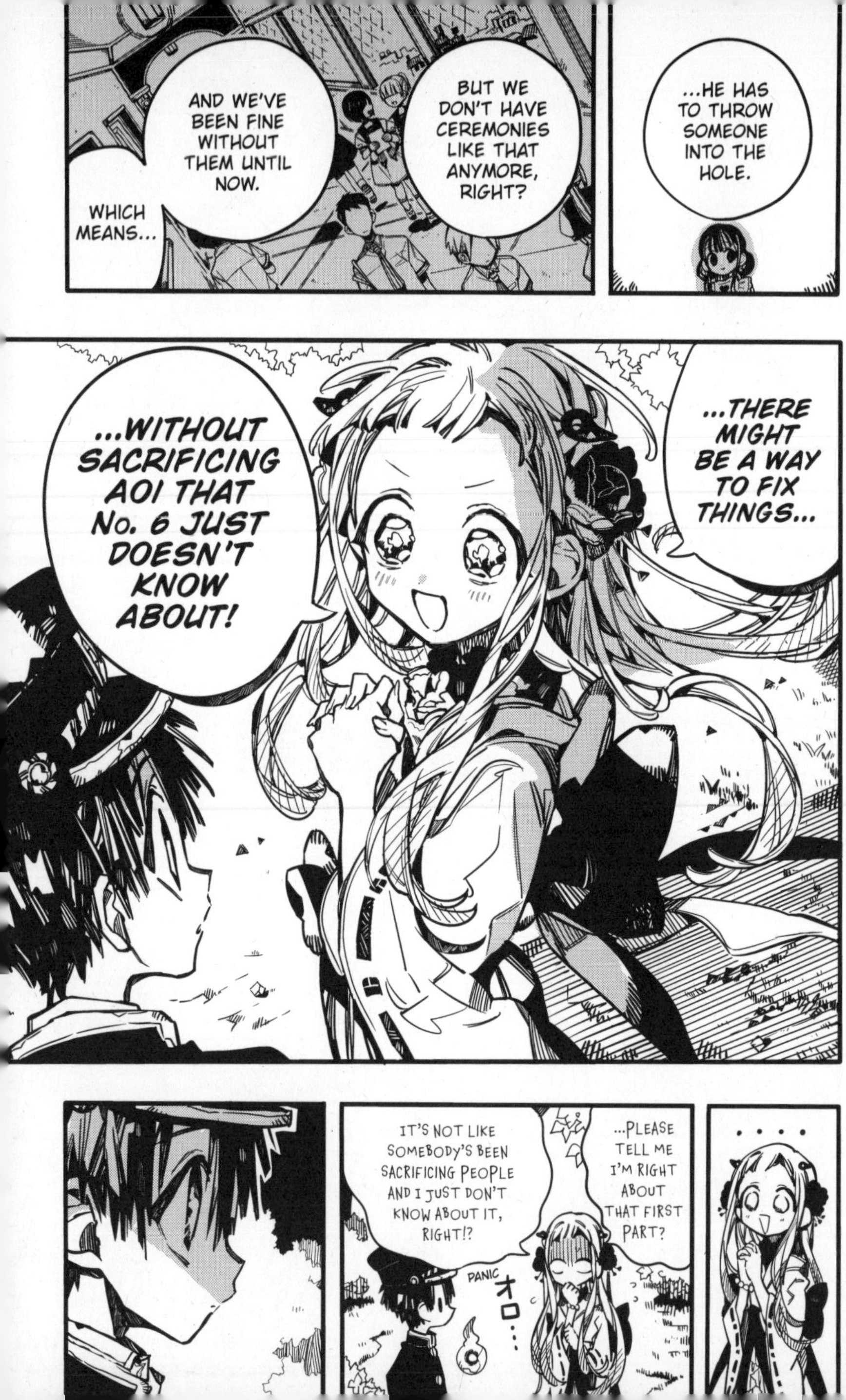
...HE HAS TO THROW SOMEONE INTO THE HOLE.
BUT WE DON'T HAVE CEREMONIES LIKE THAT ANYMORE, RIGHT?
AND WE'VE BEEN FINE WITHOUT THEM UNTIL NOW.
WHICH MEANS...
...THERE MIGHT BE A WAY TO FIX THINGS...
...WITHOUT SACRIFICING AOI THAT No. 6 JUST DOESN'T KNOW ABOUT!
• • • •
...PLEASE TELL ME I'M RIGHT ABOUT THAT FIRST PART?
IT'S NOT LIKE SOMEBODY'S BEEN SACRIFICING PEOPLE AND I JUST DON'T KNOW ABOUT IT, RIGHT!?
PANIC
オロ...

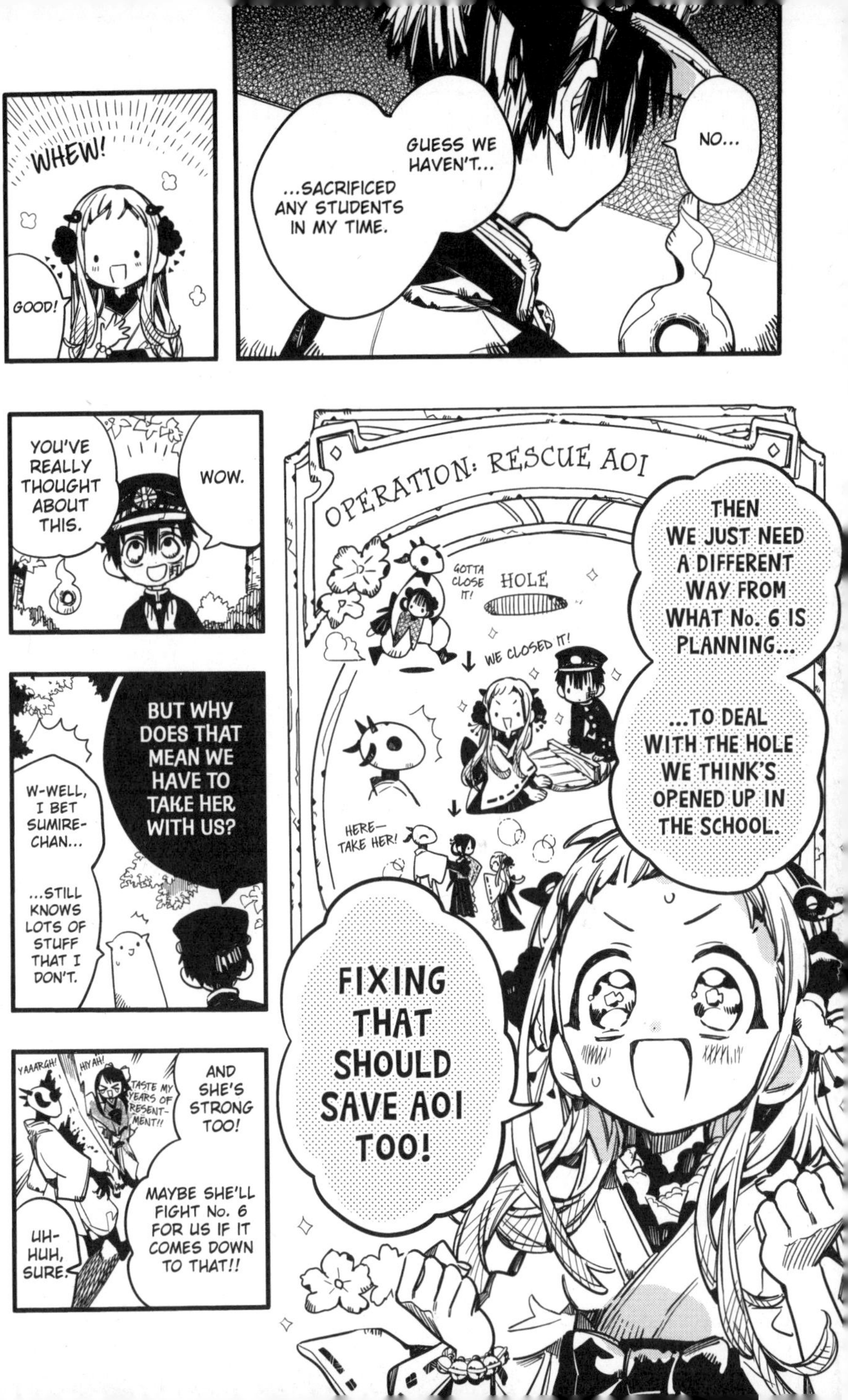
NO...
GUESS WE HAVEN'T...
...SACRIFICED ANY STUDENTS IN MY TIME.
WHEW!
GOOD!
OPERATION: RESCUE AOI
GOTTA CLOSE IT!
HOLE
WE CLOSED IT!
HERE—TAKE HER!
THEN WE JUST NEED A DIFFERENT WAY FROM WHAT No. 6 IS PLANNING...
...TO DEAL WITH THE HOLE WE THINK'S OPENED UP IN THE SCHOOL.
FIXING THAT SHOULD SAVE AOI TOO!
WOW.
YOU'VE REALLY THOUGHT ABOUT THIS.
BUT WHY DOES THAT MEAN WE HAVE TO TAKE HER WITH US?
W-WELL, I BET SUMIRE-CHAN...
...STILL KNOWS LOTS OF STUFF THAT I DON'T.
AND SHE'S STRONG TOO!
HIYAH!
TASTE MY YEARS OF RESENT-MENT!!
YAAARGH!
MAYBE SHE'LL FIGHT No. 6 FOR US IF IT COMES DOWN TO THAT!!
UH-HUH, SURE.

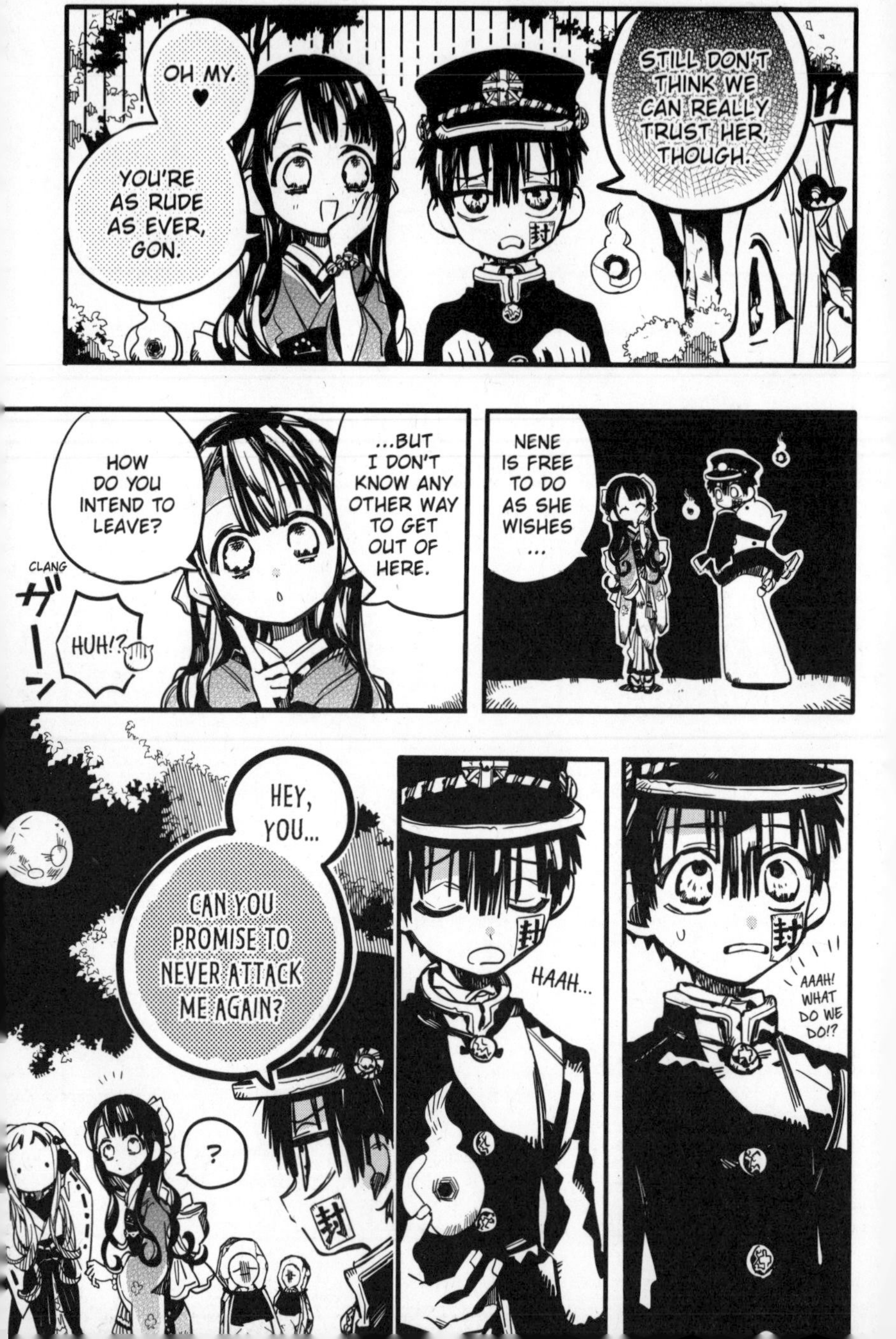
STILL DON'T THINK WE CAN REALLY TRUST HER, THOUGH.
OH MY. ♥
YOU'RE AS RUDE AS EVER, GON.
NENE IS FREE TO DO AS SHE WISHES ...
...BUT I DON'T KNOW ANY OTHER WAY TO GET OUT OF HERE.
HOW DO YOU INTEND TO LEAVE?
CLANG
HUH!?
AAAH! WHAT DO WE DO!?
HAAH...
HEY, YOU...
CAN YOU PROMISE TO NEVER ATTACK ME AGAIN?
?

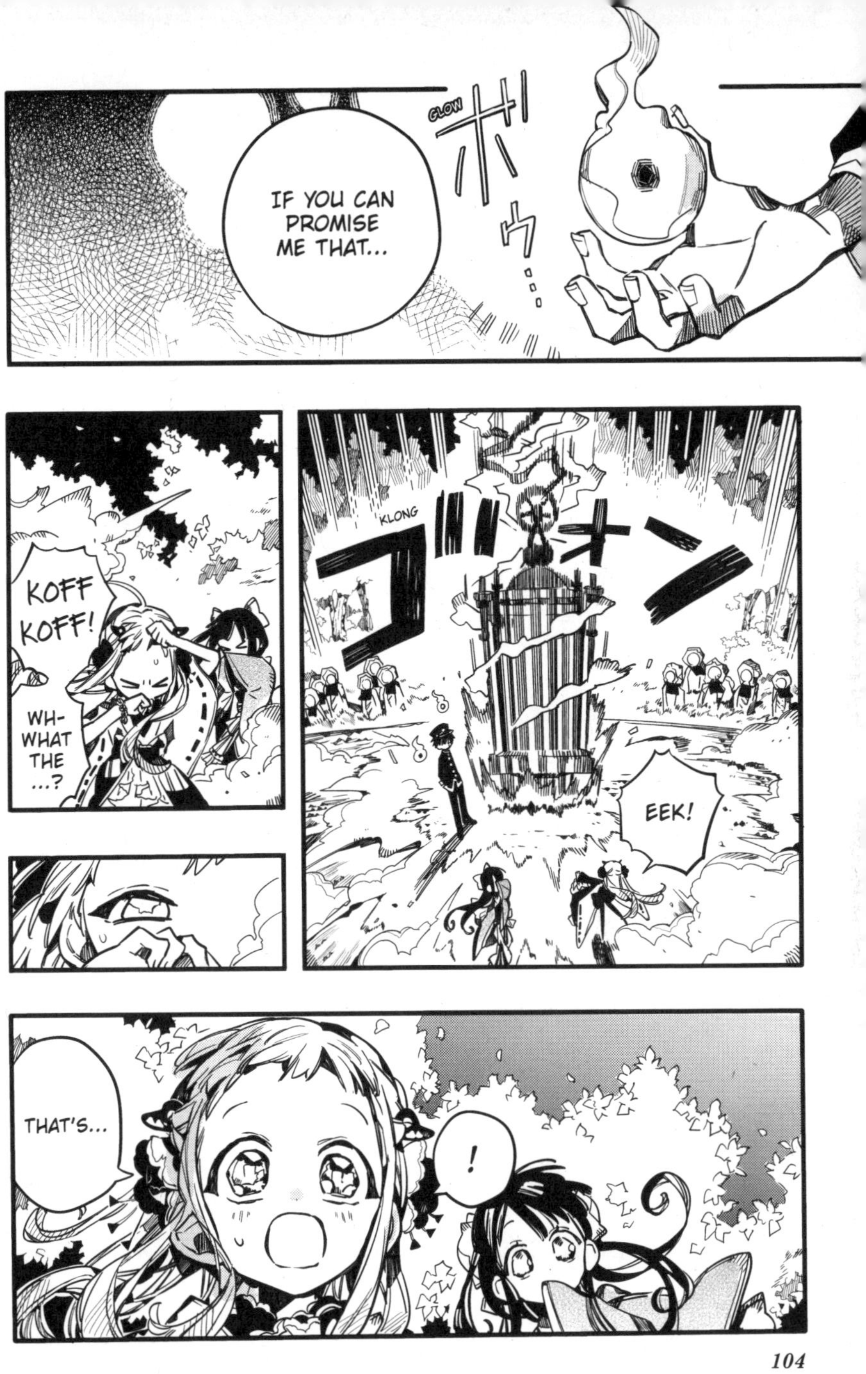
GLOW
ボゥ...
IF YOU CAN PROMISE ME THAT...
KLONG
ゴオン
EEK!
KOFF KOFF!
WH-WHAT THE ...?
!
THAT'S...

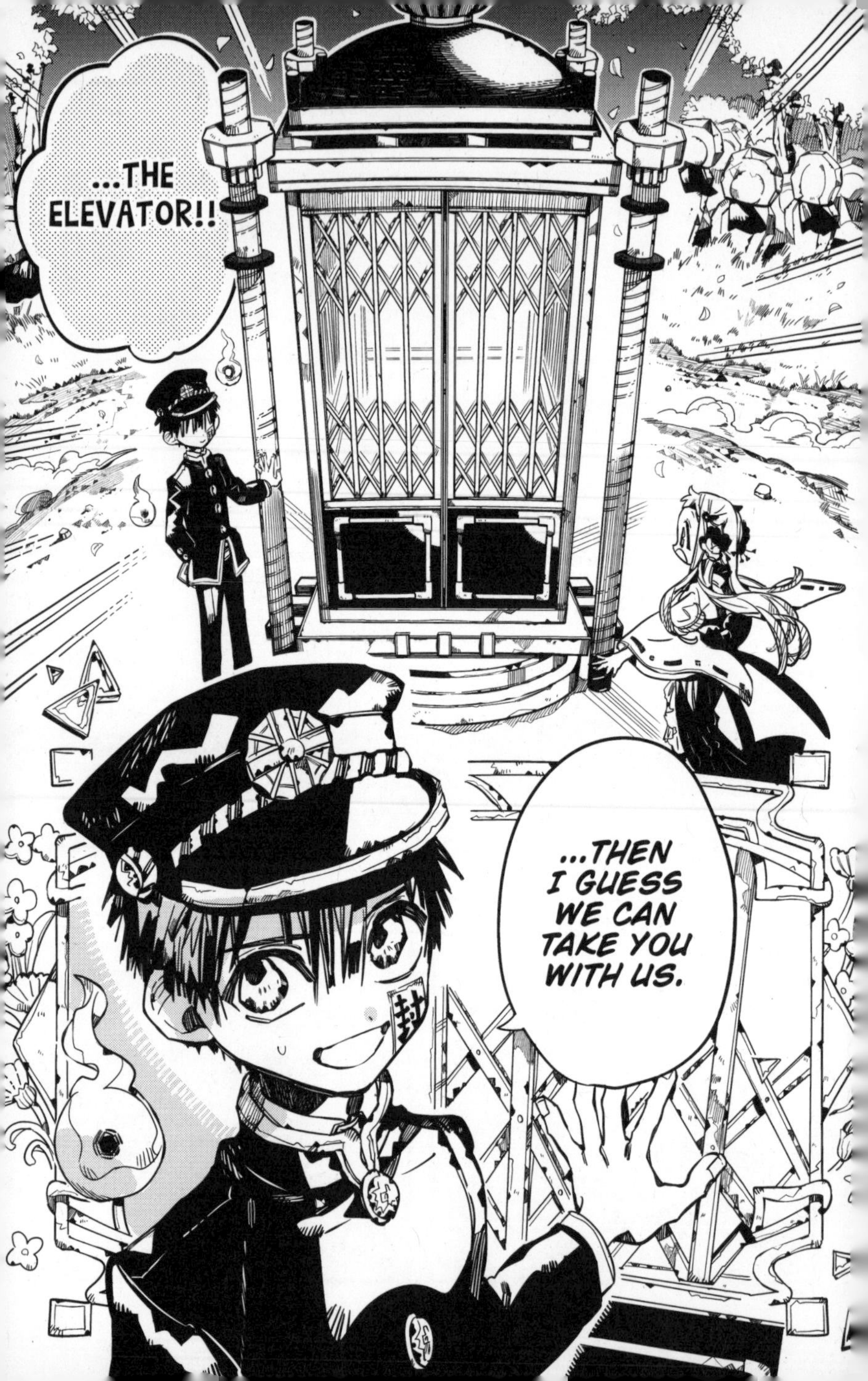
...THE ELEVATOR!!
...THEN I GUESS WE CAN TAKE YOU WITH US.

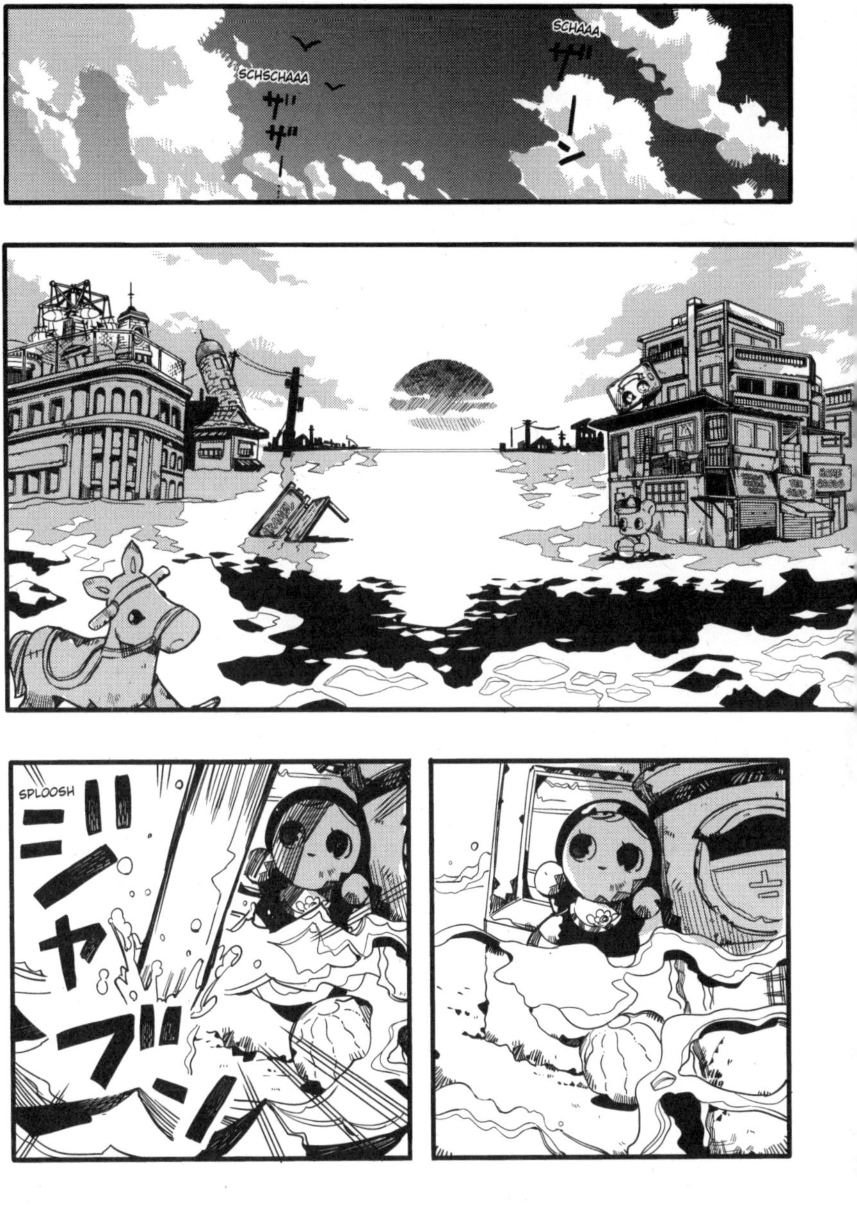
SCHAAA
SCHSCHAAA
HOME GOODS
TEA SHOP
SPLOOSH

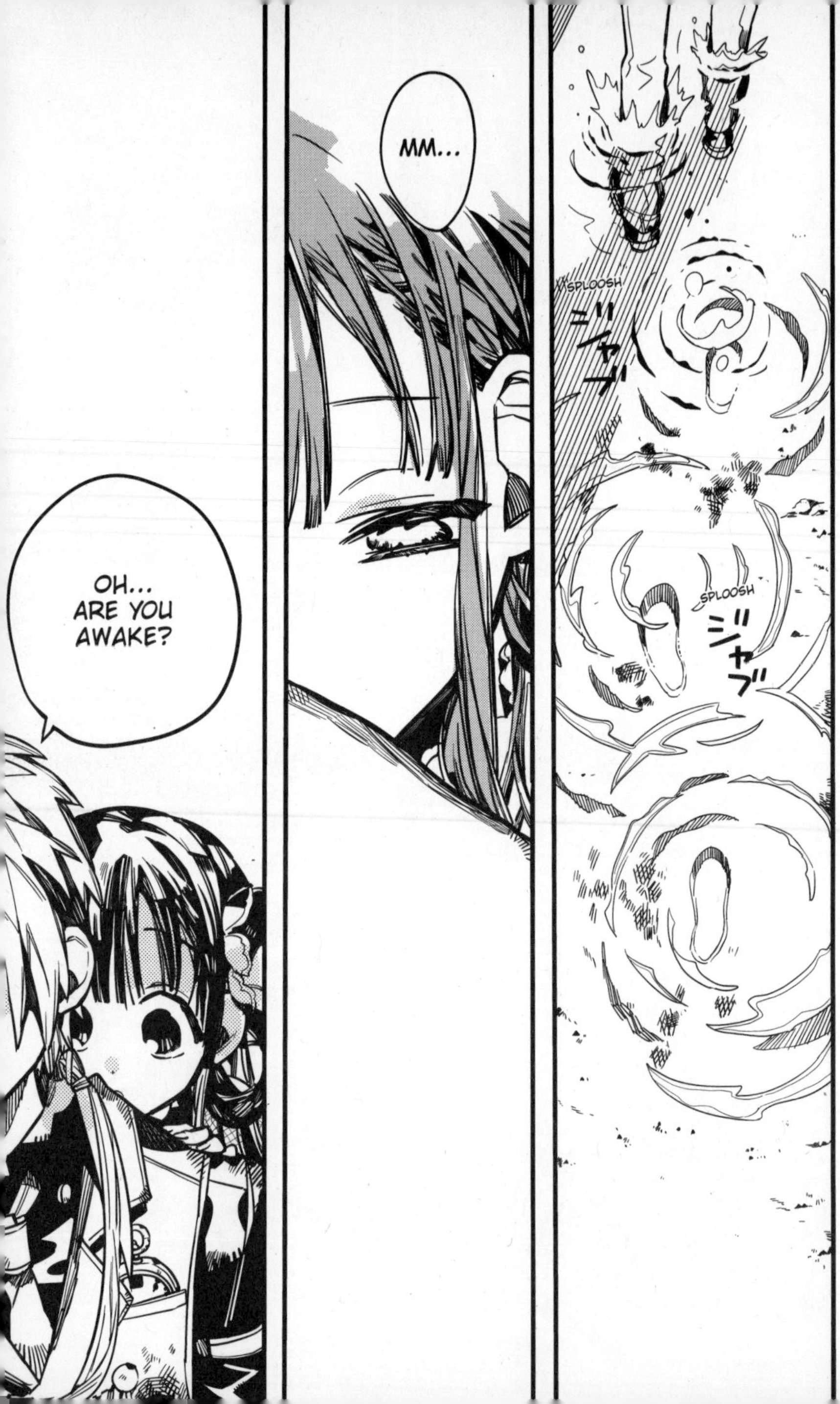
SPLOOSH
ジャブ
SPLOOSH
ジャブ
MM...
OH... ARE YOU AWAKE?

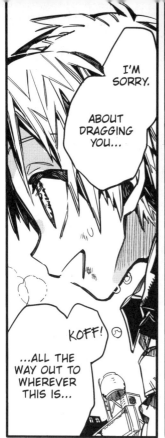

I'M SORRY.

ABOUT DRAGGING YOU...

KOFF!

...ALL THE WAY OUT TO WHEREVER THIS IS...

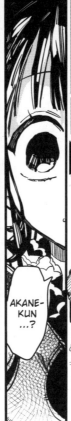

AKANE-KUN...?

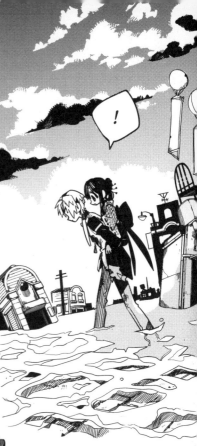

!

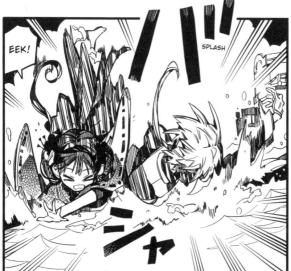

EEK!

SPLASH

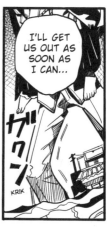

I'LL GET US OUT AS SOON AS I CAN...

KRIK

108

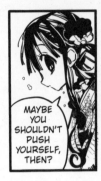

MAYBE YOU SHOULDN'T PUSH YOURSELF, THEN?

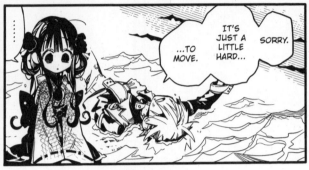

SORRY.

IT'S JUST A LITTLE HARD...

...TO MOVE.

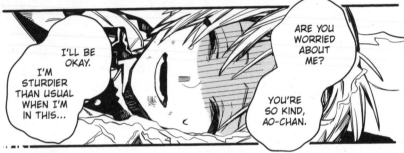

I'LL BE OKAY.

I'M STURDIER THAN USUAL WHEN I'M IN THIS...

ARE YOU WORRIED ABOUT ME?

YOU'RE SO KIND, AO-CHAN.

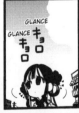

...FORM...

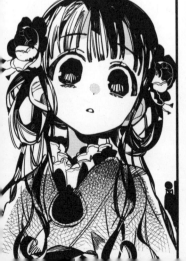

GLANCE GLANCE キョロ キョロ

TUG

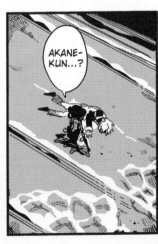

AKANE-KUN...?

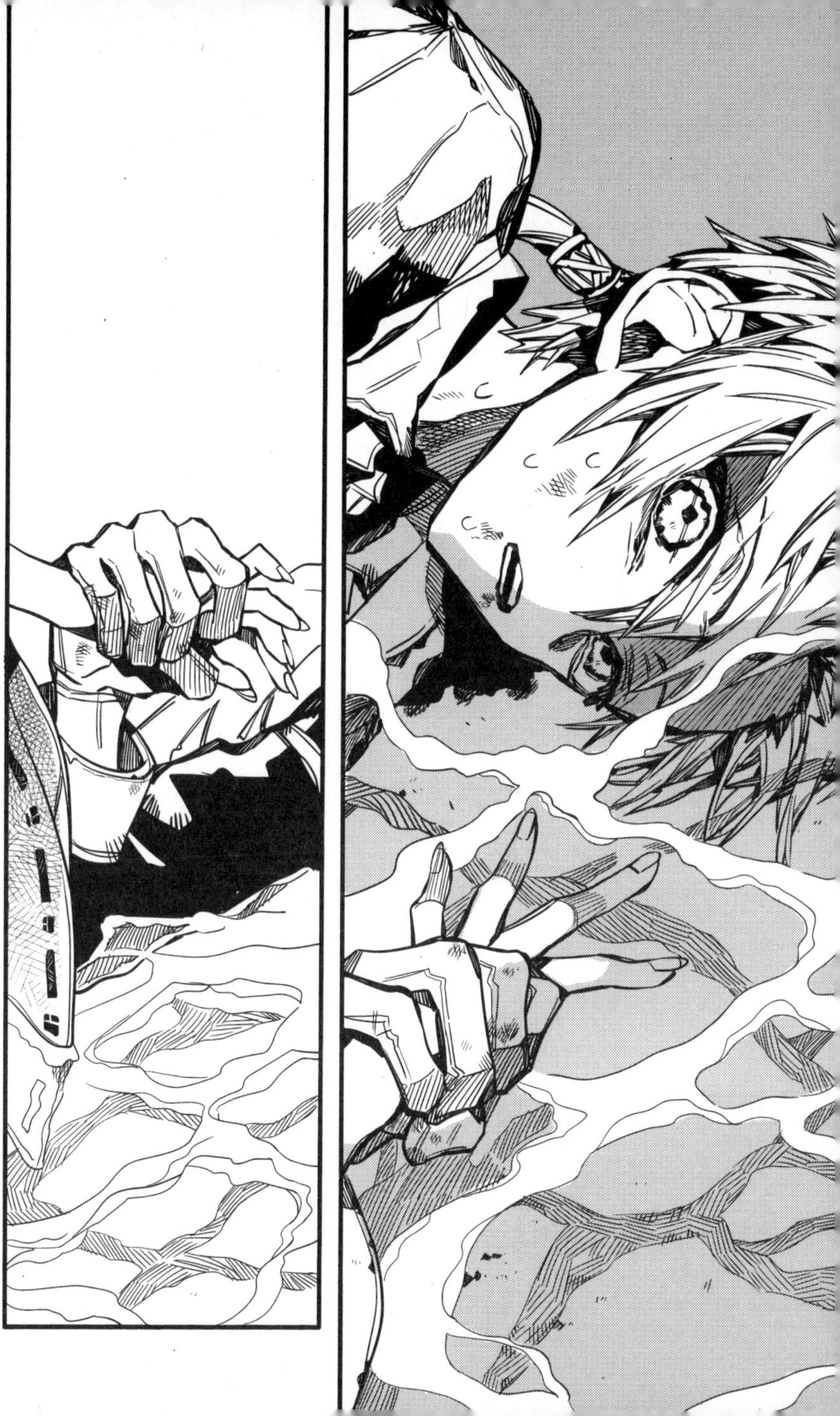

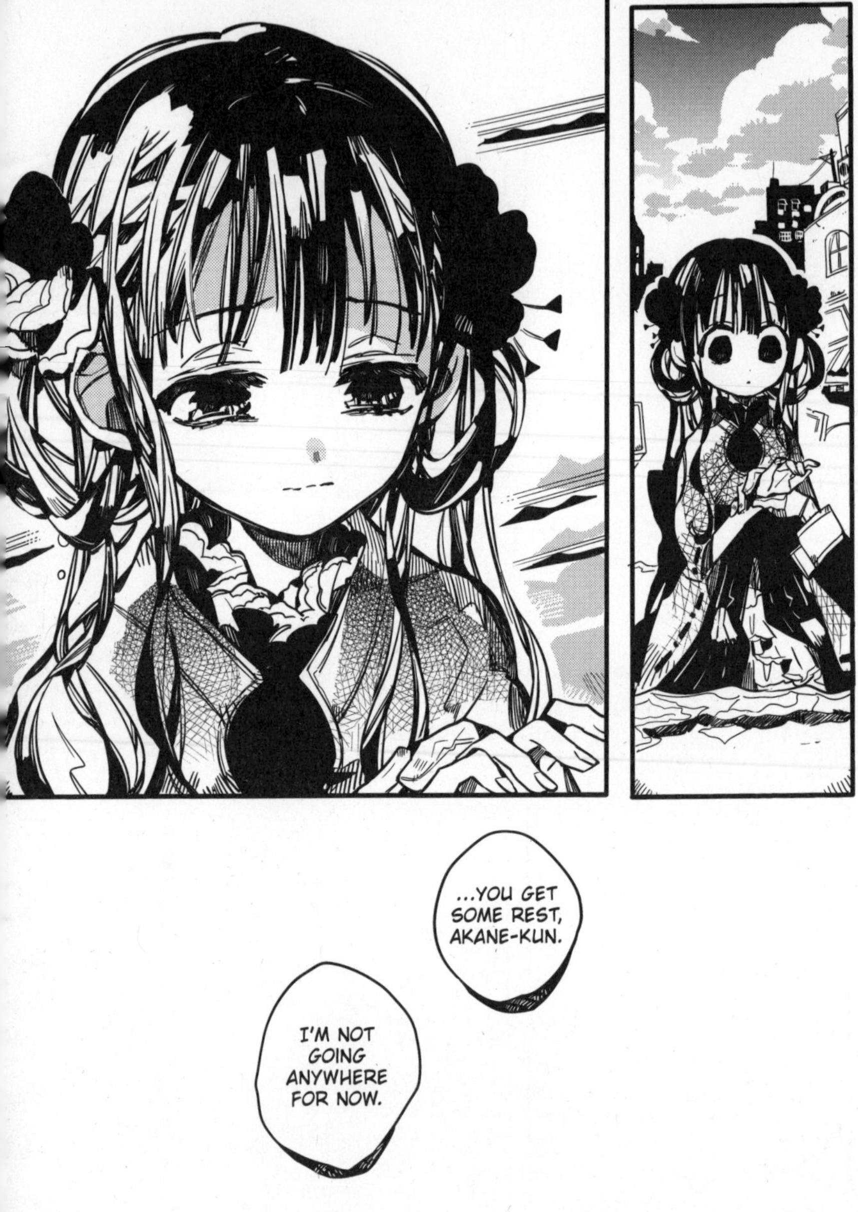
...YOU GET SOME REST, AKANE-KUN.
I'M NOT GOING ANYWHERE FOR NOW.

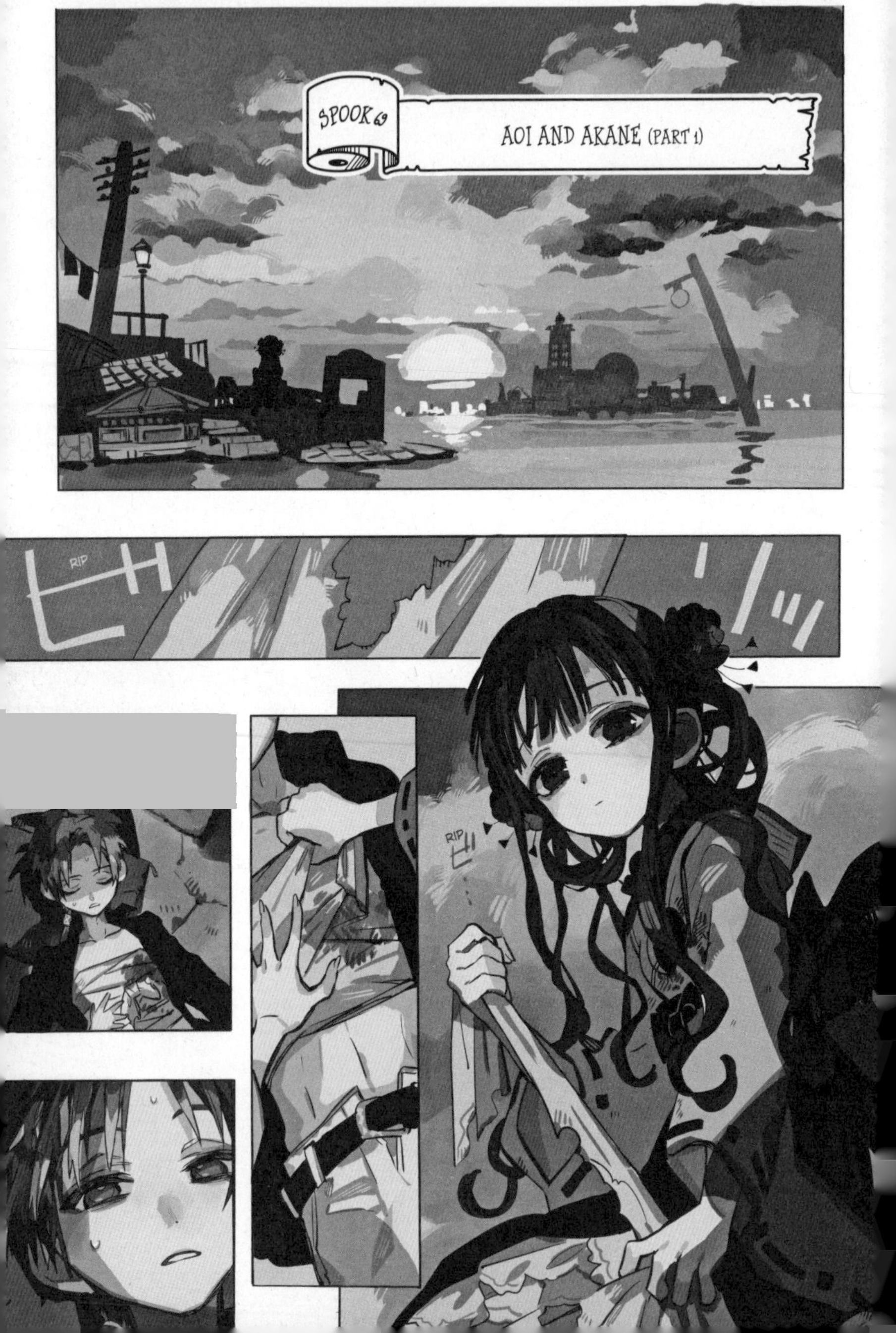
SPOOK 69
AOI AND AKANE (PART 1)
RIP
RIP

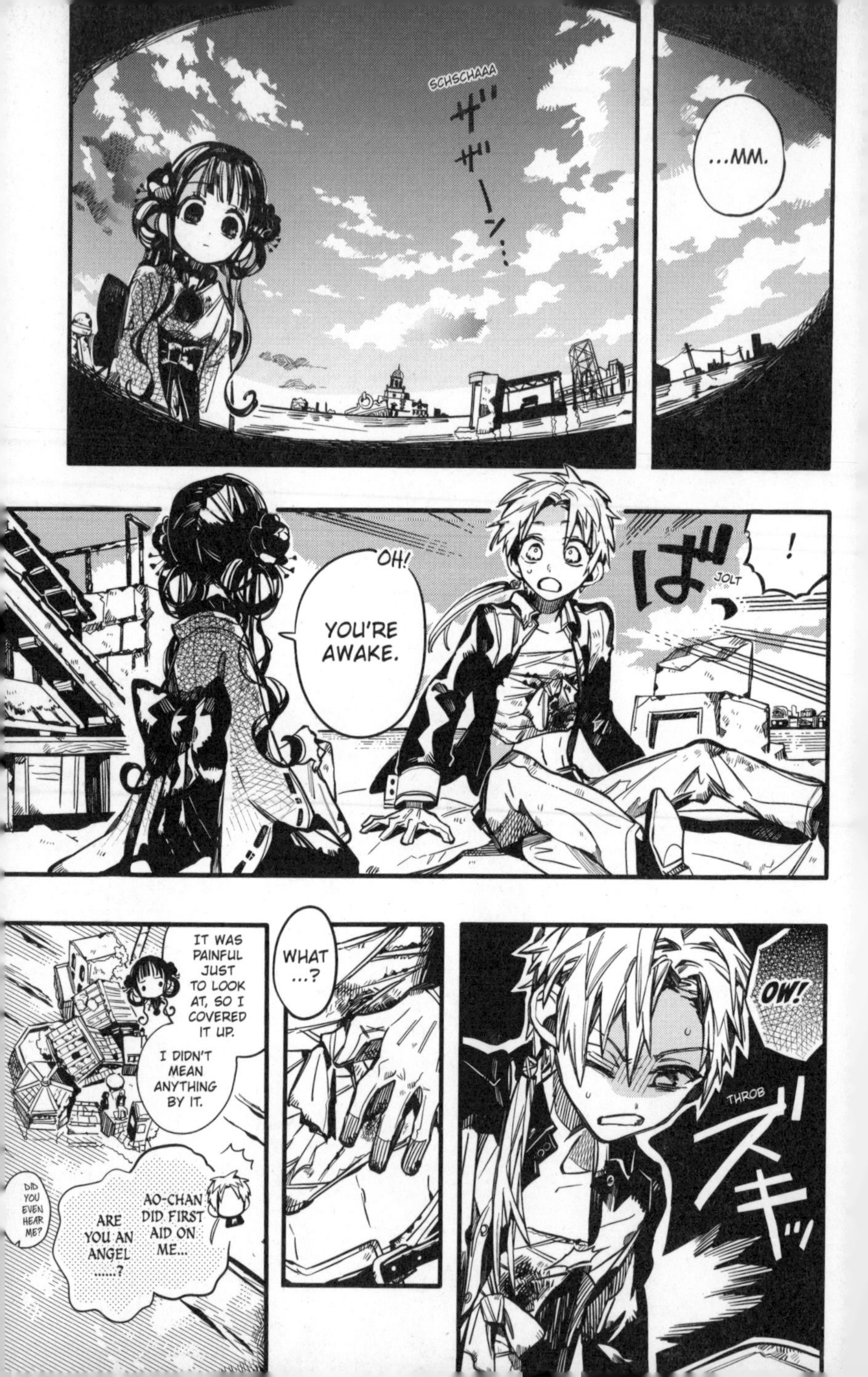
...MM.
SCHSCHAAA
!
JOLT
OH!
YOU'RE AWAKE.
OW!
THROB
WHAT ...?
IT WAS PAINFUL JUST TO LOOK AT, SO I COVERED IT UP.
I DIDN'T MEAN ANYTHING BY IT.
AO-CHAN DID FIRST AID ON ME...
ARE YOU AN ANGEL ......?
DID YOU EVEN HEAR ME?

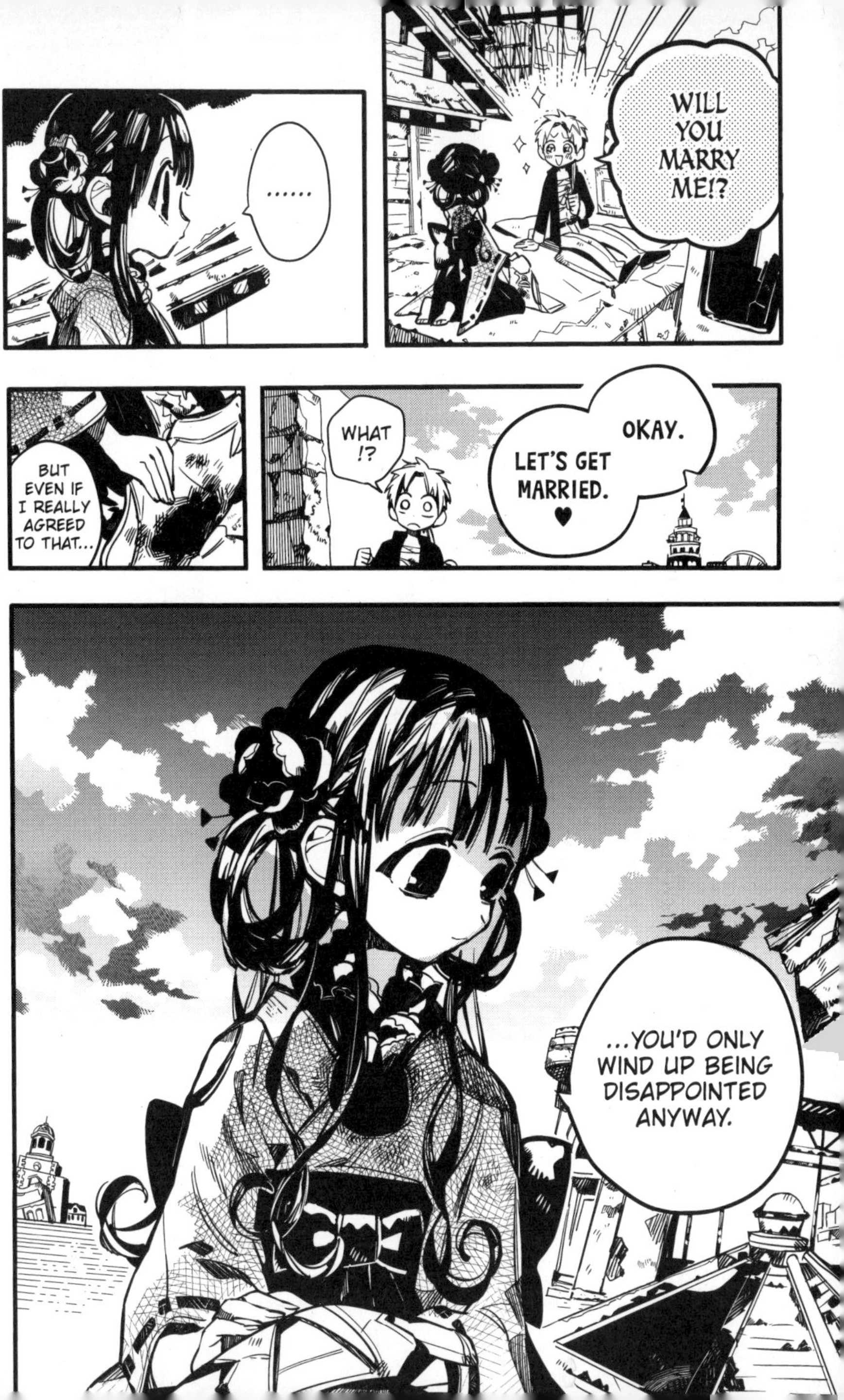
WILL YOU MARRY ME!?
......
OKAY. LET'S GET MARRIED. ♥
WHAT !?
BUT EVEN IF I REALLY AGREED TO THAT...
...YOU'D ONLY WIND UP BEING DISAPPOINTED ANYWAY.

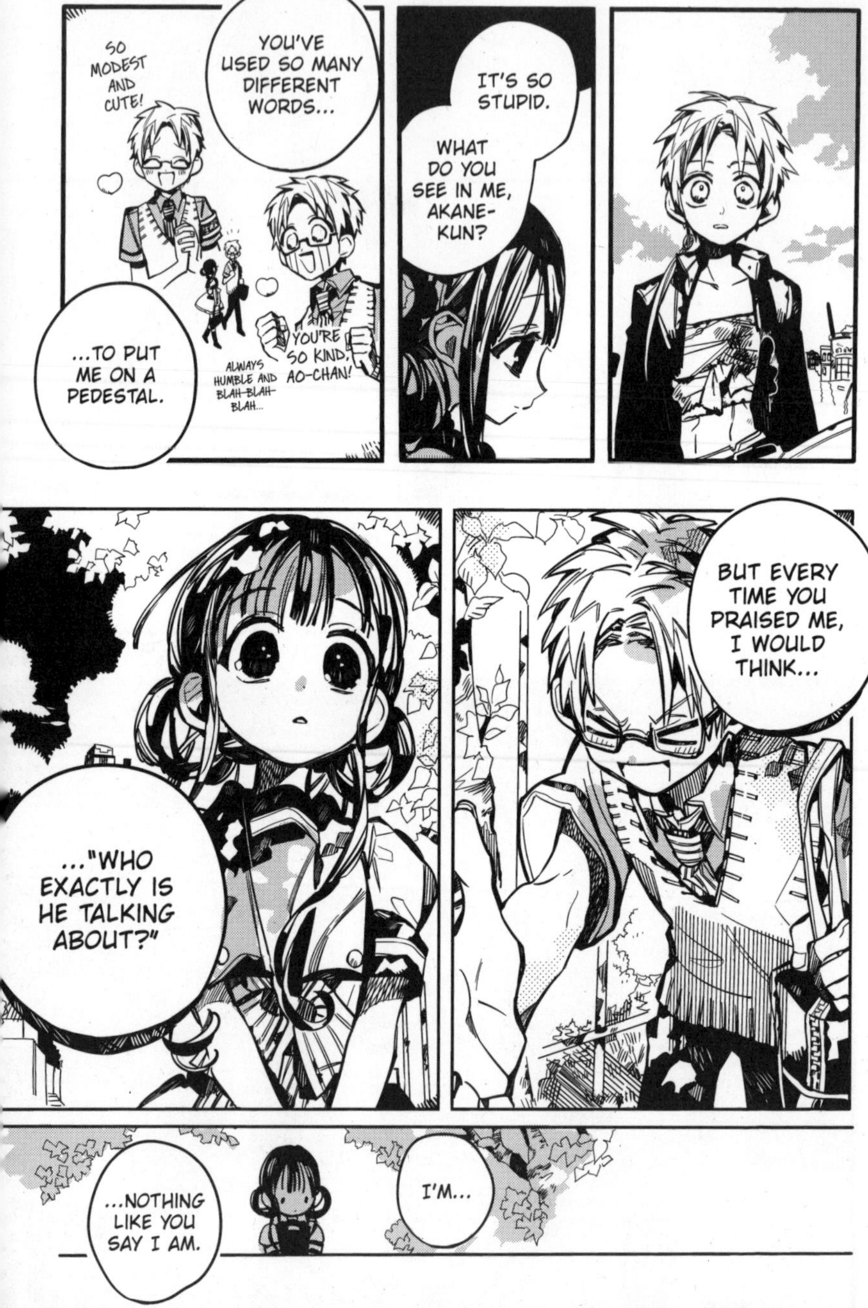
IT'S SO STUPID.
WHAT DO YOU SEE IN ME, AKANE-KUN?
YOU'VE USED SO MANY DIFFERENT WORDS...
SO MODEST AND CUTE!
YOU'RE SO KIND, AO-CHAN!
ALWAYS HUMBLE AND BLAH-BLAH BLAH...
...TO PUT ME ON A PEDESTAL.
BUT EVERY TIME YOU PRAISED ME, I WOULD THINK...
..."WHO EXACTLY IS HE TALKING ABOUT?"
I'M...
...NOTHING LIKE YOU SAY I AM.

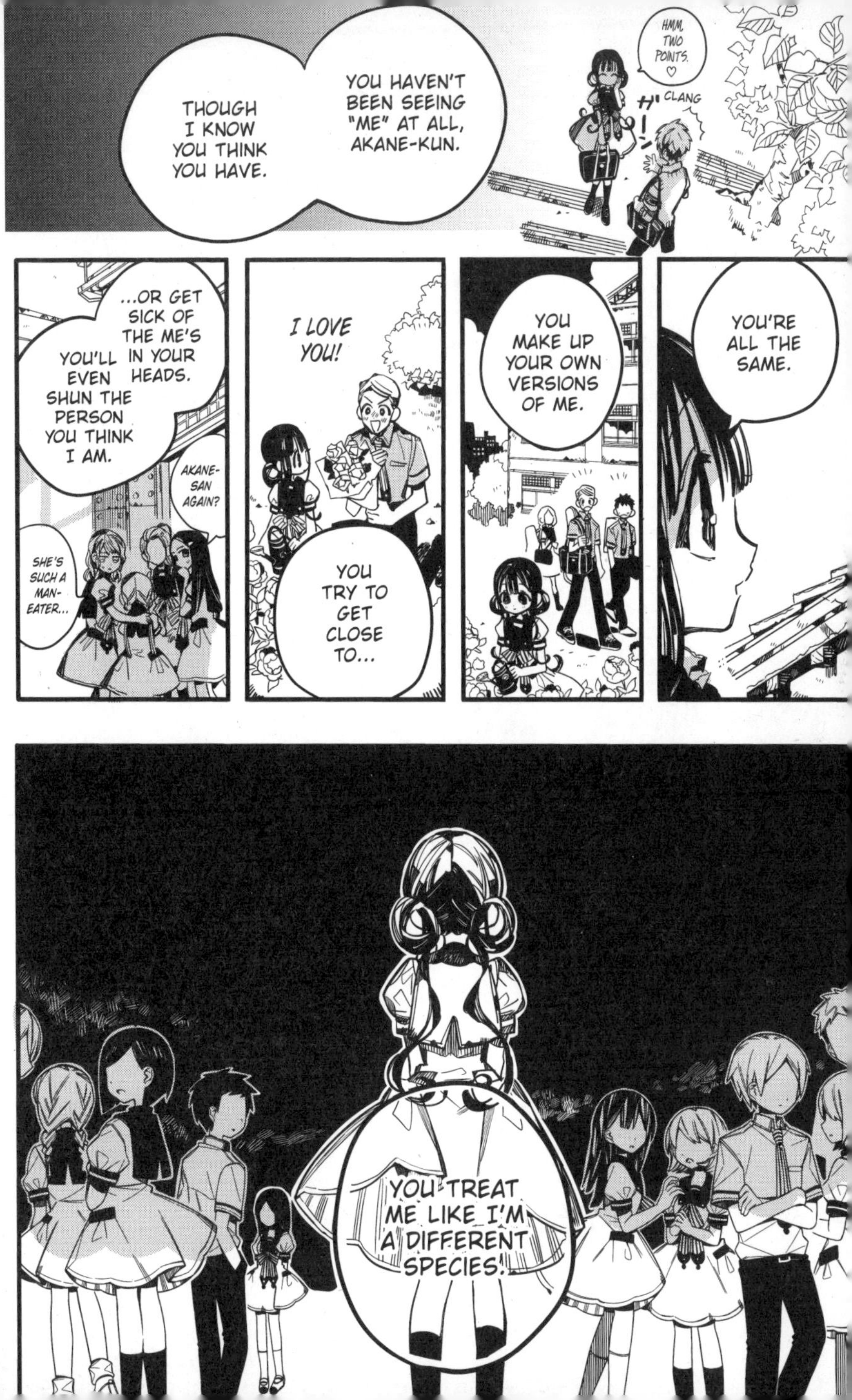
HMM, TWO POINTS. ♡
CLANG
YOU HAVEN'T BEEN SEEING "ME" AT ALL, AKANE-KUN.
THOUGH I KNOW YOU THINK YOU HAVE.
YOU'RE ALL THE SAME.
YOU MAKE UP YOUR OWN VERSIONS OF ME.
I LOVE YOU!
YOU TRY TO GET CLOSE TO...
...OR GET SICK OF THE ME'S IN YOUR HEADS.
YOU'LL EVEN SHUN THE PERSON YOU THINK I AM.
AKANE-SAN AGAIN?
SHE'S SUCH A MAN-EATER...
YOU TREAT ME LIKE I'M A DIFFERENT SPECIES.

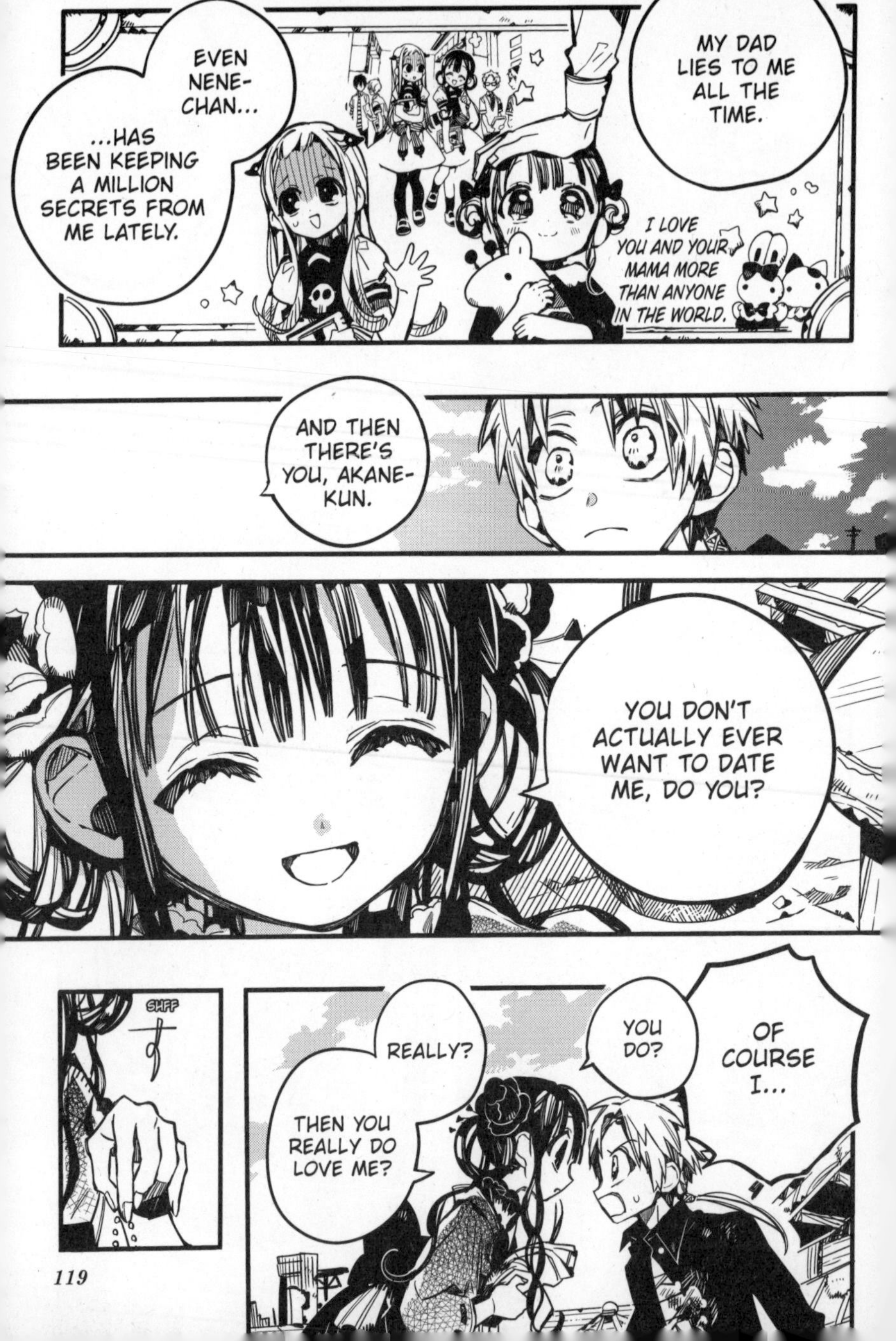
MY DAD LIES TO ME ALL THE TIME.
I LOVE YOU AND YOUR MAMA MORE THAN ANYONE IN THE WORLD.
EVEN NENE-CHAN...
...HAS BEEN KEEPING A MILLION SECRETS FROM ME LATELY.
AND THEN THERE'S YOU, AKANE-KUN.
YOU DON'T ACTUALLY EVER WANT TO DATE ME, DO YOU?
OF COURSE I...
YOU DO?
REALLY?
THEN YOU REALLY DO LOVE ME?
SHFF

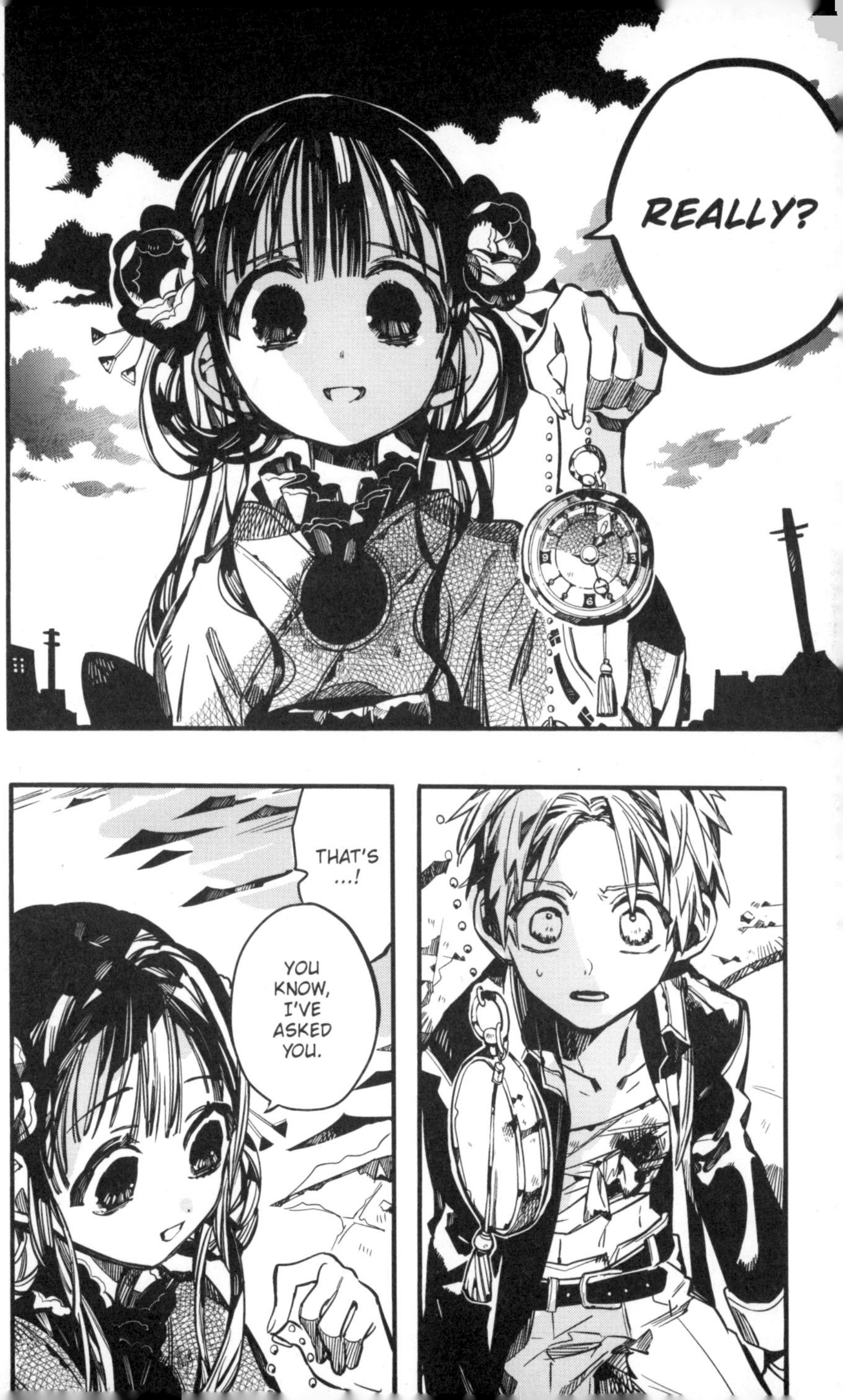
REALLY?
THAT'S ...!
YOU KNOW, I'VE ASKED YOU.

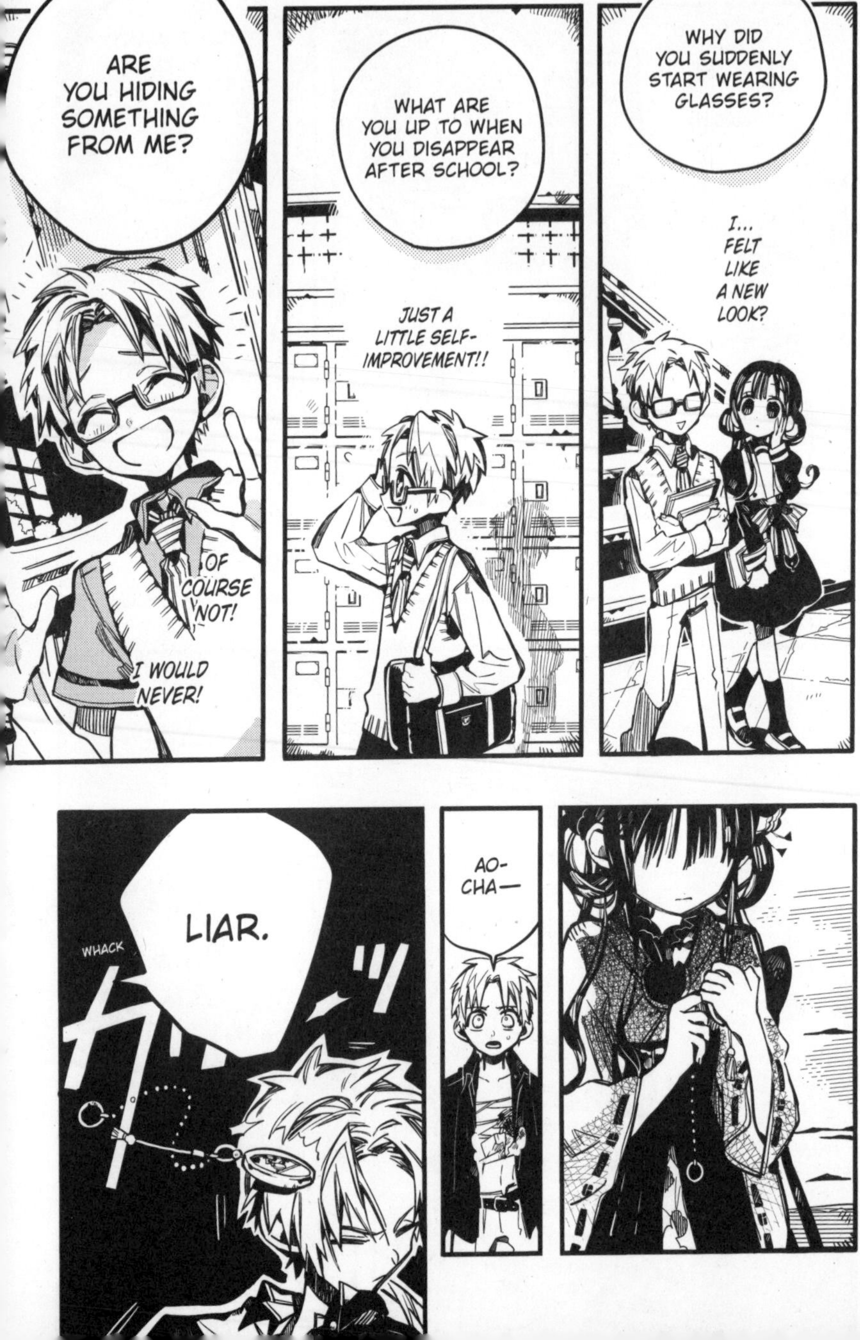
WHY DID YOU SUDDENLY START WEARING GLASSES?
I... FELT LIKE A NEW LOOK?
WHAT ARE YOU UP TO WHEN YOU DISAPPEAR AFTER SCHOOL?
JUST A LITTLE SELF-IMPROVEMENT!!
ARE YOU HIDING SOMETHING FROM ME?
OF COURSE NOT!
I WOULD NEVER!
AO-CHA—
LIAR.
WHACK

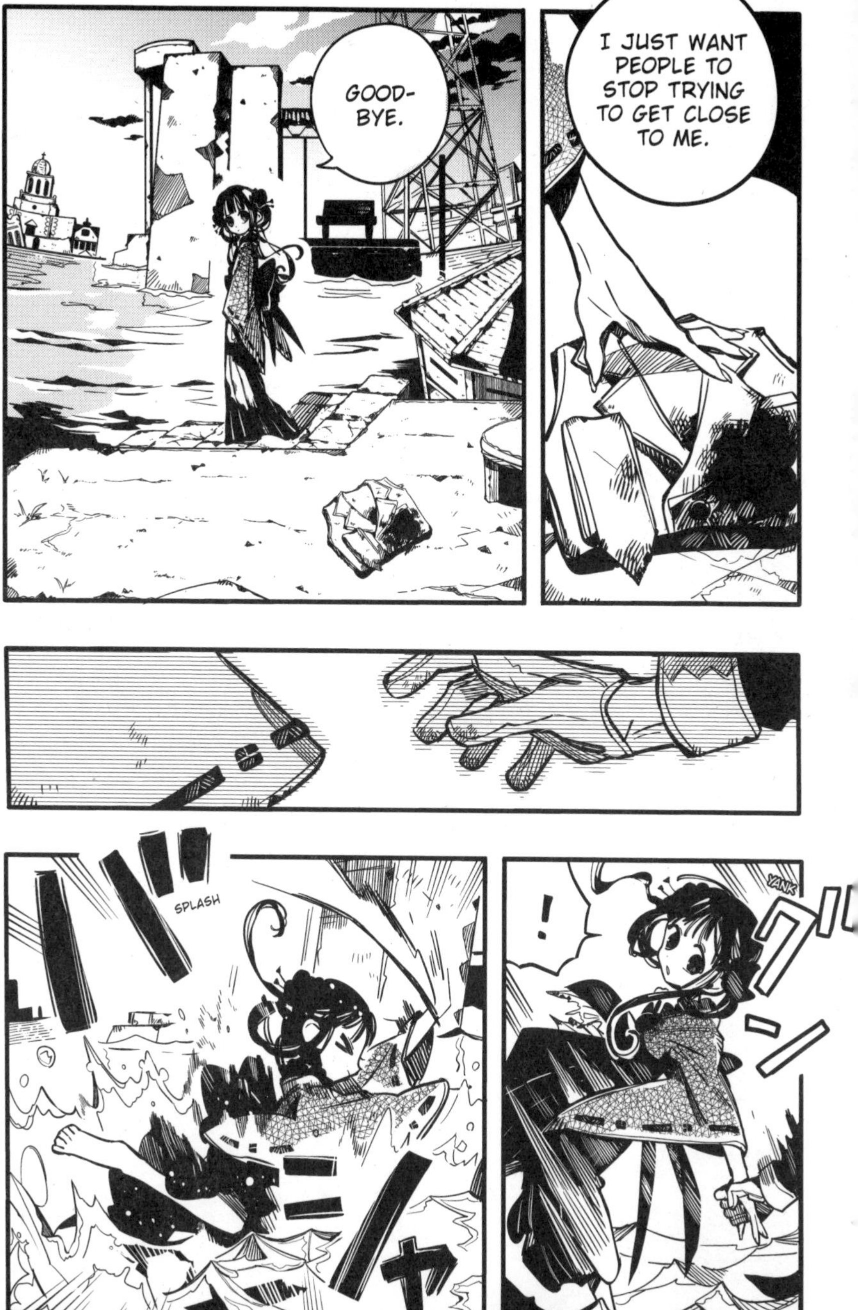
I JUST WANT PEOPLE TO STOP TRYING TO GET CLOSE TO ME.
GOOD-BYE.
YANK
!
SPLASH

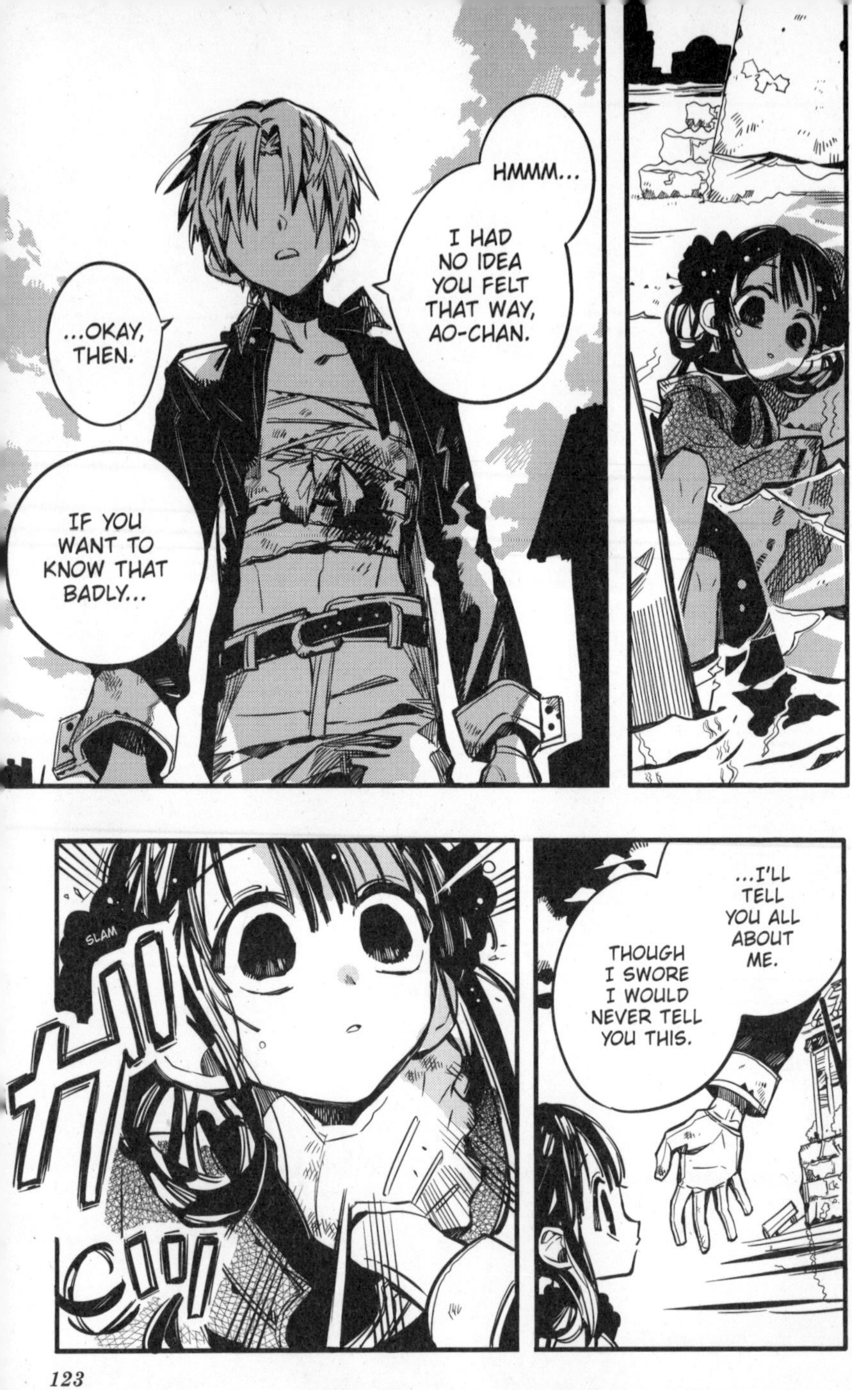
HMMM...
I HAD NO IDEA YOU FELT THAT WAY, AO-CHAN.
...OKAY, THEN.
IF YOU WANT TO KNOW THAT BADLY...
...I'LL TELL YOU ALL ABOUT ME.
THOUGH I SWORE I WOULD NEVER TELL YOU THIS.
SLAM

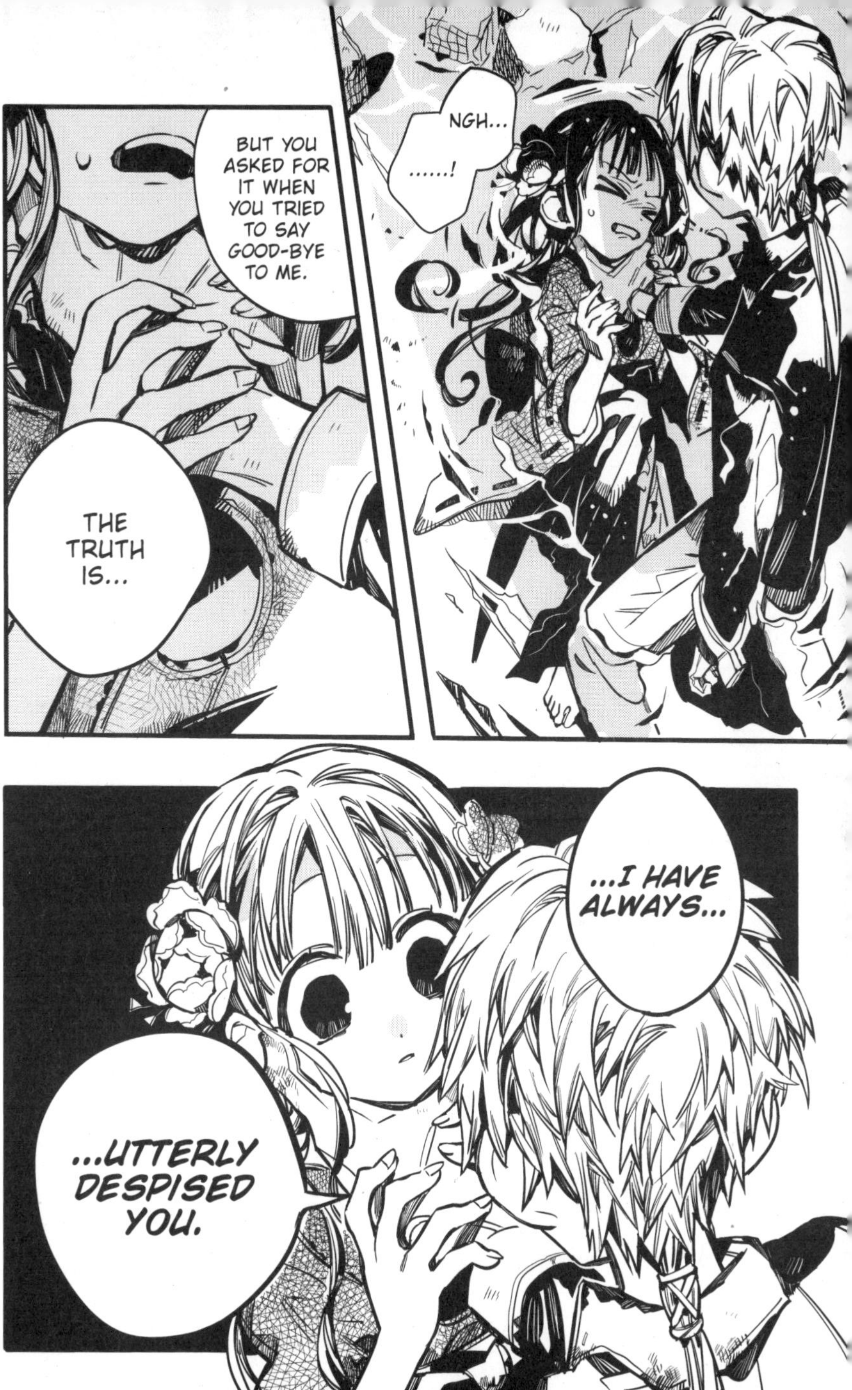
NGH...
......!
BUT YOU ASKED FOR IT WHEN YOU TRIED TO SAY GOOD-BYE TO ME.
THE TRUTH IS...
...I HAVE ALWAYS...
...UTTERLY DESPISED YOU.

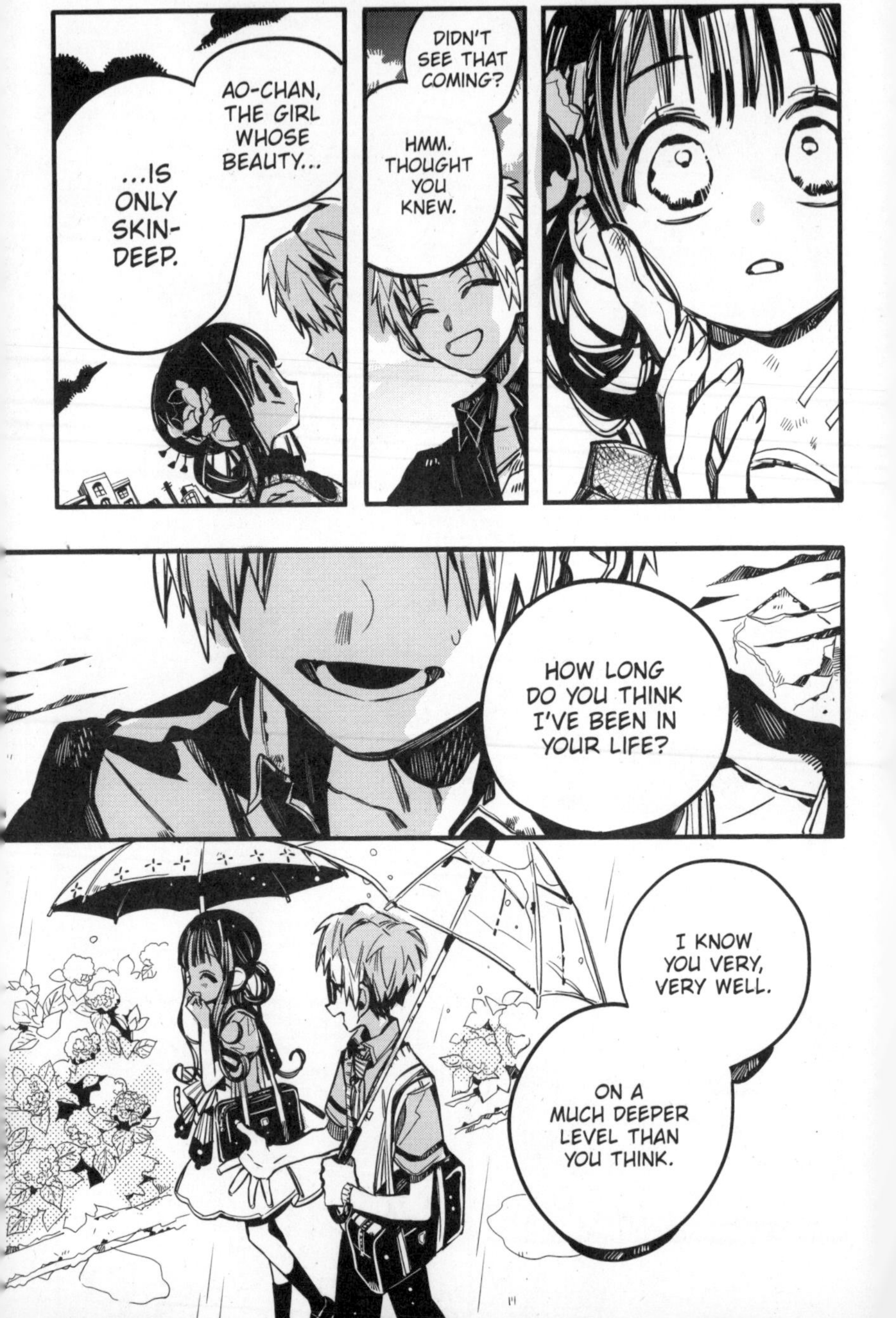
DIDN'T SEE THAT COMING?
HMM. THOUGHT YOU KNEW.
AO-CHAN, THE GIRL WHOSE BEAUTY...
...IS ONLY SKIN-DEEP.
HOW LONG DO YOU THINK I'VE BEEN IN YOUR LIFE?
I KNOW YOU VERY, VERY WELL.
ON A MUCH DEEPER LEVEL THAN YOU THINK.

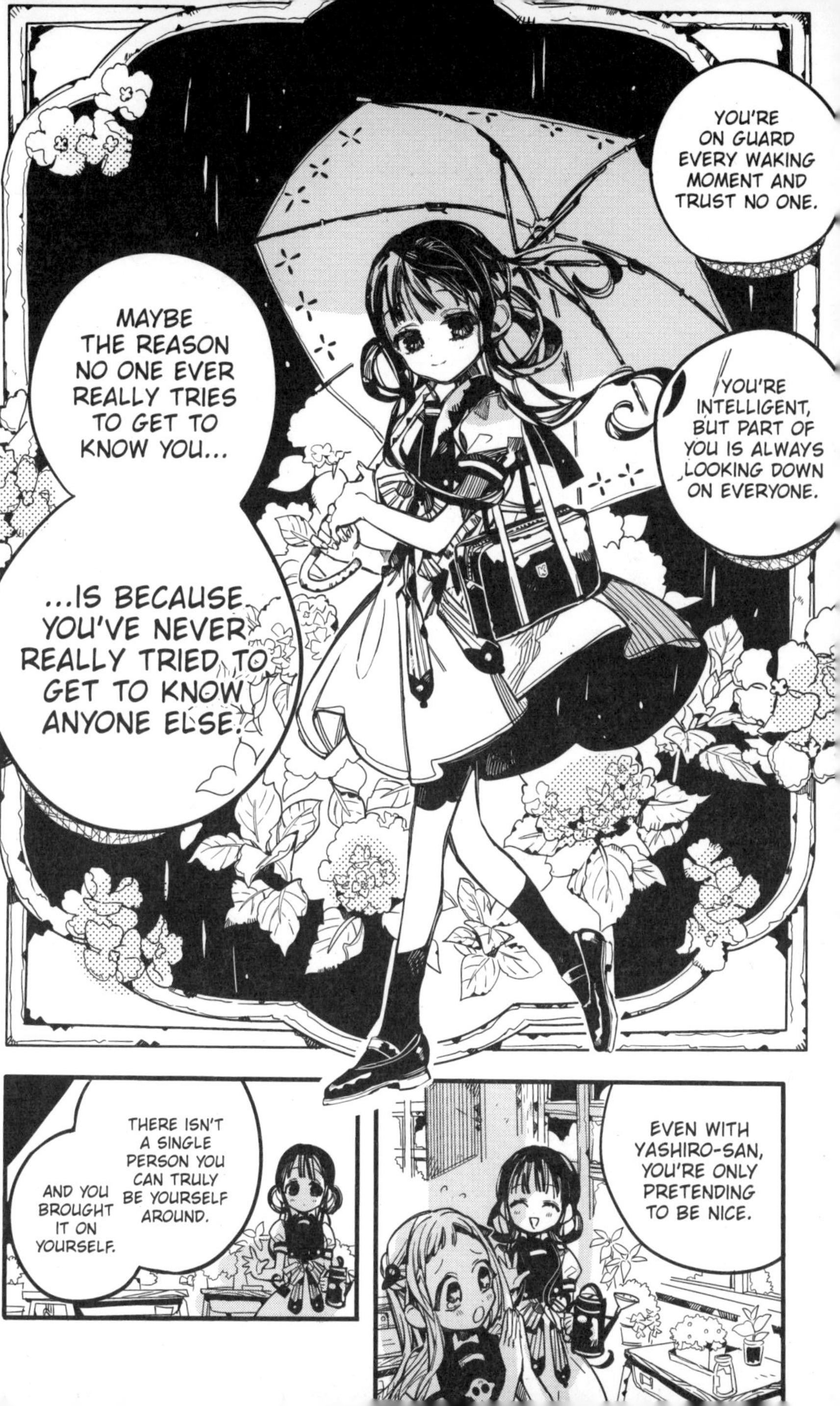
YOU'RE ON GUARD EVERY WAKING MOMENT AND TRUST NO ONE.
YOU'RE INTELLIGENT, BUT PART OF YOU IS ALWAYS LOOKING DOWN ON EVERYONE.
MAYBE THE REASON NO ONE EVER REALLY TRIES TO GET TO KNOW YOU...
...IS BECAUSE YOU'VE NEVER REALLY TRIED TO GET TO KNOW ANYONE ELSE.
EVEN WITH YASHIRO-SAN, YOU'RE ONLY PRETENDING TO BE NICE.
THERE ISN'T A SINGLE PERSON YOU CAN TRULY BE YOURSELF AROUND.
AND YOU BROUGHT IT ON YOURSELF.

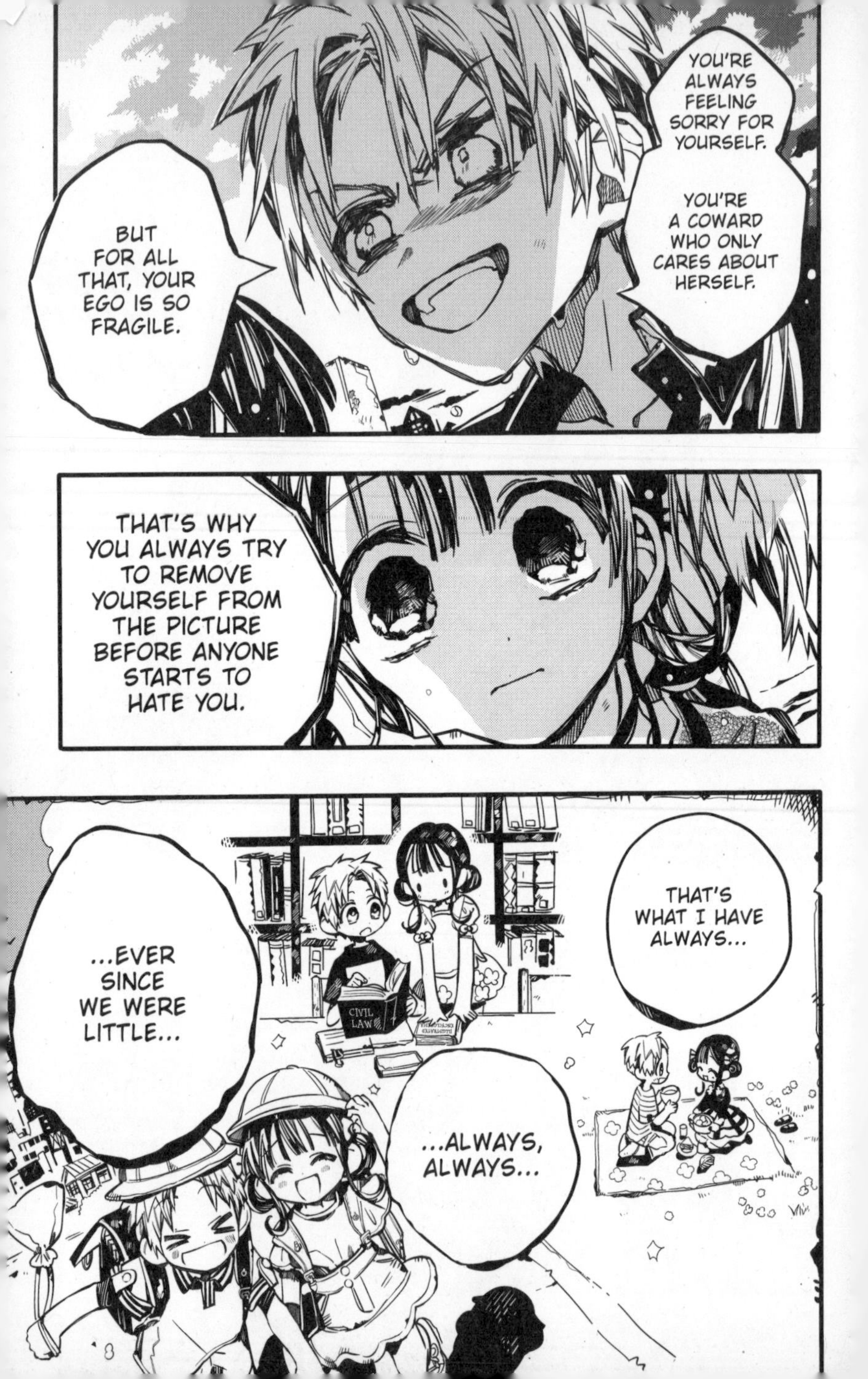
YOU'RE ALWAYS FEELING SORRY FOR YOURSELF.
YOU'RE A COWARD WHO ONLY CARES ABOUT HERSELF.
BUT FOR ALL THAT, YOUR EGO IS SO FRAGILE.
THAT'S WHY YOU ALWAYS TRY TO REMOVE YOURSELF FROM THE PICTURE BEFORE ANYONE STARTS TO HATE YOU.
THAT'S WHAT I HAVE ALWAYS...
...EVER SINCE WE WERE LITTLE...
CIVIL LAW
...ALWAYS, ALWAYS...

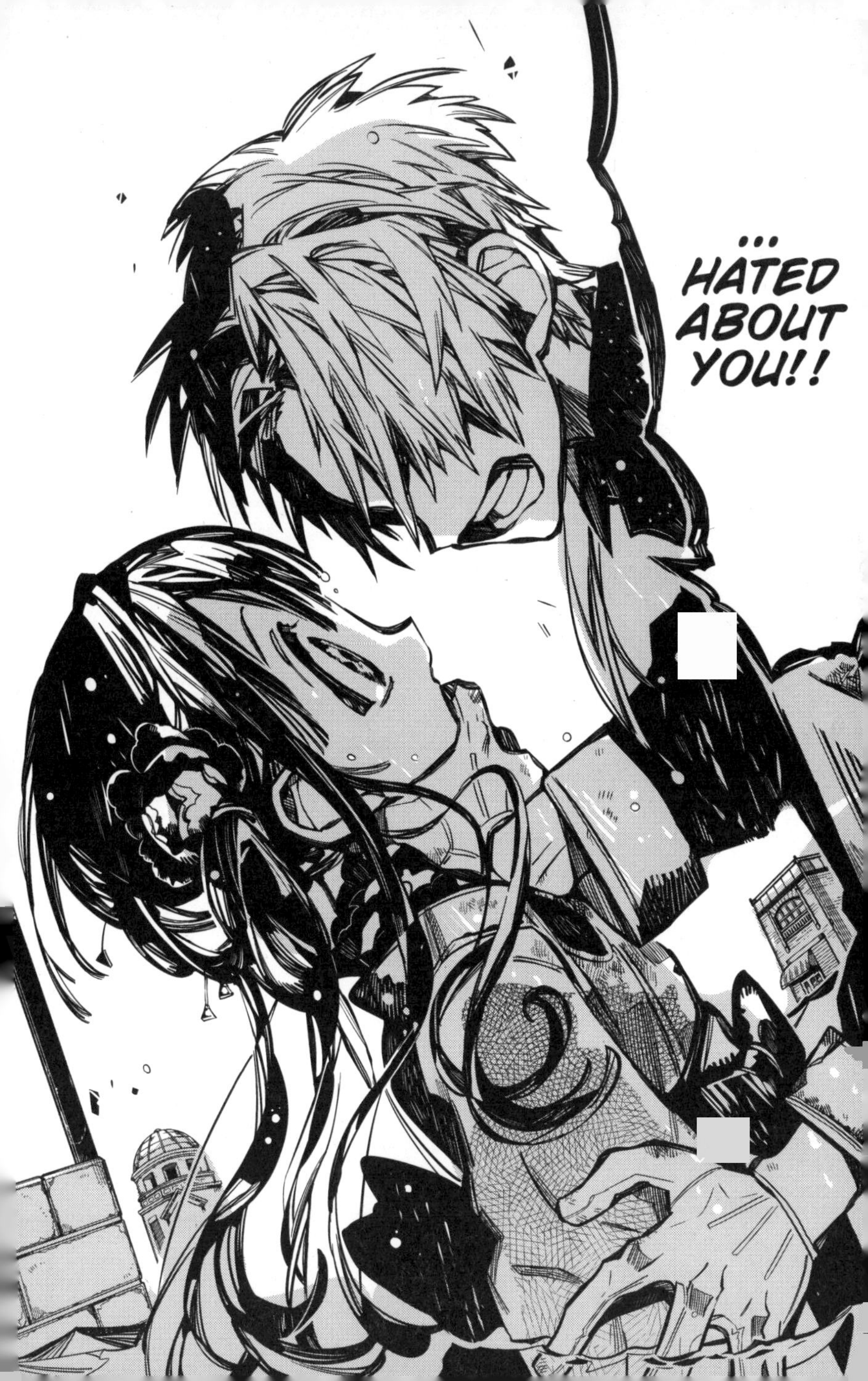
...HATED ABOUT YOU!!

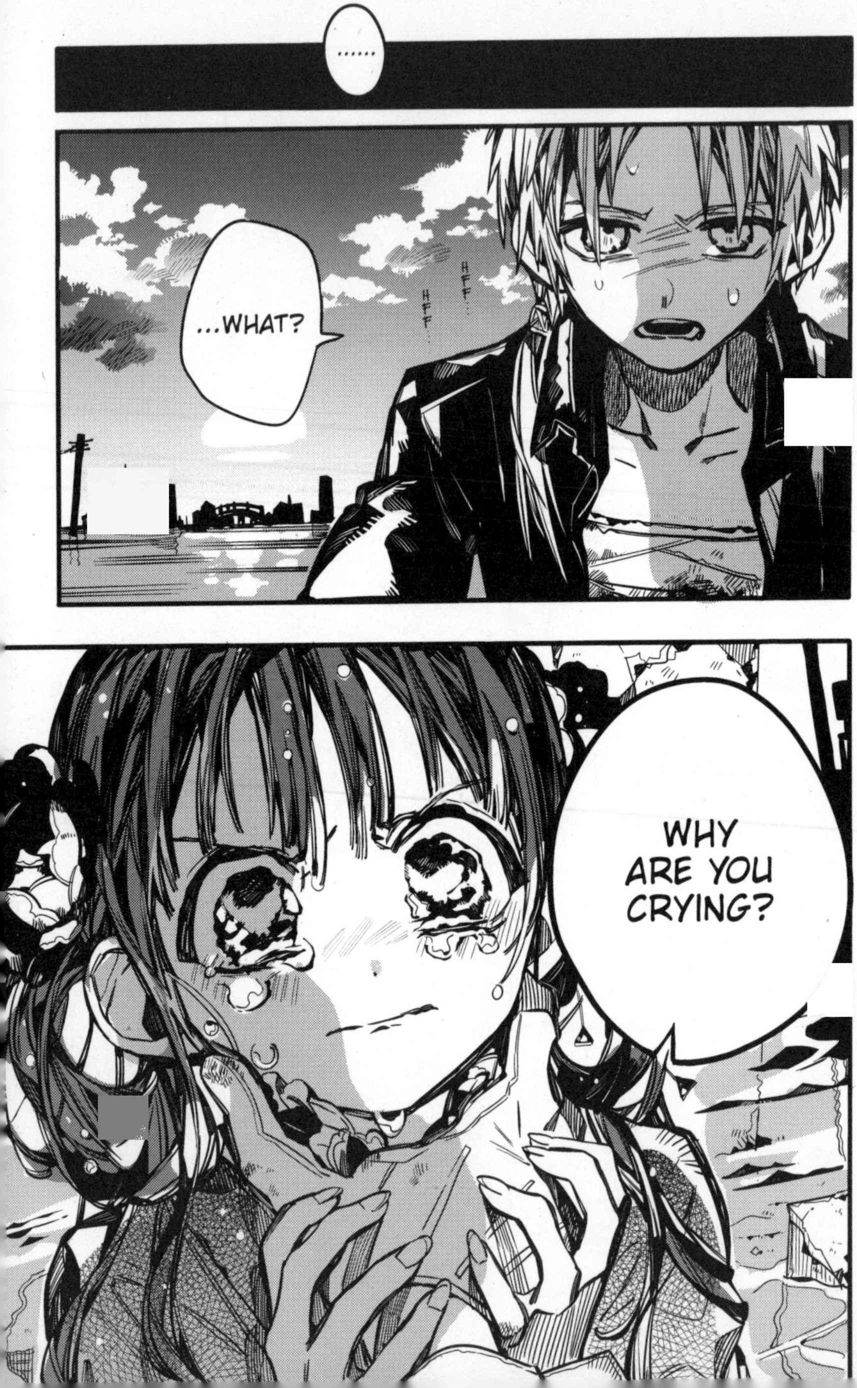
......
HFF...
HFF...
...WHAT?
WHY ARE YOU CRYING?

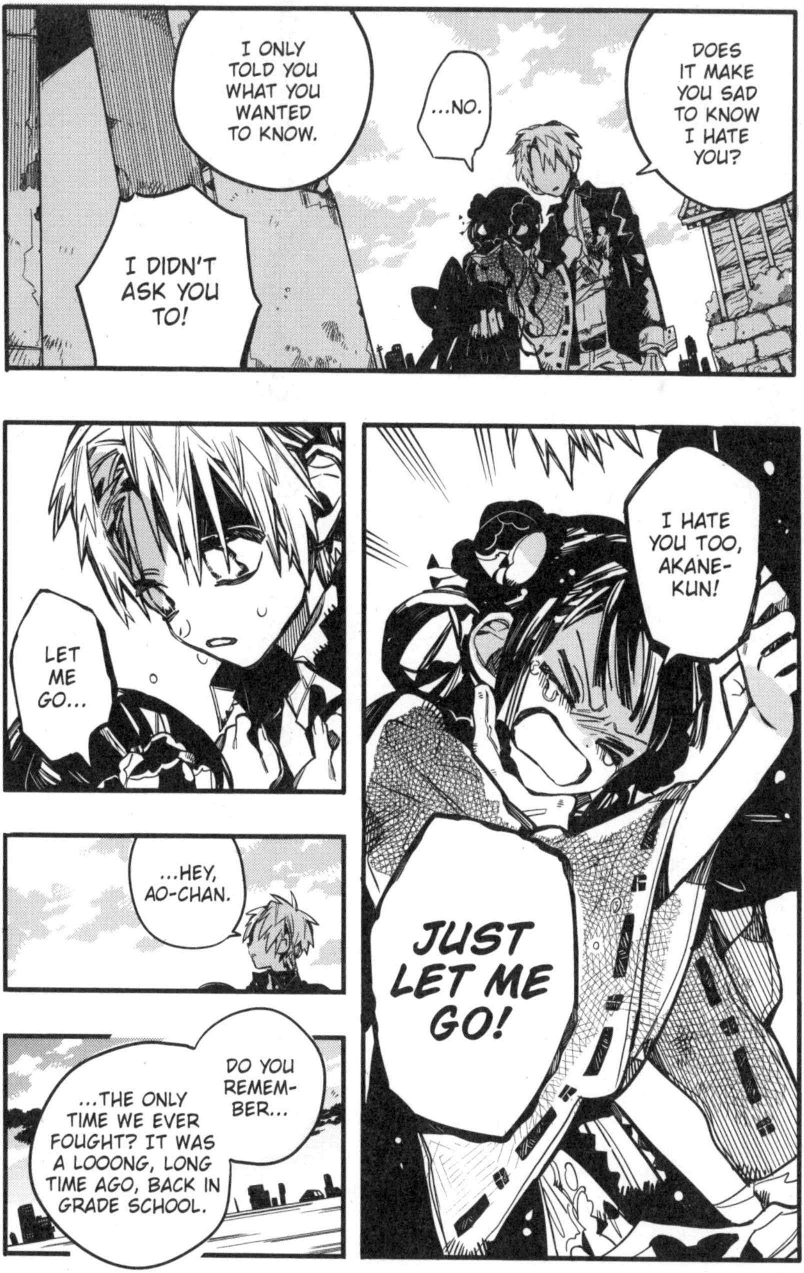
DOES IT MAKE YOU SAD TO KNOW I HATE YOU?
...NO.
I ONLY TOLD YOU WHAT YOU WANTED TO KNOW.
I DIDN'T ASK YOU TO!
I HATE YOU TOO, AKANE-KUN!
JUST LET ME GO!
LET ME GO...
...HEY, AO-CHAN.
DO YOU REMEMBER...
...THE ONLY TIME WE EVER FOUGHT? IT WAS A LOOONG, LONG TIME AGO, BACK IN GRADE SCHOOL.

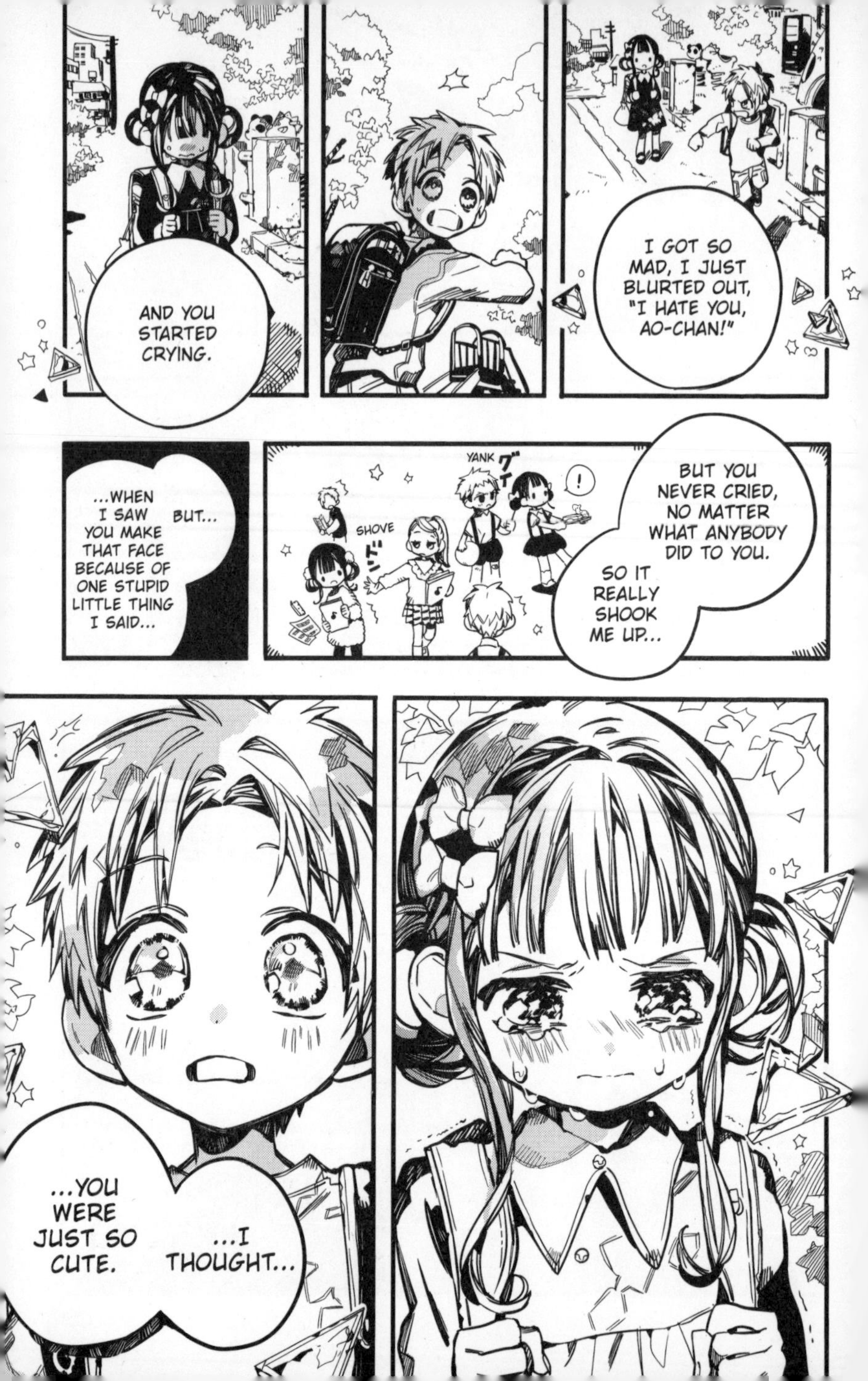
I GOT SO MAD, I JUST BLURTED OUT, "I HATE YOU, AO-CHAN!"
AND YOU STARTED CRYING.
BUT YOU NEVER CRIED, NO MATTER WHAT ANYBODY DID TO YOU.
SO IT REALLY SHOOK ME UP...
YANK
グイ
!
SHOVE
ドン
BUT...
...WHEN I SAW YOU MAKE THAT FACE BECAUSE OF ONE STUPID LITTLE THING I SAID...
...I THOUGHT...
...YOU WERE JUST SO CUTE.

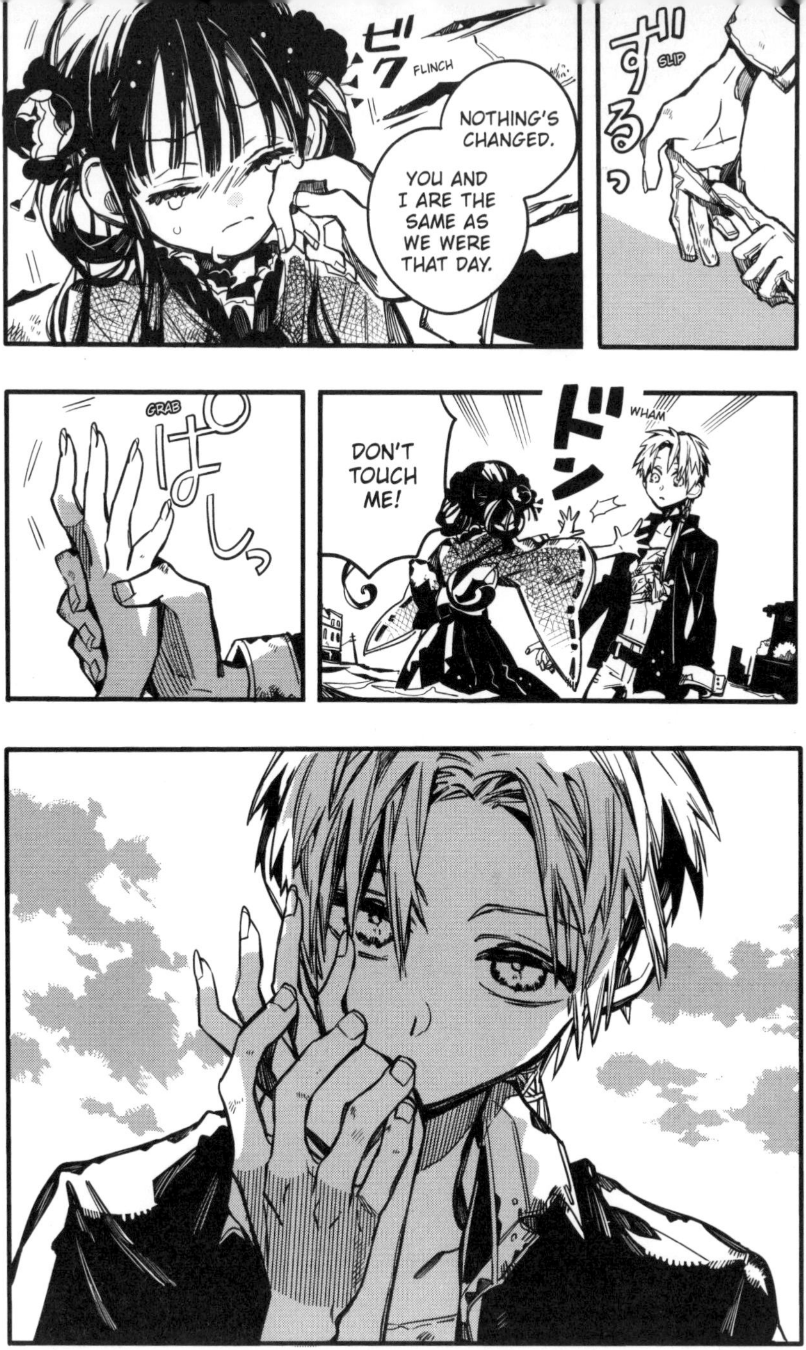
するっ
SLIP
ビク
FLINCH
NOTHING'S CHANGED.
YOU AND I ARE THE SAME AS WE WERE THAT DAY.
ドン
WHAM
DON'T TOUCH ME!
ぱしっ
GRAB

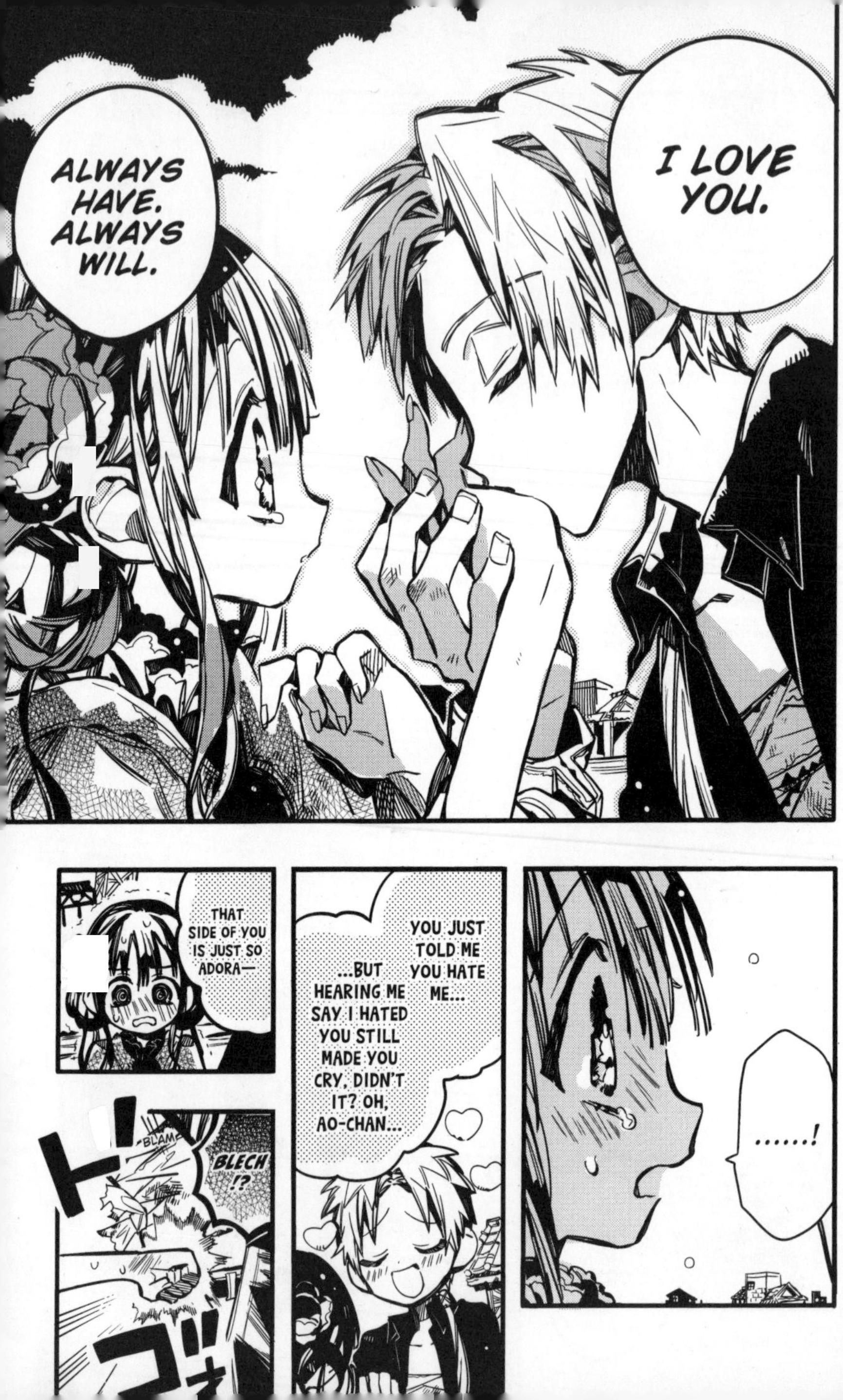
I LOVE YOU.
ALWAYS HAVE. ALWAYS WILL.
......!
YOU JUST TOLD ME YOU HATE ME...
...BUT HEARING ME SAY I HATED YOU STILL MADE YOU CRY, DIDN'T IT? OH, AO-CHAN...
THAT SIDE OF YOU IS JUST SO ADORA—
BLAM
BLECH !?

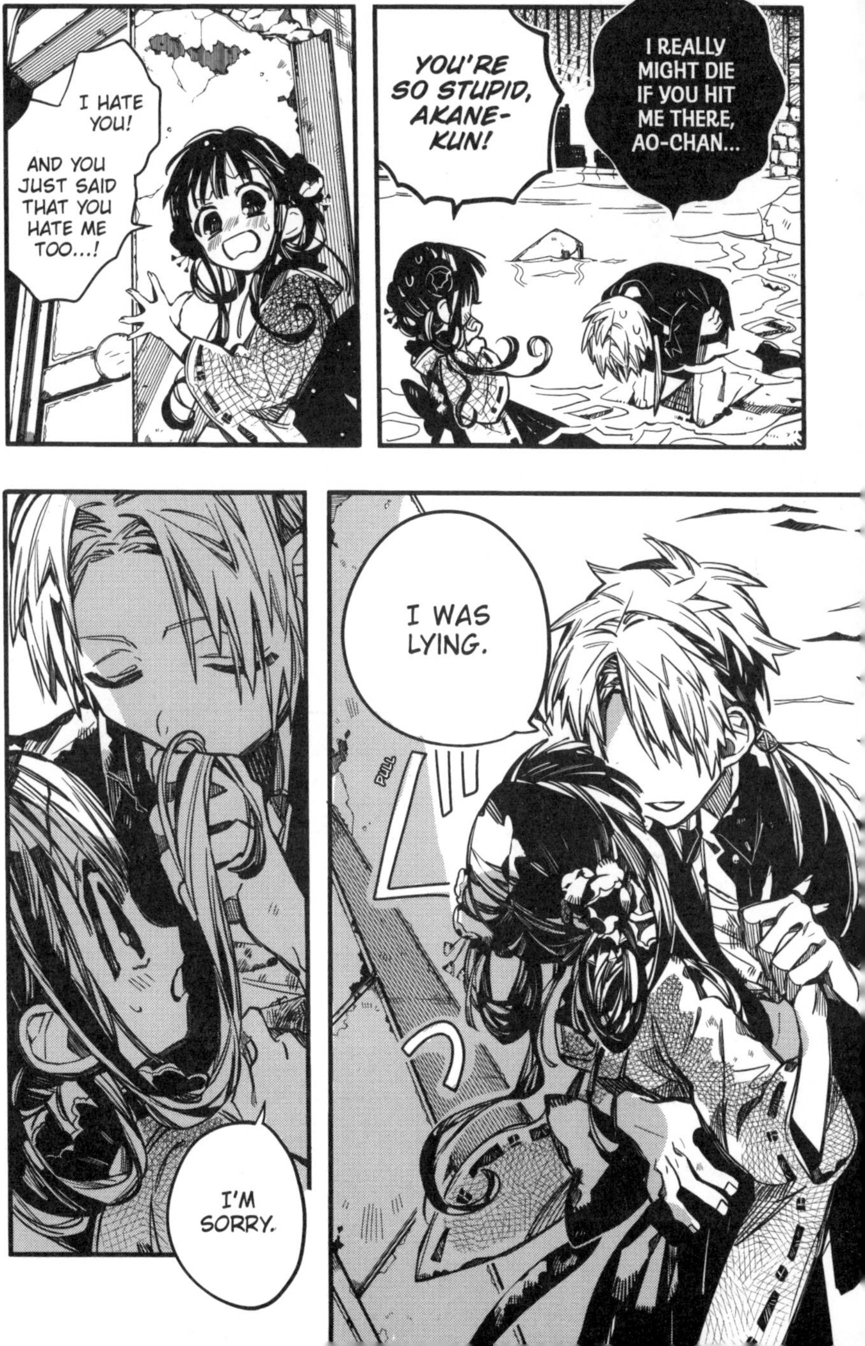
I REALLY MIGHT DIE IF YOU HIT ME THERE, AO-CHAN...
YOU'RE SO STUPID, AKANE-KUN!
I HATE YOU!
AND YOU JUST SAID THAT YOU HATE ME TOO...!
I WAS LYING.
PULL
I'M SORRY.

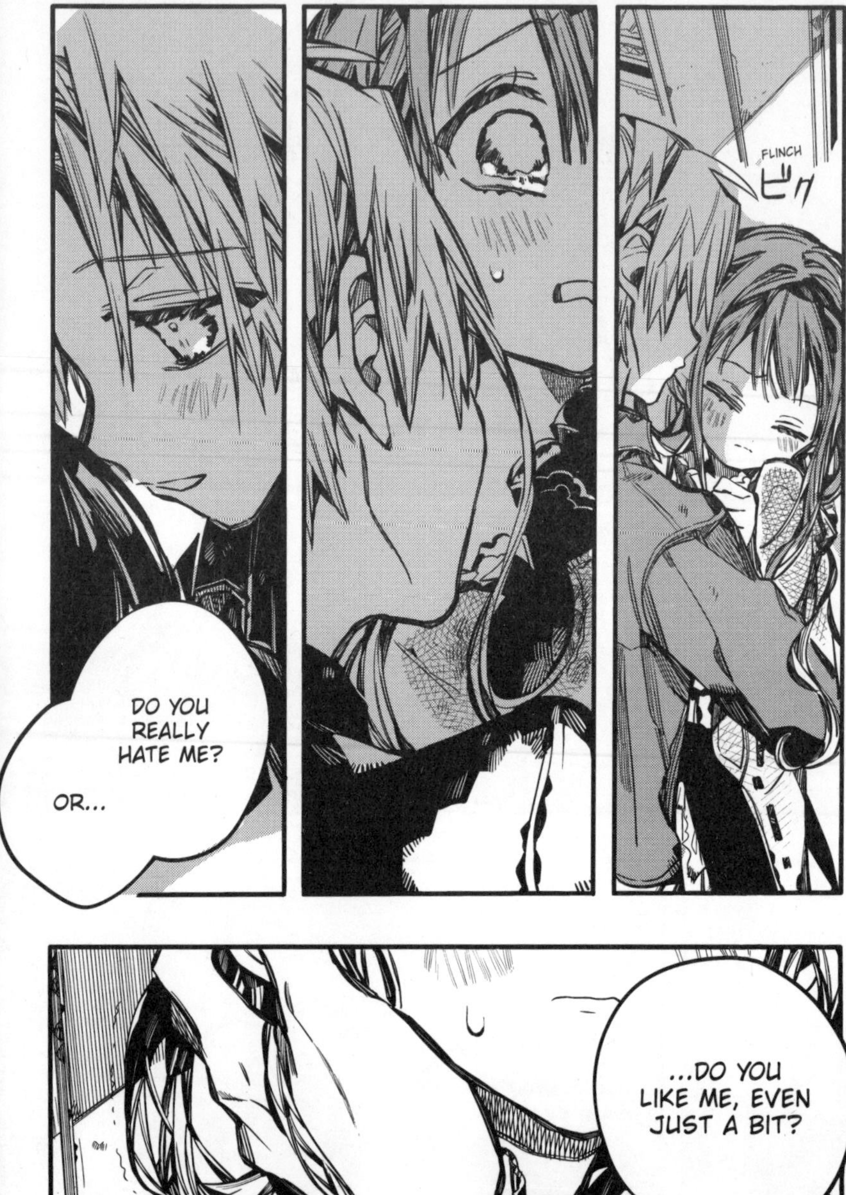
FLINCH
ビク
DO YOU REALLY HATE ME?
OR...
...DO YOU LIKE ME, EVEN JUST A BIT?

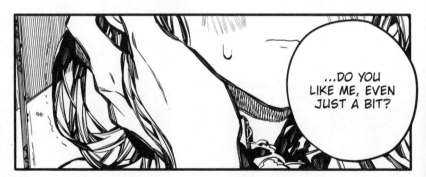

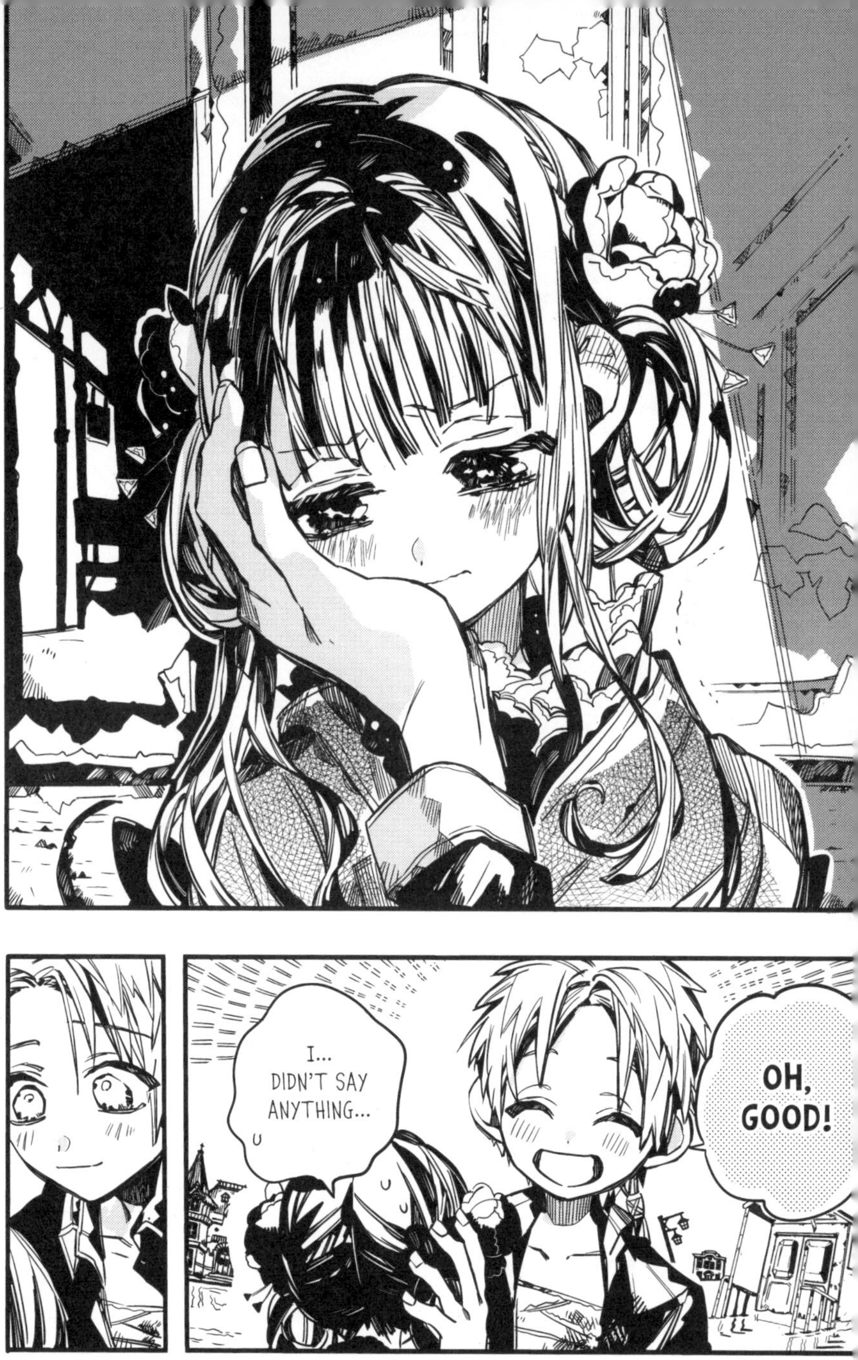

OH, GOOD!
I... DIDN'T SAY ANYTHING...

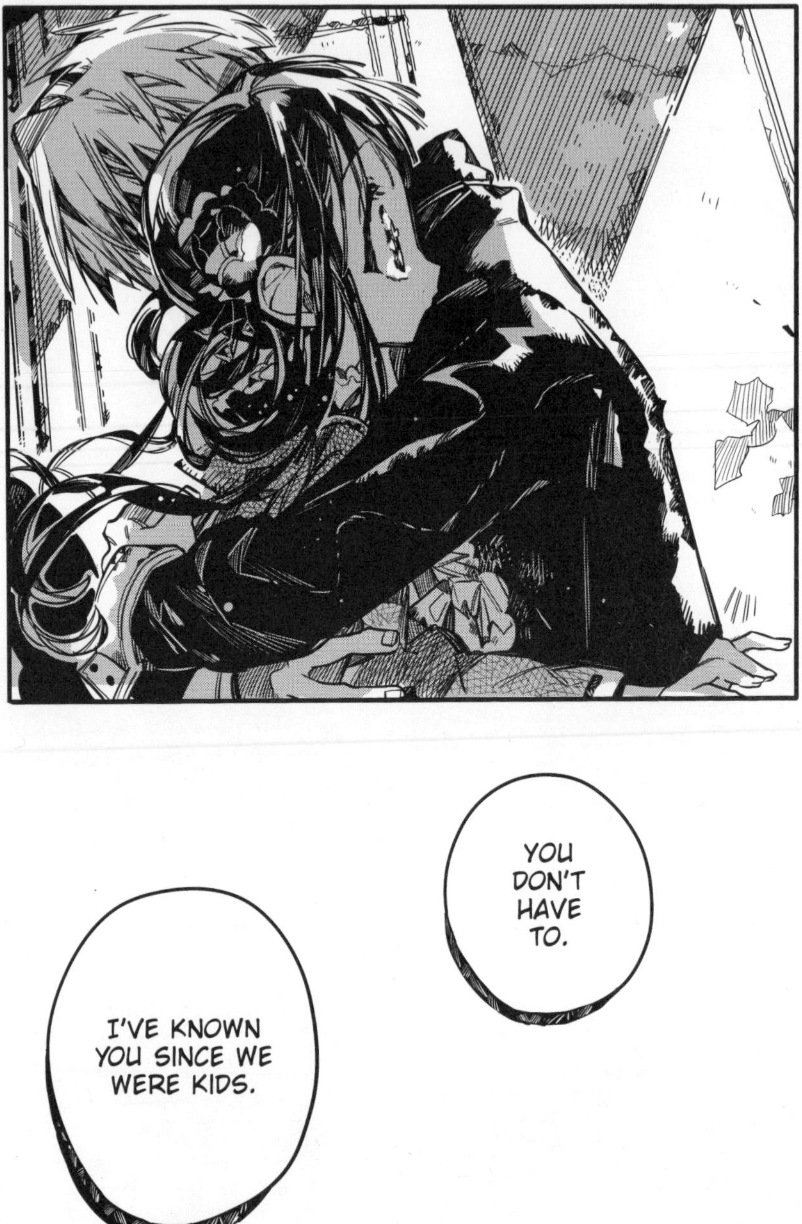
YOU DON'T HAVE TO.
I'VE KNOWN YOU SINCE WE WERE KIDS.

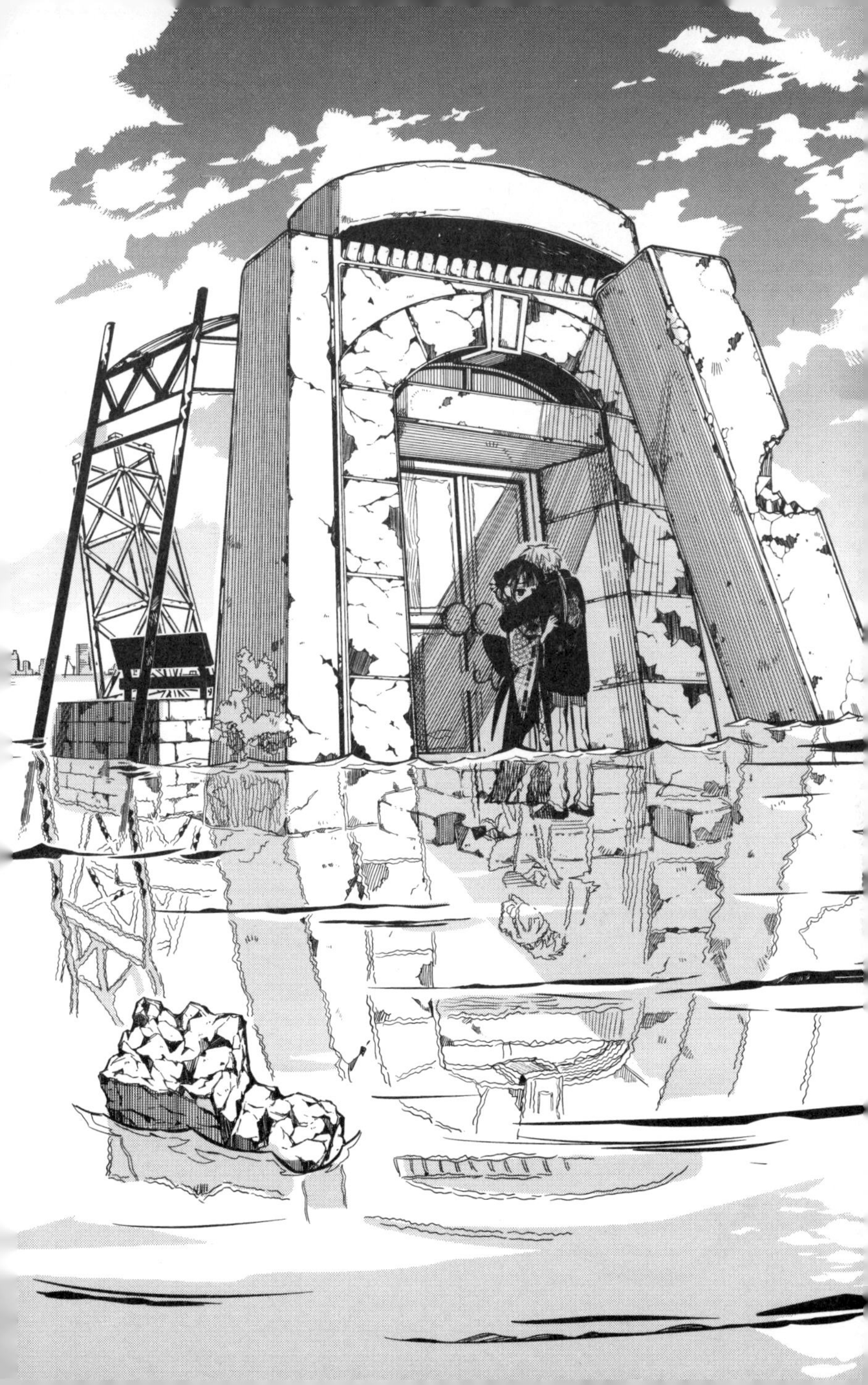

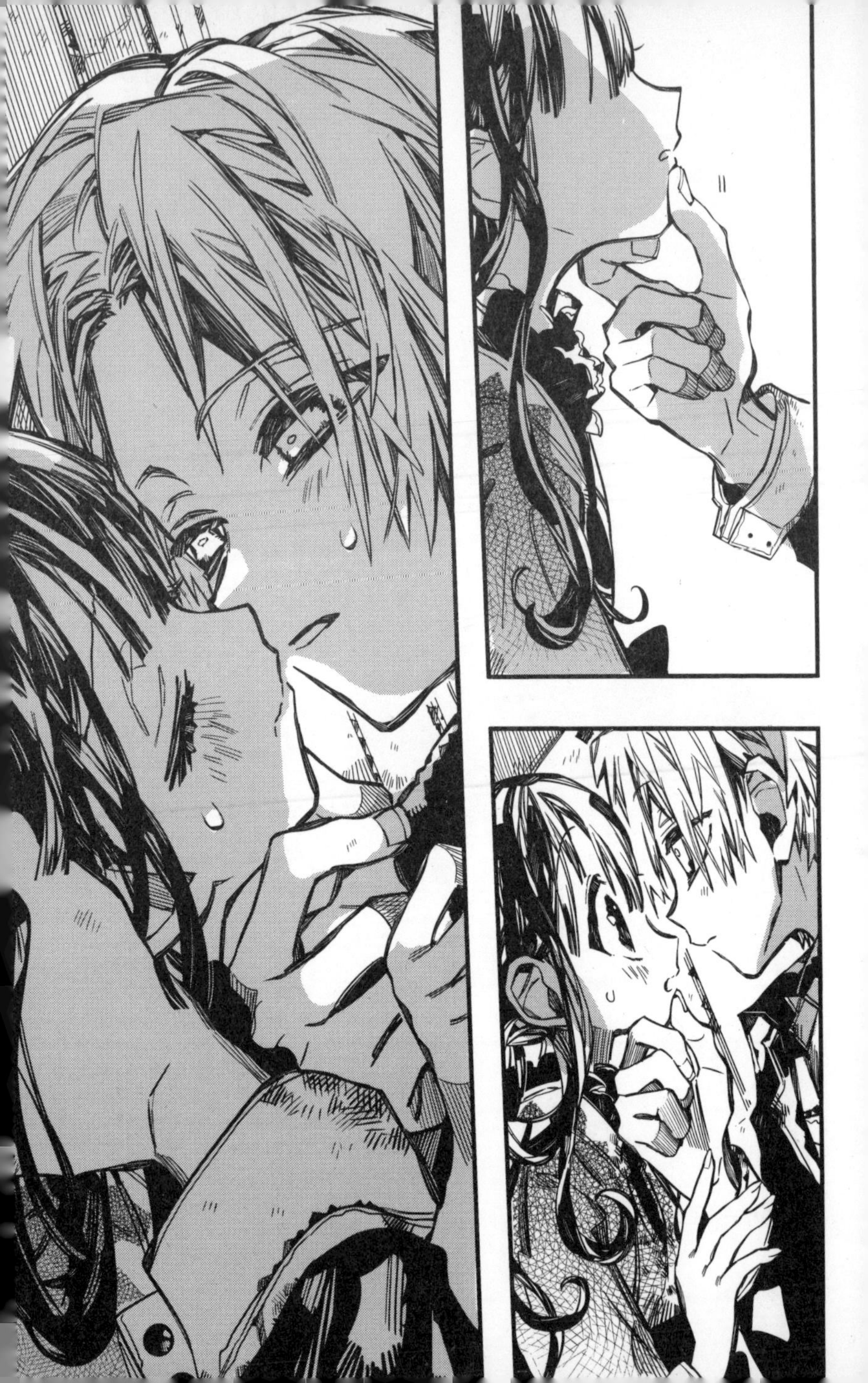

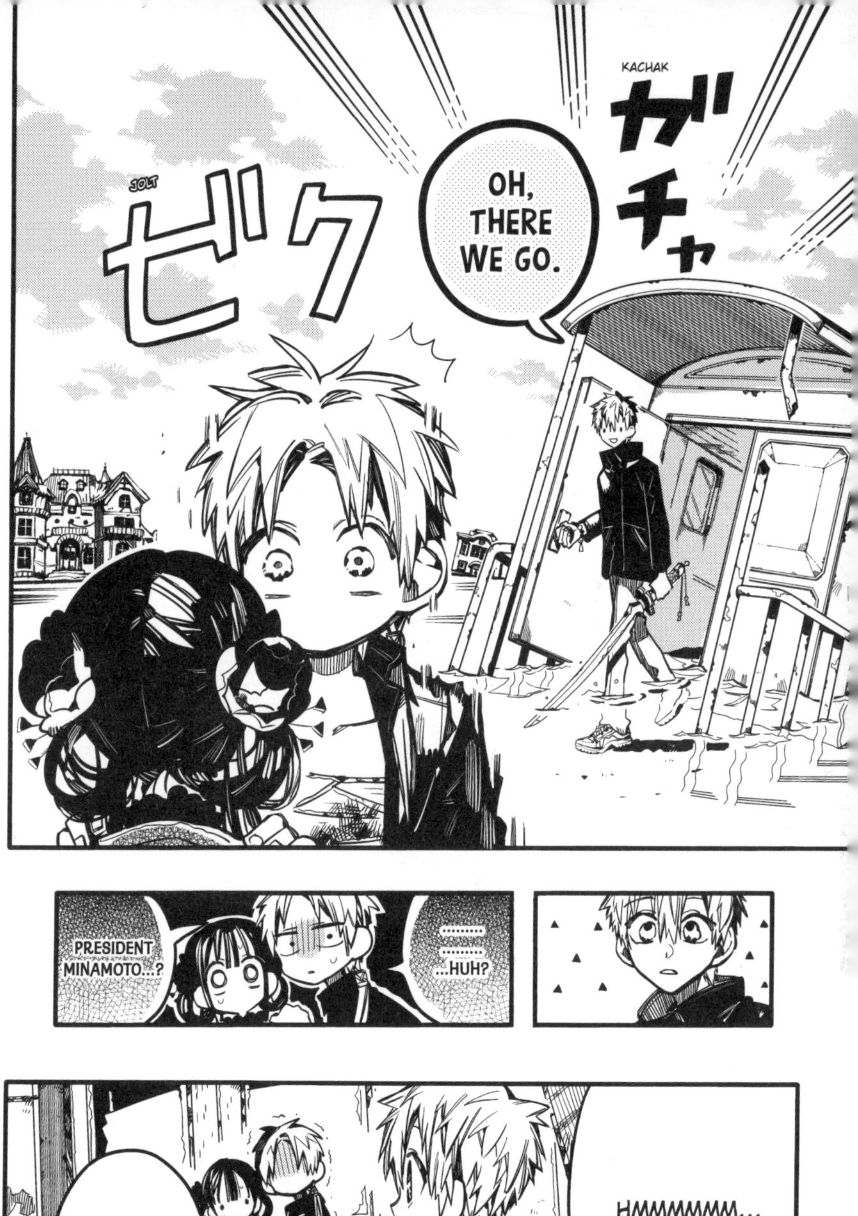
KACHAK
ガチャ
OH, THERE WE GO.
JOLT
ビク
....
....
...HUH?
PRESIDENT MINAMOTO...?
HMMMMMM...
HEY, AM I...

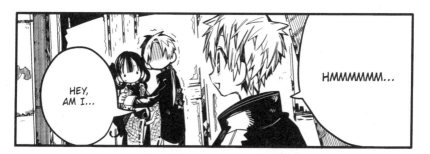

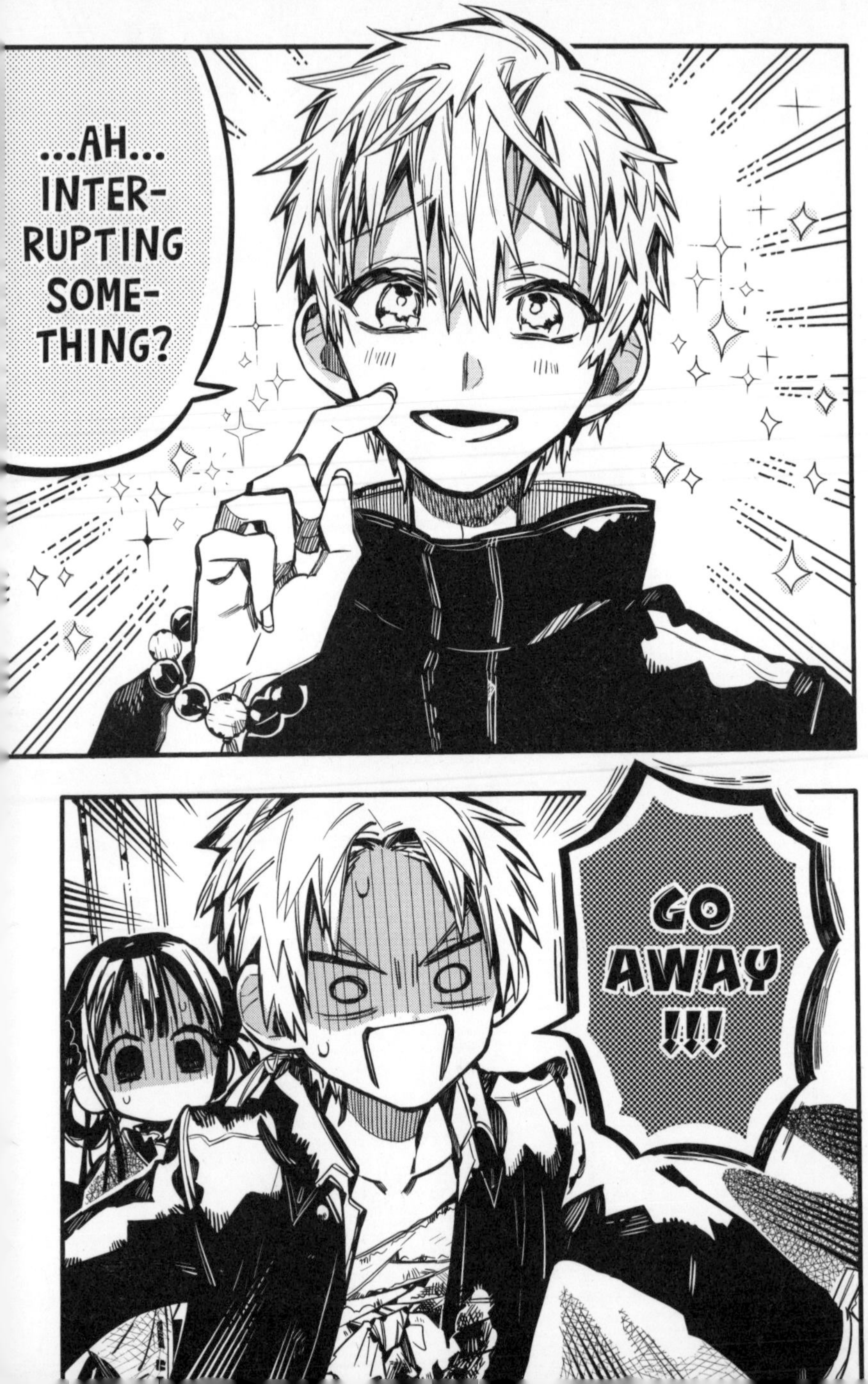
...AH... INTER- RUPTING SOME- THING?
GO AWAY !!!

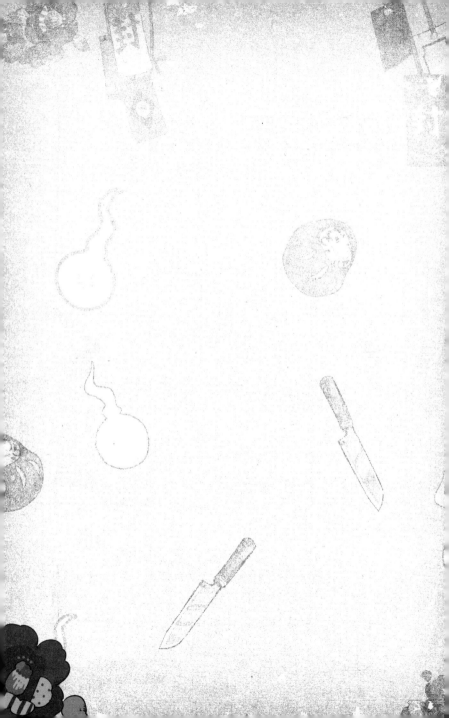

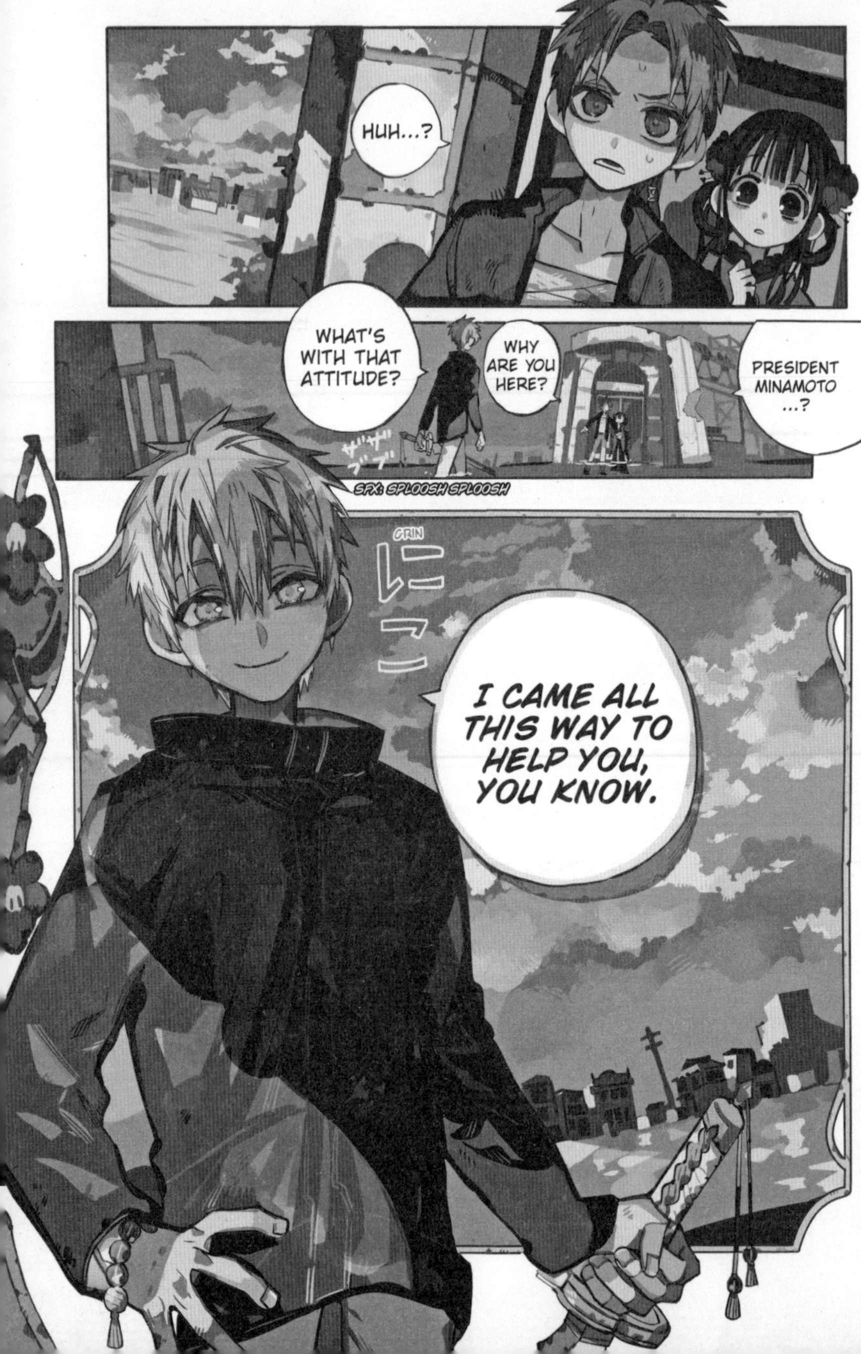
HUH...?
PRESIDENT MINAMOTO ...?
WHY ARE YOU HERE?
WHAT'S WITH THAT ATTITUDE?
SFX: SPLOOSH SPLOOSH
GRIN
I CAME ALL THIS WAY TO HELP YOU, YOU KNOW.

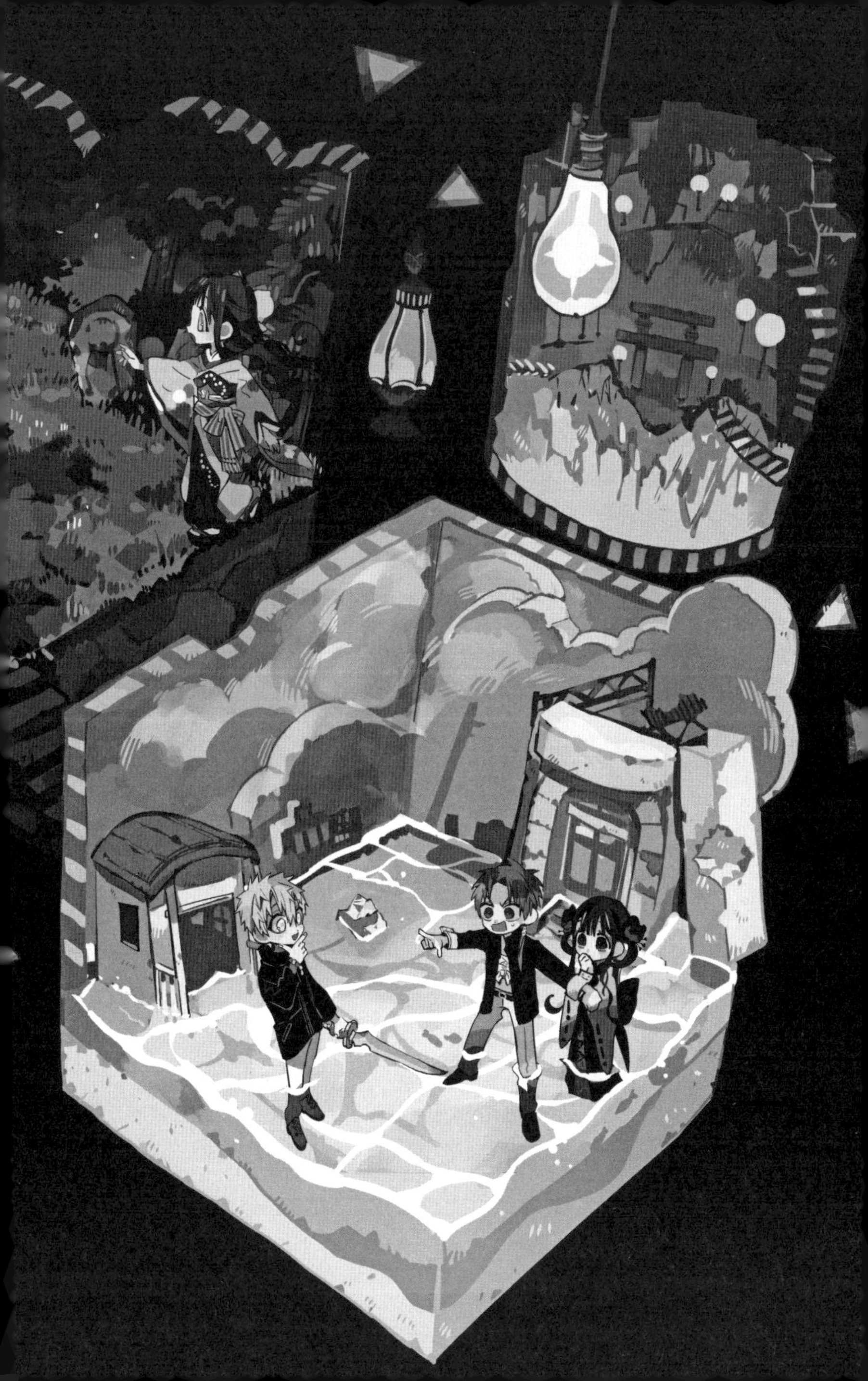

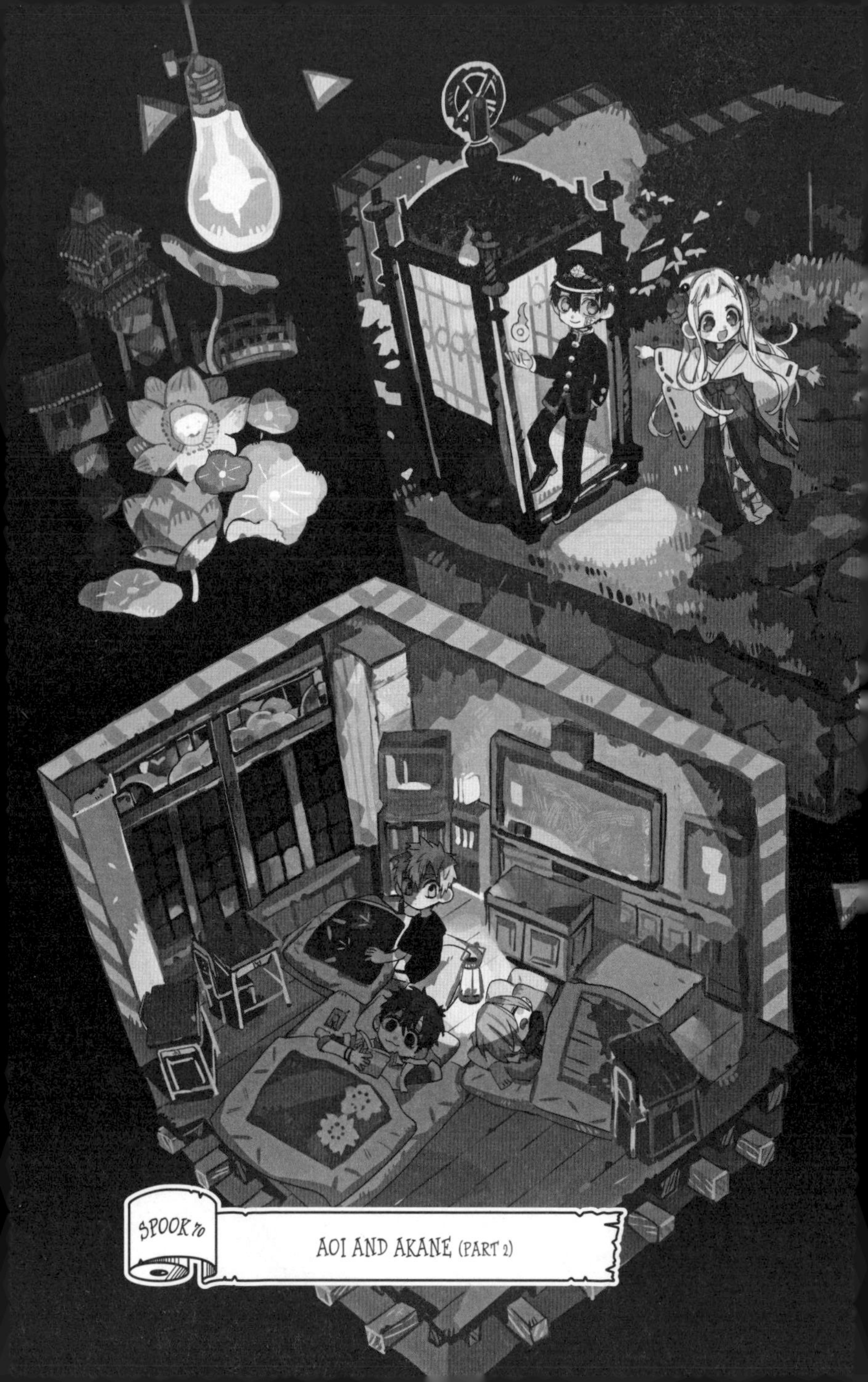
SPOOK 70
AOI AND AKANE (PART 2)

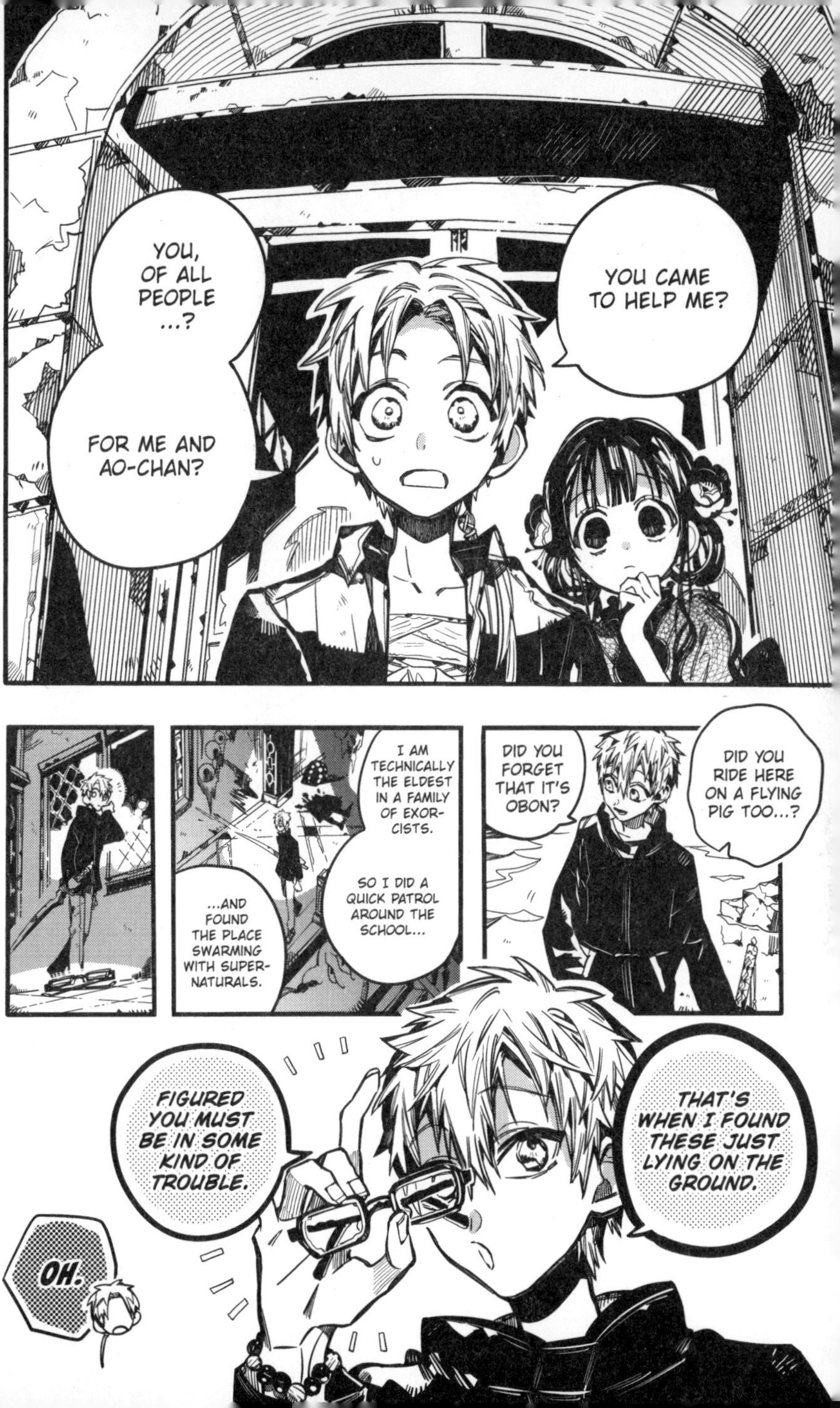
YOU CAME TO HELP ME?
YOU, OF ALL PEOPLE ...?
FOR ME AND AO-CHAN?
DID YOU RIDE HERE ON A FLYING PIG TOO...?
DID YOU FORGET THAT IT'S OBON?
I AM TECHNICALLY THE ELDEST IN A FAMILY OF EXOR-CISTS.
SO I DID A QUICK PATROL AROUND THE SCHOOL...
...AND FOUND THE PLACE SWARMING WITH SUPER-NATURALS.
THAT'S WHEN I FOUND THESE JUST LYING ON THE GROUND.
FIGURED YOU MUST BE IN SOME KIND OF TROUBLE.
OH.

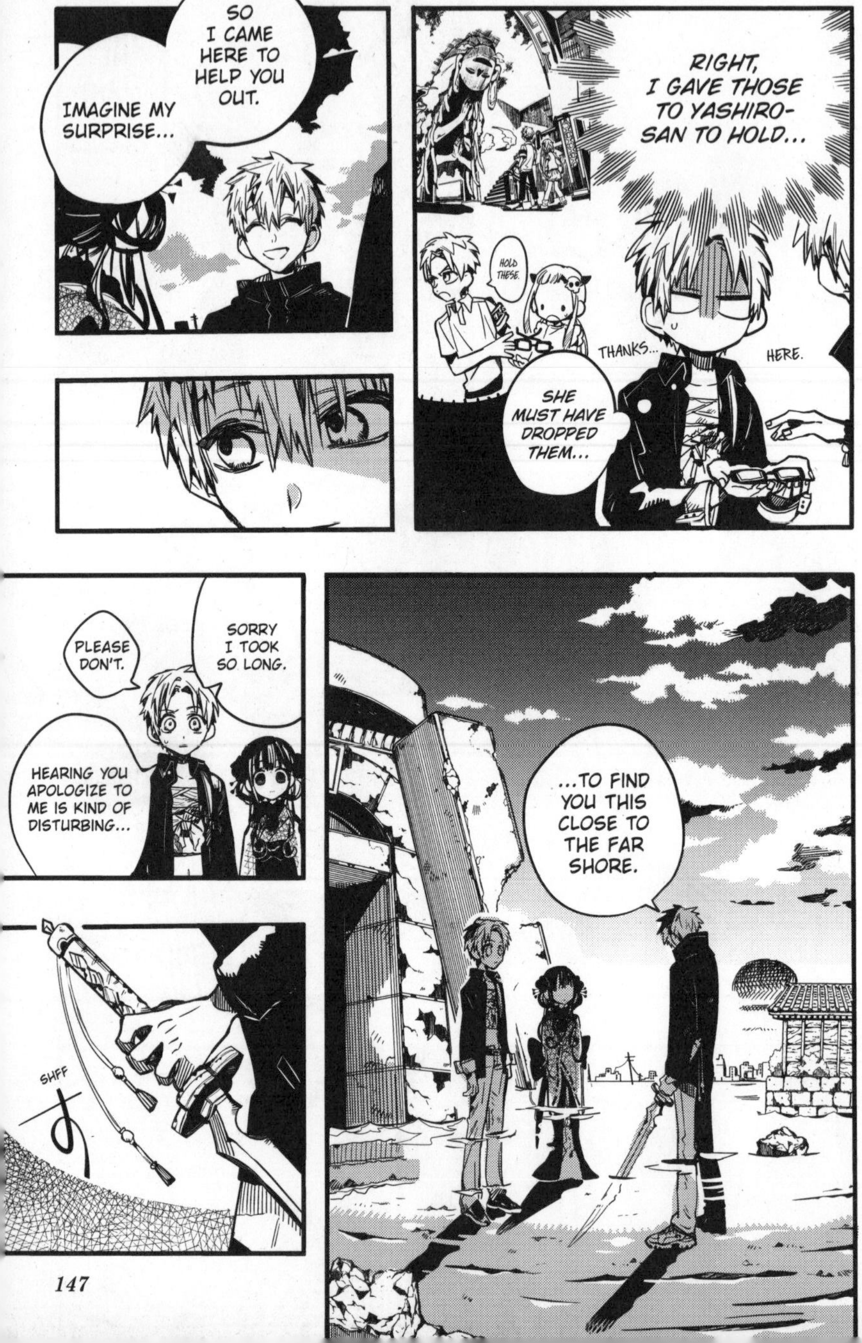
RIGHT, I GAVE THOSE TO YASHIRO-SAN TO HOLD...
HOLD THESE.
HERE.
THANKS...
SHE MUST HAVE DROPPED THEM...
SO I CAME HERE TO HELP YOU OUT.
IMAGINE MY SURPRISE...
...TO FIND YOU THIS CLOSE TO THE FAR SHORE.
SORRY I TOOK SO LONG.
PLEASE DON'T.
HEARING YOU APOLOGIZE TO ME IS KIND OF DISTURBING...
SHFF

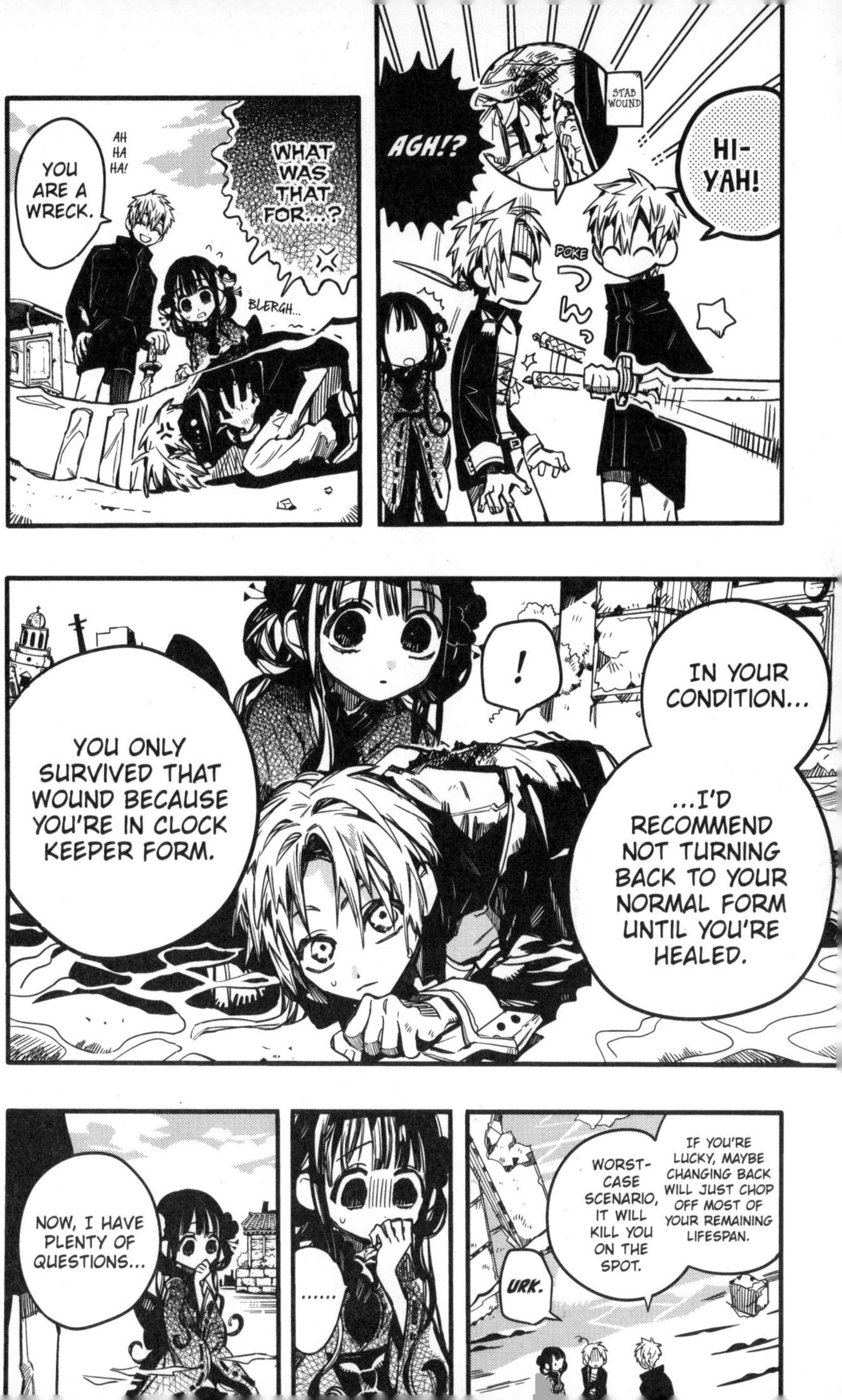
HI-YAH!
STAB WOUND
AGH!?
POKE
WHAT WAS THAT FOR...?
AH HA HA!
YOU ARE A WRECK.
BLERGH...
IN YOUR CONDITION...
...I'D RECOMMEND NOT TURNING BACK TO YOUR NORMAL FORM UNTIL YOU'RE HEALED.
!
YOU ONLY SURVIVED THAT WOUND BECAUSE YOU'RE IN CLOCK KEEPER FORM.
IF YOU'RE LUCKY, MAYBE CHANGING BACK WILL JUST CHOP OFF MOST OF YOUR REMAINING LIFESPAN.
WORST-CASE SCENARIO, IT WILL KILL YOU ON THE SPOT.
URK.
......
NOW, I HAVE PLENTY OF QUESTIONS...

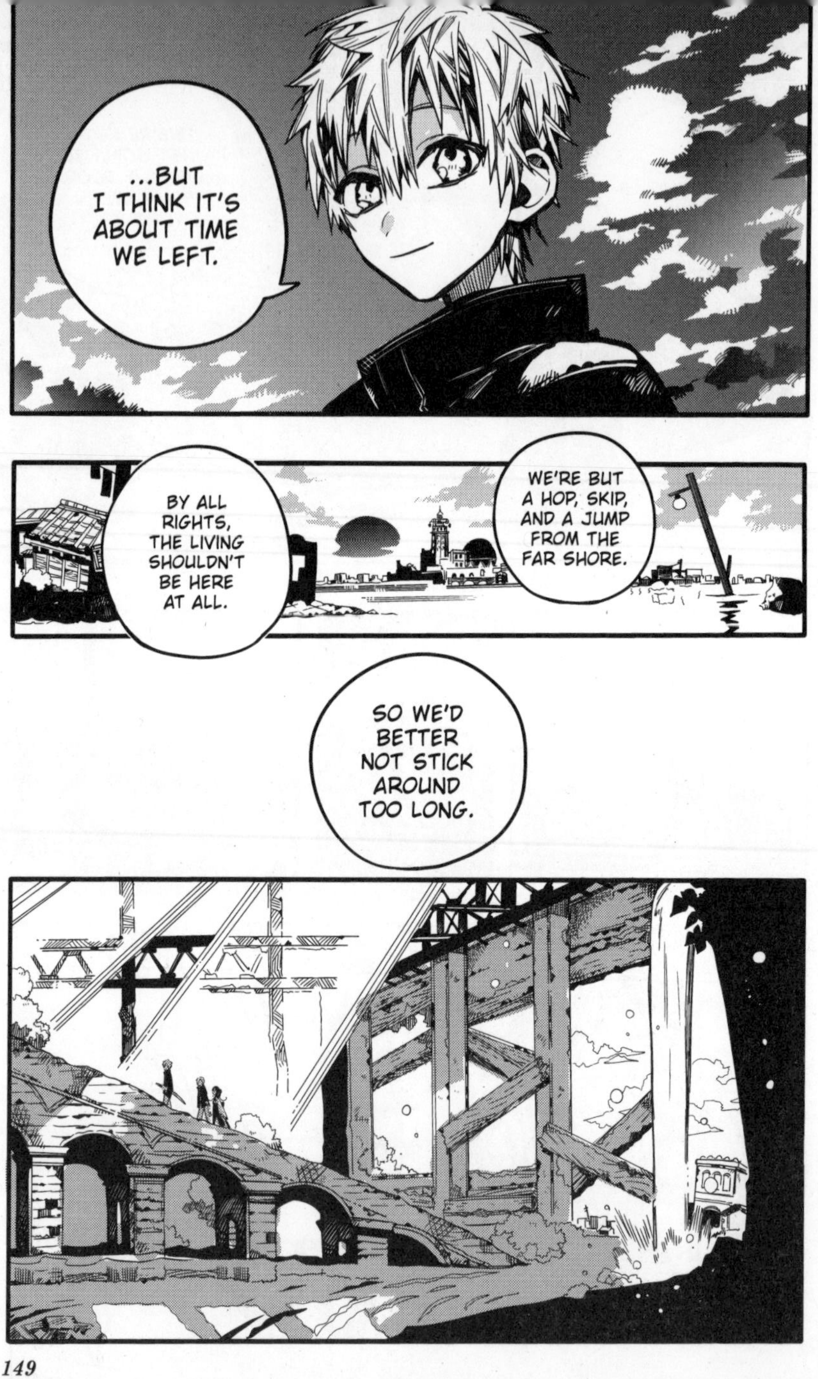
...BUT I THINK IT'S ABOUT TIME WE LEFT.
WE'RE BUT A HOP, SKIP, AND A JUMP FROM THE FAR SHORE.
BY ALL RIGHTS, THE LIVING SHOULDN'T BE HERE AT ALL.
SO WE'D BETTER NOT STICK AROUND TOO LONG.

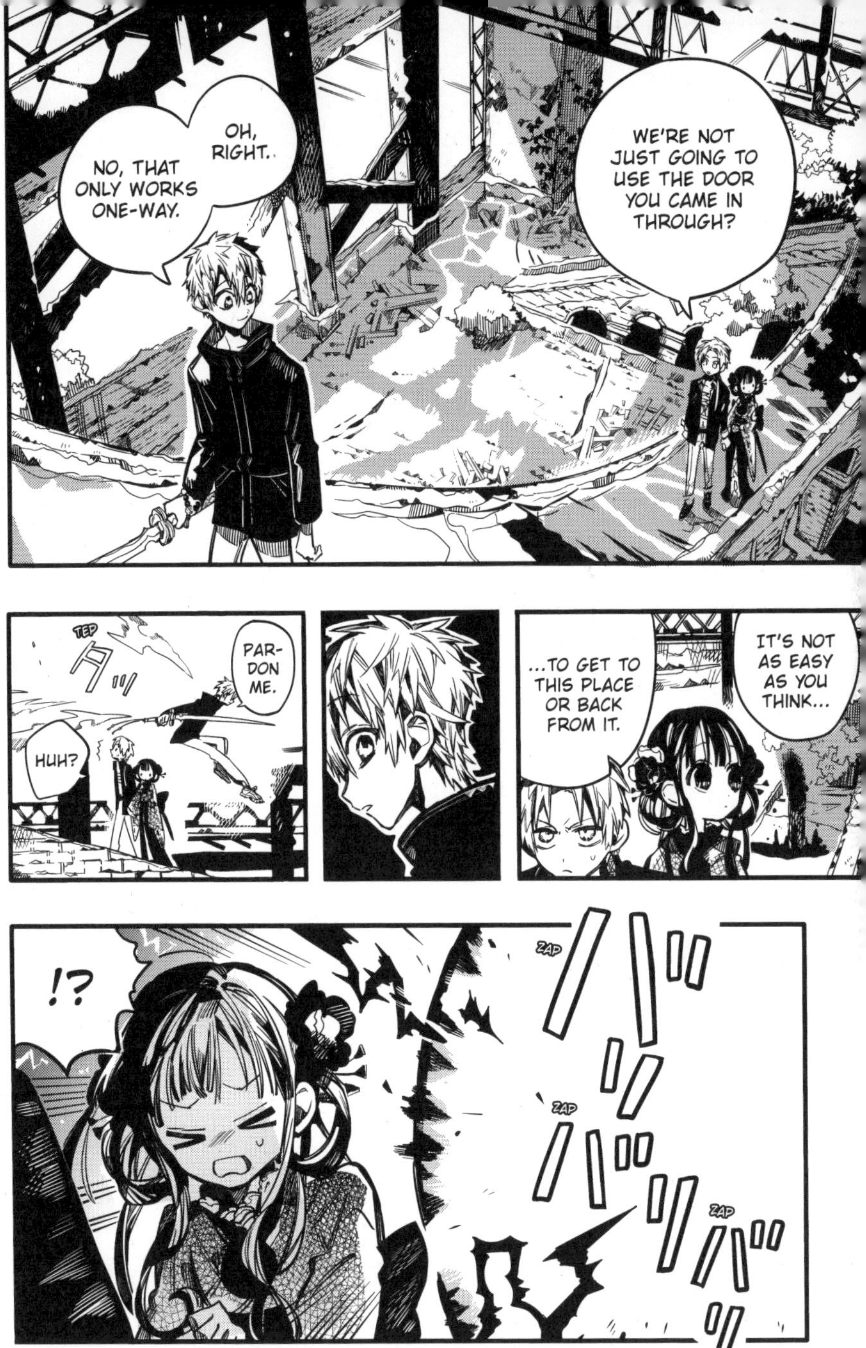
WE'RE NOT JUST GOING TO USE THE DOOR YOU CAME IN THROUGH?
OH, RIGHT..
NO, THAT ONLY WORKS ONE-WAY.
IT'S NOT AS EASY AS YOU THINK...
...TO GET TO THIS PLACE OR BACK FROM IT.
PAR-DON ME.
TEP
HUH?
ZAP
!?
ZAP
ZAP

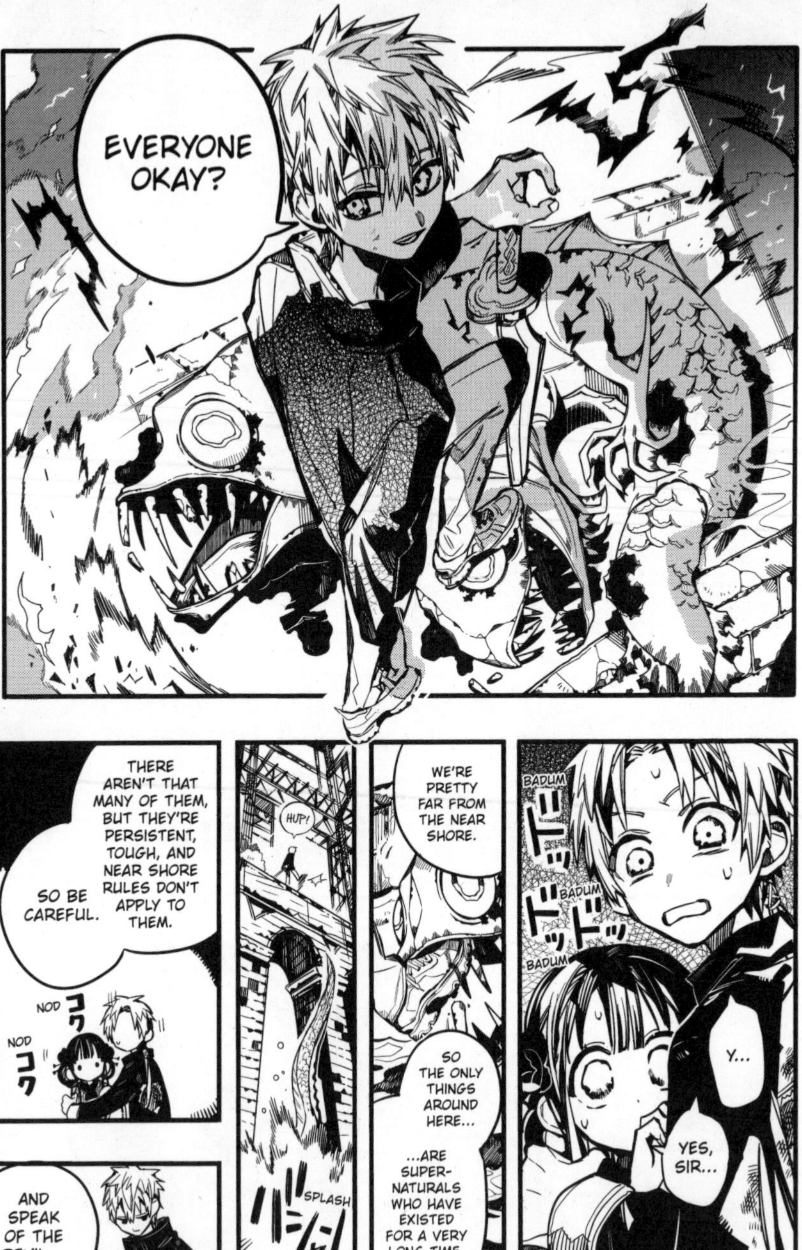
EVERYONE OKAY?
BADUM
BADUM
BADUM
Y...
YES, SIR...
WE'RE PRETTY FAR FROM THE NEAR SHORE.
SO THE ONLY THINGS AROUND HERE...
...ARE SUPER-NATURALS WHO HAVE EXISTED FOR A VERY LONG TIME.
HUP!
SPLASH
THERE AREN'T THAT MANY OF THEM, BUT THEY'RE PERSISTENT, TOUGH, AND NEAR SHORE RULES DON'T APPLY TO THEM.
SO BE CAREFUL.
NOD
NOD
NOD
AND SPEAK OF THE DEVIL...

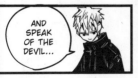

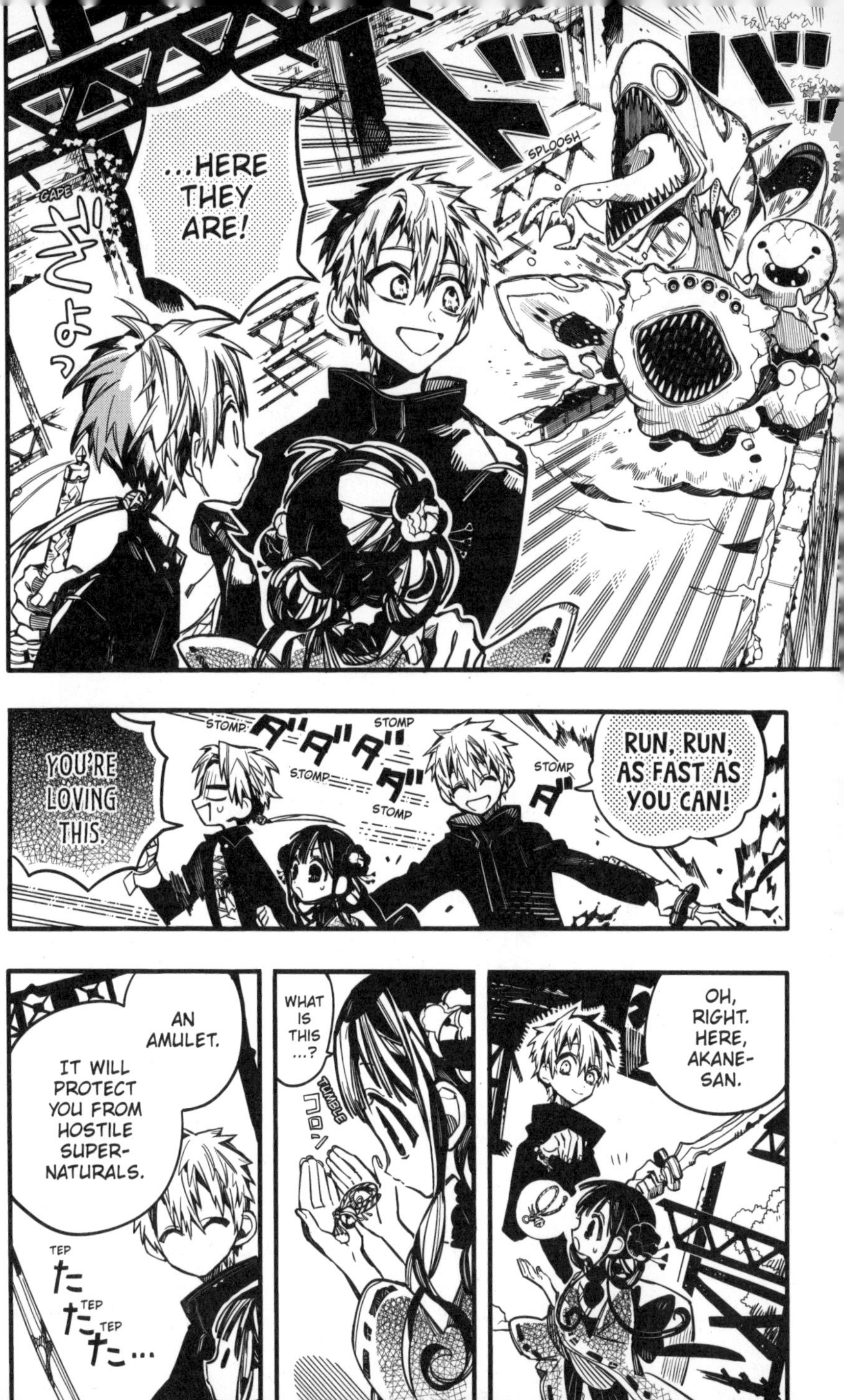
SPLOOSH
...HERE THEY ARE!
GAPE
RUN, RUN, AS FAST AS YOU CAN!
STOMP
STOMP
STOMP
STOMP
STOMP
YOU'RE LOVING THIS.
OH, RIGHT. HERE, AKANE-SAN.
WHAT IS THIS ...?
TUMBLE
AN AMULET.
IT WILL PROTECT YOU FROM HOSTILE SUPER-NATURALS.
TEP
TEP
TEP

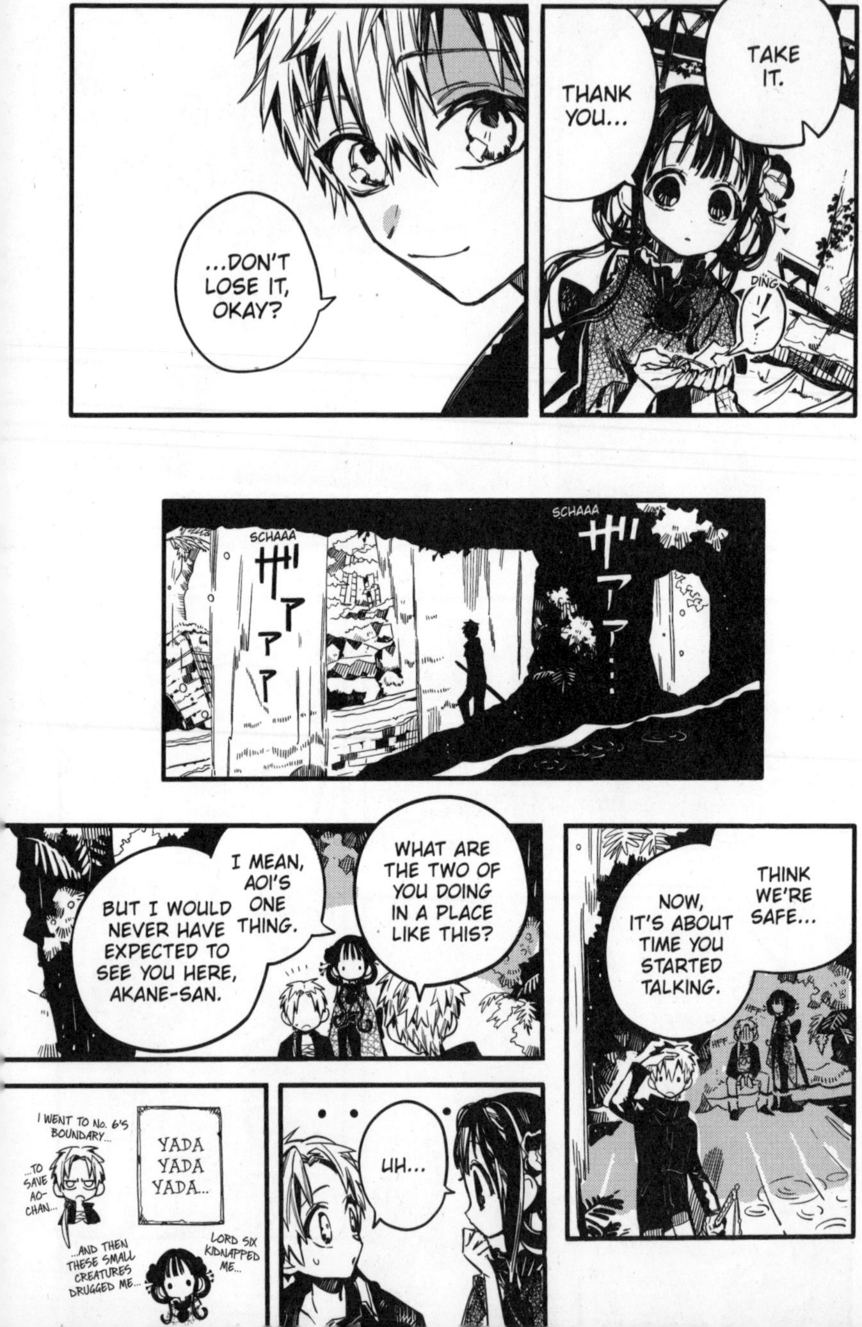
TAKE IT.
THANK YOU...
DING
!
...DON'T LOSE IT, OKAY?
SCHAAA
ザァァ...
SCHAAA
ザァァァ
THINK WE'RE SAFE...
NOW, IT'S ABOUT TIME YOU STARTED TALKING.
WHAT ARE THE TWO OF YOU DOING IN A PLACE LIKE THIS?
I MEAN, AOI'S ONE THING.
BUT I WOULD NEVER HAVE EXPECTED TO SEE YOU HERE, AKANE-SAN.
• • •
UH...
YADA YADA YADA...
I WENT TO NO. 6'S BOUNDARY...
...TO SAVE AO-CHAN...
...AND THEN THESE SMALL CREATURES DRUGGED ME...
LORD SIX KIDNAPPED ME...

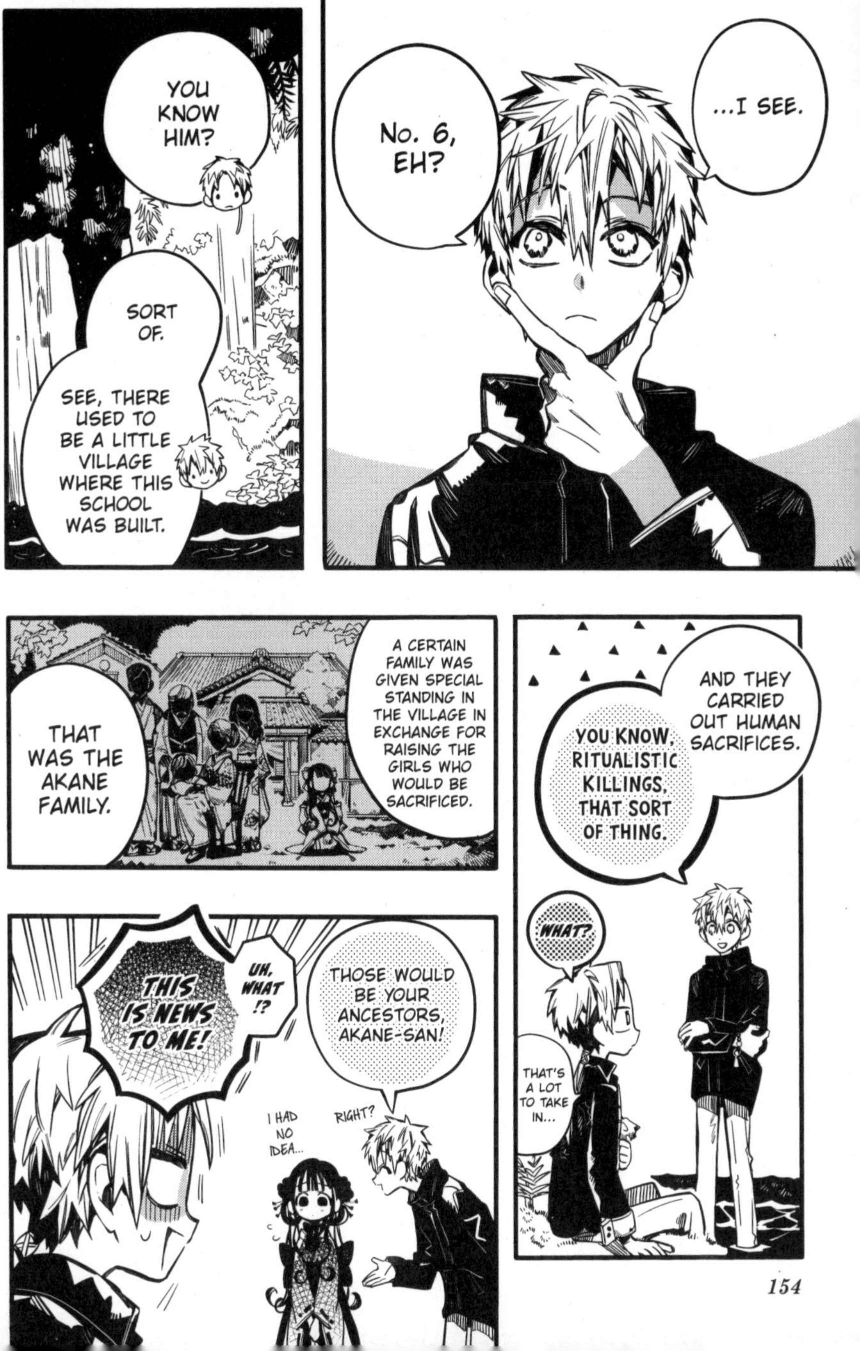
...I SEE.
No. 6, EH?
YOU KNOW HIM?
SORT OF.
SEE, THERE USED TO BE A LITTLE VILLAGE WHERE THIS SCHOOL WAS BUILT.
AND THEY CARRIED OUT HUMAN SACRIFICES.
YOU KNOW, RITUALISTIC KILLINGS, THAT SORT OF THING.
WHAT?
THAT'S A LOT TO TAKE IN...
A CERTAIN FAMILY WAS GIVEN SPECIAL STANDING IN THE VILLAGE IN EXCHANGE FOR RAISING THE GIRLS WHO WOULD BE SACRIFICED.
THAT WAS THE AKANE FAMILY.
THOSE WOULD BE YOUR ANCESTORS, AKANE-SAN!
UH, WHAT!?
THIS IS NEWS TO ME!
RIGHT?
I HAD NO IDEA...

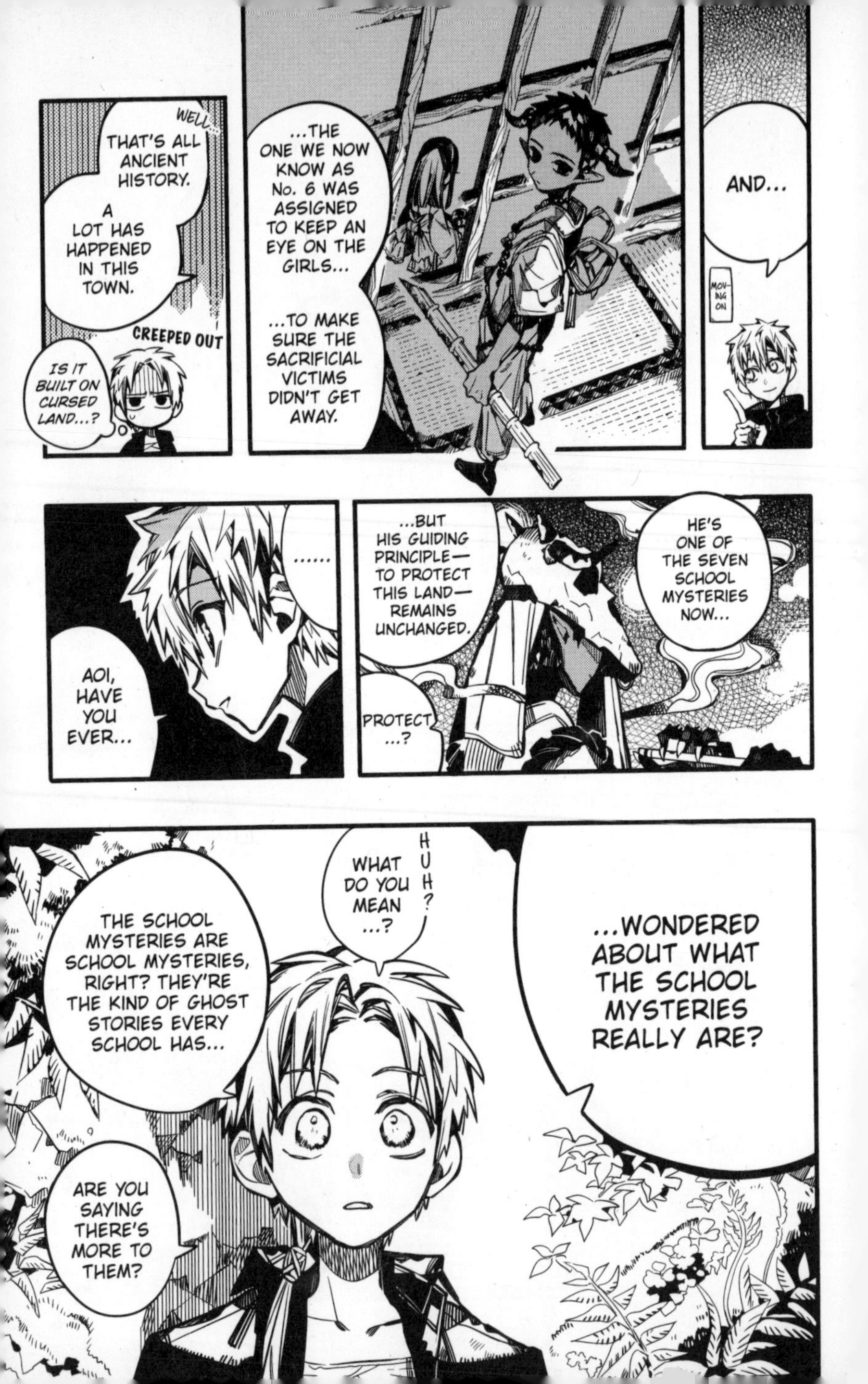
AND...
MOV-ING ON
...THE ONE WE NOW KNOW AS No. 6 WAS ASSIGNED TO KEEP AN EYE ON THE GIRLS...
...TO MAKE SURE THE SACRIFICIAL VICTIMS DIDN'T GET AWAY.
WELL...
THAT'S ALL ANCIENT HISTORY.
A LOT HAS HAPPENED IN THIS TOWN.
CREEPED OUT
IS IT BUILT ON CURSED LAND...?
HE'S ONE OF THE SEVEN SCHOOL MYSTERIES NOW...
...BUT HIS GUIDING PRINCIPLE—TO PROTECT THIS LAND—REMAINS UNCHANGED.
PROTECT...?
......
AOI, HAVE YOU EVER...
...WONDERED ABOUT WHAT THE SCHOOL MYSTERIES REALLY ARE?
HUH?
WHAT DO YOU MEAN...?
THE SCHOOL MYSTERIES ARE SCHOOL MYSTERIES, RIGHT? THEY'RE THE KIND OF GHOST STORIES EVERY SCHOOL HAS...
ARE YOU SAYING THERE'S MORE TO THEM?

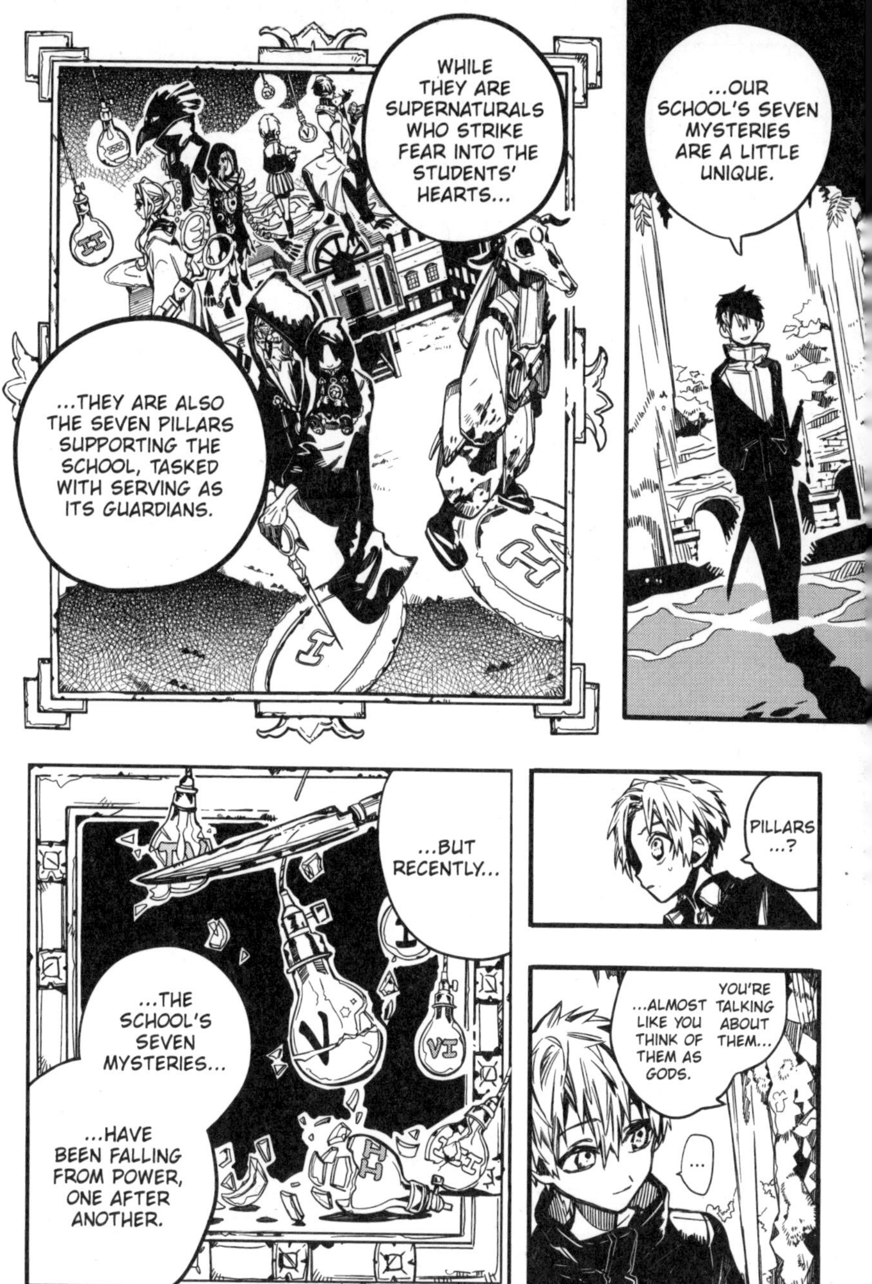
...OUR SCHOOL'S SEVEN MYSTERIES ARE A LITTLE UNIQUE.
WHILE THEY ARE SUPERNATURALS WHO STRIKE FEAR INTO THE STUDENTS' HEARTS...
...THEY ARE ALSO THE SEVEN PILLARS SUPPORTING THE SCHOOL, TASKED WITH SERVING AS ITS GUARDIANS.
PILLARS ...?
YOU'RE TALKING ABOUT THEM...
...ALMOST LIKE YOU THINK OF THEM AS GODS.
...
...BUT RECENTLY...
...THE SCHOOL'S SEVEN MYSTERIES...
...HAVE BEEN FALLING FROM POWER, ONE AFTER ANOTHER.

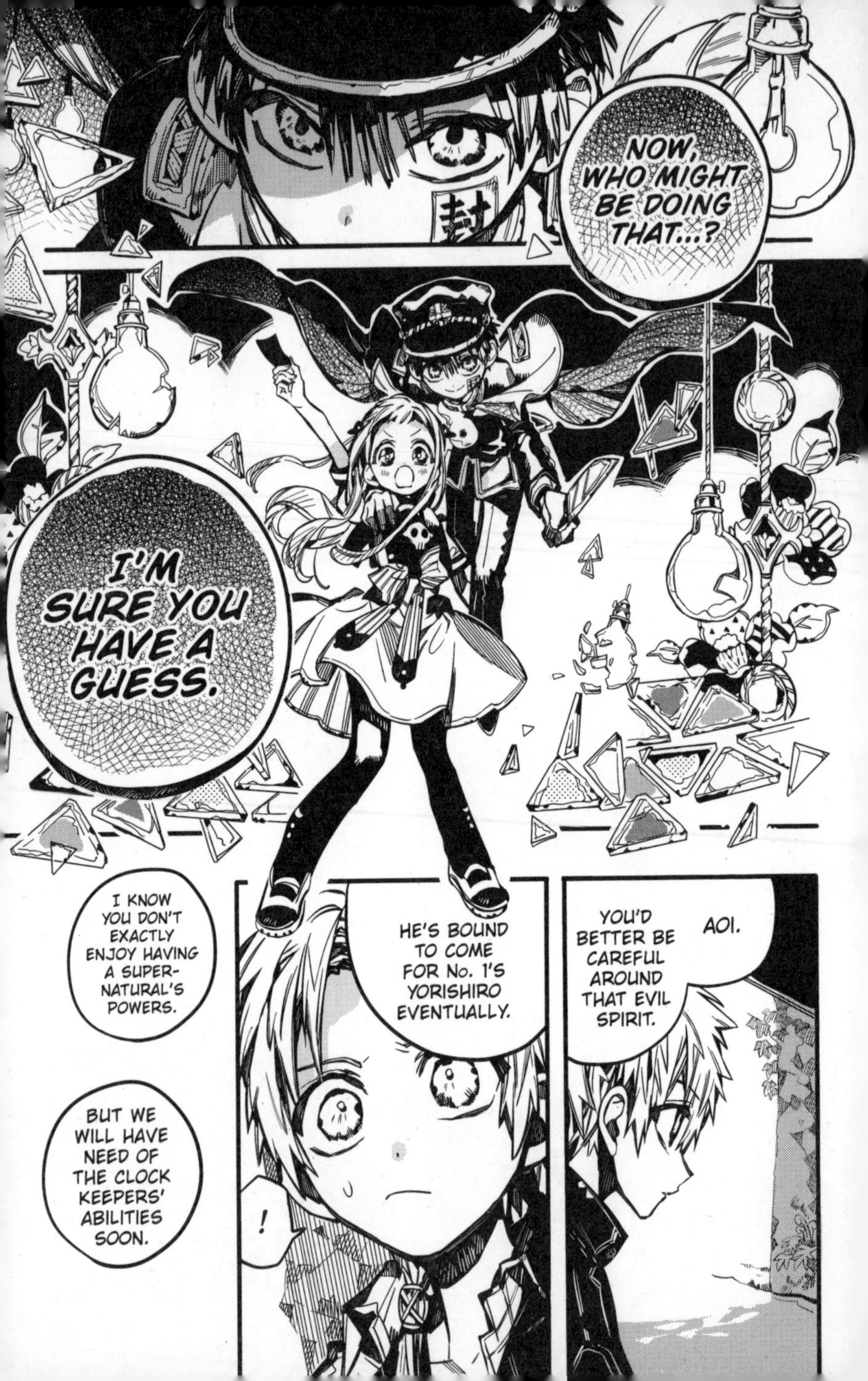
NOW, WHO MIGHT BE DOING THAT...?
I'M SURE YOU HAVE A GUESS.
AOI.
YOU'D BETTER BE CAREFUL AROUND THAT EVIL SPIRIT.
HE'S BOUND TO COME FOR No. 1'S YORISHIRO EVENTUALLY.
!
I KNOW YOU DON'T EXACTLY ENJOY HAVING A SUPER-NATURAL'S POWERS.
BUT WE WILL HAVE NEED OF THE CLOCK KEEPERS' ABILITIES SOON.

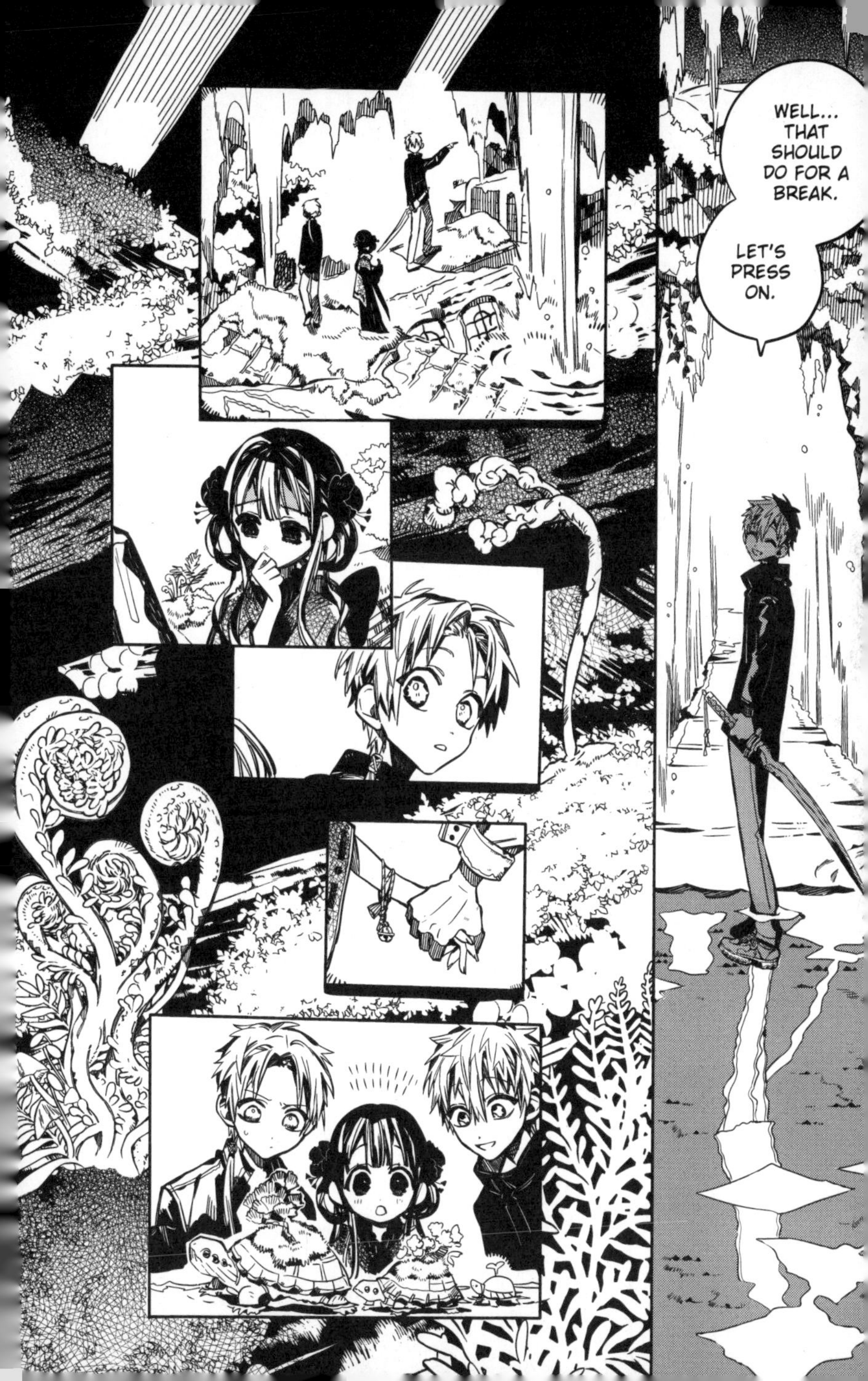
WELL... THAT SHOULD DO FOR A BREAK.
LET'S PRESS ON.

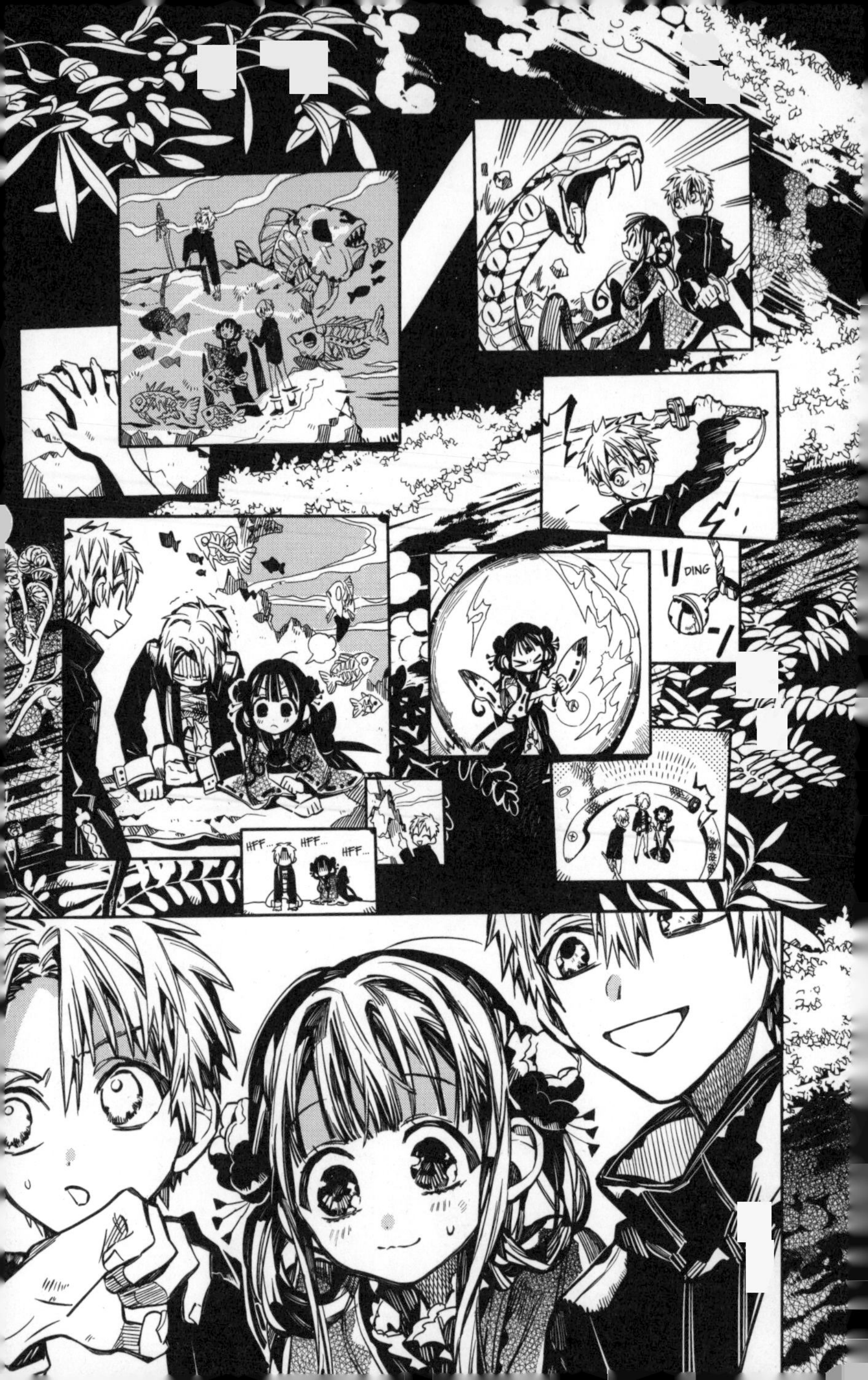
DING
HFF... HFF... HFF...

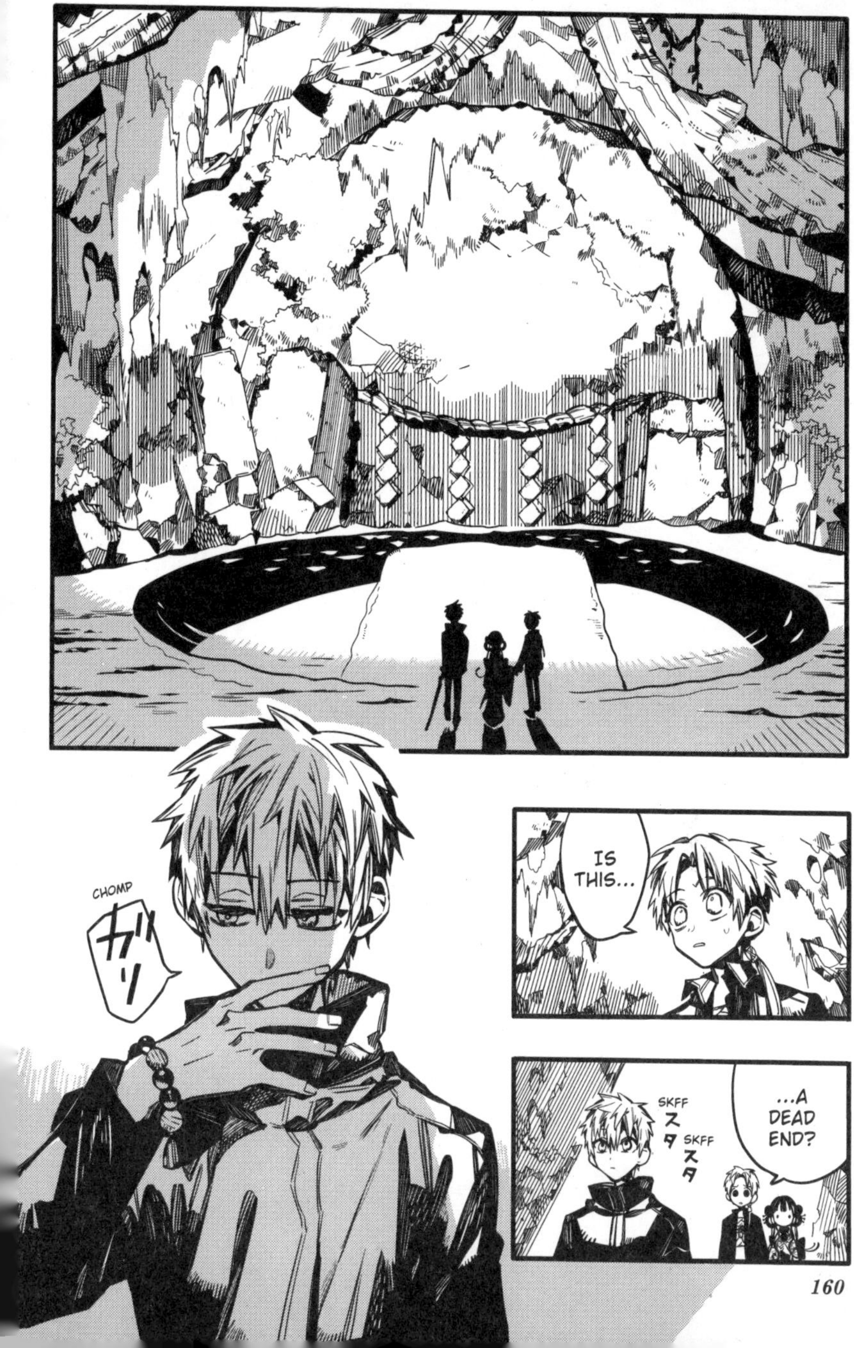
IS THIS...
...A DEAD END?
SKFF
スタ
SKFF
スタ
CHOMP
ガリッ

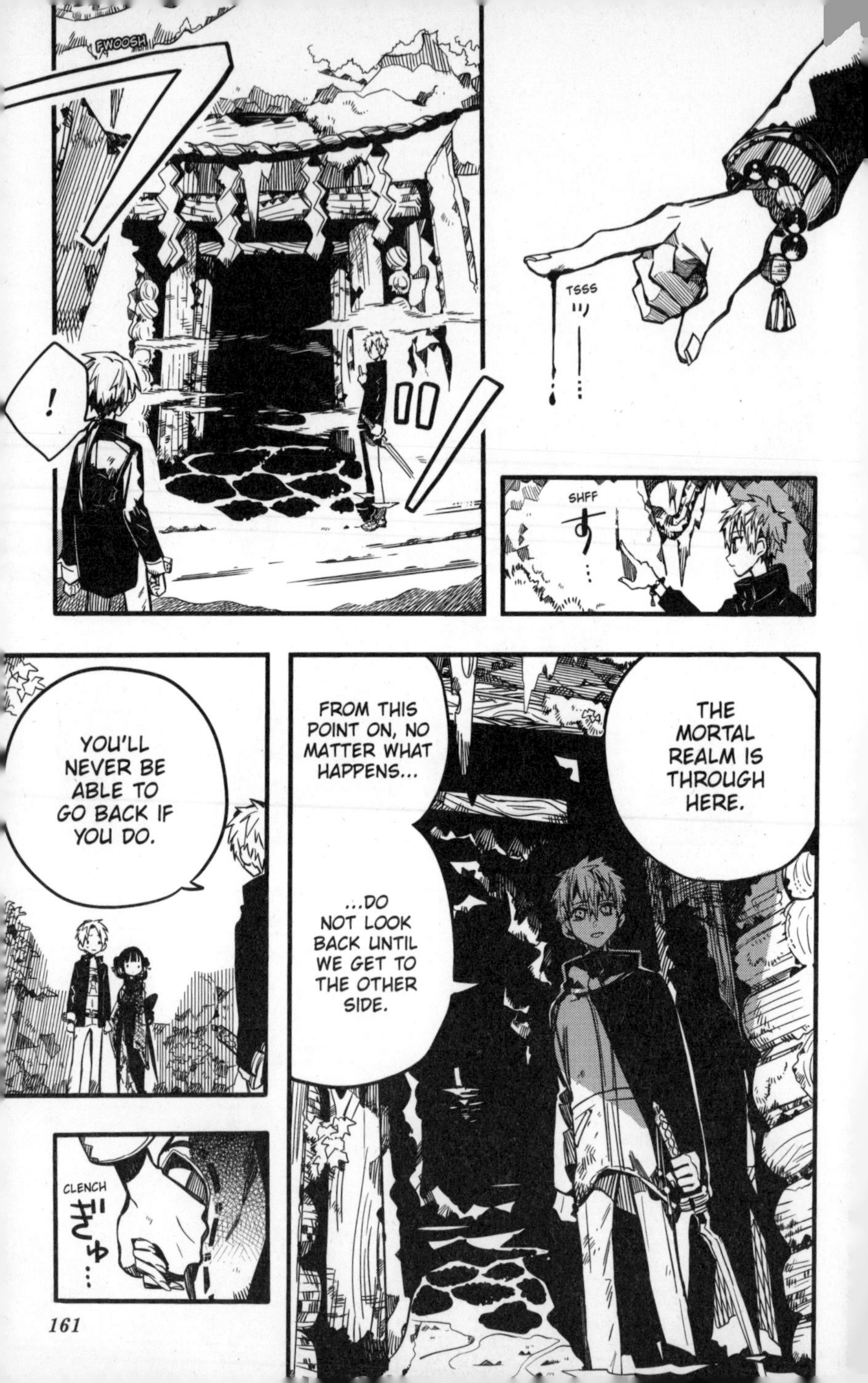
TSSS
ッ
SHFF
す…
FWOOSH
!
THE MORTAL REALM IS THROUGH HERE.
FROM THIS POINT ON, NO MATTER WHAT HAPPENS...
...DO NOT LOOK BACK UNTIL WE GET TO THE OTHER SIDE.
YOU'LL NEVER BE ABLE TO GO BACK IF YOU DO.
CLENCH
ぎゅ…

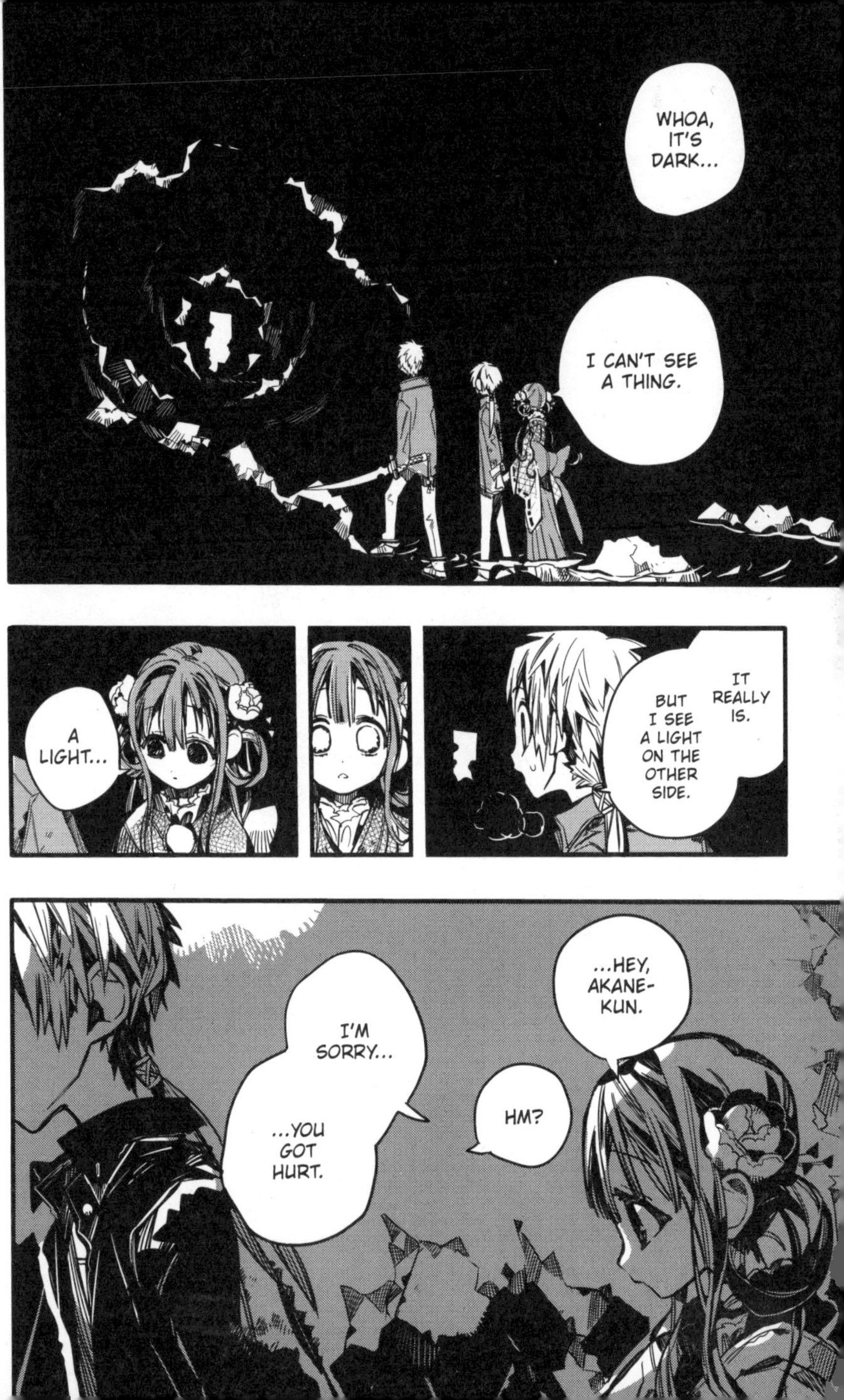
WHOA, IT'S DARK...
I CAN'T SEE A THING.
IT REALLY IS.
BUT I SEE A LIGHT ON THE OTHER SIDE.
A LIGHT...
...HEY, AKANE-KUN.
HM?
I'M SORRY... ...YOU GOT HURT.

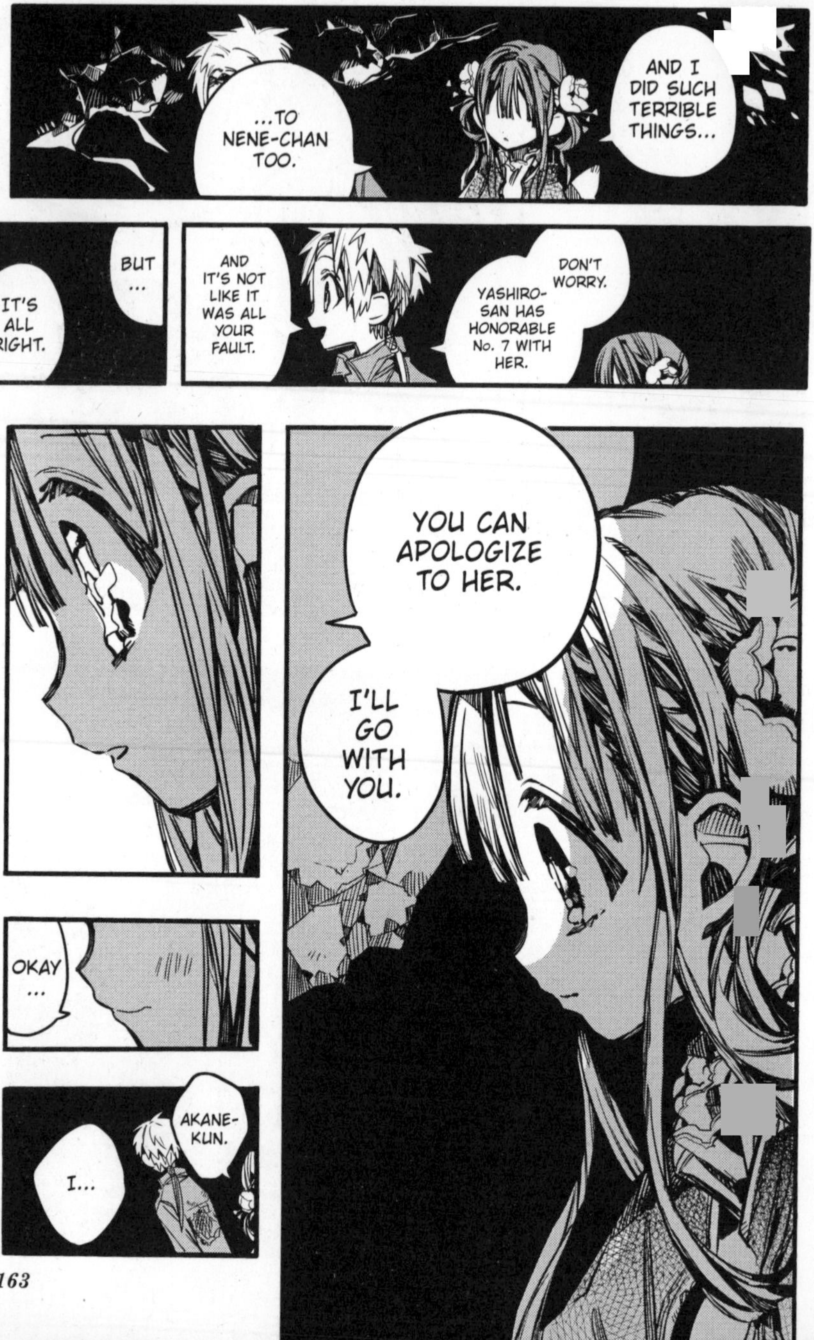
AND I DID SUCH TERRIBLE THINGS...
...TO NENE-CHAN TOO.
DON'T WORRY.
YASHIRO-SAN HAS HONORABLE No. 7 WITH HER.
AND IT'S NOT LIKE IT WAS ALL YOUR FAULT.
BUT...
IT'S ALL RIGHT.
YOU CAN APOLOGIZE TO HER.
I'LL GO WITH YOU.
OKAY...
AKANE-KUN.
I...

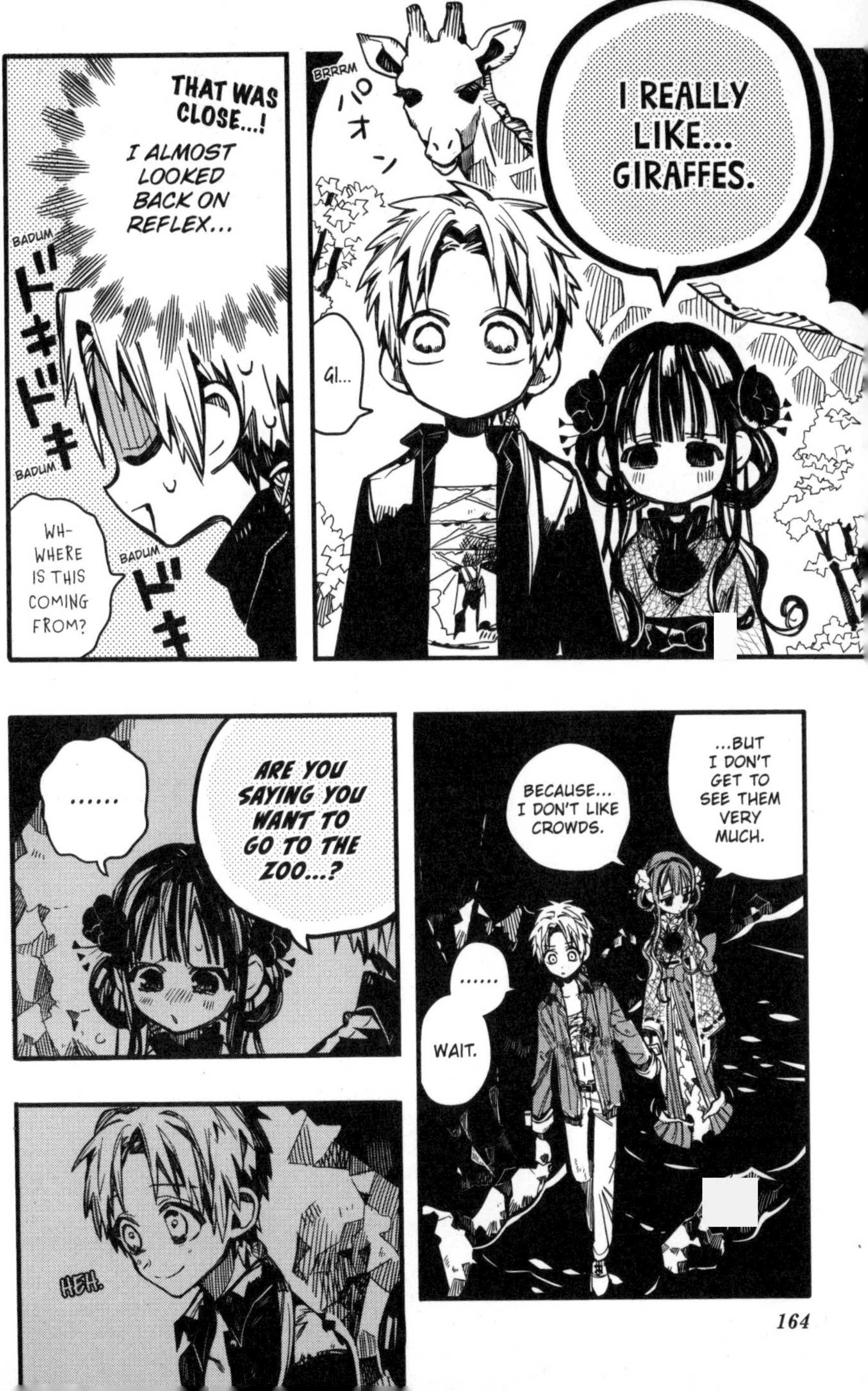
BRRRM
パオーン
I REALLY LIKE... GIRAFFES.
GI...
THAT WAS CLOSE...!
I ALMOST LOOKED BACK ON REFLEX...
BADUM
ドキドキ
BADUM
WH- WHERE IS THIS COMING FROM?
BADUM
ドキ
...BUT I DON'T GET TO SEE THEM VERY MUCH.
BECAUSE... I DON'T LIKE CROWDS.
......
WAIT.
ARE YOU SAYING YOU WANT TO GO TO THE ZOO...?
......
HEH.

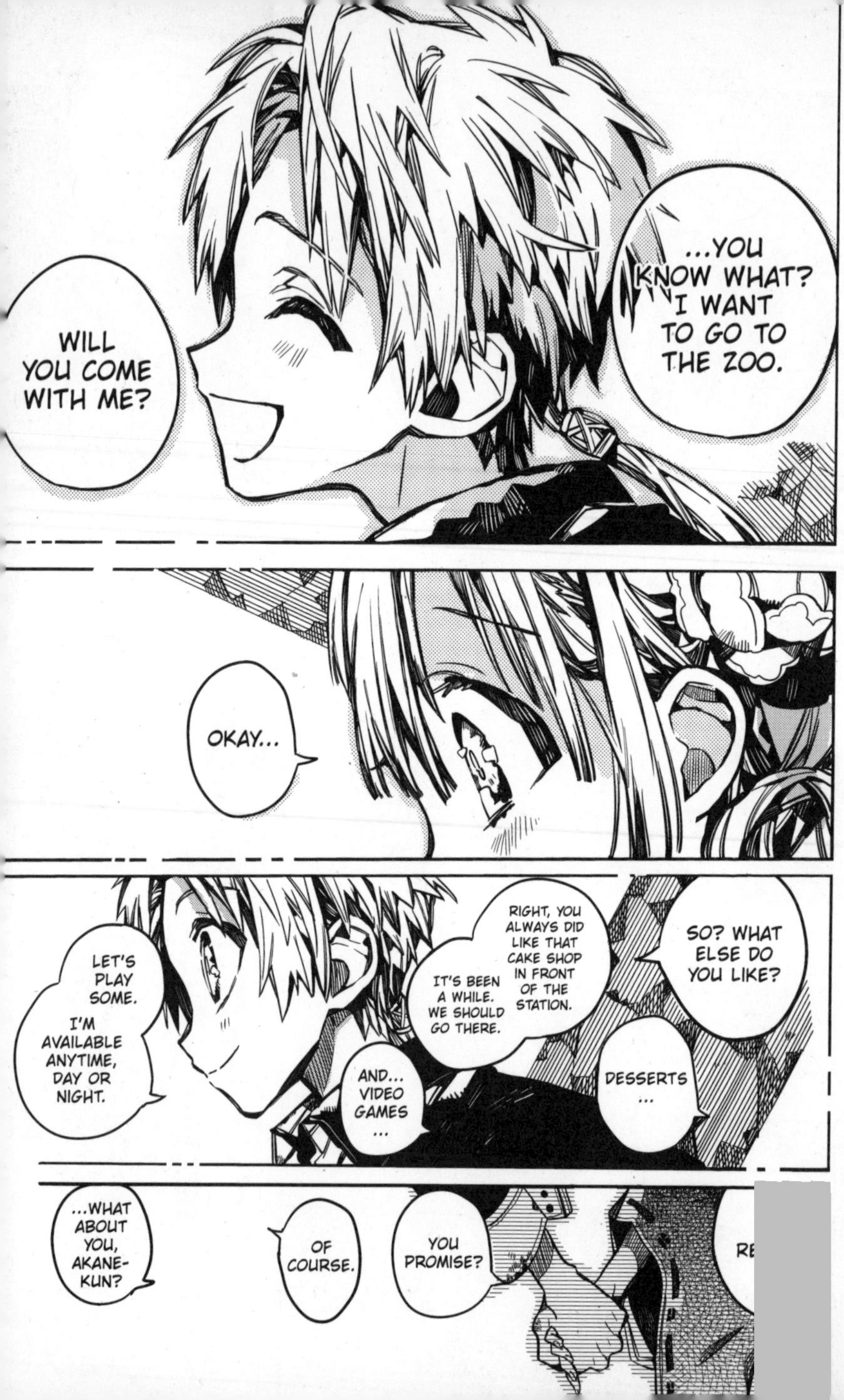
...YOU KNOW WHAT? I WANT TO GO TO THE ZOO.
WILL YOU COME WITH ME?
OKAY...
SO? WHAT ELSE DO YOU LIKE?
DESSERTS ...
RIGHT, YOU ALWAYS DID LIKE THAT CAKE SHOP IN FRONT OF THE STATION.
IT'S BEEN A WHILE. WE SHOULD GO THERE.
AND... VIDEO GAMES ...
LET'S PLAY SOME.
I'M AVAILABLE ANYTIME, DAY OR NIGHT.
RE
YOU PROMISE?
OF COURSE.
...WHAT ABOUT YOU, AKANE-KUN?

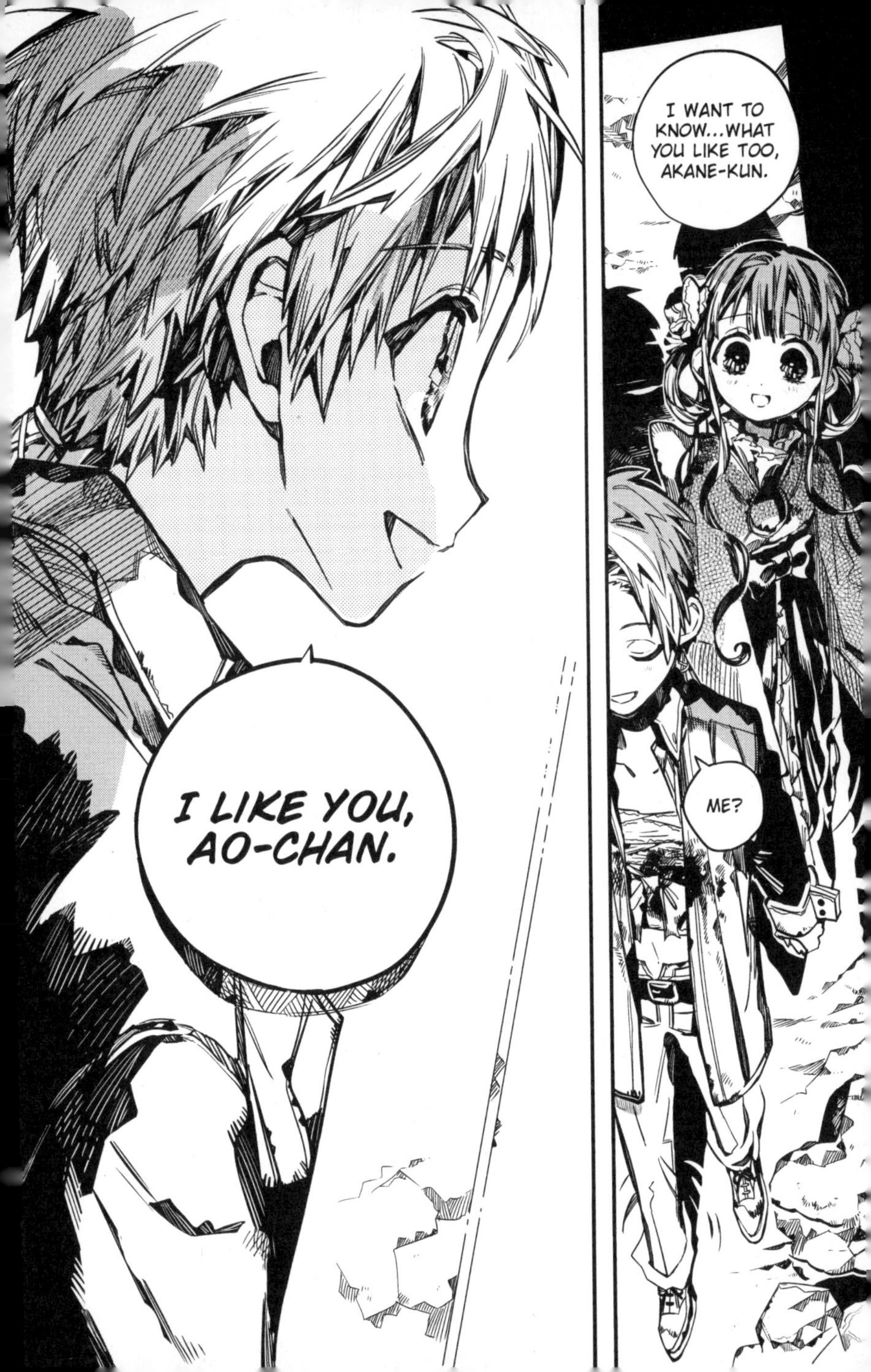
I WANT TO KNOW...WHAT YOU LIKE TOO, AKANE-KUN.
ME?
I LIKE YOU, AO-CHAN.

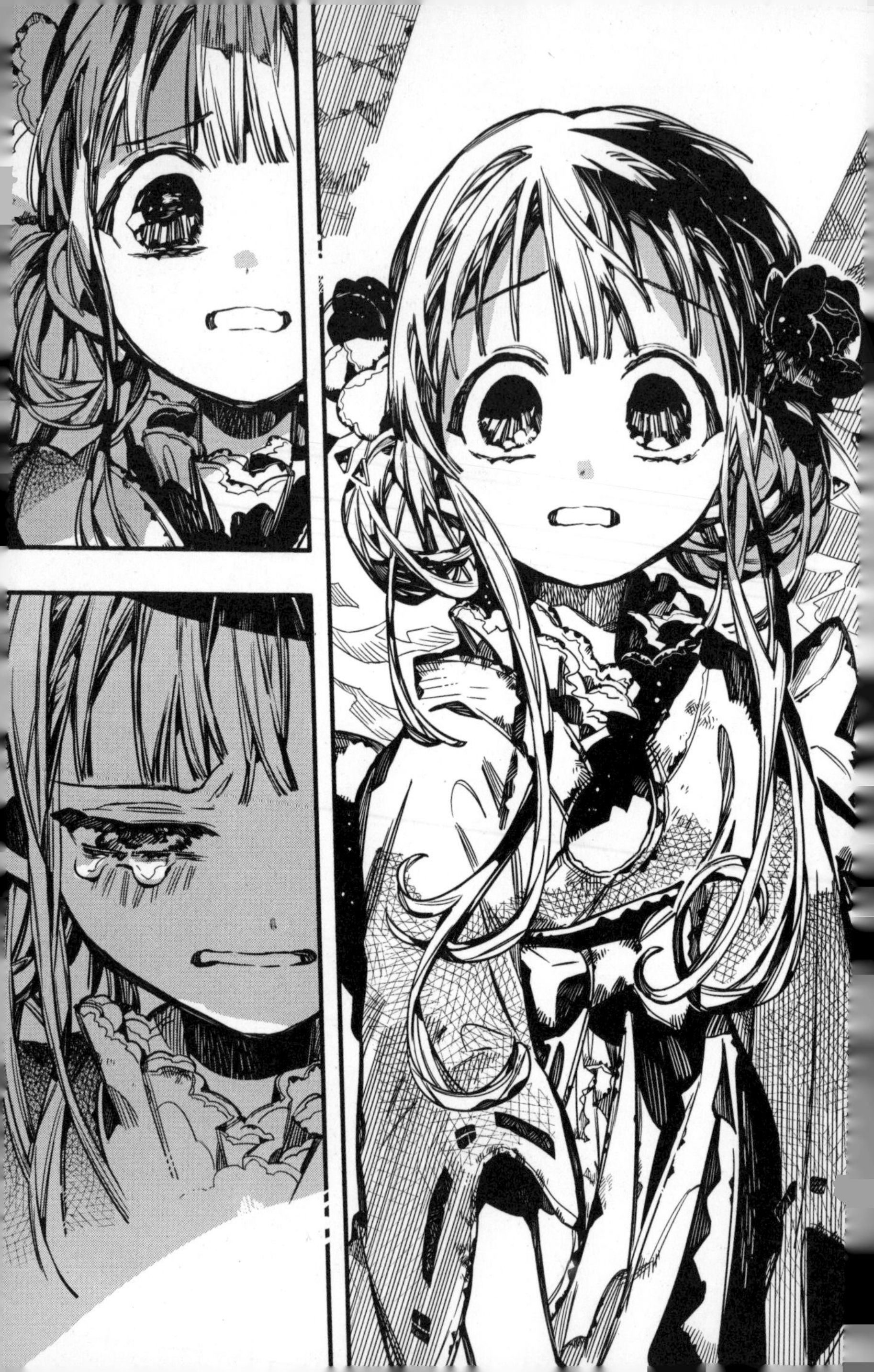

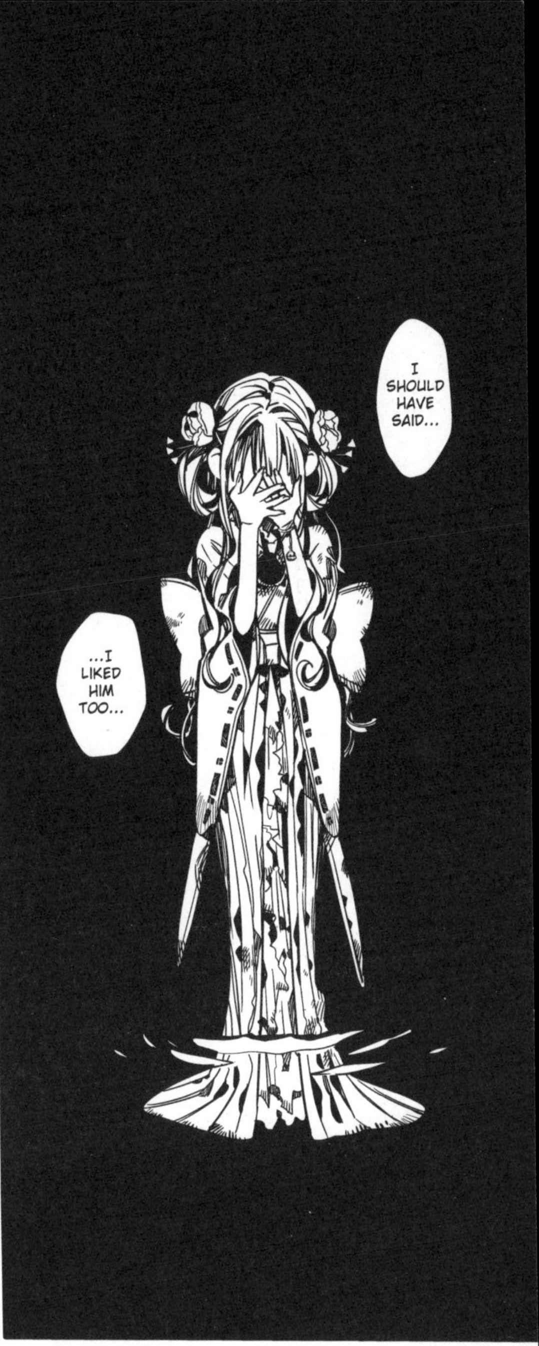
I SHOULD HAVE SAID...
...I LIKED HIM TOO...
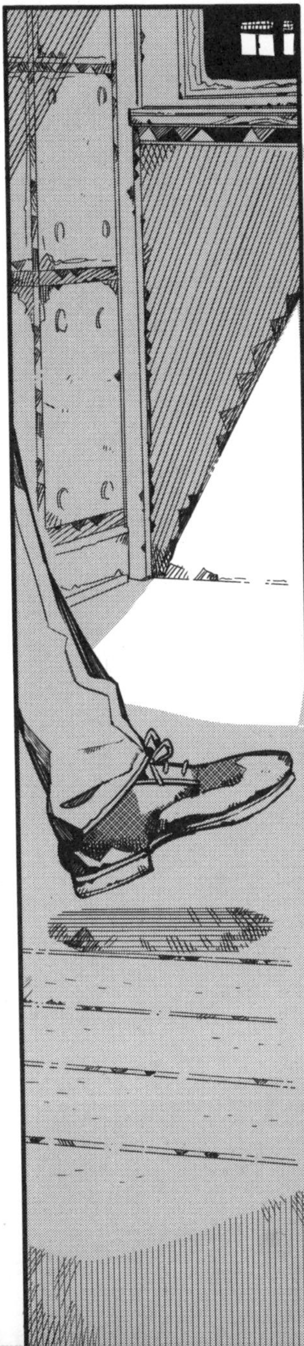

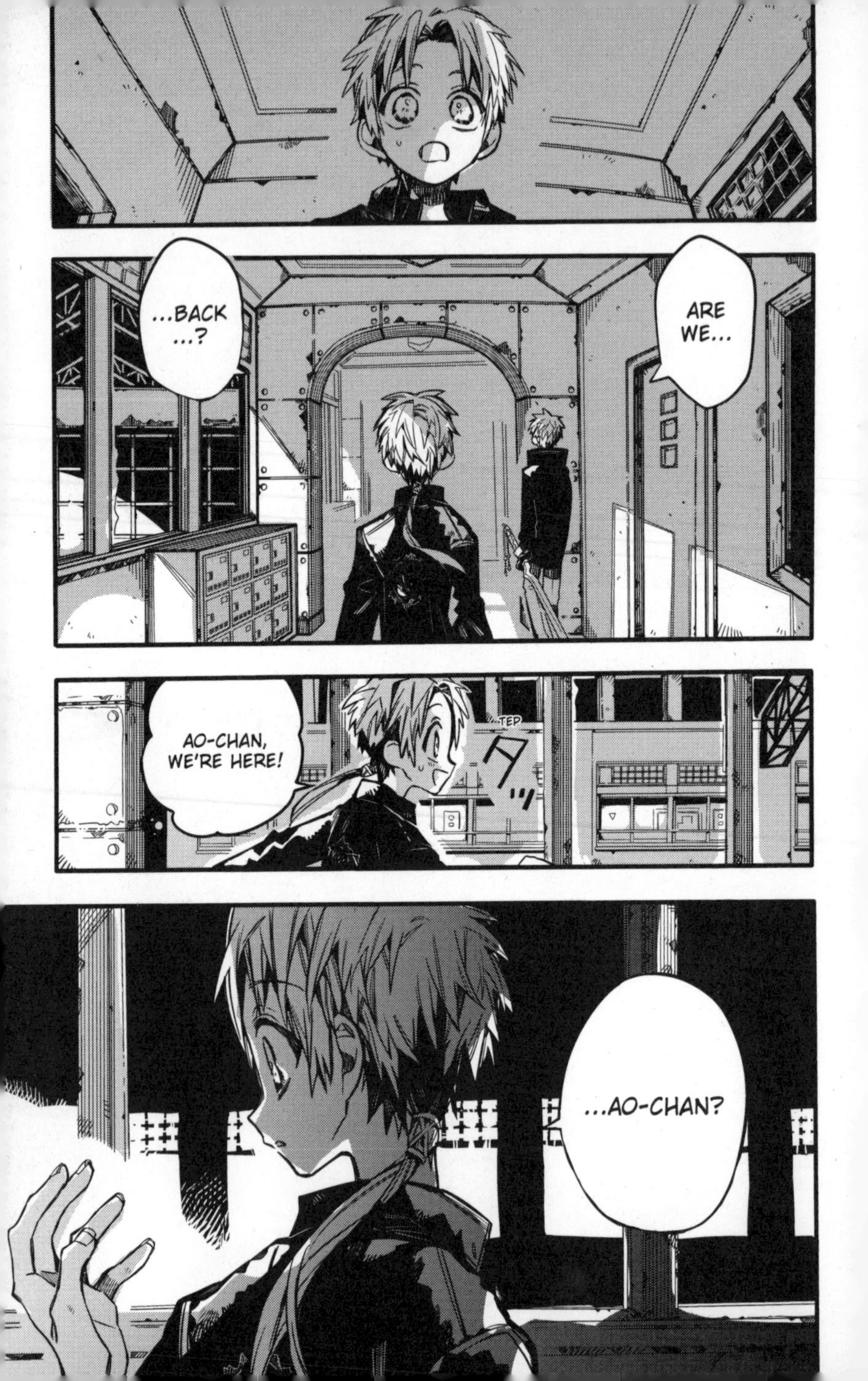
ARE WE...
...BACK ...?
TEP
タッ
AO-CHAN, WE'RE HERE!
...AO-CHAN?

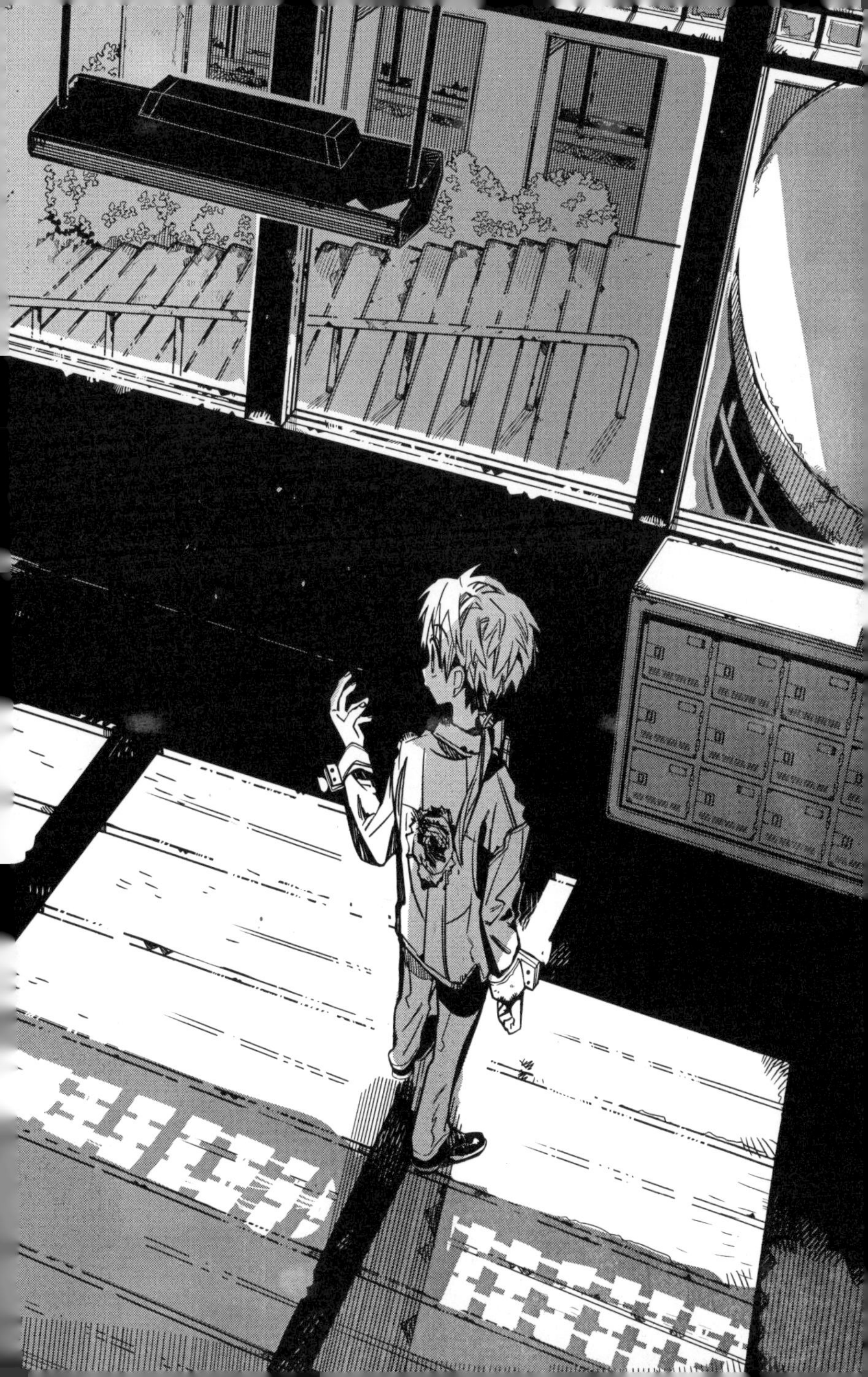

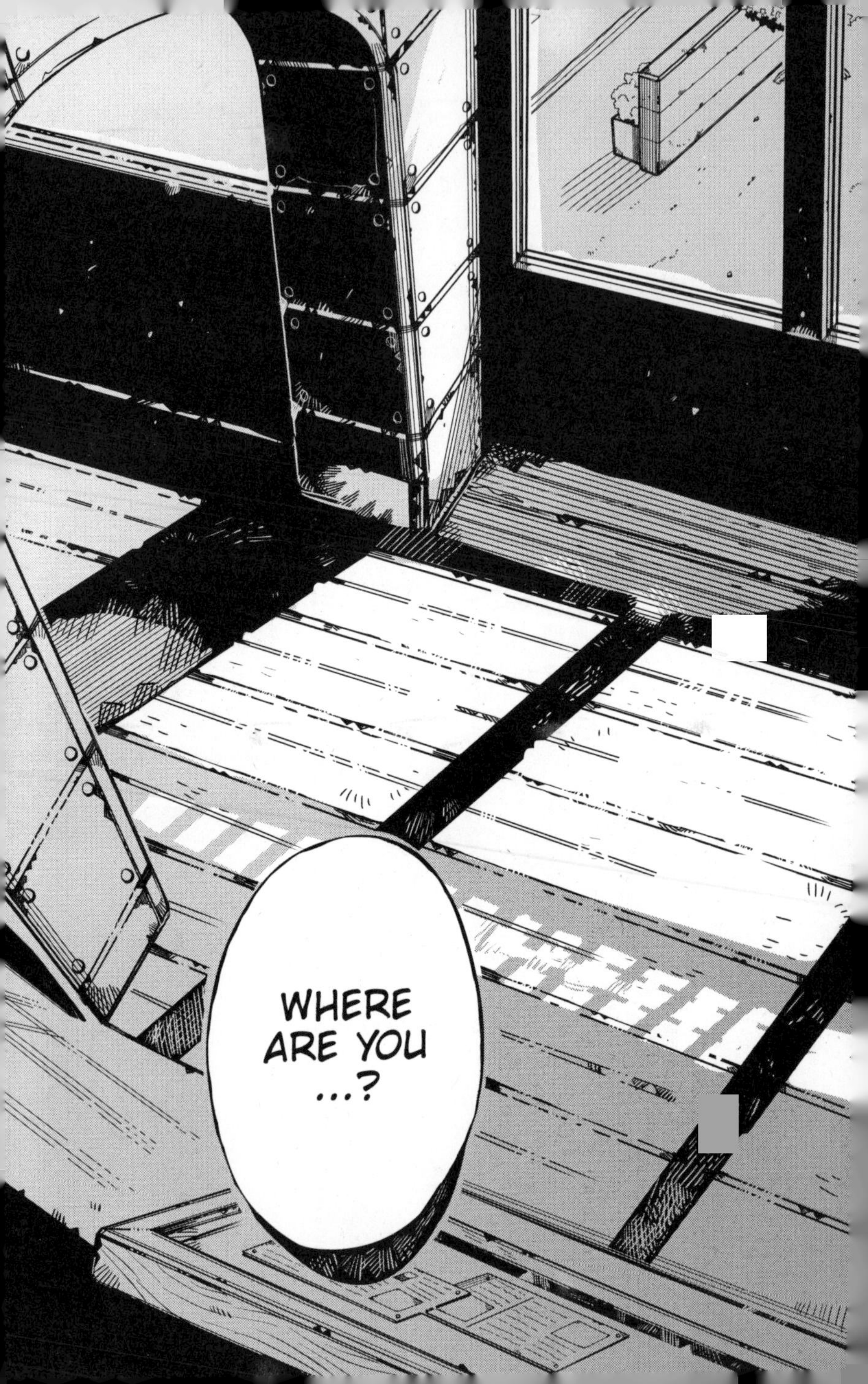
WHERE ARE YOU ...?

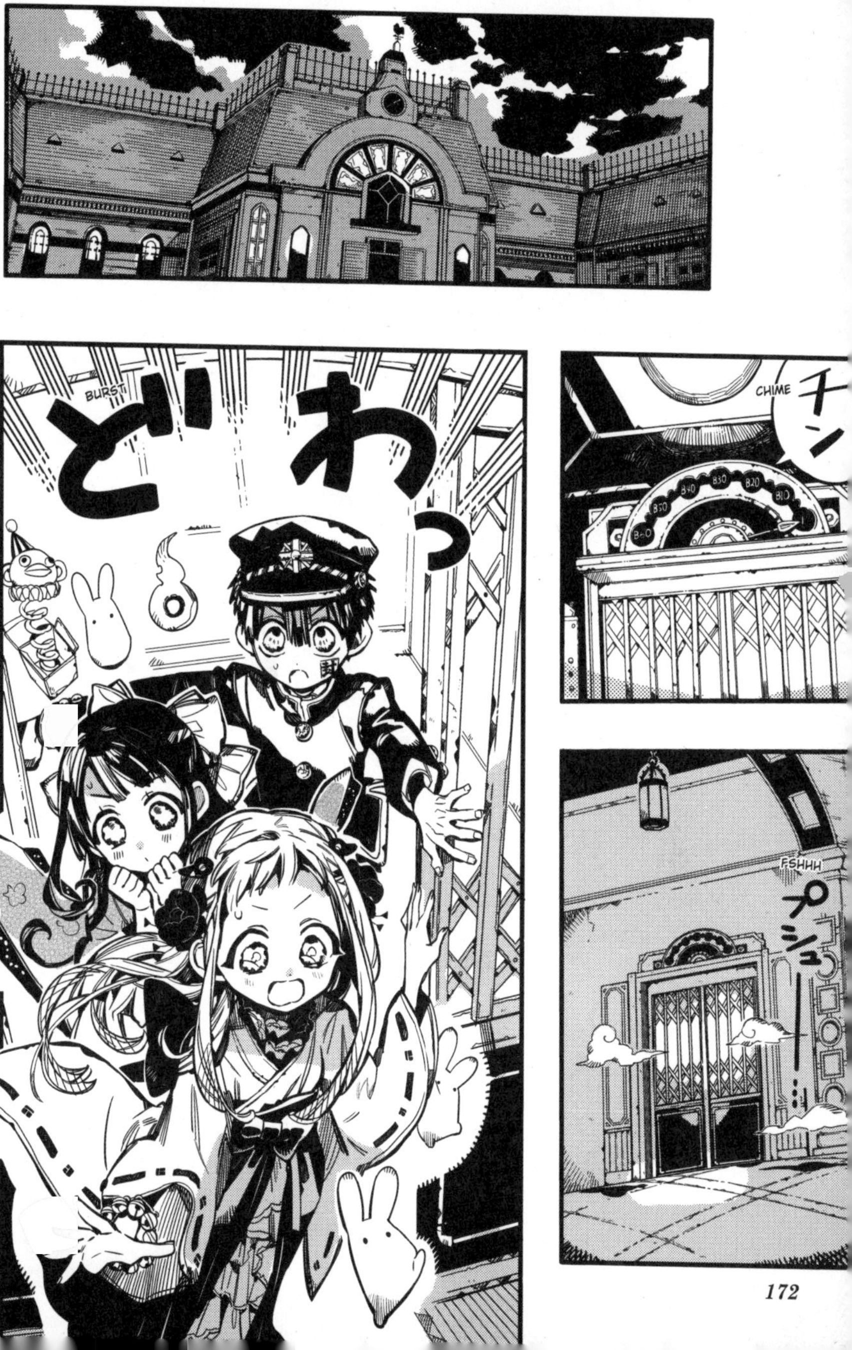
CHIME
チン
FSHHH
プシュー…
BURST
どわっ

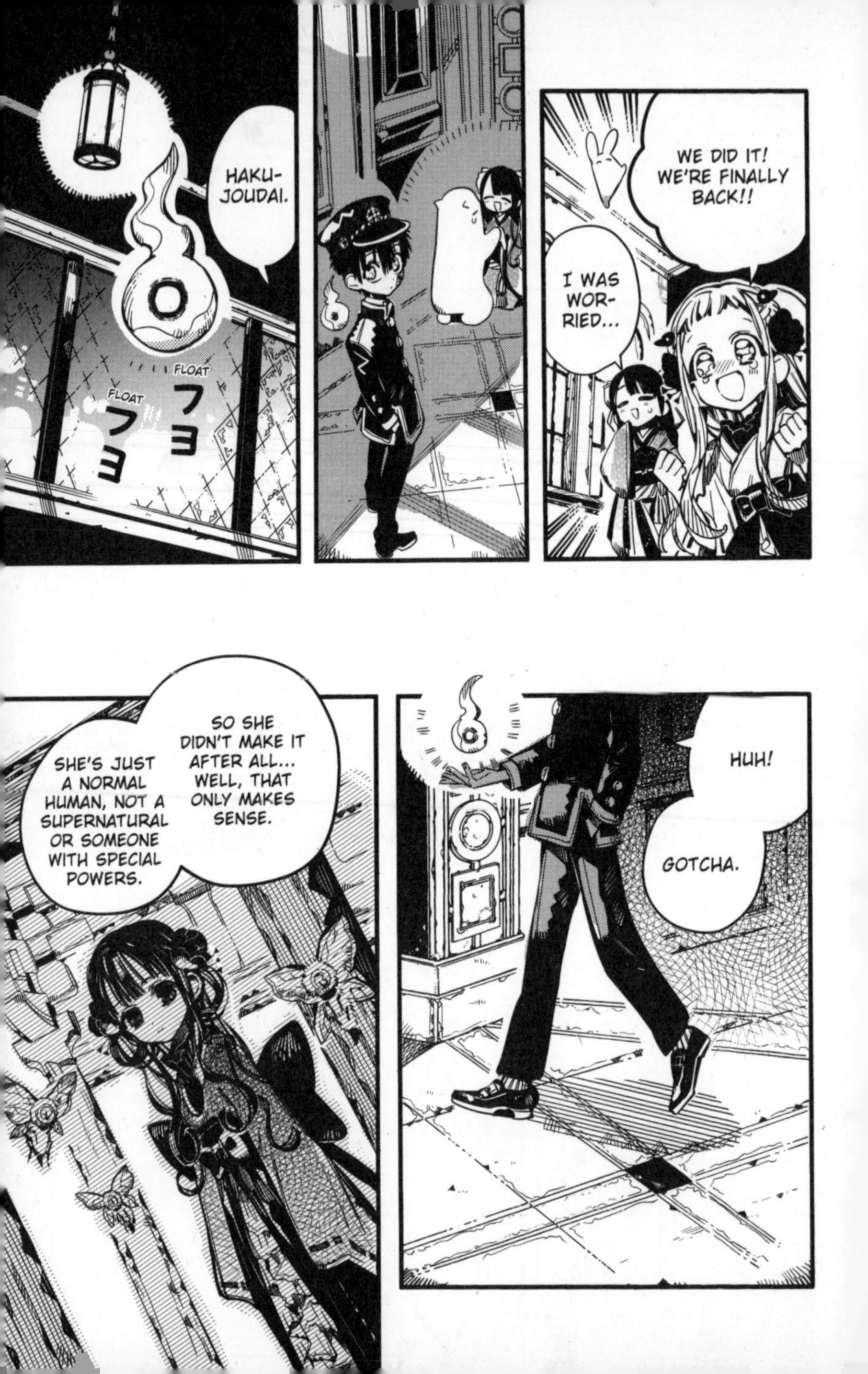
WE DID IT! WE'RE FINALLY BACK!!
I WAS WOR-RIED...
HAKU-JOUDAI.
FLOAT
フヨ
FLOAT
フヨ
HUH!
GOTCHA.
SO SHE DIDN'T MAKE IT AFTER ALL... WELL, THAT ONLY MAKES SENSE.
SHE'S JUST A NORMAL HUMAN, NOT A SUPERNATURAL OR SOMEONE WITH SPECIAL POWERS.

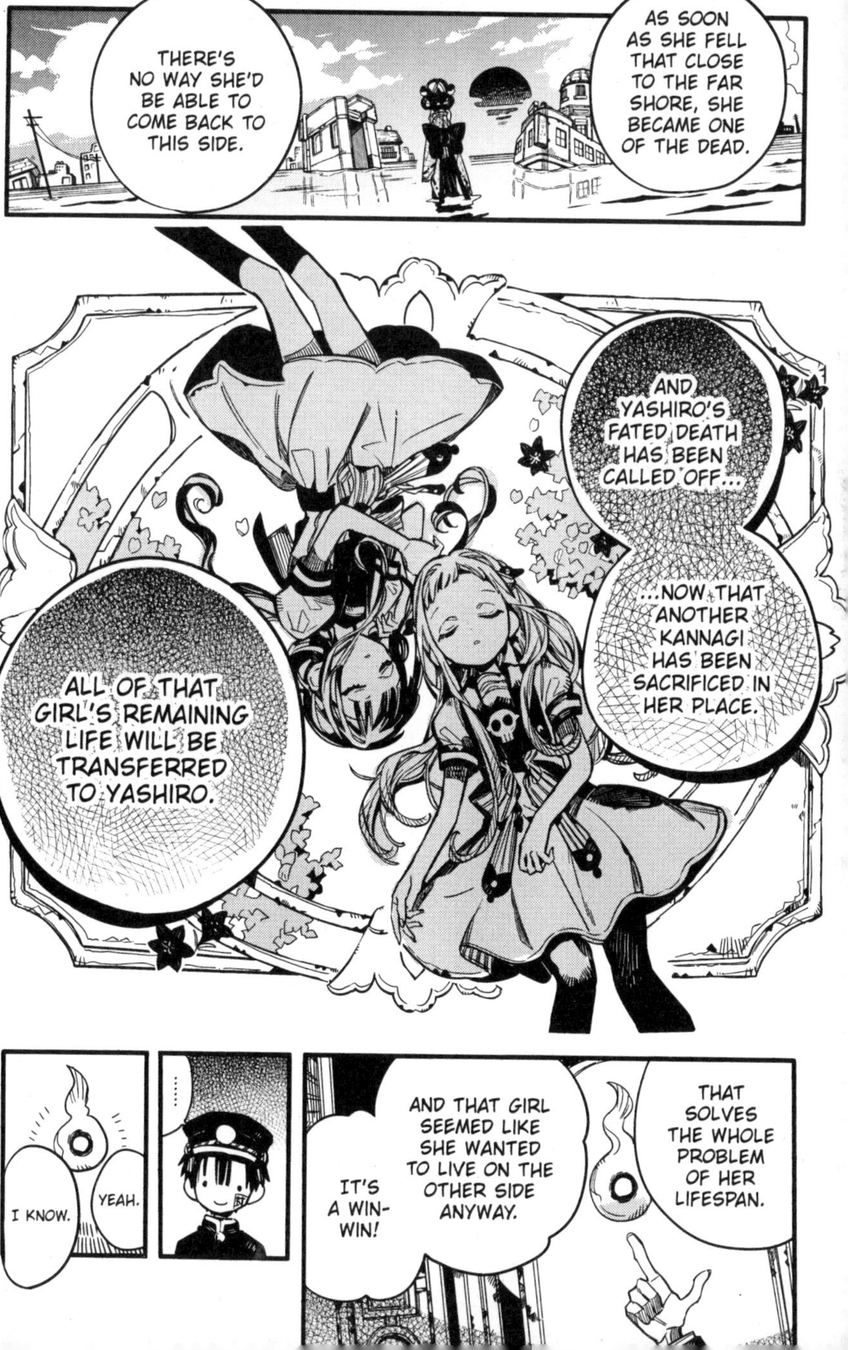
AS SOON AS SHE FELL THAT CLOSE TO THE FAR SHORE, SHE BECAME ONE OF THE DEAD.
THERE'S NO WAY SHE'D BE ABLE TO COME BACK TO THIS SIDE.
AND YASHIRO'S FATED DEATH HAS BEEN CALLED OFF...
...NOW THAT ANOTHER KANNAGI HAS BEEN SACRIFICED IN HER PLACE.
ALL OF THAT GIRL'S REMAINING LIFE WILL BE TRANSFERRED TO YASHIRO.
THAT SOLVES THE WHOLE PROBLEM OF HER LIFESPAN.
AND THAT GIRL SEEMED LIKE SHE WANTED TO LIVE ON THE OTHER SIDE ANYWAY.
IT'S A WIN-WIN!
......
YEAH.
I KNOW.

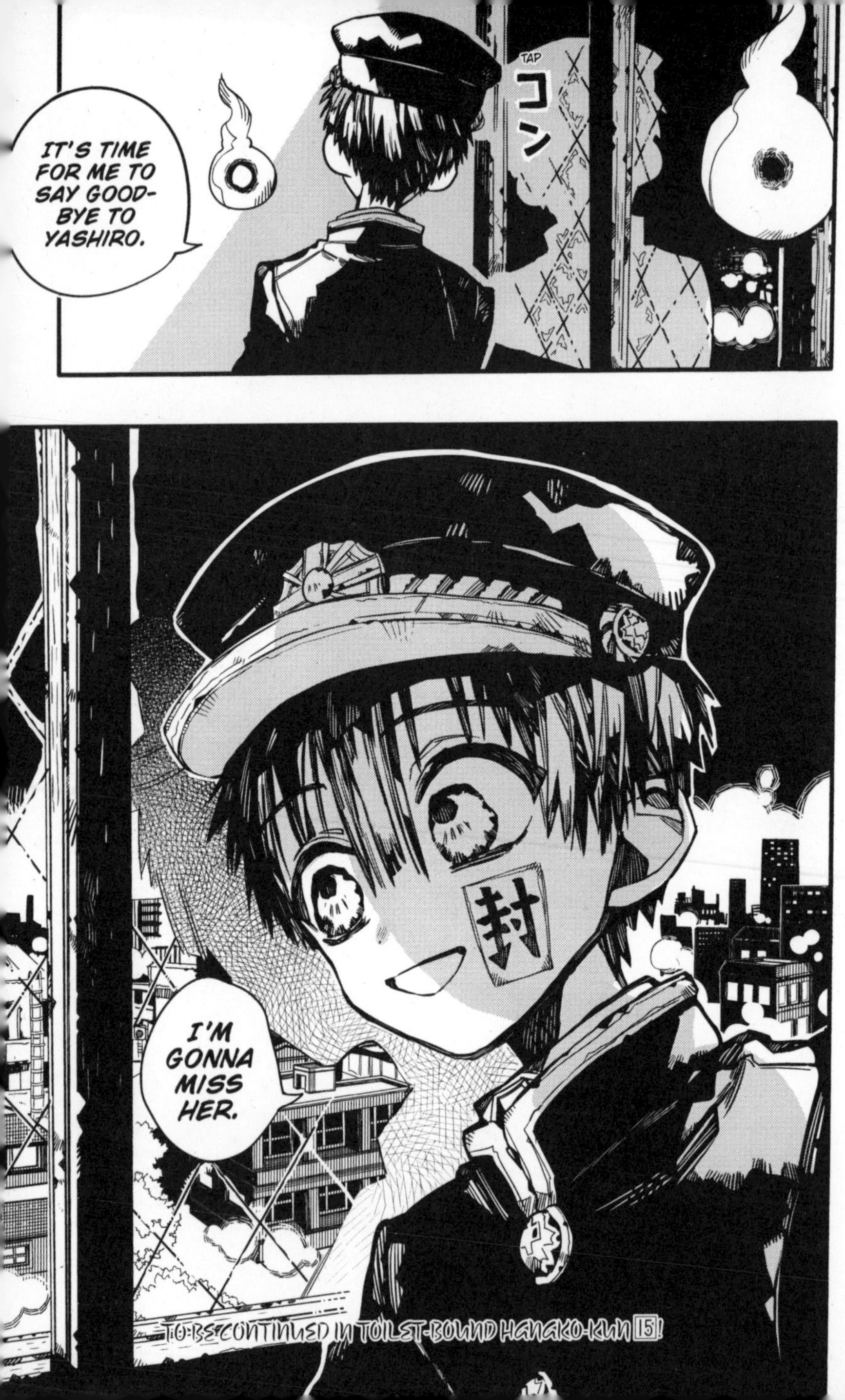
TAP
コン
IT'S TIME FOR ME TO SAY GOOD-BYE TO YASHIRO.
I'M GONNA MISS HER.
TO BE CONTINUED IN TOILET-BOUND HANAKO-KUN 15!